Praise for *Lords of* and James L. N Revolution at Sea Saga

"Swashbuckling action. . . . A swift read and a fun adventure. . . . Nelson imbues almost every sentence with the taste of the sea and the name of the sail."

—*Morning Sentinel* (Waterville, ME)

"Nelson knows sailing, and he knows people. In Biddlecomb he has an all-too-human hero willing to step over any barrier to keep the British at bay and his own career on track."

—*Houston Chronicle*

"Nelson's seagoing experience is evident in his clear, convincing description. . . . The characters are strong and realistic, the plot and action believable and brisk . . . a fine adventure."

—*Publishers Weekly*

"Splice the main brace and drink a toast to James L. Nelson. . . . Sailing in the wake of C. S. Forester, Nelson has done an excellent job of combining historical authenticity with firm characterization and lively action."

—Nathan Miller, author of *Sea of Glory: A Naval History of the American Revolution*

"Set sail with Jim Nelson into a world where he will lead you with the same command presence that he led his shipmates as Third Officer aboard the very real twentieth-century sail training ship H.M.S. *Rose*. Plant your feet firmly on Nelson's decks and you will smile as Patrick O'Brian has at Jim Nelson's grace, wit, and humor."

—Captain Richard Bailey, Sail Training Ship H.M.S. *Rose*

Also by James L. Nelson

By Force of Arms
The Maddest Idea
The Continental Risque
All the Brave Fellows

Published by POCKET BOOKS

LORDS OF THE OCEAN

REVOLUTION AT SEA SAGA

BOOK FOUR

JAMES L. NELSON

POCKET BOOKS
New York   London   Toronto   Sydney   Singapore

This book is a work of fiction. Names, characters, places and
incidents are products of the author's imagination or are used
fictitiously. Any resemblance to actual events or locales or persons
living or dead is entirely coincidental.

POCKET BOOKS, a division of Simon & Schuster Inc.
1230 Avenue of the Americas, New York, NY 10020

Copyright © 1999 by James L. Nelson

Originally published in hardcover in 1999 by Pocket Books

Nelson, James L.
    Lords of the ocean / James L. Nelson.
        p.   cm.—(Revolution at sea saga : bk. 4)
    ISBN 0-671-01383-1
    1. United States—History—Revolution, 1775–1783—Naval
operations—Fiction. 2. United States—History, Naval—18th
century—Fiction. I. Title. II. Series: Nelson, James L.
Revolution at sea saga : bk. 4.
PS3564.E4646L67 1999
813'.54—dc21   99-26943
                                               CIP

First Pocket Books trade paperback printing June 2000

10 9 8 7 6 5 4 3

POCKET and colophon are registered trademarks of
Simon & Schuster Inc.

Cover illustration by Dennis Lyall
Cover design by Matt Galemmo

Printed in the U.S.A.

In Memoriam

Ronald E. Johnson

They that go down to the sea in ships
And do their work on great waters
These see the works of the Lord
And his wonders in the deep.

Acknowledgments

My thanks to Tristram Coburn, editor and sailor, and, as ever, to Nat Sobel and all of the fine people at Sobel Weber Associates, including Laura Nolan, to whom special thanks is long overdue. Thanks to C. A. Finger for his ongoing help and to Stephanie Nelson for her ever insightful comments. And thanks to Fr. Peter Timmins and his entire research staff for assistance on the theological points and to Mark Boucher *pour le français*.

Our Cartel goes on, a second Cargo of American Prisoners 119 in Number being arrived and exchanged. Our Privateers have dismissed a great Number at Sea, taking their written Paroles to be given up in Exchange for so many of our People in the Gaols.

We continue to insult the Coasts of these Lords of the Ocean with our little Cruizers . . .

—Benjamin Franklin
dispatch to the
Continental Congress
October 4, 1779

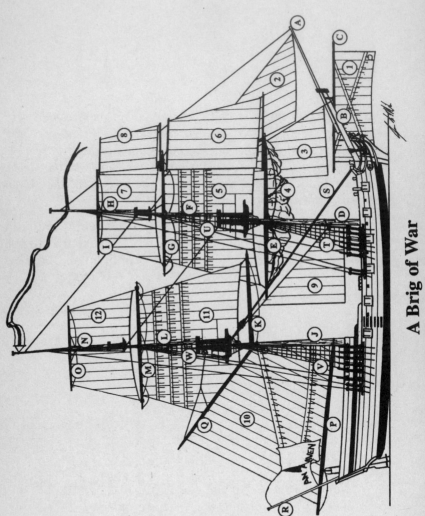

A Brig of War

Sails

1. Spritsail
2. Jib
3. Fore Topmast Staysail
4. Foresail (clewed up)
5. Fore Topsail
6. Fore Topmast Studdingsail (removable)
7. Fore Topgallant Sail
8. Fore Topgallant Studdingsail (removable)
9. Main Staysail
10. Mainsail
11. Main Topsail
12. Main Topgallant Sail

Spars and Rigging

A. Jibboom
B. Bowsprit
C. Spritsail Yard
D. Foremast
E. Foreyard
F. Fore Topmast
G. Fore Topsail Yard
H. Fore Topgallant Mast
I. Fore Topgallant Yard
J. Mainmast
K. Mainyard
L. Main Topmast
M. Main Topsail Yard
N. Main Topgallant Mast
O. Main Topgallant Yard
P. Boom
Q. Gaff
R. Ensign Staff (removable)
S. Mainstay
T. Fore Shrouds and Ratlines
U. Fore Topmast Shrouds and Ratlines
V. Main Shrouds and Ratlines
W. Main Topmast Shrouds and Ratlines

*For other terminology and usage see Glossary at the end of the book

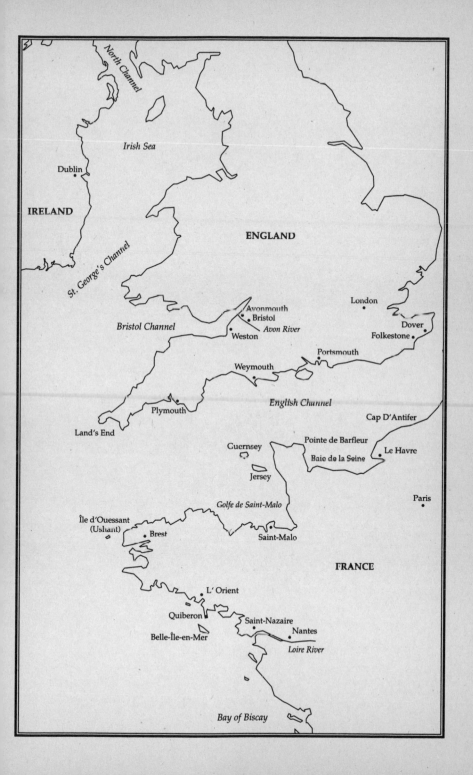

CHAPTER
1

After three days men grow Weary,
Of a Wench, a Guest, & Weather Rainy.
—POOR RICHARD'S ALMANACK, 1733

CAPT. ISAAC BIDDLECOMB STOOD IN THE POURING RAIN, HIS SHOES firmly fixed in the thick mud underfoot, the water running in three rivulets out of the corners of his cocked hat. His clothing was soaked through entirely, right down to his skin. He was more wet than he could recall ever having been while on land—it could not be called dry land—and had it been any later in the season, he might have been chilled as well, which would have made his discomfort complete.

Fortunately it was only the twenty-ninth of August, the end of the summer of 1776, and the evenings were still fairly warm in the former Crown colony of New York, which meant he was spared the misery of being both wet and cold.

He stood in the gathering dusk, confused and uncertain, while around him rushed dozens of men, hundreds of men, all of them even more confused and uncertain than he, an army apparently in full retreat. They were heavy laden with haversacks and cartridge boxes and soaked blankets tied in bundles, and they clutched muskets rendered useless by the rain.

"13th Pennsylvania, form up here! Form up!" a sergeant cried, waving his hat over his head to attract the attention

of the men who streamed by, but no one paid any attention
to him.

"Pardon me . . ." Biddlecomb took a step toward the
sergeant, and as he did so, he was bumped hard from behind. He stumbled but his shoe stayed put, held fast in the
mud, and his now stocking-clad foot came forward and sank
inches deep in the muck. "Son of a bitch . . ."

"Keep clear, you stupid whoreson," said the man who
had bumped him. The man rushed on past, bearing the head
of a litter on which lay a soldier, thrashing and moaning, his
formerly white breeches soaked with dirt, rain, and blood.

Biddlecomb extracted his foot from the mud, pushed it
back into the shoe, and made his way over to the sergeant
who had managed to round up three of the 13th Pennsylvania and was calling for more.

"Pardon me, pardon me, where might I find General
Washington's staff?"

The sergeant did not look at him but jerked his thumb
over his shoulder. "Tent, over yonder."

Biddlecomb looked in the direction the sergeant was
pointing. A cluster of tents stood one hundred yards away,
a group of smaller ones surrounding one much larger. They
looked gray and indistinct through the rain and the failing
light. "Thank you."

"If you see anyone of any rank worth piss," the sergeant
said, meeting Biddlecomb's eyes, "tell him my men skir-
mished with some pickets that was thrown out in front of
the sappers. Them saps are extending out northeasterly,
about three hundred yards now, and they're still digging
like fucking badgers."

"Yes, indeed . . ." Biddlecomb began to ask for an explanation of the sergeant's words, less than half of which he
understood, but the man had returned to calling for his
troops, so Biddlecomb left him and made his way toward
the distant tent.

He was on the Brooklyn Heights, the high, wooded ridge

that stood between the little town of Brooklyn, which he could see in glimpses through the trees down and to his right, and the rest of Long Island to his left. From where he stood he could just see the East River, but Manhattan Island and the harbor of New York were both lost in the poor visibility.

Still, he knew what was there. He knew that on Manhattan Island, behind hastily constructed fortifications, were huddled the few reserves from Washington's army, those who had not been thrown into the battle on Long Island. And he knew that in the harbor by Staten Island there were dozens of British transports, while just through the Narrows in Gowanus Bay were ten British ships of the line, twenty frigates, and hundreds more transports, the greatest expeditionary force ever mounted by the British military.

He had seen them both that morning, and had heard about the fleet beyond the Narrows, during a break in the weather, as he stood on the landing at the tip of Manhattan trying with great difficulty to find someone to ferry him across the river to Long Island.

It had taken him five days to get that far, five days from Philadelphia, which was not above ninety miles away.

The first part of the journey had been undertaken by coach, the coach that was supposed to go clear to Manhattan, crossing the Hudson at Jeffery's Hook, well north of the known British positions. The driver, however, had gone as far as Harlem and refused to go farther, swearing that he would not risk getting killed or having his horses requisitioned by plunging into the middle of a fight between them damnable German murderers and them godforsaken Whig rascals.

Biddlecomb had then been forced to walk the length of Manhattan Island, only to be stopped from his mission of seeing General Washington by the East River, which stood between him and the commander in chief.

"You don't want to go over there," said the soldier guarding the landing, turning and spitting into the East River in the general direction of Long Island. "Goddamned army's on the run. Goddamned Cornwallis marched right around the left flank, sent the bastards running. I'm just thanking the Good Lord that I ain't over there, and you should too."

But in point of fact Biddlecomb did want to go over there. He had come all of that way to see General Washington and he would not be stopped just short of accomplishing that.

Of course, when he had left Philadelphia, it had not occurred to him that he would find the general in the midst of such a crisis. After all, the British and the Americans had done nothing but stare at one another across New York Harbor for almost two months now. Only during his trip had he begun to hear disquieting rumors about British activity and the possibility of actual fighting. But he had not been dissuaded then and he would not be now.

A few hours short of nightfall, he managed to find a boat to take him across the fast-moving river.

And now, at long last, General Washington was in sight. Or General Washington's tent, at least.

He trudged on across the great expanse of mud that had once been a grassy field, pausing to let a column of men march past. They shuffled and muttered curses and their shoes made squishing sounds in the mud, but they possessed the closest thing to military order he had seen since reaching Long Island.

He could see the flare of a lantern being lit in the big tent, and then another, and soon the canvas glowed from within, an image of warmth and dryness. He looked at it longingly.

The column of men moved past and Biddlecomb continued on. He very much wanted to get in that tent and get some relief from the incessant rain, rain that he had endured with only brief respites for two solid days.

He entered the cluster of tents and crossed, it seemed, some invisible divide. On the battlefield it was all confusion and disorganization, with wounded and frightened men

4

rushing in panic. But in the cluster of tents a calm if urgent efficiency seemed to prevail. Messengers hurried in and out, and majors issued orders to captains, who issued orders to lieutenants, who moved frenetically through the headquarters. But there was no sense of panic, no sense of pending disaster. There was only the need to see things done, and quickly.

Biddlecomb paused outside the big tent, unsure whether he should enter. He took a breath and pushed the flap aside and stepped in, out of the driving rain and into the lantern light and the musty air within.

The tent was crammed with small tables, ringing the edges of the space, and at each sat a clerk scratching out copies of orders. Another dozen men at least milled around, talking in low tones, water running off their long cloaks and mixing with the mud with which the floor of the tent was evenly coated. And sitting at a big desk in the middle of the tent, enunciating orders to a lieutenant who stood before him, sat Maj. Edward Fitzgerald.

Biddlecomb pushed through the crowd of men and stood to one side of the desk, waiting for Fitzgerald to finish with the young officer. It had been almost a year since he had last seen the major, an aide-de-camp to General Washington. Fitzgerald had been instrumental in dispatching Biddlecomb to Bermuda to capture a British store of gunpowder in what had turned out to be nothing more than a plot to capture him.

The major had won no small degree of glory in driving off a British regiment that was attempting to take back the British merchantman that Biddlecomb had captured and brought into Boston Harbor, and though the major would not say as much, Biddlecomb also believed that the major had personally killed the traitor who had engineered the trap.

Fitzgerald was intelligent and charming, the loftiness of the Southern aristocracy coupled with a handsome face and athletic bearing. But despite those irritating qualities, they had become friends during Biddlecomb's time in Cambridge.

"Yes, I am in no doubt that Fort Putnam is well manned," Fitzgerald was saying to the lieutenant, "but you go and tell *General* Putnam that General Washington wants him to personally make certain there are troops clear to Wallabout Bay. That left flank must be anchored down thus or Cornwallis shall steal a march on us again. Now go."

The lieutenant swept off his hat in salute, then spun on his heel and was gone. Fitzgerald turned to Biddlecomb with an expression of a man ready to deal with yet another annoyance. Then he frowned and his eyebrows came together. "Isaac Biddlecomb? Capt. Isaac Biddlecomb, could it be? What in all hell . . . ?"

He stood and extended his hand and Biddlecomb shook it with pleasure. "What in all the world are you doing here, sir?" Fitzgerald asked, smiling, quite in contrast to his expression of a moment before. "Of all the people I would have thought would have enough sense to keep clear of this debacle!"

"I'm . . . actually, I must have a word with General Washington."

"The general is out on the lines at the moment, left me here to deal with this nonsense."

"I understand things have not gone well these past days?"

Fitzgerald smiled. "You could say that. General Sullivan failed to hold the Jamaica Pass. Hell, he failed to even try to hold it. Cornwallis marched right around our left flank, and before we knew it, his whole damned army was in our rear. It was a rout. They drove us clear back to the Heights with the damned East River at our backs. We lost a great deal of men, good men."

"Sir? Sir?" A drenched, muddy soldier stepped up to Fitzgerald's desk and saluted. His cheek was smeared with blood that was diluted to a thin red wash by the rain. "Corporal Mulligan, sir, 13th Pennsylvania. Lieutenant says for me to report to you that we had a skirmish with some pickets protecting the sappers, sir. The saps is three hundred yards long now, extending northeast, and they're still digging."

"Thank you, Corporal," Fitzgerald said, and the soldier saluted again and left.

"Oh, yes," said Biddlecomb with a flush of guilt, "what does all that mean?"

"General Howe is digging regular approaches to get at us. By that I mean saps . . . trenches . . . and breastworks, getting his troops closer."

"But it appeared to me as if the Continental Army was in full retreat. Are the British not in close pursuit?"

"What? Oh, do you mean the men out there? No, they are just stragglers, wounded men or men separated from their companies or skulkers. The main part of the army is still well entrenched. Please, Captain, have a seat." Fitzgerald gestured toward a chair in front of his desk. Biddlecomb sat and Fitzgerald did too.

"And Cornwallis is digging approaches?" Biddlecomb asked. "I should think he would prefer a headlong assault, with his greater numbers."

"Apparently he had a bellyful of frontal attacks at Bunker's Hill and we can thank the Lord for that. Had he pressed his attack of the other day, he would have overrun us. He still could, especially in this rain, as we have precious few bayonets amongst us. Fortunately he does not seem inclined to try. But tell me, how has it been with you? I heard some of the captains were court-martialed for that affair with the *Glasgow?* I would wish you were not one of them."

"I was not," said Biddlecomb. The affair to which Fitzgerald alluded was a night battle, one that pitted the entire American fleet, two ships, three brigs, and a sloop, against the British frigate *Glasgow.* And despite the overwhelming odds the *Glasgow* had managed to inflict considerable damage and then escape.

7

"Apparently my chasing the *Glasgow* nearly into Newport, as stupid and ill-considered as it was, was thought valiant enough to put me above suspicion. It was Whipple that was court-martialed, at his own request, to quash the bloody stupid talk of cowardice that had started. If ever there was a man who was not a coward, it is Abraham Whipple. He was acquitted of course. Hazard of the *Providence* was cashiered, as well he should have been. Hopkins was just censured by Congress a few weeks ago."

Fitzgerald nodded. "So the fleet is still in Providence?"

"For the most part. The first on *Alfred*, a Scotsman by the name of Jones, has command of *Providence* now in Hazard's stead and he has been cruising, as has *Andrew Doria* and *Cabot*. I have mostly been tied up with business in Philadelphia."

"Not so tied up, I should hope, that you have been unable to see Virginia? Virginia Stanton?"

Biddlecomb smiled at that. Virginia was the daughter of his mentor, William Stanton. He had been courting her, to the extent that his time ashore and his courage would allow, for almost two years. Fitzgerald had met her, during the Bermuda affair, and Biddlecomb was not insensible to the effect that she had had on him. She had that effect on most men.

"Yes, I have seen her," said Biddlecomb, "though I fear you mistake her name. She is no longer Virginia Stanton. She now goes by the name Virginia Biddlecomb."

At that, Fitzgerald's fine-tailored composure fell apart, to Biddlecomb's delight. The major sat forward and his mouth hung open. "I . . . I . . . ," he stammered while Biddlecomb leaned back and folded his arms, savoring the moment.

And then he was back in Philadelphia, a hot, humid July day. And then he was back in her bed, their bed, her lithe body moving under him, and despite the heavy, soaked clothing he felt a warmth inside, the beginnings of arousal.

"Well, man, congratulations!" Fitzgerald said at last, his

8

usual cool demeanor returning. "You are married? Why, you lucky dog! I am with child to hear the particulars, though I fear this is not the time or place."

"Indeed." Biddlecomb shook his head, like shaking off comforting sleep. He was again aware of the pelting of rain on the roof of General Washington's tent as he stared at the flame in the lantern, flickering and dancing in the many and conflicting drafts. "Forgive my distraction, I beg. I find the memory more pleasing by far than the present circumstance."

"Of course you do. I do too, and I wasn't even there. But pray, what is it you wish with the general?"

"Oh." Biddlecomb hesitated. It seemed such a silly thing, given the predicament in which the United States Army found itself. But he had come all that way.

"The fact is this. You recall Ezra Rumstick, my first officer during the Bermuda affair? Well, the Marine Committee has failed to recognize Rumstick's seniority based on the commission that the general issued him last summer. I have been to every person I can think of, and none feel willing or able to help in this measure. I thought perhaps that if the general could write a letter to the committee . . ."

At this, Major Fitzgerald burst out laughing. Not a smile or a chuckle of mirth but a full-bellied laugh that made everyone in the tent look over at him. Biddlecomb shifted uncomfortably, wanted to tell Fitzgerald, "Pray, sir, shut your bloody gob."

"Captain, forgive me," Fitzgerald began when his laughter had subsided enough for him to speak. "Your request is entirely proper, but I must say, as fortunate as you are in matters of the heart, you have the damnedest luck when it comes to military affairs. And once again you show the most exquisite timing."

"Well, sir, allow me to point out that there was not even a hint of the present battle when I left Philadelphia five days ago."

"I understand, Captain. However, I fear that the general

will not have the time tonight to write your letter, and by this time tomorrow I fear you will no longer require it."

"And why not?"

"Because," Fitzgerald said, now sounding resigned rather than amused, "once Howe completes his approaches, I believe you shall witness the entire destruction of the Army of the United States."

CHAPTER
2

Cold & cunning come from the North:
But cunning sans wisdom is nothing worth.

—Poor Richard's Almanack, 1743

"Well, indeed," said Biddlecomb, and for a moment he could think of nothing more to add. "It seems we're to witness a prodigious amount of history this season. The beginning of American independence and the end of it, all in the space of two months."

Fitzgerald nodded. "It would seem so."

"But surely there is something that can be done? Must the army just wait here to be overrun?"

"We will fight, of course, and hope for the opportunity to break out. But as it stands we are surrounded by the British and the Hessians in the front and water behind and on either flank."

The mention of water made Biddlecomb brighten. It was his element, and the thought of its proximity gave him a spark of optimism, as baseless as it might be. "Of course. Why do you not just ferry the men back to Manhattan? There are no men-of-war in the river to stop you now, nor can there be as long as this wind holds northeasterly. Glover's regiment from Marblehead is here, is it not? They should be more than able to handle the boats."

"Ah, therein lies the rub, as the old boy said," Fitzgerald replied, leaning back in his chair. "We've but a half dozen

11

boats. Less, actually, I believe. Those boatmen we hired to bear the army over fled with their precious boats at the first sign of fighting. We had considered an evacuation, and we would do it, gladly, but for want of boats."

Biddlecomb frowned and stared into the flame. "You have searched along the island, I presume, and on Manhattan?"

"We have. We have hired every boat there is for hire. Half a dozen."

Biddlecomb felt his thoughts wandering, sailing out across the black, rain-swept harbor. To most it was a frightening and dangerous place, but to him it was a sanctuary. On the water one could not become trapped as easily as one could on land. On the water there was always someplace to run, and once clear of the constricting land one could circle the globe on the contiguous seas.

But those thoughts would not save the Army of the United States. It seemed that nothing would, save for boats.

And the irony of the thing was that there were boats aplenty, hundreds of boats, not above eight miles away. Unfortunately they were British, part of the great armada off Staten Island and anchored in Gowanus Bay.

He glanced down at his coat—blue with white facings and cuffs—and his white waistcoat and breeches, now quite splattered with mud. It had not occurred to him until that moment that his outfit was all but identical to that of a lieutenant in the Royal Navy. Certainly on a night such as this there would be no distinguishing the two. He felt the first stirrings of an idea, the telltale tingling on the soles of his feet.

"It occurs to me, Major, that perhaps there are more boats to be had," he said before he had given any thought to the words.

"Pray, Captain, go on," said Fitzgerald, leaning forward. "We might save the entire army but for want of boats."

So I shall once again rescue the fine Mr. Fitzgerald, shall I?

Biddlecomb thought. He pictured his friend Fitzgerald in slavering gratitude, and the image was warm and gratifying.

"Well, sir, it occurs to me that there are a great number of boats to be had among the British fleet. It wants only a good, big boat of our own, well manned with sailors, which are to be had in abundance from Colonel Glover's men . . ."

It was eight miles by water to Staten Island, eight miles to the roadstead where a small portion of the fleet of British transports lay moored in what little shelter they could find. And across that stretch of water known as New York Harbor sailed a single boat, crammed to the gunnels with men, quite invisible in the dark and the rain.

Biddlecomb sat in the stern sheets, wrapped in a borrowed boat cloak, the tiller held lightly in his left hand. There was quite a bit of wind for an open boat, gusting to twenty-five knots, but it was nearly dead astern, and with the big boat's mast and lugsail rigged they were making six knots at least through the water, and with the ebbing tide even more than that over the ground.

The crew, thirty well-armed men, sat huddled together in the bottom of the boat, attempting to keep their powder dry and on occasion bailing a few scoops of water back into the harbor. They were well outfitted in oilskins and tarred hats, lashed fast under bearded chins. They were handpicked men from the 14th Continental Regiment, Colonel Glover's regiment from Marblehead in Massachusetts.

The 14th Continentals were sailors to a man, fishermen mostly, bred to the sea, who had joined the militia when the British restrictions on fishing had ruined their livelihood and left them with little to do beyond seeking vengeance. They sat calmly now, quite unperturbed by the wild motion of the boat as it pounded through the chop or the rain that came in lashing gusts and blotted out everything ten feet outboard of the boat.

It had not taken Biddlecomb long to convince Fitzgerald

to allow him to give his idea a try. Indeed, there was little for the army to lose, and survival to gain, if he was able to secure boats for the evacuation of Long Island.

A messenger was dispatched to Glover with orders for thirty of his best men while Fitzgerald and Biddlecomb made their way to the ferry landing to survey the boats that were available.

Biddlecomb had little difficulty choosing the one that he wanted. Only six boats were there. Two of them were little bigger than yawls, and one already had six inches of water in the bottom that he did not believe to be the result of rain.

But one of them was ideally suited to the purpose. Though Fitzgerald did not know its origins, Biddlecomb suspected that it had once belonged to a British man-of-war. Twenty-five feet in length, it looked very much like one of the barges carried by the smaller ships of the navy. And if that was not enough, it mounted in its bow a small swivel gun, and beneath the forwardmost thwart, kept perfectly dry in an iron box, were cartridges, round shot, and grape for the same.

Glover's men arrived, led by a sergeant, Noah Wilbur, who looked and acted much more like a veteran navy boatswain than the sergeant of infantry he purported to be.

"You men, get this sailing rig set up," he growled, nodding with his chin toward the boat, and with a speed born of an intimate knowledge of their task the Marbleheaders stepped the mast and rigged the lugsail and jib.

No more than fifteen minutes later, the Americans were under way, running down the East River to New York's Upper Bay. Governors Island loomed on the starboard bow, the wind- and tide-driven water flashing white as it piled up on the weather side. A moment later they left the island astern as Red Hook hove into view to larboard.

Biddlecomb felt the wind build in a sudden gust, felt the bow dig in as the boat tried to round up, and he tightened his grip on the tiller.

"Let's stand by to jibe, men," he called out, the first words he had spoken since getting under way. The water that streamed down his face, half rain and half spray, filled his mouth as he spoke and made him sputter, but he could see hands reaching automatically for the sheets of the jib and the lugsail.

He shifted in his seat, waiting for the gust to diminish a bit. It blew again, harder, heeling the boat away, and then, as if it had expended its breath, eased off to its former strength.

Biddlecomb eased the tiller over and the stern swung up into the wind and the men at the lugsail sheet hauled with a will, dragging the canvas toward the centerline of the boat until the wind caught the sail on the other side and snapped it over.

The men at the jib eased away the larboard sheet as the starboard took up the strain, and the men at the lugsail sheet eased that away too, until the sail was well out over the starboard side and the boat began its run down bay.

What a pleasure, Biddlecomb thought, to work with these men! After having one crew after another of landsmen aboard the *Charlemagne* who needed to be trained in the very basics of seamanship, it was such a joy to have with him a boatload of men—men with whom he had never sailed before—who could jibe a boat in a driving storm, at night, with never a word spoken. If he could have an entire crew of such men, what a burden would be lifted from his shoulders.

He leaned outboard and peered forward through the dark. Five miles distant he could just see the twinkling of the anchor lights from the fleet of transports anchored near Staten Island. That would be the place to get boats, from the lightly manned merchantmen who were more likely to be cowed by the officious demands of a lieutenant of the Royal Navy, or someone whom they took for such.

He felt the boat heel and glanced down at the small compass by his knee, noting the heading that would take them to the fleet. He looked up again, but now another squall was on them. He felt the speed of the boat increase, heard the strain of the rigging on the light mast, and then all visibility was gone as the brunt of the storm rolled over them.

It was one of those moments—he had had them before, many times—as he sat in the dark, driving the boat by instinct through the rain-swept night, that he wondered what in all hell he had been thinking. This was insane. He was seriously intending to sail straight into the British fleet and demand the use of their boats.

But what made it most insane was his motive for doing it. It was not for the cause of independency, not because he was brave, not out of concern for the men trapped on Long Island.

He was doing it because Major Fitzgerald had annoyed him by laughing at his request for a letter from Washington, because Major Fitzgerald always annoyed him, always made him feel as if he had to prove himself. He had undertaken this mission primarily to show the major up. And that was not much of a reason to get killed, he knew, or much of a reason to get these other men killed along with him.

Well, he thought, *the reason is of no matter*. If he could pull it off, then he would have done a good thing, a great thing, of enormous benefit to his country, his own silly motives notwithstanding. And then he could get Washington to write the goddamned stupid letter for which he had come.

The chop grew steeper and the wind stronger as they left Red Hook astern and headed out across the open water of the Upper Bay. The boat pitched and yawed in the following sea, and the waves on occasion broke over the gunnels, forcing the Marblehead men to bail in earnest. But the wind was a blessing now, hurling them across the bay. On their return trip it would be a curse as they would be forced to row straight into it, while with any luck towing at least two dozen empty boats.

They were in blackness, a wild, wet, buffeting blackness where nothing could be seen beyond the tiny orb of light from the sheltered glim that illuminated the compass. Biddlecomb pulled his watch awkwardly from his pocket and held it near the light. It was near ten o'clock, just over an hour since they had left from the ferry landing on Long Island. By his reckoning they would be in among the fleet of transports momentarily.

"We're almost there," he said to the men huddled in the bottom. "Let's strike this sailing gear and approach under oars." He thrust the tiller over, easing the bow of the boat up into the wind. The canvas snapped and flogged until the men cast off halyards and wrestled it down.

The squall, with its poor visibility, would be a good thing now, Biddlecomb realized. It was cover, another impediment to their being discovered.

And then with that vindictive, malicious caprice with which all weather systems seem to operate, the squall blew past. The rain eased away, and with it the fog, and in less than a minute they went from their dark and watery tomb to a good two miles of visibility at least. Only the strong wind was left, the one thing that was pure hindrance to them.

"Well, thank the Lord that's blown past, at least," Biddlecomb said, trying to sound sincere. Just off the larboard quarter, two hundred yards away, the anchor lights of the transports burned like a city at night. The Marbleheaders, without a word, dropped the oars in the tholes and took them up, double banked because of the great number of men aboard. Biddlecomb pushed the tiller over and they resumed their course toward the transports.

He steered past the first ship—he could see no boats on her booms nor any floating alongside. This, to his thinking,

17

did not bode well. But the ship moored astern of her and closer to shore had two boats bobbing under her counter.

Biddlecomb called, "Toss oars!" and the two banks of oars came up with a precision that was as good as anything one might expect from the British navy.

"The transport, hoay!" he called out. He had thought at first to just steal the boat, but if he was discovered doing so, then the game would be up. Better to try to bluff the transports out of dozens of boats than to just steal a few.

A moment later, having received no response, he called again. "The transport, hoay!"

At length a figure appeared over the bulwark of the quarterdeck. "What do you want, then?"

"Beg your pardon," Biddlecomb said, trying to sound clipped and officious, "I'm from the flag. We've need of the use of your boat."

"Use of our boat? You've already got near every boat in the fleet. Ain't you got bloody boats of your own?"

"Yes, but we've need of more. We are shifting troops by water."

"What, on a night like this?"

"If you think it unwise, I suggest you speak with Admiral Howe about it, but I haven't the time to discuss it. Now by your leave I shall take the boat. You should just be glad I have no need of men as well."

"Oh, bloody hell. You give me a receipt for that, them boats is dear, we don't get 'em free like the bloody navy."

Biddlecomb nodded at the oarsmen and the oars came down. "I've no time to give out receipts for each boat. I'm keeping a log of which boat we get from whom. What ship is that?"

"*Elizabeth Clare* out of Plymouth."

Biddlecomb brushed his boat cloak aside, enough to give a glimpse of his ersatz uniform, the blue coat with white facings and the white waistcoat and breeches. Across his chest was a leather shoulder belt, also white, from which was slung his sword. The belt was adorned with an oval-shaped brass plate that sparkled as the light from the various lanterns glinted off the water beaded on the metal and made the plate look like something more precious than it was.

He pretended to jot down the name in a book hidden under the cloth. "Very good, then. We shall be returning the boats within a day or two," he called, but by the time he finished speaking, the man on deck was lost behind the looming counter of the merchantman.

"Backwater, larboard, there," Wilbur growled, and the larboard side backed their oars and the boat spun on its length. Another of the boat crew untied the painter on the merchantman's boat and made it fast to their transom, and the first capture of the night was complete.

And so it went through the fleet, with Biddlecomb demanding boats in his best imitation of a British naval officer and then patiently fending off various degrees of abuse and invective. None of the merchantmen were polite, and none cooperative, but neither did any of them refuse, and soon the string of boats grew until they looked like ducklings following their mother through the water.

But the words of the first merchantman, to the effect that the navy already had every boat in the fleet, proved to be prophetic. They encountered that objection many times over, and what was worse, it appeared to be true.

As they passed out of the merchant fleet, Biddlecomb looked at the string of boats astern. They had visited every one of the transports off Staten Island and had collected only seven boats. It was a start, but they would need at least twice as many, three times as many, to get Washington's nine-thousand-man army, as well as the artillery and other equipment, across in one night. If it could be done at all.

A nearby merchantman began to ring its bell, and then another and another, three sets of two quick strikes, a single one, and then silence again. Seven bells. Eleven-thirty at night.

"I believe we've gleaned what we can from these transports," he said to the men of the 14th, resting on their oars and waiting further instructions. He steeled himself to give his next order, one that was completely outrageous, in a matter-of-fact tone.

"I need ten of you to go off with this lot of boats and bring them back to the ferry landing. It'll be a hard pull in this wind, but I can't spare any more men. The rest of us will head over to Gowanus Bay and see what we can pick up there."

It was the most insane suggestion yet, that they should row right in among the moored men-of-war and continue pretending to be a part of the Royal Navy, but it received no more than a murmur and a few nods of approval. In the bow Sergeant Wilbur barked out ten names and those men clambered out of the boat and into the captured one that had been pulled alongside. "Step that mast again, Captain?" the sergeant asked.

"Aye. We've work enough tonight, let's let the wind do what it will for us."

Ten minutes later the longboat was racing across the Upper Bay, heeling over with the wind abeam. It was livelier now, on that point of sail, and absent the weight of the ten men who were pulling back to Brooklyn with the first of their catch. The twenty men still aboard huddled up on the weather side, enduring the spray that broke frequently over the gunnel.

Twenty minutes later they were in among the fleet, a sight the likes of which none of them had ever seen. There were ten ships of the line, huge, ponderous two- and three-deck men-of-war, the broad yellow stripes running the length of their hulls and delineating their gun decks, barely visible through the gloom. They were moored, two anchor cables coming from each bow and jutting out straight like solid beams, holding them in place against the rising wind. Scattered among them were the frigates and sloops of war, twenty or more of them, the smallest of which was at least as powerful as the most powerful ship in the American navy.

The navy ships were all clustered near the northern end of Gowanus Bay, while to the south and east, nearer to shore, were the transports. There were hundreds of them, three times the number that had been at Staten Island. Biddlecomb was stunned at the sight. He had been with the British fleet during the siege of Quebec in 1759, he had been among the big convoy that resupplied Boston, he had been to sea for seventeen years, but he had never seen anything the likes of that.

"Dear God, looks like we found the happy hunting ground, Captain," Sergeant Wilbur growled.

"Indeed, Sergeant, and I reckon it will be better guarded than the last. Let's luff up for a moment and see our muskets are charged with dry powder and see that swivel gun loaded."

The wind was blowing harder now, gusting to thirty knots, as the Marblehead men struggled in the tossing boat to unstep the mast and ship oars. Soon they were under way again, firearms ready, pulling for the merchant fleet.

They were still one hundred yards away when Biddlecomb realized why there had been so few boats among the other transports. They were all here, where they had been used for the landing on Long Island a week before. Three or four boats were trailing astern of every ship at anchor, and each boat was twenty feet or more in length.

The Marblehead men pulled for the nearest transport. "Hoay, there!" Biddlecomb called over the whistling and moaning sound of the wind through the rigging. "I'm from the flag!" Unobtrusively he shouldered his boat cloak aside to reveal the white facing on his coat. "We've need of your boats!"

Two minutes and several pointed words later Sergeant Wilbur made fast to a cleat a string of three boats from the transport.

It took no more than fifteen minutes for that number to rise to a dozen, and another ten men of the 14th were sent off to pull that covey of watercraft back to Brooklyn ferry landing.

Biddlecomb and his remaining men worked their way north through the transports, closer to the navy ships but closer to the American lines as well.

Isaac had all he could do to avoid laughing out loud at how simple the whole thing was. A touch of arrogance, an air of superiority, white lapels on his coat and he was indistinguishable on that dark night from a genuine lieutenant in the British navy. And apparently these transport captains were so accustomed to such demands from the navy that they gave it not a second thought, after putting up what useless protest they might.

Hubris, he thought. Beware, beware of hubris. It had done for the Greeks and it had done for him on plenty of occasions. Hubris had him out on this filthy night to begin with, and if he allowed his arrogance to become real, and not just an act to fool these transport captains, then it would do for him again.

These thoughts tumbled around in his head as he watched Wilbur make fast the last of the boats. They had commandeered twelve more, and with only ten men left to man the oars, it was time to head for Brooklyn. But he had managed to gather thirty or so all told, good boats, and that should be sufficient to evacuate the army.

"Boat's coming. Looks like a guard boat," one of the Marbleheaders muttered, nodding over the starboard quarter.

Biddlecomb swiveled in the stern sheets and looked in the direction that the man had indicated. A boat was approaching, its two banks of oars moving together with a symmetry that bespoke the British navy. It seemed to resolve out of the mist that had been building for the past hour, creating halos around the anchor lights and blurring the images of the more distant vessel.

"Eyes inboard," Biddlecomb hissed. "Just keep rowing as if you were doing what you were supposed to be doing." He stared forward, past the men at the oars. They were heading for the moored fleet, the ships of the line and the frigates and sloops, and once past them they would be out of Gowanus Bay and lost in the darkness again, with the British navy astern. They had only to get that far.

"The boat, hoay!"

Biddlecomb jumped at the hail, though he had entirely expected it.

"Hoay, the boat there!"

"Keep rowing," Biddlecomb hissed, and then turning again to the guard boat replied, "Holloa, there!"

There was a moment of silence as the guard boat, moving much faster than the Americans with their stolen boats in tow, pulled closer, until they were abeam and twenty yards away. Biddlecomb eased his boat cloak open so that his uniform coat was just visible.

"I say, who are you and what are you about?" called the officer in the stern sheets of the guard boat. At least Biddlecomb figured him for an officer; he appeared as little more than an amorphous shape in the dark and the mist.

"Lieutenant Biddlecomb, fourth in the flagship. I've orders to bring these boats to the beach. Some shifting of troops, or some such. Bloody army, you know how it is."

There was a pause, a silence, not the response that Biddlecomb had hoped that his jovial reply would receive. Out of the corner of his eye he could see the men of the 14th slowly picking up their muskets with movements too subtle to be seen from the guard boat.

"Fourth in the flagship? The *Eagle* flagship?"

"The *Eagle* is the only flagship in the fleet, is it not?"

Biddlecomb asked. In point of fact he did not know if the *Eagle* was the flagship at all, but nothing in his voice gave that away.

"Well, this is queer," the officer of the guard boat called back, "because, you see, I am the fifth lieutenant in the flagship. And I daresay I've never heard of you."

CHAPTER
3

Those who in quarrels interpose
Must often wipe a bloody nose.

—POOR RICHARD'S ALMANACK, 1740

"KEEP THOSE GUNS OUT OF SIGHT, NO FIRING BUT ON MY COM-
mand," Biddlecomb said in a whisper. "We'll try to take
them silent, if we can.

"Now see here," he called to the guard boat, which was
ten yards away and coming straight at them. "I am tempo-
rarily assigned to the flagship and am not at liberty to discuss my orders. I have been strictly commanded to secrecy
and have been enjoined to hurry." His weak attempt at sub-
terfuge drew no response from the approaching boat.

Five yards away the guard boat turned parallel to the
Americans and the boat crew tossed oars. The officer in
the stern sheets was younger than Biddlecomb, in his early
twenties, if that. Guard boat duty on a night such as that
was not work for more senior officers.

"I shall have to ask you to follow me," the young lieutenant said. Biddlecomb could see the officer's uniform under
his boat cloak; it was nearly identical to his own, and it
occurred to him that the British might hang him for a spy
if they thought he was wearing one of their uniforms, which
inadvertently he was. "We shall return to the flag," the
young man said, "and have them straighten this out."

"I do not have time for this, Lieutenant. Cornwallis himself is waiting . . . ," Biddlecomb began, then saw the officer's attention drawn to the men of the 14th, saw the lieutenant's eyes go wide, saw him pull awkwardly at a pistol in his belt. Biddlecomb looked forward at his men. Their muskets could clearly be seen, and their feeble attempts to hide them made them that much more conspicuous.

"Throw those weapons down, all of you!" the lieutenant shouted, struggling with his pistol as his own boat crew reached for something—guns, presumably—in the bottom of the guard boat. Five yards of water still separated the Americans from the British. There would be no taking them silently.

"Fire!" Biddlecomb shouted, and the muskets came up to the boat crew's shoulders and ten flintlocks came down on frizzens, and of those, five actually fired.

It was like a miniature broadside, and at that distance the Marbleheaders could not miss. Three of the guard boat's men were blown from their thwarts and fell from sight to the bottom of the boat. Several more howled in surprise and pain and grabbed at shoulders and arms.

The five who had misfired reprimed their weapons and this time discharged them, just as the men in the guard boat who still could aimed and fired their own muskets. The gunshots in the mist made a weird, glowing flash. One of Biddlecomb's men fell, a hole through his forehead, dead even before he splashed in the water in the bottom of the boat.

"To the oars, to the oars, let's go!" Biddlecomb shouted, and muskets were flung to the bottom of the boat as the men took up the oars and bent their backs to escape.

The guard boat was drifting away, out of control, half her crew dead or wounded as the lieutenant rallied those left and pushed them to the oars.

"Damn it!" Biddlecomb said out loud. Of all the damned luck.

The guard boat was under way now, coming after them

again, slower, the oars single-banked. But the lieutenant could dog them all the way to Brooklyn, blasting them with musket fire, but of course they would not make it that far. The Americans could either continue to row and be shot at their oars, or could stop rowing and shoot back, but in either case they would not escape.

Soon the guard boat was all but lost in the mist, a vague shadow, as the Americans pulled for all they were worth. Biddlecomb looked astern at the long train of empty boats being towed behind. The last one was over three hundred feet back, he could not even see it.

The thing to do was to just cut them loose, but he could not. And he hoped that no one else would suggest it, because he did not want to try to explain his irrational reluctance.

Pandemonium had broken out in the fleet, the raucous sound of chaos, audible even to Biddlecomb's ears, dulled by the musket fire. Bells were ringing from all corners of the bay, and out of the mist he could hear shouted orders and the stamp of feet. He imagined that a few captains at least, unsure of what was happening, were clearing their ships for action.

He felt a jerk in the boat's motion, just the subtlest of tugs that most would have dismissed as the effect of the chop.

He glanced astern again, but could see nothing beyond dark and ill-defined shapes. But he did not have to see to know what it was.

The lieutenant from the guard boat had hooked on to one of their stolen train, and he and his men had climbed aboard and were working their way forward, clambering from boat to boat to get at the Americans.

"You four men," Biddlecomb hissed at the four aftermost oarsmen. "Stow your oars and load your muskets, and make certain you have cutlasses. Quickly now. Sergeant Wilbur, lay aft and take the tiller, please."

A moment later the muskets were ready and the big sergeant was settled on the stern sheets, the tiller in hand. Biddlecomb pulled the next boat in line up to the transom of the longboat and hopped over, the four Marbleheaders following on his heels.

"Get down, get down in the bottom," Biddlecomb whispered, "and on my word stand and fire, then at 'em with cold steel." The men obeyed, half crouching and half lying on the bottom of the boat. Biddlecomb crept aft, keeping low, until he was kneeling by the stern sheets as if at an altar, peering aft into the dark and the mist.

In less than a minute he saw movement, a dark shape stepping silently forward, moving with infinite care, three boats back. Behind him moved another shape, and another, more than Biddlecomb could count. They climbed with some difficulty from the bow of one boat over the transom of another, then made their way across that boat to the next, just one back from the boat in which the Americans were hiding.

Biddlecomb ran his thumb over the lock of the pistol he was holding under his boat cloak. This kind of waiting, this tension, was all but intolerable. It made him want to scream.

He heard a footfall in front of him, a pause, and then a surprised voice calling, "Here, now—"

"Fire!" Biddlecomb whipped the pistol out from under his cloak, pointed it at the dark figure looming over his head, and pulled the trigger. In the subsequent flash he had a glimpse of the young lieutenant, a look of profound shock on his face, before the officer tumbled back into the bottom of the boat. Four musket balls screamed over his head, and the report of the guns mixed with the shouts of surprise from the clandestine boarding party.

"At them!" Biddlecomb shouted, drawing his sword and leaping to his feet, and in that instant he realized he had done a stupid thing.

Three guns exploded in front of him, and he felt the punch of a musket ball striking him square in the chest. The impact flung him back into the bottom of the boat, and his head struck a thwart as he came to rest in two inches of water.

There was no air in his lungs; he was incapable of drawing breath. His arms and legs thrashed out, kicking and striking at the sides of the boat, trying to find air, trying to draw the others' attention to his plight.

A horrible, horrible hurt in his chest, the Marbleheaders stepping around him, going after the enemy in the next boat aft. He felt death overwhelming him, felt he would never draw breath again.

His fist pounded against the gunnel, his mouth and eyes went wide as he sucked in, and suddenly, like catching a foothold just before falling, there was air in his chest.

He sucked deeper, taking in great mouthfuls of the cold, wet air. It was the most delicious taste he had ever experienced and he breathed greedily. The panic subsided, and as it did, he became aware of the terrific agony in his chest where the musket ball had struck. He lay still, his chest heaving, the pain coming in spasms with each deep breath.

He was aware of the sounds of fighting in the next boat, now steel on steel, his people engaged with the guard boat's crew, ignoring him and his wound.

Yes, yes, just leave me, he thought. *The boats, get the boats to Washington . . .*

It was dramatic, and he hoped he would be able to say it out loud to someone before he died. He wanted them to fight on. But still he found he was a bit put out that no one had even inquired as to how he was. He was dying, there in the bottom of the boat, the water sloshing around, and no one had even asked if he was hurt.

So this is death, he thought. He had cheated it so many times, but now at last it had him. He thought of Virginia, and how sorry he was to leave her, how much he did not want to die, on her account. But he had been shot in the chest, and there was no hope for it.

Sharp, agonizing pain, stabbing him again and again with

each breath. It was like nothing he had ever experienced before.

He wondered if he would bleed to death before anything else. *Yes,* he thought, *that's what will do for me.* He knew he was losing blood rapidly, he had to be, and as the thought came to him, he realized that he could not feel any blood on his skin.

Perhaps I've lost feeling already, he thought. But no, his chest still hurt like a son of a bitch.

With a tentative hand he reached under his coat to feel for the blood. The cloth was cool and damp from the mist, not warm and soaked through with blood as he would have expected. He felt around, growing bolder as he encountered nothing out of the ordinary. His hand reached the leather shoulder belt. His fingers were just inches from the wound, from the hub of the pain, but still no blood.

He moved his fingers up the smooth leather of the belt and onto the cold oval-shaped brass plate that covered the buckle. To his surprise it was no longer smooth, but rather twisted and jagged in places.

He ran his hand over it. It felt as if someone had beat it with a hammer. And embedded in the middle, still warm, was the musket ball, badly deformed. He touched it with his fingertip, and even that slight pressure on his bruised chest caused him to suck in his breath.

"Captain, you shot?" a voice spoke in the broad accent of Marblehead.

Biddlecomb rolled onto his side and struggled to his knees. "Ahhhhhhhh!" he shouted through clenched teeth. The pain was all but overwhelming. His breastbone was broken, he was certain, but he was equally certain that he could fight through the pain, as long as he did not have to move too much. "I'm all right, I'm all right," he gasped, thinking sheepishly of the great drama in which he had been indulging himself. "What of the guard boat?"

"We run 'em off, shot three of them, one dead, and the officer in the shoulder. They're still in the boat yonder."

"Very well, we'll leave them for now." He made his way forward, every step an agony, and climbed with care into the stern of the longboat. "Pray, Sergeant, keep the tiller," he said to Wilbur. He could barely lift his arms. Manning the tiller was out of the question.

The four oarsmen resumed their duties, and Biddlecomb, settled in the stern sheets, looked about as best he could.

The situation was getting worse, getting worse quickly.

Another boat was visible in the dim light cast by the ships' deck lanterns, no doubt launched from one of the two-deckers, sent to find out what all the shooting was about. It was two cable lengths away and pulling for them fast, much faster than they could hope to pull, encumbered by all of those boats. He could see at least two other men-of-war launching boats.

And now his men were pulling straight into thirty knots of wind.

Think, think, he had to think, but the throbbing in his chest blotted it all out, fogged his brain like strong drink.

"Keep this heading, Captain?" Wilbur asked.

"Yes, yes." The course they were on now would take them right past the moored men-of-war, but it was the most direct heading out of Gowanus Bay. And the men-of-war would not stop them. It was the boats astern, quickly overtaking, that would make them prisoners or make them dead.

Three minutes later they were up with the moored ships of the Royal Navy, passing the last in a line of the great ponderous brutes that stretched half a mile in front of them. Biddlecomb read the name, *Asia*, in the light of the big lanterns that glowed over the ornate stern of the two-decker. They pulled past the transom, past the poop deck. A voice from the quarterdeck hailed, "Hoay, the boat! What was all that shooting?"

"A boatload of those bloody rebels causing some mis-

31

chief!" Biddlecomb called back. "The guard boat and the others are running them to ground!" This seemed to satisfy whoever it was who had hailed, for no further word came from the *Asia* and the Americans pulled past.

The big men-of-war were moored one in front of the next, with no more than one hundred feet separating the bow of one from the stern of the next, and all were pointing like wind vanes into the stiff breeze. There would be anxious eyes on the anchor cables, Biddlecomb thought, and officers of the deck taking frequent bearings to see that the anchors did not drag. If one of the windward vessels started to go, then it would be a disaster.

And despite the pain in his battered chest, Biddlecomb smiled to himself. Yes, indeed, it would be a disaster. And a disaster was just the thing that they needed to give them cover for an escape.

And he had something of a penchant for manufacturing disaster.

"Sergeant, pray steer for that man-of-war, the one moored at the head of the line," Biddlecomb said, and when the sergeant had repeated the order, Biddlecomb pushed himself to his feet, gritting his teeth against the wave of pain, and stepped carefully forward, making his way between the men at the oars. At last he flopped down on the forwardmost thwart and sat for a moment, catching his breath. He looked at the iron box at his feet.

"You there," he said to the man at the nearest oar, "load this swivel gun with grape, if you would." He had intended to do it himself, but that was out of the question.

"In the boat, toss oars, we are coming alongside!" a voice called from one of the men-of-war's boats, one of the boats that was quickly overtaking them.

"Damn it," Biddlecomb hissed. He needed another four minutes, three at the very least. "Keep rowing."

"Toss oars, now, or we shall fire into you!" the voice called. Biddlecomb grit his teeth. He was in absolute agony,

32

with his breastbone and every rib in his chest broken, he was now certain. And there was nothing he could do. He could not stop for them.

The dark and the mist were rent with the blast of a bow gun, a wide, muted blossom of flame, and the air was filled with the shriek of grapeshot whistling overhead.

The other boat was no more than fifty feet away, but the mist had grown thicker, and even in the flash of light Biddlecomb had not been able to see the enemy, which meant that the enemy could not very well see them. And that no doubt was why they had fired high; they were not certain of what or whom they were firing at.

"What in all hell are you doing?" Biddlecomb shrieked. "We're British, damn your eyes! Fire at the bloody rebels!"

There, he thought, that should give them a moment's pause. "Sergeant Wilbur," he hissed, "come left, under this two-decker's counter."

The sergeant put the tiller over and the longboat turned to pass under the great jibboom of one ship of the line, thrusting up into the fog seventy feet above their heads, and the high stern section of another. Biddlecomb could see the name *Augusta* carved deep in the counter planking.

Behind them, snakelike, their string of boats turned as well in a great sweeping arc. He could not see the guard boat, or the boat that had fired at them.

"Fire!" a voice called out from somewhere in the dark, and another bow gun fired, and this time grapeshot slammed into the Americans' longboat, sending shards of wood whistling through the dark. One man cursed and dropped his oar and it was lost over the side.

"Damn it, damn it all," Biddlecomb said out loud. Two of the boats were on them now, at least two. He could just barely see them. "Sergeant, make for this man-of-war's bow!" Biddlecomb shouted, and the longboat turned again. Musket fire crackled in the dark, twin explosions of priming and cartridge, sharp points of light from the muzzles, the whine of lead balls in the air.

And then the muzzle flashes were lost from sight as the Americans pulled around the far side of the *Augusta* and the big ship came between them and their pursuers. Ten pulls and they were under the big ship's bow as the last of their stolen boats came around the ship's stern.

Overhead, the *Augusta*'s huge anchor cable, hemp rope ten inches in diameter, ran from the hawse pipe in a long straight line to where it disappeared into the water. "Sergeant, lay the bow against that anchor cable," Biddlecomb called aft, and with two strokes the bow of the longboat butted into the cable and stopped as if hitting the trunk of a tree.

Another bow gun fired in the dark, at what Biddlecomb did not know, and from the *Augusta* Biddlecomb heard someone call, "Hey, there, what are you about?"

Let me show you, Biddlecomb thought as he swiveled the longboat's gun around until it was pointing at the anchor cable a foot away. He drew his pistol, cocked the lock, and snapped it over the powder in the gun's touchhole.

The gun went off with a concussion that shook the longboat from bow to stern, blasting its load of grapeshot into the cable and shredding it as if it were packing string.

Biddlecomb's cry of agony took up where the gun's report left off, but no one seemed to notice. The *Augusta* slewed away, twisting in the wind as the strain was taken up on the one remaining cable. From the deck above he could hear shouts of panic, calls for all hands, and the high-pitched squeal of boatswain's pipes, even before the echo of the gun had died away.

"Next cable!" Biddlecomb gasped aft at Wilbur. Wilbur, grinning like a lunatic, shouted, "Give way!" and the men leaned into their oars again.

"Are you all right, sir?" asked the man who had loaded the swivel.

"Yes, fine . . . ," Biddlecomb said, then sucked in his breath against the stabbing in his chest, waited until the pain had subsided, and then said, "please load the fucking gun again, if you would."

The man was pouring the powder in the touchhole as the bow of the longboat ran into the second cable. It was even tauter than the first, having on it all of the weight of the *Augusta*, holding the ship of the line against the pressure of thirty knots of wind. Musket fire came from the foredeck of the man-of-war, and Biddlecomb could see little spouts of water leaping around the longboat, but he was not concerned with that. He was concerned only with the boats that were pursuing them, the boats that in a second would be right in the path of the drifting ship.

He aimed the swivel at the remaining anchor cable. This time it was no more than five inches away. He gritted his teeth, knew what would come, the shock of pain when the gun went off. He pressed his free hand against his chest and held the lock of his pistol over the touchhole of the swivel. He hesitated a second, then squeezed the trigger.

In the flash of light, with his head swimming in pain, he had an image of the huge rope flying back through the air as the two-decker, cut free from the bottom, drifted helplessly downwind, turning out of control, gathering speed and momentum as it swept away everything in its path.

"Give way! Give way!" Sergeant Wilbur cried, he alone resisting the temptation to sit back and enjoy the havoc they had wrought. The men leaned to the oars and the long train of boats was under way again. Biddlecomb peered aft, trying to see through the fog and the bright spot on his eyes left by the flash of the gun. He could see no boats pursuing them now, nor was it likely that anything to leeward would get clear of the drifting man-of-war.

It did not drift far, no more than fifty feet, before it slammed into the next ship astern, tangling itself in the other's headrig until the two vessels were locked together. The impact tore the second ship's anchors free from the bottom, and the two ships, fully at the mercy of the gale, drove into the next in line.

They could hear the panic sweep like fire through the anchored fleet, and in that confusion and madness not another thought was spared for the rebels and their string of stolen boats.

It took the Americans another half an hour to round the northern point of Gowanus Bay, putting the wooded shoreline between themselves and the scene of utter chaos to the south. Once well away from the fleet, they put the wounded men from the guard boat into the smallest of the stolen boats and let them drift back to the fleet, then pulled for the relative safety of the American lines.

Two hours shy of dawn, they finally arrived at the Brooklyn ferry landing. The weather had turned in their favor at last, with the wind dying away and a thick fog settling over the entire harbor.

The landing was crowded with men, with equipment, with artillery and casks full of everything needed to sustain an army. Muddy, bedraggled, dispirited soldiers moved in and out of the fog like ghosts, loading the boats and clambering in themselves to be pulled away into the mist.

Biddlecomb and the men of the 14th, arriving with a dozen more boats, were greeted with an enthusiasm akin to that with which the Israelites greeted manna from heaven.

A regiment from Salem, as adept as the Marbleheaders at boat handling, took charge of the new arrivals, and soon they too were plying the East River, evacuating the last of the men and supplies to the relative safety of Manhattan Island. One by one the American units pulled back to the ferry landing, while out in the night and the mist General Howe's army dug their approaches, drawing ever closer to the now empty American entrenchments.

The rising sun turned the black fog into a white, opaque fog as the last boat, save for Biddlecomb's, pulled away from the ferry landing. Major Fitzgerald materialized out of that damp gray cloud, looked around, and then stepped down into the boat, taking a seat beside Biddlecomb. "Well done, Captain, I must say it again. The army is once more in your debt."

"I won't say it was nothing, or that it was my pleasure, because you would never believe that, nor would it be true. But I am genuinely pleased to be of help."

There was something anticlimactic about the major's show of appreciation, something not quite satisfying. *But what would satisfy me?* Biddlecomb wondered. *If the major went down on bended knee and groveled in his gratitude?*

Yes, that would do nicely.

"Pray, Biddlecomb, we have a few moments. Won't you tell me about your wedding to Virginia?"

"Yes . . ." Isaac grimaced as a fresh wave of pain swept over his chest. He let it pass. "Yes, I would be delighted."

And that was true. It was a story that he enjoyed, a story that made him happy to think on. A story that he knew would tweak the unflappable major.

CHAPTER
4

You cannot pluck roses without fear of thorns
Nor enjoy a fair wife without danger of horns.

—POOR RICHARD'S ALMANACK, 1734

IN JUNE OF 1776, ISAAC BIDDLECOMB HAD RETURNED TO PHILA-delphia, a hot and humid place, quite in contrast to the frozen, bitter, windswept city from which he had sailed half a year before. Now the city seemed to radiate heat, enveloped by the smells from the waterfront and the horses that crowded the streets. The air was filled with noise, with the tension that attended the ever escalating war, and with the ubiquitous flies.

He arrived by coach, accompanied by Lieutenant Rumstick, the acting first officer of the Continental brig-of-war *Charlemagne.* Biddlecomb's command.

Rumstick, being as he was over six feet tall and twenty stone, took up more than one person's share of the coach, so that none beyond he and Biddlecomb could occupy the rear-facing seat. For that reason they actually had more room than the three men crowded into the seat across from them. And though Biddlecomb found it necessary on occasion to give Rumstick a sharp elbow when his snoring became intolerable, the trip was no great discomfort to them.

Across from the two younger men (Biddlecomb was twenty-nine, Rumstick thirty-one) sat Commo. Esek Hopkins, commanding officer of the small American fleet now at anchor in Providence, Rhode Island. Next to him was Dudley Saltonstall, captain of the flagship *Alfred,* and next to him Abraham Whipple, captain of the *Columbus,* the second-largest vessel in the fleet.

Together, and with the other ships and men of the Continental Navy, they had that spring captured the British colonial island of New Providence and carried off a prodigious amount of military stores for use by the struggling Continental Army.

They had been hailed as heroes for that act, but once the adulation had died down, the questions had begun. Certain congressmen, for instance, wished to know why Hopkins had utterly ignored the orders given him by the Continental Congress and acted entirely on his own accord.

And Whipple was demanding a court-martial to clear his name of mutterings of cowardice based on his inability to get into the fight with the frigate *Glasgow,* an inability, Biddlecomb knew, that owed nothing to a lack of courage and everything to a lack of wind.

And Congress wished to hear from Biddlecomb about the death of his first officer, Roger Tottenhill, and the several riots and open mutiny that had broken out aboard the *Charlemagne.*

While the city was all but unbearably hot, it was hotter still in the small, private room in which the seven-man special committee appointed by Congress to investigate these naval affairs met to hear testimony.

Biddlecomb's case was heard first, being, so he supposed, the matter of least consequence. He stood before the long table at which sat the committee and described in bland words the events that had transpired over the past ten months, since the *Charlemagne* had pushed through the ice-choked Delaware River, bound for sea.

He described how Tottenhill had become increasingly suspicious of Biddlecomb and the other officers, described how one man among his crew had used this to inspire the others to rise up in mutiny during the pivotal moment in two separate sea fights.

"Now, Captain Biddlecomb," said Richard Henry Lee, looking not at Biddlecomb but rather at the table as he rubbed his forehead with a weary gesture, "pray tell us, in your opinion, what is the cause of all this and where might we mend it? I think I may speak for the other gentlemen when I say we are not at all pleased with the internecine fighting within our naval forces."

"Well, sir," said Biddlecomb, clearing his throat and straightening. This was the moment for which he had been waiting, the moment when he could either see himself cashiered from the navy or see that not another word of the affair was mentioned. It would take some clever rhetorical twists, but fortunately such things were his forte.

"I honestly do not know why this happened, sir, save to think that Mr. Tottenhill had a tendency toward suspicion. I can see no common thread between his actions and those of the mutineers. Except, of course, that they were from the same state. As you know, sir, Mr. Tottenhill was a native of North Carolina, as were all but a few of the men who mutinied. But as they were not acquainted with one another prior to joining the *Charlemagne*, I can only reckon that as a coincidence."

Biddlecomb stood in respectful silence and watched the uneasy glances shot between the members of the committee. Of all the areas of distrust between the colonies of the north and those of the south, the navy was one of the foremost. Biddlecomb knew that the southern states were convinced that the navy was being run by the northern states for their own benefit, and the northern states were trying to assure the south that such was not the case, even though it pretty much was.

To further assuage the south, the congress was making a great effort to include the southern states in naval operations. And now here was a captain suggesting that as soon as southerners had become active in the Continental naval force, they had mutinied, officers and men. This was not the

4 0

kind of rumor that they would wish to be generally known, especially not Lee of Virginia.

"Well, very good, Captain Biddlecomb," said Lee. "I think we have heard all that we need hear. Gentlemen?" To a man the committee members nodded their agreement. "You are dismissed, then, Captain. We shall discuss your case and render you a verdict."

The verdict arrived at breakfast the next day. A messenger delivered it to Biddlecomb just as he was sitting down to his coffee. He broke open the wafer that sealed the note and read it through, then read it aloud to William Stanton and Virginia, with whom he was sitting.

Sir

Upon hearing the testimony of Yourself and Others regarding the activities aboard the Continental brigantine *Charlemagne* during the recent Cruise to New Providence and the Engagement with the frigate *Glasgow,* and after considerable discussion of the Same, this Committee has concluded that the misfortunes that you have suffered were the work of Various and Perfidious men whose activities you were not able to discover.

We are satisfied with your account of the Brave and Unhappy Death of Lt. Roger Tottenhill in the defense of the said brigantine, and with your own conduct in the above affairs.

Your Bold Pursuit of the *Glasgow* nearly to the harbor at Newport renders you above suspicion of negligence or want of courage. This committee thanks you for your efforts toward our glorious cause.

Your obedient Servant
R. H. Lee

To Isaac Biddlecomb
Commander of the *Charlemagne*
Stone House, Philadelphia

41

Officially, nothing more was ever said.

And Biddlecomb was happy for that, for he still had two important pieces of business to attend to while he remained in Philadelphia. One of them was to see Rumstick posted as first lieutenant aboard the *Charlemagne*. The other was to marry Virginia.

Rumstick had sailed with him as first officer when the *Charlemagne* had been a part of the Rhode Island navy, before there even was a navy of the United States. But once the federal navy had been established, the naval committee failed to recognize his seniority and had made him second lieutenant, which, in Biddlecomb's mind, had led to the trouble aboard the *Charlemagne*. He was determined to see Rumstick made first, and once he himself had been cleared of any wrongdoing, he began that campaign in earnest.

As to Virginia, he had proposed to her before he had sailed and now was the time to make good on that proposal.

"Isaac," Virginia said as they walked arm in arm through the small garden behind their lodging at Stone House, "I fear the circumstances under which you proposed to me were . . . not ideal. I would not have you coerced into this. If you wish to withdraw your proposal, I shall not hold you to it."

Biddlecomb squeezed her small hand. "I have had ample time to consider that proposal, my dearest. Many a late night pacing the quarterdeck or staring out of the stern windows, and I would never in life withdraw it. But if you wish to decline . . ."

"Decline? No, never."

The wedding was set for the eighth of July, a Monday, in the small church that stood across Walnut Street from the courtyard of the State House.

William Stanton, Virginia's father and the man who had taken Biddlecomb on as an apprentice seaman after the death of Isaac's mother and father, was less surprised than Biddlecomb had thought and indeed feared he might be.

Rather, he was elated, calling for toasts and pounding Biddlecomb on the back with a bonhomie that grew tiresome after the first hour. But on the whole it was more agreeable than being thrown bodily out of the house, which is what Biddlecomb had half expected.

It was all but intolerably hot on July eighth, just as it had been on July seventh and July sixth and every day since the rain of a week before had let up. Biddlecomb stood by the altar, the sweat creeping down the edge of his scalp and down his back, under his shirt, waistcoat, and coat. He was happy, at least, that, being a seaman, no one expected him to wear a wig.

It was miserable in the church, and little relief was to be gained from the few doors that were flung open, one on either side of the back of the church and the big doors in the front that looked out on the State House courtyard. It was stifling, but Biddlecomb was aware that the heat accounted for only a certain degree of his discomfort.

Looming over his shoulder and grinning like some kind of idiot was Ezra Rumstick, newly outfitted in a blue coat with white lapels and cuffs, a white waistcoat and shirt, white breeches and silk stockings.

The door to the vestry opened and the minister stepped around the altar, a Bible in his hands, his long white vestments immaculate. Biddlecomb felt his stomach twist, felt a tingling on the soles of his feet, and his left hand reached automatically for the hilt of his sword.

Like going into bloody battle, he thought, and it did seem that way, including the occasional reassuring glance at the stolid and unflappable Ezra. Ezra in turn seemed to be enjoying this moment even more than he enjoyed plunging into battle, and he always seemed to enjoy that very much.

The organ player took his place and, after a preliminary sour note, began the wedding march. Biddlecomb and Rumstick turned toward the front of the church. The pews were not filled to capacity, not even close, but neither was the church deserted. William Stanton had made a number of friends and associates during the ten months he had been in Philadelphia, as had Virginia, and they were all in attendance, though most of them Biddlecomb did not know. Several members of Congress were there, as well as Hopkins, Saltonstall and Abraham Whipple, who had the look and demeanor of a kindly uncle.

William Stanton emerged from a side door, Virginia on his arm. She looked beautiful in her white gown, stunning, the kind of beauty that gives men a visceral longing. The dress was cut to accentuate her slim, athletic physique, kept that way by hours of hard riding on horseback, a consuming passion with her, second only to her passion for the cause of American independence.

Isaac felt a thrill run through him, despite his nerves. The moment had come, the end of all the uncertainty and the frustrated desire, the beginning of a new epoch in his life.

But despite this alluring sight, Isaac's eyes were drawn past his bride-to-be, past the confines of the church and through the front doors to the State House courtyard where a group of people seemed to be gathering. Odd. Rarely were more than one or two idlers to be seen wandering about, and here were two dozen or more standing before the low stage, and more joining them.

Virginia continued down the aisle at her slow and solemn pace, stepping to the lugubrious rhythm of the wedding march. Isaac shifted his eyes; at that distance he could not see her face under her white, gauzy veil, but as she walked, she half turned and looked out the door as well, no doubt curious as to what besides herself could have attracted her bridegroom's attention.

She walked a good part of the way half turned around, looking out the door, until her father gave her arm an un-subtle jerk that brought her attention back to the immediate business.

At length they reached the front of the church, and William Stanton handed her off with a half smile and what looked to Isaac to be tears forming in his eyes. Isaac looked from the old man down at Virginia. Through the veil he could see her bright eyes and her teeth as she smiled.

They turned toward the minister as he began, "Dearly beloved . . ."

Then from the courtyard of the State House they heard a handbell ringing, and together they turned back again and looked, as did Rumstick and a better part of the people in the pews. A man was standing on the low stage, ringing the bell and calling more and more people to the crowd gathering around.

"Dearly beloved," the minister said again, with greater emphasis, and all heads turned back. "We are gathered here today . . ."

Biddlecomb made a great effort to concentrate on the words, but he was only in part successful, so distracted was he with the heat and Virginia's presence at his side, how lovely she looked, and the profundity of what he was about to do. He was about to marry! And all the while he could hear the swelling noise of the crowd in the courtyard, the ringing of the bell, and now the cry of "Hear, ye! Hear, ye!" from the man on the stage.

Out of the corner of his eye he caught Virginia glancing back over her shoulder, and he fought down the urge to do the same.

"And why do two people enter thus, into the bonds of holy matrimony?" the minister intoned.

"Pray, sir," Virginia whispered, just loud enough for the wedding party to hear, "but might we hurry this up a bit?" She jerked her head in the direction of the courtyard, just the briefest of motions, but enough for the minister to get her meaning.

"Oh, yes, ah . . . ," the minister continued. "Ah, do you, Virginia Stanton, take this man to be your lawfully wedded husband, to have and to hold, for better or worse, for richer for poorer, in sickness and in health, from this day forward?"

"I do," she said.

"And do you, Isaac Biddlecomb—"

"I do," he said, and he did.

"The rings, please."

Isaac turned to Ezra, and Ezra held out the ring, sitting on the palm of his hand as if on a cushion. It looked like the frailest of objects against his huge, scarred, and calloused hand. Biddlecomb took it and slipped it on Virginia's finger, and she slipped her ring on his.

In the ensuing silence they could hear the crier from the stage in the courtyard calling out in his clear tone, "The Right Honorable Col. John Nixon, of the Philadelphia Committee of Safety." There was a shuffling and murmur from the people stuck in the pews of the church, and Virginia and Isaac together glanced over their shoulders.

"I now pronounce you man and wife," the minister said. "You may kiss . . ."

Isaac flipped the veil over Virginia's head and gazed for a second—less than a second—on her lovely face, her dark brown eyes, her white skin with just a hint of a tan. She reached up and wrapped her arms around his neck and drew him near and he kissed her, a light touch, like a warm breeze on his face. "I love you. My wife."

"My husband," she said, then nodding toward the front door added, "let's see what's acting."

She grabbed his hand and together they turned and ran down the aisle for the courtyard of the State House. With her free hand she held her dress up and away from her feet to prevent it from tripping her, and Biddlecomb clasped the hilt of his sword to keep it from getting caught between his legs. He could hear the pews emptying as the rest of the wedding party raced out behind them to hear whatever was about to be said.

Together, as man and wife, they ran across Walnut Street,

blinking in the glare of the noonday sun, ignoring the glances of those people who had seen them race from the church. They stopped at the edge of the crowd, Rumstick on one side of them and William Stanton on the other. The minister, who was shorter than Biddlecomb had realized, stood beside Stanton, craning his neck to see.

Colonel Nixon held up a printed sheet and read in his best commanding voice, "In Congress, July fourth, 1776. The unanimous declaration of the thirteen United States of America."

The anticipatory buzz of the crowd died away as Nixon read those words. The colonel paused and looked out over the audience, then once again his voice filled the silent courtyard. "When in the Course of human Events, it becomes necessary for one People to dissolve the Political Bands which have connected them with another . . ."

Biddlecomb felt a thrill of excitement and anticipation, of closure and a new beginning. As when Virginia had stepped up the aisle. One life ends, another begins.

This was it then, the declaration, the final break with Great Britain, the moment toward which all of the past year and a half of his life had been building.

"We hold these Truths to be self-evident, that all Men are created equal, that they are endowed by their Creator with certain unalienable Rights, that among these are Life, Liberty, and the Pursuit of Happiness—That to secure these Rights, Governments are instituted among Men . . ."

Biddlecomb felt Virginia's small hand squeeze his tighter, and he squeezed back, then they looked at each other and smiled.

"Is this something you had arranged for my wedding present?" Virginia asked.

"Indeed, I had Congress declare independence last week, just as a gift to you. And here this Colonel Nixon has made a hash of the thing. I told him to wait until after the ceremony to read this."

"But when a long Train of Abuses and Usurpations," Nixon continued, "pursuing invariably the same Object, evinces a Design to reduce them under absolute Despotism, it is their Right, it is their Duty, to throw off such Government . . ."

Biddlecomb was enraptured, listening to the words. Here some writer unknown to him had set down in solid and unadorned prose all of those thoughts that had drifted unformed and ephemeral through his head for the past year. And now, as he heard them, all he could think was yes, yes, indeed, yes.

Now Nixon was reading off a list of the many abuses that King George had heaped on his once mostly loyal subjects, and heads from one end of the courtyard to the other were nodding their agreement.

Isaac stole a glance at Rumstick. His friend was standing like a statue, hands clasped behind his back, his chin slightly raised. Rumstick was one of the Providence Sons of Liberty. More than just agreeing with the cause, he had been fighting for it, literally fighting, for a decade at least. Biddlecomb could well imagine what this moment meant for him.

"And for the support of this declaration, with a firm Reliance on the Protection of Divine Providence, we mutually pledge to each other our lives, our Fortunes, and our sacred Honor."

Colonel Nixon looked up from the broadside. The courtyard was silent, like a church. From somewhere in the city a bell began to ring, and it was joined by another and another and soon half a dozen more. And then the cheering began.

Isaac and Virginia Biddlecomb made love for the first time that evening, nervous and awkward at the outset, and then with increasing passion as their mutual embarrassment foundered in long-pent-up desires. Isaac ran his hands and his lips over Virginia's beautiful, strong body, loving her, taking in as much of her as he could while Virginia in turn gave as much of herself as her inexperience and modesty would allow her to give.

At length they lay together, naked, wrapped in each other's arms, reveling in the heat of the night and of one another. From somewhere beyond the Stone House people began to cheer. A cannon fired, followed by another and another until a dozen at least were shot off. And then the bells, which had enjoyed less than an hour's respite, started in again, blanketing the city with their sound, and shot through here and there with musket fire.

"Is that for us, my love?" Virginia asked in that imitation of sincerity of which she was a master.

"I have no doubt, and well deserved it would be. But I believe I heard a rumor of the Declaration being read tonight on the Commons, and it might be that that the people are reacting to."

"Perhaps," said Virginia, shifting her position on his chest and running her fingers through his hair.

He listened to the gunfire, to the peeling bells and the cheers. Perhaps they were not for him, but they certainly echoed to perfection the way he felt.

He let the memories of his wedding night run unfettered through his mind. They gave him some warmth and mitigated somewhat the misery of his present circumstance, his exhaustion, his wet clothing, the throbbing, all-consuming agony that was his chest.

"Well, that was indeed quite a day, what?" Major Fitzgerald said, startling Biddlecomb from his reverie. He wondered how long he had been sitting there, staring silently into the fog. "A wedding and independence all in one afternoon. Almost more than a man could hope for."

Another figure appeared out of the swirling mist, a tall man, striding with great purpose toward the boat. He stopped, looked back into the fog, then turned and stepped with a surefooted grace into the stern sheets and settled on the seat opposite Biddlecomb and Fitzgerald.

"General, shall we be under way?" Fitzgerald asked.

"Yes." Washington nodded. "There is no one left." He looked over at the two younger men and smiled, a look more of resignation than mirth. "The army lives, at least, to fight again."

"Indeed, sir," said Biddlecomb, nodding to the men to give way. They leaned once more into the oars, and with one stroke the landing was lost in the fog as Sergeant Wilbur pushed the tiller half an inch to larboard.

"General," Biddlecomb said, "I wonder if I might trouble you about a small matter. You recall, I am sure, the blank commissions you gave me last summer . . ."

CHAPTER
5

Three may keep a secret, if two of them are dead.

— POOR RICHARD'S ALMANACK, 1735

To the Honorable Silas Deane, Esqr.
Hôtel d'Hambourg, Rue de l'Université
Paris, France

Sir
                                      Philadelphia, October 2, 1776
   We have this day received from the Honorable Congress of the United States of America the important papers that accompany this letter, being,
   first, a Treaty of Commerce and Alliance between the Court of France and these States.
   second, instructions to their commissioners relative to the said Treaty.
   lastly, a Commission, whereby you will see that Doctor Franklin, the Honorable Thos. Jefferson, Esqr. and yourself are appointed Commissioners for Negotiating said Treaty at the Court of France.
   These papers speak for themselves and need no Strictures or remarks from us, neither is it our business to make any. You will observe, that in case of the absence or disability of any one or two of the Commissioners the other has full Power to Act.
   We thereby think it proper to inform you that Doctor

Franklin and Mr. Jefferson will take passage with all Speed but it is necessary that their appointment on this business remain a profound Secret and we do not choose even to trust this paper with their route. Should you think proper to disclose this Commission to the Ministers of France, enjoin the Strictest Secrecy respecting the Names, because if that Circumstance reaches England before their arrival it will evidently endanger their persons.

We most fervently pray for a successful negotiation and are with the utmost attention and regard Dear Sir Your affectionate Friends and Obedient Servants

> B. Franklin
> Robt. Morris
> Committee of Secret Correspondence

To Captain Isaac Biddlecomb
Stone House
Philadelphia

Sir

October 10, 1776

This Committee, being informed by you of your current State of Fitness to resume duty, having recovered sufficiently from the Noble Wounds suffered lately during the withdrawal of the Army of the United States from Long Island, we forthwith transmit these Orders and Instructions to you.

This Committee being very desirous of sending the *Charlemagne* under your command on immediate service—desire that you forward her outfit, take in provisions and Stores for two Months, and get ready for sea with the utmost expedition, and all commanders and officers of the fleet now in the Port, as well as all other persons in the Continental employ, are hereby desired to aid and assist you in getting your Ship immediately fitted and manned.

Having Manned and Provisioned said *Charlemagne* you are to proceed, as quickly as wind and weather shall allow, to the docks at Marcus Hook, below the town of Chester on the Delaware River. There you are to make contact with a Mr. Henry Whitley, from whom you shall receive your further Orders and Instructions from this Committee.

We greatly regret any Inconvenience that might be caused by our not being able to give you here any further Particulars of your orders. Suffice it to say that this current undertaking is of the most Vital Nature, and might be expected to greatly advance us in our Mutual Cause of Liberty. It is likewise for that reason that the Utmost Secrecy must be maintained, for we are much of the opinion that were any word of this mission to be heard abroad it would place the people and the vital mission in the gravest Jeopardy.

As to your petition that Lt. Ezra Rumstick be posted as first officer aboard the *Charlemagne*, which you submitted with a Request from General Washington, we must note that the esteemed General is Commander-in-Chief of the land forces alone, and is not in a position to influence this Committee. This Fact notwithstanding, it is the policy of this Committee to look with favor upon the recommendations of the Masters of Vessels regarding the appointment of the inferior officers, and so we have on this date posted Lt. Rumstick as first officer aboard the *Charlemagne*.

We hold you in much esteem, and flatter ourselves your conduct in the service will always be such as to meet the continuance of it.

We remain, sir, your Obedient, Humble Servants,

> John Jay
> Robt. Morris
> Marine Committee

To the Right Honorable David Murray, Seventh Viscount
Stormont
Ambassador of Great Britain to the Court of France
British Embassy, Paris

My Lord,

October 14, 1776

I received your correspondence of the 3rd instant and
am inclined to agree with you that there might be some
Great Mischief done were the French to become involved in the current troubles, though I cannot but
think they will be disinclined to help in any great Manner and thus incur once more the Wrath of Great Britain, particularly as it becomes increasingly clear here
that the rebels have not the least hope of achieving
anything, and that the Entire Destruction of their army
is but a matter of some small time.

You have already received intelligence of the Distressing manner in which Mr. Washington and his rebel
army slipped away from General Howe when they
were all but Trapped on Long Island. The British
Troops might well have made good use of their Bayonets and ended this whole shameful affair in a matter
of hours, had the General seen fit to make a bold assault. What is worse, it is generally rumored around
here that the boats used in Mr. Washington's Escape
were that night stolen from the British Transports,
under the very nose of the Navy, but I have no proof
of that.

During the middle part of last month the rebels
achieved some small thing on Harlem Heights against
a regiment of our Light Infantry, which they style a
Great Victory, the likes of which has not been seen since
the Greeks at Thermopylae. How they can reckon that
I do not know, as their victory was accomplished in the
midst of a retreat, the one military evolution in which

the rebels have, through much practice, perfected to a degree that far excels our own.

Two days ago Admiral Lord Howe landed on Frog's Neck with Four Thousand men, and it is presumed that they will once more steal a march on Mr. Washington, and if they can do so before the rebels put into effect their considerable skills of Flight, it is possible we shall see an end to this, perhaps even before you receive this note. Let us pray that such is achieved, so that we might once more turn our attention to those things that will bring further Honor to Our King, Our Country and Our Lord. I remain your most Obedient and most Humble Servant,

Grey Cooper
New York

P.S. I now have some reliable word that Mr. Jefferson, lately appointed one of the rebel commissioners to France, has declined that office, giving as his reason the ill health of his wife. In his place it is presumed they will send Mr. Arthur Lee, who, as you know, is currently in London. It is still intended that the Arch Villain Dr Franklin will soon take passage to Paris, I should think in this month. This is generally known among the people here, though the Congress and their Committee of Secret Correspondence think it the Great Secret of the Ages.

G.C.

CHAPTER
6

Keep your eyes wide open before marriage,
half shut afterwards.

—POOR RICHARD'S ALMANACK, 1738

ISAAC ROLLED FROM HIS BACK ONTO HIS SIDE AND PUT HIS ARM
around Virginia's waist. She felt tiny, almost like a child,
when he held her like that. Virginia in turn made a sound
midway between a moan and a sigh and pushed herself
closer against him.

The *Charlemagne*'s carpenter, by way of a wedding present
for his captain, had constructed a new hanging cot for the
sleeping cabin. It was half again as wide as the former one,
but it was still of no great width, and it forced the new-
married couple to squeeze tight against one another, which
neither found to be inconvenient.

He ran his hand down her waist and her hips and along
her strong thigh, feeling her warm skin under the silk of
her sleeping gown. Then he reversed direction, moving his
hand over her stomach and under her breasts. She made
another little guttural sound and squeezed his hand as she
slowly came awake.

Isaac felt himself becoming aroused again, despite the
fairly energetic time they had had before falling asleep the
night before, and he warned himself to stop now before
stopping became unbearable.

It was not out of any thought of Virginia's reluctance that

he feared being brought up all standing, not at all. She had expressed nothing even akin to reluctance since their wedding night and grew more bold as she grew more comfortable with her matrimonial state. For the three weeks after Isaac's return from Long Island, while his chest caused him so much pain that he could not even roll over in bed, she had demonstrated a creativity that surprised and delighted him.

No, it was not a fear of rejection that made him cool his ardor.

He heard footsteps in the alleyway outside the great cabin door, heard a muffled voice speaking to the marine sentry posted there. Here, at last, was the reason that he did not think it wise to begin anything in the carnal line.

Through long habit he tended to wake every hour, quite involuntarily and never for more than a minute or so, and take note of the ship's state, or what he could tell of it from the motion and the sound. Thus he knew that the tide had begun to turn an hour before and that the *Charlemagne*, anchored in Delaware Bay, would be able to continue upriver to Marcus Hook. And once the tide had turned, he knew that he would be disturbed by someone telling him as much. He had left orders that they should do so.

Careful footsteps padded across the canvas-covered deck in the great cabin. It sounded to Isaac like an assassin come to murder him, but he knew that it was only the freshly promoted Lieutenant Weatherspoon, who always tried not to disturb him, even when coming to wake him up. The footsteps stopped and were followed by a gentle knocking on the cabin door.

"Sir? Tide's turned, sir, and wind's light out of the east northeast."

"Very good, Lieutenant." Isaac rolled onto his back once more. "I shall be up directly." He swung his right leg out of bed, but before he could further extricate himself, Virginia pounced like a cat, pulling him back into the cot.

"No, don't leave me," she said, "stay and keep me warm."

"In faith, there is nothing I would more wish to do, but there are some things that take precedence even over the duties of a husband."

"Well, if reason or kindness will not sway you, perhaps I should use some of my other God-given wiles," Virginia said in her most enticing, husky whisper. She threw a leg over Isaac's; in the dim light of the predawn he could see her smooth, white skin where her nightdress was hiked up her thigh, and she began to kiss his neck and run her hands through the hair on his chest.

"Stop, Mephistopheles," Isaac said, and using a considerable degree of strength and will he pushed her aside and climbed out of the cot. From the great cabin he fetched a lantern and brought it into the sleeping cabin, where it cast a warm, faint yellow light over the cramped space.

Virginia lay under the covers, propped up on one arm. With her thick chestnut hair tousled, a few stray strands hanging across her face, and her make-believe pout, she was more enticing than ever, and Biddlecomb forced himself to pull on his breeches and shirt.

"I don't see why they need you on deck," Virginia said. "Ezra is perfectly capable of getting us under way. He is every bit as good a sailor as you."

"No doubt he is as good a lover as well. Shall I send him down to perform the office that your husband so callously ignores?"

Virginia smiled and flopped back in the cot. "Now who is leading whom into temptation?"

But of course Virginia, whose father was a sea captain and a shipowner who employed dozens of sea captains, understood full well why he was needed on deck. Isaac knew she would have thought less of him if he had succumbed to her temptation.

Ten minutes after he arrived on the quarterdeck, she appeared as well, fully dressed and carrying three pewter mugs of coffee like a barmaid, one for Isaac, one for Lieutenant Rumstick, and one for herself. They stood there for a moment, silent, like three conspirators, while sleepy men staggered up from below and milled about waiting for orders.

And there were quite a lot of men, over one hundred now in the *Charlemagne*'s company. Fifty of them were old Charlemagnes and the rest were culled from the other ships in the fleet, which they had left at anchor in Providence, Rhode Island, two weeks before.

Biddlecomb had found reason to remain in Philadelphia for as long as he could, convalescing, enjoying his new life as a married man, until the explicit orders from the Marine Committee had forced him to return to his ship. Virginia had accompanied him to Providence and sailed with them to the Delaware Bay, as unwilling as Isaac for them to be parted.

He drained the last of his coffee and said to his two lieutenants, Rumstick and Weatherspoon, and the bosun, Mr. Sprout, "Very well, let us loosen off all plain sail and get the ship to short peak. We'll have Ferguson in the chains with the lead, if you please."

Half of the men were new to the *Charlemagne*, and thus the weighing and getting under way was not as smooth as might be hoped. But most of the new men were able-bodied seamen, could hand, reef, and steer, and so the evolution was not the low comedy that it had been in times past.

By the time the sun made its appearance over the hills that edged the bay, tinting the topgallants orange while the lower sails were still gray with shadow, the brig was moving at a stately four knots, standing northwest. They were making for the entrance of the Delaware River, where the *Charlemagne* and the rest of the American fleet had spent so many miserable weeks frozen in the ice that January past.

Marcus Hook was fifty miles away, halfway between

Reedy Island, at the entrance to the River, and Philadelphia. It took the *Charlemagne* twelve hours to cover that distance, with the hands employed around the ship, drilling at the great guns and overhauling running gear.

The brig sailed easily northwest, then north and northeast, following the river around. The wind remained steady at ten knots and the weather was cold, but not miserably so, particularly not in the brilliant sunshine, and the run up the bay had the quality of a yachting holiday.

It was two hours after sunset and quite dark when the *Charlemagne* finally dropped her anchor at Marcus Hook. The warps were passed to the warping posts and the men laid into the capstan, heaving the brig up to the dock. On shore, half lost in the shadows, Biddlecomb could see a short, portly man whom he took to be the enigmatic Mr. Henry Whitley, pacing back and forth. The man stared at the ground as he walked and only looked up now and again.

Biddlecomb felt a tingling on the bottom of his feet, the harbinger of pending action. He was excited and intrigued by this mission, so secret that the Marine Committee would not even commit it to paper.

Because of the importance of this meeting he had dressed in his uniform.

It was a real uniform this time, an official uniform established by Congress a month before for the officers of the Continental Navy. It consisted of a blue coat with red facings and red slash cuffs, flat yellow buttons, a red waistcoat, and blue breeches.

He had had it made by one of Philadelphia's better tailors, and he secretly thought that he looked quite dashing in it, which made him protest even louder about the foolishness of the whole thing.

"My dear husband," Virginia had said as he dressed in the cabin, "if you so hate that uniform, then pray stop stealing glances at yourself in the mirror," and that had silenced his protest.

But for a meeting of this importance the uniform was only appropriate. He felt his pulse quicken when the brig was finally close enough for Whitley to step across to the boarding steps, which he did awkwardly. He clambered aboard and hurried aft to the quarterdeck.

"Captain Biddlecomb?"

"I am he, sir." Biddlecomb extended his hand.

"Henry Whitley, sir." Whitley gave Biddlecomb's hand a brief shake. "The committee no doubt alerted you to my meeting you here?"

"They did, though I've no notion of why I am here, or where I am to go."

"No, of course you haven't. A secret. Can't trust it to the mails, or even couriers. But there, that is what you have come for." He pointed to a great stack of barrels at the landward end of the dock.

"I see." Biddlecomb looked with dismay at the stack. There had to be forty of them at least. "What might they contain, sir?"

"Indigo."

"Indigo?"

"Indigo. Valuable stuff, it'll go far to help finance this war. You're to transport it and sell it at the most favorable price. Can't fight a war without money, you know."

"Oh, for God's sake." Biddlecomb shook his head in disgust. "This is the great secret? To where am I to convey this indigo?"

"Oh, I wouldn't know, Captain. I ain't privy to that information. It's—"

"—a secret?"

"Just so, sir. You should receive a letter from the Committee of Secret Correspondence come morning."

Biddlecomb scowled at the barrels. Under normal conditions they would pose no problem, but he had been ordered to provision for two months at sea and in his enthusiasm had laid in stores for closer to three. The hold was entirely filled, as was the bread room, the pantry, the spirit locker, bosun's stores, carpenter's stores, armorer's stores, shot locker, and magazine. There was not even room to store all of the provisions he had wanted to bring.

"Son of a bitch," he muttered.

"Captain?"

"I'll have to break everything out again, restow it, and leave a good portion of my food and water here if I am to take all that."

"Well, if it must be done, it must be done. This is the highest priority, this indigo."

"Very well. At first light we shall break open hatches."

"Oh, no, sir," said Whitley. "I expect you'll receive your instructions by first light, and you'll have to be under way on the first tide tomorrow. We must see this stowed down tonight."

"Indeed. And did you think to employ any laborers to help with this?"

"Certainly not. This must be kept an absolute secret."

Ten minutes later the hatches were broken open and Biddlecomb and Rumstick found themselves walking, squeezing, and crawling through the *Charlemagne*'s hold, discussing what could be left behind and what could be moved to make way for the indigo.

Biddlecomb had changed from his good uniform into his working clothes. He was embarrassed now by his self-importance. It was not the first time he had indulged in the trappings of a naval officer and been humiliated as a result.

The stay tackle was overhauled and the hands set to swaying up from below those items that could be left behind, and shifting those others so that the indigo could be stowed down in the bottom where it would not prevent their getting at more necessary items, such as food, water, and gunpowder.

Biddlecomb stood on the quarterdeck, watching the activity in the waist. With Rumstick, Weatherspoon, and Sprout overseeing the work there was little for him to do.

"Sir?" Lt. Elisha Faircloth, the officer in command of the *Charlemagne*'s twenty marines, stepped up to the quarterdeck and saluted. He was in his late thirties and sported a big mustache in a fashion rarely seen among Americans, but it was much in keeping with his expression, which was friendly and generally amused by the world.

He wore a green regimental coat with white facings and a silver epaulet on his right shoulder. On his head was a small cocked hat. Like Biddlecomb's, the marine's uniform had just been made official by Congress, that body finally deciding that the war might last long enough to warrant uniforms for naval officers.

"Yes, Lieutenant?"

"I posted a picket line along the road leading up to the dock, sir, and I have a guard around the indigo casks."

"Thank you, Lieutenant. That was very thorough." It was also quite unnecessary, given the absence of any appreciable enemy within fifty miles. Faircloth loved to play with his marines, like a boy deploying tin soldiers. And because Faircloth had already proven himself to be unflinching in battle, and because Biddlecomb liked him, he let Faircloth do whatever he wished.

It took them until eight bells in the middle watch, or four o'clock in the morning, to make room for the indigo, stow it down, restow the more vital supplies, and secure the whole thing against the pitch and roll of a seaway.

At last the hatches were battened down again. On the dock sat forty barrels containing salt beef, salt pork, tar, dried peas, and wine, those things that had to be left behind to make room for the secret cargo of purplish-blue dye. Biddlecomb gave all hands a double tot of rum and sent them to bed.

Virginia left before dawn the next morning. She dressed quickly in the dark cabin, despite Isaac's attempts to lure her back into bed. "Your orders are going to arrive soon, and then it shall be all hands about ship and everyone needing your help and you won't have a moment to see me off, you'll just wave good-bye as you sail away. And I don't want that. I want a long, drawn-out, tearful farewell. I want to make certain that you realize all that you are leaving behind."

"But I do, my love, and if you would get undressed and get back in the cot, you could make me realize it even more. There will be no orders today. Do you expect a committee of the Congress to do anything promptly?"

But Virginia would not be persuaded and so she left in the dark, taking passage up to Philadelphia in a coach she had hired the day before. It was a long farewell, and a tearful one, despite Isaac's silent oath that it would be neither. In truth they did not know how long they would be separated, or by how many miles of ocean, and it was a thought that neither cared to contemplate.

No orders arrived that morning, just as Biddlecomb knew they would not, no instructions from Congress or the Marine Committee or the Committee of Secret Correspondence. Not even Mr. Whitley made an appearance. It was as if the *Charlemagne*'s mission were simply to load the indigo, no more.

Rather than putting to sea, Isaac spent the chief of the morning in his great cabin, witnessing wills.

It was not uncommon on shipboard for one or two men to get a notion in their heads and to have that notion spread like yellow fever through the entire crew. That morning the cooper and the sailmaker decided that they needed to prepare a last will and testament before putting to sea. By noon half of the crew needed them as well.

As captain, Biddlecomb had to witness the documents, and dreary as it was, he did not feel he could refuse. Even if Congress had not prescribed it as one of his duties, he knew that not doing so would ruin the morale of the superstitious lower deck.

"Very well, Henderson, let me read this to you." Able-bodied seaman Henderson was standing uncomfortably in front of the desk, hat in hand, stooped slightly from embarrassment and the low deck beams overhead. Isaac carefully lifted the document so as to not smear the wet ink.

" 'I, Malachi Henderson, seaman, being of sound mind and body, do bequeath all of my worldly goods and possessions . . .' "

Biddlecomb glanced up at Henderson. All of the money he had earned on the *Charlemagne*'s last cruise had been stolen by a whore in Providence, and he had sold nearly all of his clothing to buy liquor. His trousers, shirt, and jacket were all slops from the *Charlemagne*, and he had not yet earned enough wages to cover their cost. What possible worldly possessions could this man have?

" ' . . . as well as any future wages and prize money to Miss Ann Butler of Providence, Rhode Island. Signed this day by my hand.' Is that in order, Henderson?"

"Aye, sir."

"Very good. You need only sign here."

"Beg your pardon, sir, but I ain't no scholar."

"Then pray just make your mark there and I shall put your name. Yes, right there. Just a cross will be sufficient."

Henderson took the quill in an uncertain hand and made a shaky, blotted X where Biddlecomb had indicated, then handed the quill back to his captain, who wrote, "Malachi Henderson, his mark."

This Ann Butler has made her mark as well, Biddlecomb reflected as he wrote. At least two other Charlemagnes had bequeathed all of their worldly goods to her. He hoped for the sake of harmony on the lower deck that they did not find out about each other.

Overhead the bell rang out, four bells in the afternoon watch, and with relief Biddlecomb replaced the quill in its stand and said to Weatherspoon, who was acting as his secretary, "Four bells. I'm to meet with the carpenter to have a look at those breast hooks, so I'm afraid that will be all for wills for today." Even crawling through the dark and filthy hold up to the bow and listening to the prolix carpenter drone on about the degree of rot in the breast hooks seemed preferable to facing one more long and morbid face.

Biddlecomb changed from the tolerably decent clothing he was wearing to slop trousers, a wool shirt, and a tattered blue jacket. He looked like some down on-his-luck jack-tar, stumbling back aboard after a long night ashore, but those clothes were more appropriate for a tour of the hold.

Ten minutes later he and the carpenter were making their way along the carpenter's walk, the narrow passageway between the lowest tier of casks and the side of the ship.

The carpenter led the way. With his thick white beard and the lantern held over his head, he reminded Isaac of Diogenes, though any men they found lurking there in the most secluded part of the ship were unlikely to possess those virtues that the Greek philosopher was seeking.

"Now all them cant frames and right aft to here was replaced in the yard, and they're still sound enough," the carpenter was saying, "but I've got my eye on some further aft, and some of the planking amidships, under the turn of the bilge I reckon is about gone, but we'll need to careen her to have a look."

He continued in this manner until the two men reached the bow, the actual subject of their meeting. It was cold and damp there, and a trickle of water ran from under the breast hook down the apron to where it disappeared into the bilge. Biddlecomb pulled a folding knife from his pocket and, leaning over the breast hook, probed the wood with the point. It was soft and wet and the blade sank an inch deep with little thrusting at all.

"I see," was all he said.

They stood there for some time, lost in a discussion so technical that anyone ignorant of the sailor's vernacular, or the shipwright's, might have thought they were speaking some kind of code, if not a foreign language.

They were interrupted at last by the voice of one of the

ship's boys as he scurried like another of the many rats through the hold. "Captain? Captain, sir?" he called.

"Here, up at the bow."

"Oh, Captain, sir." The boy emerged from the darkness. "Mr. Rumstick's compliments, sir, and there's someone here which he says you should talk to, sir."

Oh, bloody hell, Biddlecomb thought. "Very well, pray tell Mr. Rumstick I shall be up directly."

Here was some other idiot from some committee or other, come to plague him with further orders. Just a few days ago he would have been excited at the prospect, before Mr. Whitley had forced him to remember that congressional plans were best greeted with cynicism.

He wished that they would cut him free to cruise against the enemy as he saw fit. They had given the sloop *Providence* to John Paul Jones, former first officer of the *Alfred,* and let him do just that, and Jones had less seniority than he.

With the carpenter in the lead, Biddlecomb made his way aft and up to the berthing deck and then up to the weather deck above. It was twilight as he stepped out of the scuttle. The sun was just over the low hills to the west, and the whole western horizon was a bright orange, fading to yellow then white then ever darkening shades of blue, arching overhead and terminating in black in the eastern sky.

He thought briefly about his dress. Slops were not quite the thing for a formal meeting, but he had been humiliated before by wearing his best uniform for the lackey Whitley. He doubted that his current visitor was any more important. He stepped quickly up the quarterdeck stairs and aft.

The strangers—there were three of them—were standing around the binnacle box, engaged in a quiet conversation with Lieutenants Rumstick and Weatherspoon. Biddlecomb's first impression was of some invalid with his nurse and assistant, for in the dark it seemed as if one of the party was quite old and infirm, while the other two were much younger, one around twenty years old, the other just a boy.

As he crossed the deck, the faces around the binnacle became more distinct, and as they did, Isaac felt a growing uneasiness. He paused and looked down at his clothes. His pants were smeared with some black, unidentifiable substance, and his jacket had a new tear in it from where it had caught on a broken barrel hoop.

"Captain Biddlecomb," said Rumstick in his most formal tone, and Isaac saw the first officer's eyes run over his captain's tatty clothing. "Pray let me introduce you to Dr. Benjamin Franklin and his party."

"Had we known you were coming, sir . . . ," Biddlecomb stammered, but Franklin shook his head and said, "No, no, I would never have you make a fuss."

Biddlecomb extended his hand. In the dim light he saw that it was filthy, so he wiped it quickly on his jacket and extended it again, thoroughly embarrassed, even as Franklin took his hand and shook it. In that way Captain Biddlecomb welcomed aboard the *Charlemagne* the most famous man in America.

CHAPTER
7

*This matter of lightning, or of electricity,
is an extreme subtle fluid, penetrating other bodies,
and subsisting in them, equally diffused.*

—BENJAMIN FRANKLIN
PARIS, SEPTEMBER 1767

THE *CHARLEMAGNE* WAS HALFWAY DOWN THE DELAWARE BAY when the fine weather deserted them and the first of what was to be a plague of winter storms overhauled them from the northeast. The blue sky was blotted out by degrees, hidden behind the thick, variegated blanket of gray and black, until the storm clouds were all that could be seen from horizon to horizon.

Then came the lightning, illuminating the distant clouds with flickering yellow light and slashing at the bay and the frozen shoreline. And then came the freezing rain, and the last vestige of physical comfort was gone.

The night before had been a long one for Biddlecomb, with little opportunity to sleep after greeting Franklin and his entourage. To his relief the great man had seemed not in the least put out by his perfunctory welcome aboard the ship, or by the captain's shameful appearance. Rather he had taken Biddlecomb's hand in a warm greeting and expressed his pleasure at being aboard.

"Captain," he had said, "I should like to introduce my

traveling companions. This is my grandson William Temple Franklin." Franklin indicated the older boy, who, on closer inspection, appeared a bit younger than Isaac had at first thought. Sixteen or seventeen, he guessed.

"Temple is to be my secretary. And this young man bears the unhappy name of Benjamin Franklin Bache. He is my other grandson and is bound for school in France."

The second grandson was a young man indeed, no more than seven years old. Biddlecomb shook hands with both of the Franklin grandsons.

"I have for you, Captain, orders from the Marine Committee, but in substance they say that you are now to follow the orders of the Committee of Secret Correspondence. And so you will not be surprised to find that I have orders from them as well." Franklin handed a large, heavy, bound packet to Biddlecomb. "Perhaps you would care to review these while the boys and I are settled in?"

Isaac stared at the packet, then at Franklin. His usual quick wit was deserting him in the presence of this man, generally considered to be one of the greatest wits and thinkers on either side of the ocean. He was suddenly afraid that Franklin would think him a bit slow.

"Of course, sir. Mr. Rumstick." Biddlecomb turned to the lieutenant and began to issue orders, a thing that always cleared his mind wonderfully. "Dr. Franklin and his party will have the great cabin, of course. Pray set a gang to removing my personal belongings and see their dunnage stowed down properly."

"Of course, sir. And, Captain, where will you be . . . oh, in my cabin, of course."

"Please, Captain," Franklin interrupted. "I would not have you endure the inconvenience of being put out of your cabin." Franklin had an old-fashioned quality, a formality that seemed to come from an earlier, simpler time, and Biddlecomb found it quite charming.

"Sir, I insist. As you see, I merely pass any inconvenience

along to my officers, who will do the same to the warrants. It is in the nature of things maritime."

In fact, moving out of the great cabin was very much an inconvenience, Isaac's assurance to Franklin notwithstanding. Rumstick's entire cabin, the second largest on the *Charlemagne*, was no bigger than the sleeping quarters in the great cabin.

Once Franklin and his party were escorted below, a slow process, as the philosopher was once more suffering from an attack of the gout, Biddlecomb retreated with a lantern and his packet of orders to his new and cramped quarters. He settled in at the tiny desk and broke the seal and removed the sheet of lead inserted to assure that the orders would sink if it became necessary to toss them overboard. He unfolded the page and read.

To Captain Isaac Biddlecomb, Esq.
Commander of the Continental brig-of-war *Charlemagne*

Sir:
The Honorable Dr. Franklin being appointed by Congress one of their Commissioners for negotiating some publick business at the court of France, you are to receive him and his suite aboard the *Charlemagne*, as passengers, whom it is your duty, and we dare say it will be your inclination, to treat with the greatest respect and attention, and your best endeavors will not be wanting to make their time on board the ship perfectly agreeable.

When they are on board, you are to proceed, with the utmost diligence, for the port of Nantes, in France . . .

Biddlecomb leaned back in his chair. France. He was bringing the great Benjamin Franklin to the court of Louis XVI. Now it would be his name in the newspapers, couched in the phrases he had so often read about others. "Dr. Franklin was conveyed safely to France in the brig *Charlemagne*, Capt. Isaac Biddlecomb, commanding, and while making a quick passage of forty days Captain Biddlecomb also managed to secure six prizes . . . ," It was not an unpleasant thought.

France. And while the port of Nantes was on the Bay of Biscay, and not the English Channel, it was still within two hundred leagues of England, and all of the shipping around that island. The Irish linen fleet, naval stores from the Baltic, the Lisbon packet, all would be prizes within his grasp.

Of course, along with that great concentration of prizes came the greatest concentration in the world of ships of the Royal Navy, sallying forth from Plymouth and Spithead, Portsmouth and Torquay. He wondered what the papers would say about the captain who allowed Franklin to be, captured by the British.

Biddlecomb stood on the quarterdeck, the rain running off his hat and oilskins and joining the narrow, fast-moving river coursing down the waterways and jetting out of the scuppers. The eastern shore of the bay was just visible through the fog, a low-lying, dark stretch of land. It was good weather for sneaking out to sea, if nothing else. The visibility was bad and he did not imagine that any lookout, high up in the crosstrees of some British man-of-war, would be too attentive to his duties in that miserable driving rain.

"Sir?" Mr. Mid. Samuel Gerrish approached, streaming water like Biddlecomb. Gerrish had just recently been appointed to the *Charlemagne* to take the place of the newly promoted Weatherspoon. His family had influence enough to get Gerrish an appointment, but not enough to secure an appointment above the rank of midshipman.

What made the situation odd was that Gerrish was, by Biddlecomb's best guess, in his midthirties, which seemed a bit old for a midshipman, though of course there was no real reason why a midshipman had to be young. And Gerrish was an experienced seaman and a reliable hand, surprisingly nimble aloft despite his corpulent figure. His wit was sharp and dry. He couched everything he said in the same deadpan expression.

At the moment his wit was the only thing about him that was dry.

"Yes, Mr. Gerrish?"

"Dr. Franklin's compliments, sir, and he is about to dine and asks would you join him, if at all convenient?"

Biddlecomb ran his eye over the *Charlemagne*. They were reaching under single-reefed topsails, foresail, mainsail, and fore topmast staysail in about twenty-five knots of wind, and despite the miserable rain, the weather did not really pose any danger to the vessel, nor was the navigation terribly complex.

"My compliments to Dr. Franklin and I shall join him momentarily."

After a brief word with Lieutenant Weatherspoon, the officer of the watch, Biddlecomb stepped through the scuttle and into the gunroom, through which he had to pass to reach the great cabin. He walked quickly, automatically, across the room, moving by instinct the way an old horse heads for its barn at the end of the day. The marine sentry at the door to the great cabin stepped aside with great precision.

Isaac had his hand on the doorknob and was ready to twist when he realized that the great cabin was no longer his to barge in on. He paused, embarrassed that the sentry had seen him make such a silly mistake, further embarrassed that he should care what the sentry thought. A puddle of water was forming at the foot of the door, running off his oilskins.

"Um, yes, indeed," he said, straightening and crossing over to the first officer's cabin and stepping inside with what dignity he could muster. He cursed under his breath as he struggled out of his oilskins in that confined space, spraying

water over everything. At one time in his life the first officer's cabin had seemed like the pinnacle of luxury, a vast
expanse of private domain, but now it seemed cramped
and annoying.

A minute later, in his best uniform coat, he approached
the great cabin again. The marine sentry, thoroughly confused, stepped aside, but Biddlecomb said, "Pray announce
me to Dr. Franklin."

"Aye, sir." The sentry opened the door and with a glance
back at Biddlecomb said, "Captain Biddlecomb, sir."

"Yes, yes, do come in!" Franklin's voice was loud and
jovial.

Biddlecomb stepped through the door. Franklin was sitting on the settee under the stern window, his gout-ridden
foot propped up on a chair. He was dressed in a maroon
velvet coat, waistcoat, and breeches. His long, fine, gray hair
framed his face and fanned out over his shoulders. He was
portly and his face was deeply lined with heavy jowls and
a double chin, but he was not an ugly man. Indeed, there
was something kindly and attractive about him.

His two grandsons, Lieutenant Rumstick, and Obadiah
Grim, the surgeon, were already seated around the table,
like the retinue of Franklin's court. But the hub of the room,
the focus, was Franklin.

"Please, Captain," Franklin said, "I would never have you
knocking at your own door. Pray, come and go as if we
were not here. Some wine with you? It comes from the very
region to which we are bound."

"Very kind of you, sir." Biddlecomb took his seat at the
table and accepted the glass that Temple held out to him.

Franklin turned to Grim. "To conclude, sir, let me just say
that I believe the illness we call a 'cold' comes not from the
cold at all, but from a certain closeness of the air and an
exhaustion of those good parts. The very best thing to prevent that affliction is a surfeit of fresh air, warm or cold.

74

That is why I always sleep with a window open, in all but the most extreme of weather."

"Indeed, sir. Most enlightening."

Franklin then turned to Biddlecomb. "All is well with the ship, I trust, Captain?"

"Well enough. This is hardly the best weather for standing a deck, but it is excellent weather for eluding British patrols."

"It's just as well. If we fail to elude the British, it will be stormy weather indeed. Now, let us not delay the feast a moment longer. Please, sir, have some of this pie. Temple, do cut the captain a piece. This is the last of the food we brought with us. I'll confess I am somewhat concerned about how my old teeth will fare with shipboard food."

"As to that, sir," said Biddlecomb, surveying the marvelous dinner spread before him, "I have laid in a tolerable amount of cabin stores, which should prove more palatable than the usual salt pork and dried peas. Perhaps you saw the chicken coops in the launch?"

"I did, and I thank you, sir, for your generosity. However, it has been my experience, in several ocean voyages, that your seagoing fowl is very much a tougher bird than the land-based chicken. A tougher bird altogether. Much like men, I suppose."

"No doubt you are right, sir," interjected Rumstick, "but it's still better fare than the barreled meat, which I'll warrant is as salt as Lot's wife's arse . . ." He glanced around the table, then sheepishly added, "Ah, or so the sailors are fond of saying, sir."

With that the dinner party fell silent, as each man attended to his meal, which was indeed excellent. Biddlecomb knew that Franklin was right insofar as he would not dine this well again until they reached France.

The brig heeled in a gust of wind, enough to make those at the table grab for their wineglasses, and the cabin grew darker as the storm outside increased. Then suddenly the entire space was illuminated with a flash of lightning, freezing everyone in his place for that second and washing them with white light, like a faded fresco.

"Perhaps I should have asked earlier, Captain," Franklin said after the startling crack of thunder had passed, "but are you familiar with the use of the lightning rod?"

"I have seen them employed on several buildings, sir. And I have read your work on the subject."

"You flatter me, Captain. But are you not familiar with their use on shipboard?"

"No, sir. I had thought that the bitter end of the wire, as you describe it, had to be sunk some several feet in moist ground in order for the thing to work."

"Just so. But one can place a rod at the top of a ship's masts and run the wire down a shroud and into the water and the device will be just as effective."

"Indeed? I had no notion. Then with your permission I shall send for the armorer after dinner to take instruction from you on how to rig the thing."

"I would be delighted to show him. Now tell me, Captain, why is it that I detect such a sour disposition among the people?"

At that Biddlecomb smiled. He had noticed it as well, the grumbling, the scowls, the dirty looks shot aft. He had given it a moment's consideration and he had dismissed it. It was as much a part of shipboard life as bad food and the steady chiming of the bell. He had never known of a ship's company that did not spend at least a portion of their time growling about their miserable lot.

"They're sailors, sir," Rumstick supplied, "which is as much to say they are a bunch of grumbling malcontents."

"I would disagree, Lieutenant," said Grim. "It is my belief that a monotonous diet such as the seamen eat results in a certain imbalance in the humors. What else could explain the frequency of ill temper among ships' companies?"

"This lot's been eating like lords for the past month and

more," Rumstick said. "We've been at anchor the chief of the time, with all the fresh food you could want."

"Actually, sir," Biddlecomb interjected, "I think they are upset about our mission." Once the *Charlemagne* was out of the Delaware River, Biddlecomb had let it be known that they were bound for France. That was when the muttering had begun.

"Oh, indeed?" Franklin looked upset by that news. "And why should that bother them? Are they not aware of the excellent opportunity this will present for taking prizes?"

"I reckon they're thinking more about sailing right into the arms of the Royal Navy. And some of them, the older hands, still have a hard time thinking of the French as our friends."

"But that makes no sense, Captain. Surely they see that the British are now our enemies, and thus the French must be considered friends, after a fashion. And that the Royal Navy is more active in our own waters than off the coast of France?"

Biddlecomb smiled and shook his head. "No one ever accused a sailor of rational thought, sir."

Two hours later Isaac regained the quarterdeck, his appetite sated to the point of discomfort by the thoroughly enjoyable meal. Beside him stood Franklin, who had insisted on coming topside over the badgering protest of Temple and the somewhat maternal concern of Grim and Rumstick. They had agreed at last to let the old man (whose authority in all matters not related to the running of the *Charlemagne* exceeded even Biddlecomb's) go up on deck only because the driving rain had passed to the southwest and only a light mist remained.

The two men, Biddlecomb and Franklin, were staring aloft, their hands held over their eyes to shield them from the falling mist. Standing on the main topgallant yard with one arm wrapped casually around the halyard was Midshipman Gerrish.

He too was looking up, at George Woodberry, foretopman, who was at the very top of the mast, his legs wrapped around the royal backstays, seizing a pointed rod to the top of the royal pole.

This kind of wildly perilous position would make an onlooker gasp and feel sick, but Woodberry was a strong, wiry type who seemed to have no regard for gravity nor a natural respect for heights. He worked calmly, as if standing on deck, and when he was done, he slid down the backstay to the topmast crosstrees and then inboard to the mast.

At various positions in the main shrouds, the main topmast shrouds, and the main topgallant shrouds other Charlemagnes were seizing in place a wire that ran from the pointed rod down past the starboard main channel and into the water.

"Yes, that should answer famously, Captain," Franklin said, smiling.

"Very good. I thank you, sir, and shall put my faith in your science." Looking around, Biddlecomb could see that his faith was not universally shared. In the waist and on the forecastle men looked with suspicion and loathing at this new rig. Sailors hated anything new, and in their already black mood they saw the lightning rod as just one more thing that would bring on some terrible fate.

"Bloody fucking stupid, that just attracts the lightning, like a lodestone," someone said, and a quirk of wind drifted the words back to the quarterdeck.

"Just ignore them, Doctor," Biddlecomb said. "A little blue water will clear their heads."

Blue water. Yes, but they had to get there first, which meant running out of the bay and past any British ships that might be cruising just beyond the capes.

The Delaware Bay had seen quite a bit of activity over the past year. In the spring a British force had tried to push upriver to Philadelphia, only to be worn down and beaten back by a combination of shore batteries, chevaux-de-frise, state and Continental ships, and a fleet of thirteen clumsy, absurd row-galleys.

The British had been pushed back, but they had not left, and Biddlecomb knew that the *Charlemagne* would be fortunate indeed to reach the deep water without encountering an enemy of superior strength.

For that reason he decided to press on and shoot through the capes in the dark rather than anchor that night in the shelter of Cape May. It was a risk; running aground in the Delaware Bay was easy enough to do in good visibility; but he wished to put as much distance as he could between himself and the shore, particularly while he had the advantage of darkness.

He stood the deck as the gray evening light faded to the black of night. The watches changed around him, the officers reporting to one another in their formal, naval manner, the men huddling under oilskin hats and tarpaulin coats, reluctantly coming on watch or eager to get below.

The mist gave way once more to driving rain, with lightning flashing on the horizon and striking the water within half a mile of the brig. Biddlecomb saw eyes in the waist staring up, accusingly, at Franklin's lightning rod, faces scowling at the contraption as if it alone had brought on the terrifying bolts.

Then the rain was gone and the mist was back as a succession of storms swept in from the northeast, drenching them, threatening them with their lightning bolts and then moving past. At five bells in the night watch Biddlecomb felt the loom of the land to starboard and he was certain that Cape Henlopen was abeam, but too far off to see, even when the flashes of lightning lit up the sea.

At eight bells, four in the morning, Rumstick came aft to relieve Weatherspoon of the watch. They made a formal greeting, as if they barely knew one another, though together they had seen more action than any two men might see in a lifetime. Weatherspoon went through the routine of telling Rumstick the course and speed and the few other pertinent details of the brig's operation.

Biddlecomb had to marvel at how very like a real navy this Continental force was becoming. In just over a year and a half he had seen it grow from sundry tag-and-rag groups of men putting out in longboats to a few disjoined collections of vessels fielded by the various states to something that could be called, without fear of ridicule, a national navy.

By the time Weatherspoon's watch was below, Biddlecomb knew that they were free of the land. He did not need to see the capes over the taffrail to know that. He could feel it underfoot as the *Charlemagne*'s motion changed from the quick jerk of pounding through the chop of the bay to a long, swooping rise and fall as she met the Atlantic rollers. It was a good feeling. It meant freedom to Biddlecomb, the open ocean, independence and possibilities.

They held that course for another two hours before he judged it was time to turn.

"Mr. Rumstick?"

"Aye, sir?"

"Make her head northeast by east." Isaac felt the enthusiasm welling up in him and with a smile he added, "Take us to France, if you please."

"Hands to braces!" Rumstick called out, and Biddlecomb saw men moving ghostlike in the dark. "Helmsman, northeast by east. To France, the captain says." Rumstick was smiling as well.

Ten minutes of activity and then the *Charlemagne* was silent again, close-hauled on a great-circle route to France. In the dark and the mist Biddlecomb could barely see the bow. Anything beyond the confines of the brig was blackness.

"Captain?" Rumstick stepped across the quarterdeck to the weather side. "Do you think she'll bear topgallants over single-reefed topsails?"

"I think not. It's well enough now but I believe we shall

have another of these lightning storms within the next few hours, and they have some wind in them. Let's wait for first light."

"Aye, sir."

The two men were standing side by side, staring out at the blackness to weather and astern. "Also, Ezra, I think we will clear for action before dawn. We had best get into the habit of doing so every morning."

"Aye, sir. Should have first light in an hour or so."

Biddlecomb was about to continue with a discussion of the gun tackles when a light caught his eye, a glowing, orange light off in the darkness astern, just the tiniest pinprick. "Do you see that?"

"Aye. What in all hell . . . ?"

The orange light seemed to float, though whether in the water or in the air they could not tell. It grew larger and more brilliant, though it was still no more than a tiny point, dancing back and forth in the dark.

"What in all hell . . . ?" Rumstick said again, somewhat more emphatically. They had both of them seen any number of phenomena at sea, many unexplained, but this was something new.

The orange light seemed to divide and divide again, until there were five or six spots, all moving in the same undulating dance, making little motions up and down, back and forth. And then they shot straight down, dividing again and flaring brighter, and then they were gone.

"What in the hell was that?" Rumstick took a step back from the rail. His eyes were wide.

Biddlecomb stared at the place where the lights had disappeared. He was no more superstitious than any decently educated mariner, which is to say that he was fairly superstitious, though he denied it to everyone, most of all himself. Still, the sight of that dancing orange light had thoroughly unnerved him. He did not know what to say, nor did he trust himself to speak. He looked forward, to see if any of the men had seen it, but apparently they had not. That at least was fortunate.

"Isaac, what do you think that was?" Rumstick asked, an edge of panic in his voice.

"I don't know." Biddlecomb's first reaction, irrational as it might be, was to clear for action. He had no hopes that the great guns would be any defense against the supernatural, but the defensive posture made him feel more secure.

In his mind he envisioned the men clearing away the guns, casting off lashings, sanding the deck, Mr. Sprout rigging chains to the yards, the cook and his assistant dumping the galley fires overboard.

Oh, hell . . .

He stared out in the dark again, felt his stomach twist a half turn. "It's a man-of-war."

"What?"

"It's a man-of-war, clearing for action. Those were the coals, the coals from the galley fire. We saw them throwing the coals from the galley fire overboard."

Rumstick was silent as he considered that. "You could well be right," he said at last. "What should we do?"

"First we'll shake out the reefs in the topsails and set topgallants and stuns'ls, if she'll bear it, as quietly as you please. And then we best pray that this fellow is not British."

"You think there's any chance of that, sir?"

"No, none at all."

CHAPTER
8

Courage would fight, but Discretion won't let him.

—POOR RICHARD'S ALMANACK, 1747

SHE WAS A MAN-OF-WAR, AND SHE WAS BRITISH, BUT IT WAS TWO more anxious hours before they would know that.

The Charlemagnes moved quickly, running up from below and swarming up the weather shrouds to lay out on the upper yards. The order to set more sail was entirely unexpected on that wild night, but the rumor of a British man-of-war had spread quickly, and that inspired them to speed and silence.

Biddlecomb could feel the *Charlemagne* surge ahead as the sail area increased. He could feel the blunt bow slamming into the seas, sending a shudder through the fabric of the vessel. He thought of the rotten breast hooks. Water would be spouting in around the stem like a fire hose, but there was nothing for it. They had to put as much distance as they could between themselves and this stranger before daylight gave them away.

Once the men had spread all of the canvas the *Charlemagne* would bear, he set them to clearing for action. Again they moved silently, more silently than was quite necessary given the rising wind, but Biddlecomb knew that it made them feel better to be stealthy.

The first hint of light in the east, a dark gray band along

the horizon and a general diffusion of the black sky, and the last of the gun crews reported themselves ready.

There was no promise of fine weather in that first light, no hint of a glorious day dawning. Rather it was dark and foreboding. The sun, somewhere behind all of that thick cloud, served only to reveal the miserable conditions that lay in store for all mariners that day. And along with the dull light came more flashes of lightning, coming up over the horizon as another of those squalls was carried down on them by the building wind.

An hour later there was enough light to see several miles of the lumpy, dull gray sea through which they were pounding, the same color as the low-hanging clouds that occasionally showered them with rain.

"On deck!" shouted Mr. Gerrish. Biddlecomb had sent him to the main topgallant to see what he could of the man-of-war.

"Deck, aye!"

"Strange sail right astern, two or three miles off . . . ship rigged . . . under reefed topsails . . . course approximately south southeast . . . big bastard, sir, beg your pardon. Looks like *Roebuck.*"

And no doubt it is, with my damnable luck, Biddlecomb thought. *Roebuck* had been hovering around the capes for months, plaguing American shipping. She was the one, along with the *Liverpool,* that had tried to force her way up to Philadelphia.

She was a frigate technically, but Gerrish had been right in describing her as a big bastard. She mounted forty-four guns, more firepower than the frigates *Rose* and *Glasgow* combined.

"She's hauling her wind, sir!" Gerrish called down. "She's seen us! Making right for us, sir!"

"Did I hear that hateful name *Roebuck?*" Franklin said, stepping awkwardly up onto the quarterdeck and limping toward the weather rail, wincing each time his gout-ridden foot touched the deck. One arm was over Temple's shoulder, for support.

"Good morning, sir," Biddlecomb said. "You know, I once read something to the effect of 'Be temperate in wine, eating, girls, and sloth, or the gout will seize you and plague you both.' "

"Pray, Captain, do not quote me to myself, not at this time of the morning. Now what of this *Roebuck?*"

"We passed her close by in the dark. Now she's two miles or so astern and just taking up the chase."

"I need not remind you that your orders are to not engage with the enemy, if it can be avoided."

"I do recall that, sir, and believe me, I shall try with all of my effort to avoid any such thing."

Biddlecomb waited for the commissioner to ask what he planned to do, but Franklin, unlike other important men whom Biddlecomb had known, had sense and discretion enough not to inquire.

The ensuing silence left Isaac with nothing to do but to try to answer that question for himself.

The first objective, of course, was to elude capture and continue on to France. To help in eluding capture it would be beneficial to throw overboard everything they could— food, water, stores, the damned indigo, even guns—but that would put an end to their voyage. The *Roebuck* was between them and the coast, so trying to run back into some American port would only bring them under the frigate's broadside.

No, he could do nothing but continue to run as fast as he could on the course he was on. That was not much of a plan, but there it was.

The lightning beyond the bow grew more distinct as the *Charlemagne* and the storm raced toward each other. There was some hope. If they could get into the squall and lose sight of the *Roebuck,* they could tack and run away on a different course, gaining some distance until the visibility improved. That was something, at least.

"Could I interest you in some breakfast, Dr. Franklin?" Biddlecomb asked.

"Breakfast? Why, you're a cool one, Captain, thinking of breakfast with a British frigate on our tail."

"Well, sir, as to the *Roebuck,* we are doing all we can at the moment to elude her, as little as that might seem." In his brief naval career Isaac had spent an inordinate amount of time being chased around the ocean by British men-of-war. He had learned that after the initial excitement of setting sail and clearing for action, there was only boredom and anxiety, and the latter was more acute if the former was too much indulged. He would see that the men had plenty to occupy their hands and minds, and then he would do the same for himself.

Since the *Charlemagne* carried all her guns on the weather deck, clearing the brig for action happily did not entail tearing down the great cabin. Thus Biddlecomb and Franklin and his entourage were able to breakfast as if nothing out of the ordinary were taking place, save for the fact that it was a cold breakfast, due to the galley fires having discreetly been thrown overboard.

But it was excellent nonetheless, consisting of cold roast beef, cold meat pies, still soft bread with still fresh butter and jam, and eggs that had been hard-boiled before the fires went out. Only the hot coffee was wanting to make it a perfect meal.

"Tell me, Captain," Franklin said as he deftly cut the kidney pie, "are you familiar with this oceanic river we call the Gulf Stream?"

"Yes, sir. Moderately so," Biddlecomb began as Temple appeared in the cabin, an elegant wooden case in his hand.

"Ah, Temple, you have found it! Good man!" Franklin said. Temple placed the case on the deck and opened it.

Wrapped in its velvet lining were several thermometers and a length of line, like a deep-sea lead.

"Pray, tell me what you know about it."

"No more than that it flows one hundred miles or so off our coast, south to north, at a prodigious rate. When crossing, one must take account of the set or miss one's landfall entirely. The water tends to be a lighter color than most open ocean and warmer. And it's a rather stormy place."

"Excellent, quite right. Tell me, do you think it would be an aid to mariners to have a map of the Gulf Stream, to know exactly its boundaries?"

"I think it would be very helpful indeed."

"Well, that is what I am attempting. I intend to measure the water temperature each day, and I have other captains doing the same, and when we are done, I hope we can use that information to create something of a map of this phenomenon."

Franklin's mind was amazing, unlike anything else Biddlecomb had encountered. He had known any number of men, of course, who could move rapidly from one subject to another, but in most instances he found they knew little about any of them. Franklin, it seemed, could discourse on virtually any topic with knowledge and insight and a prodigious amount of original thought. And he made his audience feel not in the least bit uncomfortable or stupid.

Breakfast passed swiftly by, taken up by a highly detailed discussion of navigation, which was endlessly fascinating to Biddlecomb and Franklin, though Temple seemed quite bored and young Benjamin occupied himself by reenacting naval battles with his silverware.

By the time Biddlecomb had eaten the last bite that he could possibly eat, the *Charlemagne*'s motion had become far more wild and the sky through the stern windows noticeably darker. "I think I best get back on deck, sir, if I may beg your pardon."

"Of course, Captain, never let me detain you. I think the

boys and I shall remain below stairs . . . forgive me, just *below*, I believe, is proper . . . lest we get in your way."

"Your choice entirely, sir. You are welcome wherever you choose," Isaac said, and oddly enough he actually meant it. Franklin was a pleasure to have around, as unobtrusive a man as he had ever known. He seemed so pleasant and disingenuous that Isaac wondered how he would ever fare in the court of Versailles.

Biddlecomb stepped through the scuttle and ran his eyes over the waist. Rumstick had rigged lifelines running the length of the deck, double-gripped the boats, and had storm gaskets passed around those sails that were furled. He had housed all of the guns as well and replaced the tampions.

And it was well that he had. The sea was rising, with a steep chop breaking on the backs of the big swell, and it was already too rough to have the guns cast off.

Overhead the sky was low and black and lightning was flashing in the distance, now no more than a mile ahead. *There'll be a lot of wind in this one,* Biddlecomb thought as he mounted the steps to the quarterdeck, grabbing on to the main-topsail halyard to steady himself as the brig lurched under him.

"Mr. Rumstick, what of the *Roebuck?*" he called.

Rumstick stepped over to the weather side and joined him. "She's hull up when she rises on the swell, sir," he said, gesturing aft. A big sea rolled away from the *Charlemagne*, obscuring the horizon. Then the brig lifted on the next wave, going up with a motion that left one's belly in the trough, and as the apex of the wave passed under, Biddlecomb could see the big frigate, now just over a mile and a half astern.

She had quite a bit of canvas showing, more than the *Charlemagne*, because her heavy spars could carry more, and the seas would not slow her down as much as they would the brig. If she was going just one knot faster than the *Charlemagne*, which no doubt she was, and she was one and a half miles astern, then it would take her only an hour and a half to be up with them.

Lightning struck the sea less than a mile ahead, followed a few seconds later by a crack of thunder so loud that Biddlecomb saw men leap in surprise. Several heads turned and looked up at the main truck, up at the accursed lightning rod that was somehow responsible.

"Lieutenant, we had better get the topgallants off her and the topmast stun's'ls," Biddlecomb called over the increased hum of the wind. They had probably carried those sails too long as it was. They would be lucky to get the canvas in before it blew out.

The brunt of the storm hit just as the main topgallant yard was settling in its lifts. It hit like a solid thing, like a rogue wave, slamming into their weather side and rolling them over, down and down.

Biddlecomb grabbed on to a backstay, held it with an aching hand, struggling to keep his feet as the *Charlemagne* rolled. "Come along, come along," he said out loud, waiting for the vessel to stop her heeling, to come back up on her keel, but she did not.

Over and over she went. Isaac grabbed on with another hand, felt his feet sliding from under him, and then he knew that the ship was not going to come upright again.

One second they were rising and falling on the swells, heeling fifteen degrees to starboard, and the next they were knocked down flat, the end of the main yard plunging into the sea, the water pouring over the lee rail, as the vessel slewed around.

Biddlecomb heard shouts and screams from forward as the Charlemagnes' whole world turned over. A frigid and watery death roiled below, ready to sweep over them if the brig continued to roll, continued to turn until she was upside down. He felt his feet sliding out from under him. He jammed a foot against one of the legs of the binnacle box as the brig rolled on her side, then pulled himself up to where he could see the length of the deck.

The *Charlemagne* was nearly on her beam ends, the yards and sails half in the sea, the once horizontal deck now nearly vertical. The guns on the windward side were literally hanging from their tackles; if any of those tackles carried away, then one and a half tons of cannon and carriage would plunge down the deck and smash through the leeward bulwark.

Biddlecomb ran his eyes over the masts and yards, buffeted by the waves to leeward. One of the main topmen had fallen into the sea and was clinging to the bitter end of a topgallant gasket as his mates, entwined in the rig, tried to haul him in.

A wave washed over him, obscuring him for a second, and then he was visible again. The topmen hauled away as another wave passed over him, and this time he was gone. He surfaced again, twenty yards downwind, waving in desperate panic, and then he went under once more. Biddlecomb turned away. There was no thought of rescue. It would be a miracle if they did not all drown in the next few moments.

It was quiet, unnaturally still, with the overturned hull shielding the deck from the wind, and the flogging canvas subdued by the sea. The *Charlemagne* had stopped rolling. She had turned on her beam ends and turned no further, stopped before she went clean over. But there was no knowing how long she would stay that way. Ships had lived for days on their beam ends. They had also gone down in minutes.

Rumstick appeared on the quarterdeck, half standing on the now horizontal stanchion of the rail at the break of the deck, Gerrish right behind him. They both held axes. "Shall we cut the masts away, sir?" Rumstick's voice was clear in the weird quiet.

"No!" Biddlecomb shouted back. That was the most sure-fire method of righting a ship that was laid over, but he had not forgotten the frigate charging up behind them. As ludicrous as it was, he still had hopes of escape.

He clambered up onto the high side of the binnacle box and reached overhead to the pinrail, and using the belaying pins as handholds, he made his way awkwardly forward. He gripped the pins as tightly as ever he had a shroud while going aloft. Loosing his grip meant sliding down the nearly vertical deck and disappearing into the sea swirling over the quarterdeck rail.

Lightning flashed somewhere behind him, and less than a second later the thunder cracked overhead, loud as a broadside.

"Let go the second bower!" he shouted to Rumstick, pointing toward the anchor on the leeward side, hanging from its lashings in the bow and all but submerged. "That'll bring her head around! We'll see if that rights us!"

"I'll go, sir!" Gerrish shouted. With his round face and pink cheeks he looked entirely out of place, like some store clerk or apothecary's assistant. But he turned and leapt from the quarterdeck down to the mainmast fife rail, and with the ax in his hand slid down the deck to the leeward bulwark, now awash with a foot of water, and walked and slid and pulled himself along the lifeline, working his way forward.

The *Charlemagne* was drifting fast downwind. Biddlecomb turned and looked in the direction of their drift, hoping to catch some glimpse of the *Roebuck,* but the rain had come again, driving down in sheets, and the visibility had closed down to a quarter mile at best. Most of the light on that dark morning was from the ever more frequent flashes of lightning, striking closer and closer and accompanied by the nearly constant roll of thunder.

"Mr. Weatherspoon!" Biddlecomb shouted to the second officer, struggling aft along the main hatch. "Get some men to the foremast! Cast off the sheets, see the braces manned!

Be ready when that anchor is let go! We may come upright damn fast!"

Weatherspoon waved his acknowledgment and headed back in the direction from which he had come. "Mr. Rumstick, I'll thank you to see to the mainmast."

"Aye, sir."

Gerrish had reached the bow and stood leaning over the bulwark, his feet hooked under the cathead to keep him from plunging straight down into the sea. A single cable was bent to the anchor, two hundred yards long, stoppered at the bitter end, and ready to run. If the *Charlemagne* was where Biddlecomb thought she was, then that would be just enough to reach the bottom.

The inboard fluke of the second bower thrust up out of the sea and hooked around a post as if the anchor, like the men of the *Charlemagne*, were clinging to the ship for life. Gerrish brought the ax down on the lashings, cutting rope and wood together. He cut again and again and at last the fluke let go, disappearing into the sea and tearing chunks of bulwark as it went.

He twisted around and cut the ring stopper, the last line holding the anchor to the ship. The stopper whipped through the air as the great weight was released, and the big anchor plunged toward the bottom.

"Anchor's let go!" Gerrish shouted aft, but the end of the sentence was lost in a clap of thunder.

Biddlecomb waited for the booming to subside and then shouted, "Stand ready for when she catches! Stand ready at your masts!" and then the anchor caught. The *Charlemagne* jerked as if she had struck a rock, and Biddlecomb fell backward, landing flat on his back on the steep-slanting deck.

He felt himself slide, saw the water boiling around the quarterdeck rail below him. He flailed out, clutching for something, anything, but there was nothing there. He was sliding out of control toward the gray and white sea. He had a vision of that topman; one desperate cry for help and then he was gone. He grabbed at the binnacle box as he slid past, but he could not get a grip on the wet wood.

He was past the centerline, slipping, falling toward the sea from which there would be no rescue. He twisted around and clawed at the deck, feeling the seams between the planking slide past, but there was nothing to grab. His feet hit the quarterdeck bulwark, a foot underwater.

He felt himself toppling overboard, and then he was thrown back, landing heavily on his shoulder. The sea fell away and he was lying on the deck, a deck that was still steeply canted but was no longer vertical. The *Charlemagne* was coming up again.

He scrambled to his feet and moved quickly to the high side. The anchor had held in the bottom and the *Charlemagne* had slewed around until she was head to the wind, and with the wind and the sea no longer acting on her exposed bottom, she had rolled back on her keel.

Her masts, yards, sails, and rigging came up out of the sea, rising like some ancient sea monster from the depths, and tons of water ran over her decks and shot streams from her scuppers. Those topmen still aloft clung desperately on, their arms and legs entwined in the standing rigging. The brig seemed to groan with the agony of righting herself, but up she came until she was on an all but even keel, the waves crashing over her bow as she pulled and bucked at the anchor.

The height of the storm was on them now, or what Biddlecomb hoped was the height of the storm. He did not think they could take much worse than that. The rain was coming down almost sideways, beating against the deck in a thousand spurts of water, joining the great flood of seawater coming over the bow. The thunder continued unabated, as loud and intimidating as any sea battle he had witnessed, the lightning like a battery of great guns flashing all around, hitting the sea within a cable length of the brig.

He blocked it out as best he could and plunged down into the waist, the water rushing knee high down the deck and then disappearing through the scuppers and gunports, then flooding over the bow again.

Weatherspoon, Rumstick, and Sprout the boatswain saw him coming forward and made their way to him. They stood in a circle, their heads inclined toward one another to hear over the wind and the thunder.

"We can't stay anchored like this much longer, we'll swamp for sure!" Biddlecomb shouted and the others nodded their agreement. "We haven't the sea room to run with it! We'll try reaching offshore under close-reefed fore topsail and main staysail!"

"Aye, sir!" the three officers shouted, nearly in unison.

"We'll set the staysail, then cut the anchor away, straighten the rest of it out then!"

"Any sight of *Roebuck?*" Rumstick shouted.

At that the four of them turned and looked aft, searching for the frigate. The *Charlemagne* was in a trough between waves, and they could see nothing but water rearing up around them. And then the brig lifted, a jerky, unnatural motion with the bow held in place by the anchor, and there was the *Roebuck,* not a cable length astern.

"Oh, mother of God," Sprout said. She was driving hard under reefed topsails and courses, her lofty rig already looming above them. She would have been a frightening sight in any case, but with her wet canvas reflecting the flash of lightning, and the rain and fog partially obscuring her, she seemed almost mythic as she plunged toward them, out of the gloom.

"Get that staysail set!" Biddlecomb turned and pushed Rumstick toward the fife rail. "Sprout, cut that cable away, the very second the sail is hauled aft! Mr. Weatherspoon, get some hands aloft to straighten out that mess!"

He turned and worked his way aft, his eyes fixed on the *Roebuck* as with each rise and fall of the sea she drew closer.

There's nothing she can do, he thought as he pulled himself up the steps to the quarterdeck. *What can she do in this sea?*

Then, as if to answer him, the frigate fired the foremost of her great guns, a flash of orange and yellow in the gloom. Biddlecomb could not hear the report, but a hole appeared in the mainsail where the ball passed through.

This is insane! he thought. *They're firing at us?* He did not imagine that the captain of the *Roebuck* would dare open his gunports in that weather, but perhaps he was wrong.

In the *Charlemagne's* waist twenty men struggled in the knee-high water to haul the staysail up. *Come along, come along,* Biddlecomb thought. They had to be under way before the frigate drew any closer. As it was, there was little hope of shaking them off.

The *Roebuck* was no more than one hundred yards astern. She fired her forward gun again, and one of the *Charlemagne's* main shrouds was shot through. It blew out to leeward, held back only by the ratlines. Another shot like that and the mainmast would be gone, torn down by the force of the wind. The frigate did not need to destroy them. She needed only to damage them and the storm would do the rest.

The *Charlemagne* swung off the wind, turning fast, and Biddlecomb knew that Sprout had cut the anchor away. "Steady her up!" he shouted at the helmsmen, and the two men at the tiller pushed the helm to leeward.

Now they were under the frigate's broadside, the big ship no more than fifty yards away, rising like a fortress above them. The gunports along her side swung open and the great guns ran out. *He's mad, he's mad,* Biddlecomb thought. It was insane, opening the ports, even for a second, as he was doing, but Biddlecomb knew that it would be worth it. This one broadside, so close, was sure to damage the *Charlemagne* enough that the storm would finish her off.

Biddlecomb clenched his teeth and his left hand reached for the hilt of his sword. And then the darkness was split apart by a great arc of light, reaching down from heaven and grabbing the *Roebuck*'s mainmast like the hand of God.

The entire frigate lit up as if exploding. The lightning danced over the top hamper, blowing the main topgallant mast away like a dried twig and shattering the topmast clean down to the cap. The main topsail burst into flames and Biddlecomb could see fire consuming the tarred shrouds as well, despite the rain.

In the same instant there was a terrible crash, the sound of an explosion and tearing and rendering wood. His first thought was that *Roebuck* had fired her broadside, but it was the sound of the thunder and the lightning strike and the shattering spars. The frigate's foresails were all askew now, flogging and backing, the fore braces torn away or burned through.

The great ship seemed to stop in her wake, turning out of control up into the wind. Her mainsail was on fire as well, the flames racing the length of the huge mainyard and engulfing the maintop. Biddlecomb hoped that no poor sons of bitches were caught in the top, where they would have no choice but jump to their death or burn, but he imagined that any hands there had been killed quick by the lightning bolt.

"Sir? Sir?" he heard Rumstick calling out, and he realized that the *Charlemagne*'s motion, while still wild, was more regular now, and they were leaving the *Roebuck* astern.

He turned and looked forward. The main staysail was set and drawing, as was the deep-reefed fore topsail, and the brig was plunging on, making headway through the terrible storm and away from the crippled frigate.

Rumstick was making his way across the deck.

"Rumstick, did you see that!" Isaac shouted.

"Aye, I did! Praise be to God!" The lieutenant stood beside him, holding a handful of rigging for support. They watched as the *Roebuck*'s main topmast sagged to one side and then fell, crashing to the deck, tearing up standing and running rigging alike.

"Incredible! I've never seen the like!"

"Nor I!" Rumstick shouted. "It was beautiful! Real Old Testament stuff!"

CHAPTER
9

Neither a Fortress or a Maidenhead
will hold out long after they begin to parley.

—POOR RICHARD'S ALMANACK, 1733

CAPT. JOSEPH HYNSON, AN AMERICAN MERCHANT CAPTAIN CUR-
rently without a ship, sat at the table in the none-too-clean
kitchen of Mrs. Elizabeth Jump's boardinghouse, No. 13
Stepney Causeway, Ratcliff Cross, London. Mrs. Jump's
house was his home when he was in London, which was
often. It was a convenient place where he was much loved
by the owner and other guests and was only made to pay for
his room and board when it suited him, which was rarely.

The place was lit by a low fire in the big fireplace, which
did not quite fend off the cold December drafts but was at
least dim enough to hide in shadow the horrors of the Jump
kitchen. Mrs. Jump's house was called by some a boardinghouse and by others a whorehouse. Neither description
was wrong.

Hynson was built like a boatswain or a professional boxer,
with dark hair and a dark complexion that hinted at Medi-
terranean or American Indian blood. Before him sat a half-
empty bowl of punch, a pipe with no more than a stub of
a stem left, and a pouch of tobacco that was half-scattered
across the tabletop. His legs were splayed out, feet toward
the fire, like a man very comfortable in his surroundings.

"Offers of commands?" he answered rhetorically. "Oh,

hell, yes, I've had offers and then some, but I've had to turn them all down. Why? Well, my dear, there are things happening in France, do you see, things related to the American cause, and I must hold myself in the ready for such time as I am needed."

Across from Hynson sat Isabella Cleghorn, a young woman of nineteen years who lived and worked at Mrs. Jump's. She sat huddled under a wool cape. Half of her face was illuminated by the fire, but even the orange light could not mask her pale, waxy complexion. Her eyes, big eyes, like a deer's, reflected the flames in tiny convex mirrors as she nodded at Hynson, acknowledging that she understood but was unwilling or unable to interrupt his monologue.

"I'll tell you, though, and this can go no further, I'm gettin' close to worried about turning away all these merchants who want me to be master for 'em. It'll make people suspicious, important people that are having me watched."

"Watched?" Isabella spoke at last. "Sure you're not being watched?"

"Oh, indeed I am. Don't think Lord North and that lot don't know who Joe Hynson is, what he's done . . ." *Damn, but she is a pretty little bird*, Hynson thought, even as he continued to speak. He let his mind wander off, which did not impede the flow of his narrative in the least.

He thought of what Isabella felt like underneath him, his big frame pushing her petite body down into the straw mattress on his bed, gasping, her whole body jarring with each thrust. He felt himself becoming aroused. He had been with her a dozen or so times, no more than half of which he had to pay for. He was hoping that his bravado would earn him such an arrangement tonight. It was that or nothing. He had no money.

"The rumor is that Silas Deane in Paris has a notion to go privateering and that Dr. Benjamin Franklin, who is a particular friend of mine, is soon to arrive in France with blank commissions. I reckon . . ."

They heard a step beyond the door, a shoe crunching on gravel, and then a low knock. They both froze, and Hynson felt a rush of fear. Isabella's eyes grew wider still. And then Hynson realized that he was being foolish, for despite what he had told the girl, no one in London was in the least bit interested in him. He was frightening himself with his own stories.

He stood slowly, making the most of the drama, though he knew that it was probably just some poor beggar who saw the light from the fireplace and was looking for scraps. He lifted a pistol from the nearby counter and slowly eased the lock back, noting the fear and awe playing over Isabella's wet eyes.

He moved across the room and opened the door, keeping the pistol out of sight. A young boy stood there, in common clothes, too clean to be a beggar.

"What is it?"

"I've a letter for Capt. Joe Hynson," the boy said.

Lovely, Hynson thought. Nothing like the intrigue of a late-night letter to fetch the interest of a young whore and make her more liberal in her financial practices.

"I'm Hynson," he said, reaching out for the letter. He took it from the boy and opened it, angling it toward the fire until he could make out the tight letters.

Dear Joe,

I came to town 12 o'Clock last night, my business are of Such a Nature, won't bare putting to Paper, Shall Say nothing more but expect to see you Immediately, I Shall leave Town early the Morrow Morning, therefore begg You will not loose A Minute time Coming here, as I have business of Importance for you which must be Transacted this day, Your

Friend & Country Man
Sam Nicholson

P.S. I begg my Name or my being in Town may not be known to any one, to prevent wch I shall not Stur Out of the House this Day, Pray take Coach & come off to me Immediately.

Portland Street
Portland Chapel
No. 94

"Well, damn me all to hell," Hynson said under his breath. It seemed they really did have some use for him in their stupid rebellion. He was not at all certain how he felt about that.

"You may go," he said to the messenger, who was still hanging around, waiting for a tip, which he would not get. With a surly look the boy disappeared, and as soon as Hynson closed the door, he heard him shout, "Cheap Yankee bastard!" followed by the sound of running feet, but the captain did not care. This letter was something that could lead to real trouble.

"What . . . whatever is it? Not some trouble, I pray," Isabella said with real concern in her voice.

"It's from a friend. A countryman, Sam Nicholson. Damned important man in this fight." That was partially true. The Nicholson family was a prominent and influential clan on the Eastern Shore of Maryland. Hynson had heard a rumor that Sam Nicholson's older brother, James, had been appointed senior captain of the American navy. Even if Sam was not in an important position now, he would be soon, and he had the ears of some influential people.

"Please . . . Joe . . . promise you won't put yourself in any danger." Hynson looked into Isabella's eyes. She was on the verge of tears. He realized that she was genuinely concerned about him, that she had feelings for him that were real and deep felt and that might easily be parlayed into a free romp in bed.

"He sends for me this instant. I must leave."

"This instant? Sure you have some time. Some time to . . . say good-bye?"

He crossed over to her, wiped the tear from her cheek, and pulled the cloak back, exposing her tiny, bare shoulders. "Of course, my dear, of course."

The sun was just showing itself over the rooftops and lighting up those dark places in narrow Portland Street, walled in by solid rows of three- and four-story buildings, when the tired but sated Capt. Joe Hynson found number 94.

He paused in front of the door, glancing up and down the street, afraid that he was being watched and equally afraid that he was being ridiculous in his histrionic caution. When he was satisfied that no one in the already crowded street was paying the least attention to him, he knocked.

The door was opened almost immediately by Sam Nicholson, in a state of partial dress: breeches with no stockings or shoes, shirt open at the neck, waistcoat unbuttoned. He was a young man, not past twenty-five, and handsome as well, with all of the enthusiasm and energy of his years. He made Hynson feel quite old and worn-out, though he was only thirty-two.

Nicholson's face lit up in a most satisfying manner as he extended his hand and said, "Joe Hynson! God, but it is good to see you, man! I had thought you would not come in time!" Still grasping Hynson's hand and putting his other on Hynson's shoulder, Nicholson half-waved and half-dragged him inside and shut the door with his foot.

"I was out on business most of the night and only just returned to my lodging to find your note. Of course I hurried over as fast as I could."

"Good man, good man!" Nicholson led him into a drawing room off the foyer. "You're looking well, though perhaps a bit tired? Working hard, are you?"

"Very. But, pray, Sam, what brings you to London?" Sam Nicholson's conversation had a tendency to wander, calling for frequent course corrections.

"Oh, yes . . . well, here's the thing of it, and this is absolutely secret, a hanging matter, really. But of course I can trust you. I've been in contact with Silas Deane, who you know is American commissioner in Paris. He's ordered me to buy a cutter, to use in the Continental service. Wants it for a packet between France and the States, which ain't exactly the service I had in mind—no heaps of glory for a mail-boat captain—but he also has an idea that she should be armed, great guns, swivels, small arms, marines, all of it. And that means privateering, rich prizes, all the glory a man could want. And this would just be the first. They've a mind to arm more. Your name has been put forth by some of your friends in the States, for command. Command of this very first vessel, if you want it."

"I see . . . ," said Hynson, and he did, quite clearly. As it happened, he had already invented for himself all of the glory he could want, and he did not care for the risks involved in earning more.

But on the other hand there was the possibility of taking rich prizes. There was no risk in boarding an unarmed merchantman in the Irish Sea, but the fiscal gain from just one such capture could be enormous.

"But what on earth are you doing in London?" Hynson asked. "It's more than a little risk, ain't it, an American wandering around England asking to buy a cutter? Don't they have any boats in France?"

"None that are suitable, that I could find. I searched Calais and Boulogne and found nothing. I . . ."

Hynson was startled to hear a door open down the hall and footsteps, feminine by the sound, approaching. And then it came back to him. Nicholson had himself a paramour in London, a lovely little tart by the name of Mrs. Elizabeth Carter.

I can well imagine, he thought, *how hard this randy bastard looked for a cutter in France before hopping the Dover packet.*

Mrs. Carter was just as lovely as Hynson remembered from the one other time that they had met. Indeed, that meeting had led him to consider calling on her himself when Nicholson was gone. He knew at least that she was no paragon of virtue.

She stepped into the drawing room and with a nod of her head and a look well short of friendly said, "Captain Hynson, a pleasure."

"And you, ma'am." She was dressed for traveling, with a small round hat on her head and a velvet coat and weskit, a smooth, clean run from her large breasts to her thin waist. She was no scrawny little wastrel like Isabella but a healthy, voluptuous woman, and Hynson, despite his hectic night, was titillated by the sight of her. Unfortunately Mrs. Carter seemed to regard him as something repulsive, which, he recalled, was what had dissuaded him the last time.

"We're off to Dover, Joe, to look for a cutter," Sam Nicholson said. "Won't you come with us? I could use your good judgment."

"Yes, well . . . ," Hynson equivocated. It was in fact treason, what Nicholson was asking, and while Hynson had no moral qualms about committing treason, he was aware that he could end up in jail, or worse.

On the other hand there was the prize money.

"Joe, I know you were hoping for more, hoping for a more significant command," said Sam, misreading Hynson's hesitation. "And I reckon there'll be one forthcoming, once things are more organized. But this is an important mission too. We need your help. I need your help."

Et cetera, et cetera, et cetera, Hynson thought, *like I give a rat's arse for this stupid rebellion.*

But why not go to Dover? He could always deny knowing the purpose for which the cutter was being purchased. He was just a loyal British citizen, helping an old friend who, unbeknownst to him, was a rebel traitor. And perhaps he could get into Mrs. Carter's good graces for the purpose of future liaisons.

"Well, of course, Sam. I'd be honored to accompany you. You know there's nothing I won't do for my country and the Glorious Cause."

"Good, good. I knew I could count on you. Do you wish to go back to your lodging, pack anything for the trip?"

Hynson thought of the ill assortment of junk and the few dubious articles of clothing that were all the possessions he kept in his room. "No."

Mrs. Jump and Isabella Cleghorn stood at the door of the Downing Street residence of the Reverend John Vardell, huddled against the wind and waiting for someone to answer their knock. Vardell was not the only man connected with government that Mrs. Jump knew—in her business she met quite a few, and most were disposed to keep in her good graces—but Vardell was an American, an American still loyal to the Crown, and thus the one most able to help her beloved Hynson.

At last the door opened and Vardell's housemaid peered out at the women. Her expression, subtle though it was, left little question as to her opinion of the two visitors, but she was polite nonetheless. "Mrs. Jump, do come in. I shall see if the reverend is available."

He was, and soon the maid led Mrs. Jump and Isabella into the drawing room where the Reverend Mr. Vardell sat before a prodigious fire. Vardell had been born in Boston over fifty years before, ironically in the house adjoining the one in which Benjamin Franklin had been born. He had been raised in that city and prior to the rebellion had returned several times, though he had spent most of his adult life in London, living on a bounty from King George III and, since '72, working tirelessly for a Tory club dedicated to the suppression of all Yankees who were anything less than loyal to their king.

In the course of that work he had made a number of well-placed associates. Mrs. Jump knew that because, like most men, important or otherwise, he could not help but brag whenever he visited her house.

It was an odd thing about men, something that Mrs. Jump could never understand. All the bragging in the world made no difference to Mrs. Jump; it was ten shillings an hour for her girls, whether the client was a mute beggar or Lord Howe himself.

"Mrs. Jump, Isabella, how delighted I am to see you," Vardell said, standing and gesturing toward two chairs arranged around the fireplace. He sounded sincere enough, if a bit uncomfortable, but the two women were accustomed to such a greeting. "How may I be of service to you?"

"Thank you, Reverend," Mrs. Jump said as she and Isabella sat. "Do you by chance know Capt. Joseph Hynson, an American who is often a resident at my house?"

"Yes, of course I've met the captain. A fine fellow, if I recall."

Mrs. Jump knew that Vardell actually thought him a drunken, overbearing lout of limited intelligence, but she still felt certain he would help, for her sake if not for his.

"Well, Reverend, last night the captain received a note from an old acquaintance, Sam Nicholson, whom I fear is a wicked rebel. He's here in London on some treachery and Joe . . . Captain Hynson . . . has gone to see him. The captain is a loyal man, loyal to the Crown, but he won't betray a friend, do you see? I fear he will be caught up in their villainy, though he has no stomach for traitors."

"I see . . . ," said Vardell. Mrs. Jump was pleased with his reaction to the news. She feared he would dismiss her, but he seemed rather to be giving it some deep consideration. "Where is the captain now?"

"He's gone off with this wicked Nicholson," Isabella

chimed in. "I . . . I stole a look at the note Nicholson sent over. This morning I went to the address on Portland Street but they were already gone. The servant told me they had left for Dover and were staying at Mr. Harvey's Ship Tavern. Oh, sir, I am so very frightened for the captain."

"Now, my dear, don't be afraid." The reverend regarded Isabella with a look that was part kindness and part rough lust, a look that Mrs. Jump knew well. "If Captain Hynson is indeed loyal to the Crown, then he has nothing to fear."

"Oh, he is that, I have no doubt," said Mrs. Jump.

"Then I can most certainly help him," said the Reverend Mr. Vardell thoughtfully. "In fact, I believe I can do even more than that. I imagine if the good captain is so disposed to helping the king defeat these damnable rebels, I can arrange it so that he plays a most active part, a most active part indeed."

CHAPTER
10

The man who with undaunted toils
Sails unknown seas to unknown soils
With various wonders feasts his sight:
What stranger wonders does he write?

POOR RICHARD'S ALMANACK, 1740

"THERE YOU ARE, SIR, ALL RIGGED PROPER."

The foretopman, standing easily on the *Charlemagne*'s quarterdeck rail, hauled and made fast the line on the corner of the small awning. He and his mates had rigged it between the boom and the main backstays to keep the sun from bothering Dr. Franklin as he took his air. "Now, come change of watch we'll readjust this, on account of how the sun'll have moved by then."

"Yes, thank you. Very kind indeed." Franklin sat in a folding chair, his hands on his lap, as several of the brig's foremast sailors, possibly the most unmaternal-looking creatures on earth, hovered around him with pillows, books, and a cup of hot chocolate. They seemed quite unaware of their captain, who stood just feet away.

The *Charlemagne* was riding at anchor in Quiberon Bay, as motionless as she had been in a month, the low, brown hills of France surrounding her on three sides. They had come into soundings five days before, picked up a pilot just past Belle Isle, and frustrated by a southeasterly wind that prevented them from reaching the mouth of the Loire River and Nantes, had stood in past Quiberon.

It was the fourth of December 1776, and the *Charlemagne*, with the Grand Union flag snapping at her ensign staff, was the first vessel of the American navy to ever sail in European waters.

"Beg pardon, Doctor." The carpenter's mate stepped up on the quarterdeck and saluted Franklin. "Beg pardon, but I finally got some proper goose feathers for the cushion on this stool here, from that bird the bumboat brought out, and I restuffed it. Be much kinder for your foot, sir." He knelt in front of the doctor and placed the stool on the deck, then eased Franklin's gout-ridden foot onto the cushion.

"Oh, very nice. Yes, thank you, my good man."

"And I'm goddamned sorry about this rutting wind, sir. Bound to change any day now."

"Yes, well, it can't be helped," Franklin said.

"Thank you, Chips," said Biddlecomb. "I think Dr. Franklin is quite well set up. You all may leave the quarterdeck now."

With muttered "Aye" 's and various dark looks shot Biddlecomb's way, the half dozen sailors shuffled forward and down into the waist. "Forgive me, Doctor, for sending your admirers away, but I can't have the quarterdeck overrun."

"Please, Captain, don't think on it. As kind as they are, they are starting to cloy a bit, I fear."

The Charlemagnes' adoration of Dr. Franklin was not new. It had begun just minutes after their blessed escape from the *Roebuck*, as they lined the rails, staring with wide eyes at the scarcely believable sight of the frigate, her rig shattered by lightning, burning and pounded by the storm.

The foul weather had lasted another forty hours, keeping Franklin below, but when at last he emerged on the quarterdeck, the men were ready with the hammock chair and the small awning and the stool, all of which they had run up over the intervening day and a half. They swarmed around him like flies, seeing to his comfort and ready to run and fetch anything that the doctor might desire.

"I say, Captain, this is all quite extraordinary, this treatment," Franklin had said that first day after the storm, once he had shooed the anxious men away. "I can't imagine why the men are so solicitous. When I came aboard, I rather thought they resented my presence."

"Do you really not know why they're fawning over you this way?"

"I do not."

"Why, it's your lightning rod, sir. They're convinced that it was your lightning rod that drew the bolt that hit *Roebuck*. They reckon that was your plan all along."

"You astonish me, Captain. Surely they can't believe that?"

"They can and they do. Every morning they send someone aloft to polish it. See how it shines in the sun?"

"But you understand that the one had nothing to do with the other? That it was a singular coincidence?"

"I do, yes, but I don't see the need to disabuse the men of their notion. It never did morale any harm for the hands to think there's a lucky man with godlike powers aboard."

"Godlike powers? Well, indeed . . ."

The remainder of the crossing had been uneventful, a progression of fine weather and foul, but never so foul as to seriously threaten the brig. The mood of the men was as good as Biddlecomb had ever seen it. They went about their work and drills with cheerful enthusiasm, glancing up now and again at their lucky lightning rod, which Biddlecomb found amusing at first, and then annoying.

On their tenth day out he caught the first officer glancing aloft. "Mr. Rumstick, what are you looking at?"

"Oh, well, sir, I was just making certain that lightning rod had not come adrift, or anything . . ."

"You are aware, are you not, that it was seamanship that got us away from the *Roebuck*? Seamanship and a damn big helping of luck, which had nothing to do with Dr. Franklin or the lightning rod?"

"Oh, of course, sir," Rumstick said, sounding entirely unconvinced.

"Captain?" asked Mr. Midshipman Gerrish. His tone, as usual, lacked any sort of expression. "It occurs to me that, were the wind to die, Dr. Franklin might just as well step overboard and walk the balance of the way to France."

"Thank you, Mr. Gerrish," Rumstick snapped. "That will be enough of that."

Biddlecomb turned and stared out at the horizon and stifled his laugh as best he could. As morose a soul as he was, Gerrish could be damned funny at times.

On the morning of the twenty-seventh of November a small brigantine hove up over the southern horizon and made to pass the *Charlemagne* about a mile ahead. The men gathered in the bow and the officers on the quarterdeck, watching this strange sail. It was the first they had seen in weeks, but more importantly by far, it was potentially a prize.

Biddlecomb stood alone on the weather side of the quarterdeck, aware that the people were waiting on him for orders of some description. But he had his own orders; he was not to pursue prizes or deviate from his mission of delivering Franklin to France.

Unless, of course, he had Franklin's permission to do so.

At last Franklin, with Temple and young Mr. Bache's help, emerged from the after scuttle, and they were immediately surrounded by Charlemagnes, who deftly helped the doctor aft onto the quarterdeck and appeared out of nowhere with chair and stool and awning.

"Thank you, my good fellows," Franklin said when he was settled. "There seems to be some commotion, Captain. I heard it below stairs."

"Yes, sir. As you can see, there is a brigantine making to cross our bows, about a mile off."

"Yes, indeed, so I see. But surely the men have seen such a vessel before?"

"Of course, sir." He tried not to stare at Franklin, but the old man did not look well and Biddlecomb feared for his health. He seemed considerably older than he had a month before, when first he came on board. The voyage had been hard on him, the rough and wet weather, the confinement below, and the poor diet. Franklin's assessment of the maritime chickens had been correct, and with his poor teeth he was not able to eat them, which forced him to exist on salt beef, well boiled and taken in small bites. "We just have not seen another sail in some time."

"And the men are thinking of prize money, I'll warrant," Franklin said.

"Well, yes. I should think so."

"Tell me, Captain, do you see any profit in speaking this vessel?"

"We are nearing France, sir, within a hundred leagues, I believe, but I have only my dead reckoning, what with the weather. They might give us a tolerable idea of how close we are to soundings."

"And if they prove to be English?"

"They would make a legitimate prize. However, the vessel would not be worth sending to America, and I don't know what the French will allow, as far as bringing prizes into their ports. That must surely be a violation of their neutrality."

"It would be," said Franklin. "It might cause quite a bit of trouble. An international incident."

"Oh."

"However, that might be just the thing for us to test how neutral the French truly are. I suggest, Captain, that you speak this vessel and see what she's about."

She was the *George*, Captain Cod, of Cork, just cleared out of Bordeaux with staves, tar, turpentine, and thirty-five hogsheads of claret. She hove to without a word once the quick *Charlemagne*, with all sail set to topgallant stud-dingsails, had closed to within two cable lengths and put a round shot over her bows. An hour later she was under way again, sailing in the *Charlemagne*'s wake, Lieutenant Weatherspoon in command.

Several hours after that, a second vessel blithely crossed their path, her master as certain as Captain Cod that there could be no armed American vessel in those waters. She was the *LaVigne* of Hull, 150 tons, loaded with five pipes, forty-seven barrels, and eleven hogsheads of cognac, six hogsheads of wine, and 1,024 sacks of linseed. A shot across her bow, a hectic hour of boats pulling back and forth, and she too was the *Charlemagne*'s prize.

Now the two prizes lay peacefully at anchor in Quiberon Bay, just to leeward of the *Charlemagne*. Their sails were neatly stowed, and like the *Charlemagne* they were all but motionless, rocking just slightly in the small chop kicked up by the southeasterly wind. In the bright winter sun they seemed as benign and picturesque a sight as one could imagine.

It was odd to think that they were in fact a little nudge to French neutrality, a faltering step toward war on a global scale.

Joe Hynson stood at the street end of one of many quays in the port city of Dover. He looked down at the cutter tied up to the seawall and floating ten feet below street level on the low tide. She looked good, as far as he could see; about sixty feet on deck, eighty tons, rigging well set up, decking in good shape, brightwork maintained, but he was having a hard time concentrating. His good friend Sam Nicholson was annoying him to the point of distraction.

Nicholson and Mrs. Carter were standing about ten feet away, talking low, giggling on occasion and playing little pinchy-feely games that set Hynson's teeth on edge. It might not have been so bad if Elizabeth Carter were some fat waterfront whore, but she was not. She was damned beautiful and looked better every time Hynson stole a leer at her, which was often. With Mrs. Carter in hand, Nicholson showed a predictable lack of interest in the cutter.

"She looks good, Sam. Tight and strong," Hynson said in a loud voice. "Could be a bit tender, though, lively when its rough, though maybe she likes it that way." He left it to Sam to decide if he was referring to the cutter or Mrs. Carter.

"I agree, Joe, but I don't know if she's just the boat we're looking for. If she don't draw more than four feet, she'll be no good as an Atlantic packet."

There's nothing bloody wrong with her, you rutting bastard, Hynson thought. He could see that Sam Nicholson would find something wrong with any cutter they found, at least until such time as Elizabeth Carter's husband was due home.

He turned his back on the cutter and the lovers and stared at the cobbled street and the waterfront buildings. Dover's was like most English waterfronts that Hynson had visited, and he had visited nearly all of them. Noisy, close. Rotting fish and tar and brine in the air. Crowds of people. The occasional gentleman strolling along, or more likely walking fast, his walking stick clicking on the sidewalk, but mostly it was poor sailors, fishermen, boatmen, and various other human flotsam. The red-brick buildings that stood shoulder to shoulder along the street housed chandlers and sailmakers, countinghouses, inns and boardinghouses. It was a busy place, a good place to disappear.

Hearing Sam Nicholson stifle a laugh, Hynson grit his teeth. He had just about had it, and only the promise of easy money in taking prizes kept him there. But tonight they would sleep in adjoining rooms at the Ship Tavern, and Hynson swore that if he could hear them through the wall making love, he would leave that night.

A coach rolled down the street slowly, as if the occupants were sight-seeing. It was a nice vehicle, its black lacquered finish gleaming dully under the overcast sky, and it caught Hynson's attention. He watched it roll slowly along, pulled by two well-matched horses. As it drew parallel with them and about fifty feet away, Hynson could see a face peering out from the dark interior, though with his eyesight being less than perfect he could make out little more than that.

The face, or so it appeared, was looking in his direction. Hynson felt uneasy. The man in the coach reached up with his walking stick and rapped on the roof and the coach jerked to a stop.

Hynson felt the beginnings of panic. The occupant of the coach seemed to be pointing in his direction and speaking, perhaps to someone else sitting across from him.

Nicholson, he thought. *They've come for bloody Nicholson, and they'll take me as well.*

"Say, Sam, I think I see an old friend of mine," Hynson extemporized. "I . . . ah . . . I'll just hurry off and see if it's him."

Two men had stepped out of the coach and were waiting for a dray to pass before crossing the street. They were rough-looking with cocked hats and heavy woolen coats and no wigs or walking sticks, which meant they were not gentlemen. In fact they did not look gentle at all. Hynson's panic was all but complete now.

"Now, don't be long, Joe, we must find a cutter soon," Sam Nicholson said, sounding a bit confused by Hynson's sudden departure.

"Oh, I shall just . . . never fear . . . I'll be right . . . ," Hynson stuttered, then abandoned any pretense of explanation as he hurried off down the street, as directly away from the two men as he could go.

He did not turn and look back as he pushed his way through the knots of people scattered along the street, though he did have the presence of mind to wave his arm as if trying to attract the attention of his friend.

He dodged a fishmonger's wagon as he crossed the street

and ducked into a narrow alley between a sailmaker's shop and a bakery. He stopped there and peered back down the street. He could just see Sam and Elizabeth through the crowd. He wondered if Sam would fight when they tried to take him.

Poor bastard, he thought. But Sam was playing a dangerous game. He wondered if he should have warned Nicholson about the men. No, he decided, then they both would have been arrested, and there was no sense in that.

Nicholson was still standing where Hynson had left him, his hand sneaking down to pinch Elizabeth Carter's ass and make her jump. There was no sign of the two villains. Hynson felt a flash of irritation and wondered where they had gone and why they had not grabbed the traitor.

He searched the crowd for the men. At last he caught a glimpse of one of them, hurrying down the street, coming toward him. The other was nowhere to be seen. They seemed to be paying no attention to Nicholson.

"God damn your eyes!" Hynson cursed at his old friend. "Drag me into this fucking rebellion . . ." He turned and hurried down the alley as the one pursuer he could still see was crossing the street. In London, they still disemboweled people for treason. Hynson thought he might be sick with fear.

He splashed through puddles of dubious liquid, dodged mounds of garbage, as he hurried toward the far end of the alley. He could see it opening up on another street and another alley across the way. He could keep running, lose himself in the back streets of Dover. He was ten feet from the end of the alley when the second man stepped right in front of him, a pistol leveled at his head.

Hynson stopped short. He looked over his shoulder, wondering on some primal level if he should turn and flee and risk the bullet. But the first man was hurrying down the alley toward him, a cudgel gripped in his big hand. There was no escaping.

"Capt. Joseph Hynson?" asked the man with the gun, and Hynson nodded dumbly.

"There's a gentleman who would like to have a word with you, if you could spare a minute."

"It's not me!" Hynson managed to croak. "It's Nicholson you want, bloody Nicholson!" He pointed in the general direction of where his friend could be found.

The man with the gun shook his head. "No, sir, it is most definitely you we want."

Hynson nodded again but did not move. They stood there for a moment, traitor and captor, staring at one another. And then Capt. Joe Hynson turned and threw up against the side of the sailmaker's shop.

CHAPTER
11

*Tricks and treachery are the practice of fools,
that have not wit enough to be honest.*

—POOR RICHARD'S ALMANACK, 1740

THE REVEREND JOHN VARDELL SAT IN HIS BLACK COACH, HIS FEET
shoved under the blanket of straw on the floor, and watched
his two assistants half drag and half carry Capt. Joe Hynson
toward him. He had recognized the captain at once, as he
had hoped he would when he set out to search the Dover
waterfront, but he had not reckoned on this much trouble
just to speak with him.

In one way it worked out well. Vardell had assumed that
Hynson would be with the traitor Nicholson. He did not
know how he would get the captain alone. Of course, the
young man whom he took to be Nicholson seemed so involved in his little trollop that he was oblivious to all else.
Vardell imagined he could have walked up to Hynson and
made his proposal without Nicholson paying the slightest
attention. But as it happened he did not have to.

He turned to Lt. Col. Edward Smith, who was seated
across from him in the coach, and nodding toward Hynson
observed, "The man does not look well."

Smith grunted. "I reckon he'll look a damned sight worse
in five minutes time."

Lieutenant Colonel Smith was a half-pay army officer and
old friend and confederate of Vardell's. Smith had seen ac-

tive service in Portugal and had for years been deeply involved in clandestine activities.

And he looked the part. He was fit and lean, his every movement deliberate, fluid. His hair was gray and black, unpowdered, and tied in a queue with a length of black ribbon. And to top it off he wore a black eye patch over his left eye, from beneath which emerged a long, smooth scar running half the length of his cheek. Put a cocked hat on his head with a feather in the band, let him grow a beard, and he would be the very picture of the Caribbean buccaneer of the last age.

Vardell had never asked him about the eye patch and the scar. In truth he did not dare.

One of the assistants, holding a cudgel under his arm like a riding crop, opened the coach door, and the other one pushed Hynson inside. The American flopped down on the seat next to Smith, opposite Vardell. He looked around like a cornered animal, and his eyes settled on the reverend. He squinted and said, "I know you . . . how do I know you?"

"I am Reverend John Vardell. We have met once or twice, I believe. The circumstances evade me."

"Mrs. Jump's." Hynson's lips spread into a suggestive leer that did not please the reverend. "We met at Mrs. Jump's."

"That is no matter, Captain. Not in the light of treason." Vardell paused for a second to watch Hynson's leer vanish and his eyebrows come together. The American glanced over at Smith, as if looking for succor from the stranger, and was greeted with an expression that appeared even less sympathetic than Vardell's. An expression made even more frightening by the eye patch and the scar.

"We are well aware of why you are in Dover," said Smith. "In the company of a known rebel captain."

"What, Nicholson? A rebel? I had no idea, sir, I swear—"

"Very well," Vardell interrupted. "Now see here, Captain, it's no use denying what you're about. We've enough evidence to convict you in any court, and I imagine you know what the penalty for treason is?"

Hynson nodded, his mouth half-open.

"But it does not have to be that way. I have always reckoned you for a good, patriotic Englishman, and not a rebel at all."

"Oh, that I am, sir, you must believe it. Why, if it was up to me—"

"Very well. I want very much to believe that, and to give you the chance to prove your loyalty. Since the rebels believe you are working for them, you could be most valuable in helping your king."

"I have no doubt of it, sir. I was thinking much the same myself when Nicholson first contacted me . . ."

Vardell studied Hynson with a growing uncertainty as the American droned on. He was awfully quick to betray his friend and his native country. Vardell had imagined that the captain would need more cajoling than this. Hynson's eagerness made his sincerity suspect.

And that was a problem, because interest in Hynson had already reached far higher than Vardell would ever have imagined. He had mentioned the possibility of a spy in the rebel camp to Smith, and Smith, who loved all intrigue, had become absolutely enthralled with the thought. He had insisted that they take it to William Eden, who was ostensibly the undersecretary of state for the southern department but was, in fact, the director of all clandestine intelligence for the current government.

Smith's enthusiasm for Hynson, more than Vardell thought was quite warranted, was infectious, and soon Eden was equally excited. He thought it might be a brilliant strategy. He would authorize the men to approach Hynson, but first he felt they must clear it with a higher authority, specifically Lord Frederick North.

And so nine hours after mentioning to Smith the possibility of enlisting Hynson to the king's cause, Vardell found himself standing in the office of the prime minister, wondering how in the world he had ended up there.

Vardell was not an important player in colonial politics, he knew that. Meeting William Eden had been a thrill, the most important meeting he had ever had. Meeting Lord North was more than he could comprehend.

Then Lord North had brought Joe Hynson to the attention of King George.

And now all of those important men were looking for something significant from him, Vardell, by way of intelligence. And for that he had to rely on Joe Hynson; tall, strong, usually self-assured to the point of swaggering Joe Hynson, who now sat babbling and swearing his allegiance to the crown, frightened nearly to insensibility.

Vardell silently cursed Smith for taking it so far and cursed himself for not taking Hynson's measure first, before he went to Smith.

". . . and so I reckoned that with me acting like I was a rebel too . . . ," Hynson was saying, but Vardell had heard enough.

"Yes, very well. I think your loyalty is well established. And you should be aware that there are significant monetary rewards for those who cooperate."

"Oh, is that a fact?" For the first time Hynson seemed to be listening.

"And for those that don't . . . ," Smith interjected. "Well, have you ever seen a man hung till not quite dead and then disemboweled?" He let the question hang in the air. Smith had a talent for such unsubtle threats.

After a pause, an uncomfortable silence in the carriage, Vardell said, "We know more or less what you and the traitor Nicholson were up to, but why don't you give us all the details."

Hynson did just that, giving more details than either Vardell or Smith really cared to hear. He told them about the American ministers' plans to purchase a cutter, to outfit it for privateering and as a mail packet to America, about Nicholson's promise that Hynson might get command of the vessel. He was moving on to describe in numbing detail each of the cutters they had looked at when Lieutenant Colonel Smith interrupted.

"You say you was to buy this boat here and take it to France?"

"Yes, sir."

"And then to get dispatches and take them to America?"

"Yes, sir."

Smith stared out the window for a moment, rubbing his jaw. The other two men were silent, waiting for Smith to speak. At last he turned to Vardell, ignoring Hynson completely, and said, "I believe I have a plan that'll render this sniveling Yankee bastard a great help to us."

The *Charlemagne* rode at her anchor just beyond the town of Nantes, a few miles upriver from where the mighty Loire emptied into the Bay of Biscay. A few lights were burning on the north bank and a few on the south. Over a mile of water was between them. The Loire was the biggest river that Biddlecomb had ever seen beyond the Chesapeake Bay.

They had arrived late that afternoon, after sitting for fifteen days in Quiberon Bay before the wind blew favorable. Franklin and his party were long gone. After three days of waiting, the doctor could bear no more and took a coach overland for Paris, leaving instructions for Biddlecomb to come around to Nantes as soon as he could, send the baggage along to Paris, and await further orders.

The men had been visibly despondent at the doctor's departure, but they took solace from their gleaming brass lightning rod, which they glanced at often.

The crews of the *Charlemagne*'s prizes, who had been shut up belowdecks, were allowed to give their parole and were set ashore in ostensibly neutral France. Biddlecomb had little confidence that they would honor any parole given to rebels, particularly not the foremast hands, but he preferred letting them escape to dealing with the endless problem of feeding and guarding them.

The question of what to do with the ships themselves was left mostly to Biddlecomb's discretion.

And that was a problem he was well qualified to solve, having been for most of his career a smuggler.

Midnight found him and Rumstick in the captain's gig, being pulled slowly around the two captured vessels. The air was filled with the sound of soft voices and paintbrushes on planking and the quiet hammering—as quiet as hammering can be—of the carpenter and his mates. The smell of paint was thick in the air, and those patches of water lit by the lanterns shone a rainbow of colors where the pigment had spilled and formed a sheen of oil on the water.

The first order of business in selling a vessel you have no right to sell, Biddlecomb knew, is to turn it into a vessel that you do have a right to sell.

"See here, Ezra, this fellow is doing an admirable job cutting a line around that badge." Isaac pointed to one of the painters on the *George*'s quarter who was carefully painting around the gilded scrollwork.

"Aye, sir," Rumstick agreed, and then in a harsh voice, just loud enough for all hands to hear, said, "Let's step it up, boys. This ain't the fucking Sistine Chapel. We haven't got but six hours to daylight." On that command the officers could see hands moving quicker as the Charlemagnes hurried to turn the once yellow-and-blue-painted vessel into one painted black and ocher.

The gig pulled on, passing astern of the *George*. But of course she was no longer the British vessel *George*. She was now the American vessel *Betsy* of Falmouth. As if to reinforce that point, the carpenter, working with his mates on the merchantman's transom, heaved with his considerable strength at a crowbar wedged under that plank into which the name *George* had been carved. With much wrenching

123

and cracking of wood and grunting and cursing of carpenter and mates, the plank splintered and cracked and came free of the stern. Eager hands pulled the broken wood away while in the boat others prepared to hand up the new piece, freshly carved with the name *Betsy.* Biddlecomb smiled and nearly laughed out loud.

"Damn me, but this is like old times, ain't it, Ezra?" In the merchant service Biddlecomb learned that honest, straightforward dealing could make a captain prosperous and well respected, but trickery and less than scrupulous attention to the law could make a man filthy rich.

"Aye, it's like old times." Rumstick, despite his more military bearing, smiled as well. He had had his own share of clandestine dealings, often while working for Biddlecomb. "We'll get these Frenchies involved in the war, whether they want to be or not."

"I hope that we can. It's not exactly in their best interest."

"Why ain't it in their best interest? After '63 I reckon they'd do anything to wipe it in King George's eye."

"Yes, but think on the example it sets. If we were to win the war, it would show the world that an oppressed people can chuck their rightful sovereign and rule themselves. It's unprecedented. I don't know if young King Louis would care to have his people realize that. As I hear it, the Frenchies have more reason to revolt than we do."

"Humph," Rumstick said as he considered this new and distressing line of thought. "Well, maybe Louis won't think on it that way."

"You may at least be certain that if any man can convince the king to cut his own throat to save ours, it will be our dear Dr. Franklin."

The weary painting crews returned to the *Charlemagne* for an extra tot and their blessed hammocks just as the first pink light of dawn was illuminating the Loire. The hammocks to which they retreated were peacefully still, the *Charlemagne*'s motion being just the slightest rocking in the tidal current.

But with both watches below at the same time, they were packed together, leaving each man a space just fourteen inches wide in which to sleep, rather than the twenty-eight he would enjoy if half the watch was on deck, as they would be at sea.

Still the men slept well, for they had put in a long night, had received an extra ration of rum, and would soon see the prizes sold for ready money. They were safely anchored in France, with all of that country's legendary pleasures waiting ashore. All was right with their world, and every man slept like some kind of burly, hairy, tar-stained, foul-smelling babe in his mother's arms.

Biddlecomb did not have the luxury of retiring to his cot, as much as he wished to, to relive in his mind all of the fine trysts that he had enjoyed there with his wife. Rather he called for his cabin steward to fetch a pot of coffee, and he and Rumstick sat on the quarterdeck bulwark, talking idly and waiting for what he hoped would be a number of anxious buyers.

He did not wait long.

"Captain, sir?" the weary lookout called down. Biddlecomb had allowed the man to sit in the maintop rather than on the less comfortable topmast crosstrees. "Boat's putting off from town, sir, and she looks like she's making for us."

"Well, Mr. Rumstick, I guess it's time to open shop."

Ten minutes later the boat pulled up to the *Charlemagne's* side. It was rowed by two dangerous-looking French seamen. In the stern sheets sat a third man, well dressed in silk coat, waistcoat, and breeches, elegant clothes but not foppish. His brilliant white wig peeked out from under a big cocked hat, and he wore a long, dark mustache in a style rarely seen in America.

"Bon matin, monsieur. Comment allez-vous?" Biddlecomb called down, nearly exhausting his French with that one greeting.

125

"I am well, *monsieur Capitain,*" the visitor called back, thankfully in English, heavily accented though it was. "And you?"

"Very well, *monsieur, merci.* Won't you come aboard?"

"With pleasure," the man said, and scrambled up the boarding steps with the ease of a man quite familiar with ships.

After a minute of bowing and introductions and offers of coffee and food, the stranger, whose name was Boucher, said, "I trust you have been made most welcome in France?"

"Most welcome indeed, thank you, sir. It seems our country now has a number of grievances in common with France, regarding the British."

Monsieur Boucher frowned and waved his hand in a very French gesture of dismissal. "Bah, politics. We now make a great show of loving the British. It is absurd, a game, *monsieur,* one in which I do not play. But I have a great love for the Americans. I have spent some time in your country. You are so . . . I say innocent for I do not know a better word. You are a new race, *Capitaine,* a new people, like Adam, remade."

"I thank you, Monsieur Boucher. I think."

"Now, I hear in town that perhaps you were interested in selling these ships that you have with you . . . ?"

Twenty minutes later the three men, Biddlecomb, Rumstick, and Boucher, clambered up the side of the *Betsy* née *George.* "She's the *Betsy* of Falmouth, built there five years ago. She's been in the coastwise trade mostly," Biddlecomb began.

"*Monsieur,* there seems to be wet paint on the hull," Boucher said, examining the five dots of ocher paint on his fingertips. He did not sound in the least surprised.

"Well, we were touching up a bit this morning, moosyer," Rumstick explained. "Hoped to get a buyer, wanted her looking nice."

"Indeed, Lieutenant," said Boucher, running his eye over

the rig while Biddlecomb and Rumstick continued to extol the virtues of the two ships. If the Frenchman was in the least curious as to why an American naval vessel would be in the business of selling merchant ships, he did not ask.

"Here are her papers, Monsieur Boucher, all in order." Biddlecomb handed the Frenchman the sheaf of documents that Gerrish and Weatherspoon had just yesterday finished creating.

Boucher thumbed through them, showing just the slightest interest. "Yes, these will be of some use," he muttered. He was going along with the charade only as far as politeness required. "Now, *monsieur*, down to business. What price do you ask for these vessels?"

The bluffing was over, all the quick talking. There was nothing more that Biddlecomb could do but name his price. "I should think twenty thousand livres for this vessel, and twenty-five for the other. It is a fair price."

It was indeed a fair price, more than fair, but Boucher just smiled. "*Monsieur*, the price you ask, well, it would be a bit high even if there were no questions being asked about these ships. But I must tell you, the authorities ashore are quite upset, quite uncertain about all this. And that too would not be a problem, but you see they are upset in Paris as well, and when Paris is upset, they have a way of making many, many others upset. No, Captain, I must ask for some small consideration, in exchange for my . . . lack of curiosity, if you understand. Five thousand livres for each ship."

"*Monsieur*, you have been gracious in your welcome, and I do not want to appear to insult you in any way," Biddlecomb began. He felt himself stepping into a role, the familiar role of negotiator, like an actor who has been playing the same part for year after year. But for all that, he knew he had little room to maneuver. There clearly was no secret as to the origin of the two vessels, and no misunderstanding of the risks involved in buying them.

They settled at last on a price of eighteen thousand livres for both ships and cargoes.

And the British call us *the bloody pirates*, Biddlecomb thought as Boucher wrote out a draft for the money. *Well, perhaps it is not too late to extract some real money from this Frenchy.*

"It is good for me, *monsieur*, that we were able to conclude this deal," Biddlecomb said as he examined the draft. "I have but one more buyer coming out today, and I do not believe he was interested in the ships."

"Oh? And who might that be, Captain, if I may ask?"

"It was a Monsieur . . . Roche? Le Roche? Rumstick, do you recall?"

Rumstick had played this game with Biddlecomb before, many times.

"Oh, these French names," Rumstick stammered. "Beg your pardon, moos-yer. Was it Le Rochelle?"

"Le Rois?" Boucher asked. "Perhaps it was Monsieur Le Rois, of Gerard, Bretagne and Le Rois?"

"Yes, precisely. That is the gentleman. I do not think he was interested in the ships, though."

"What then, may I ask?" Boucher was nibbling. In a moment he would be hooked and thrashing on Biddlecomb's line.

"Indigo."

"Indigo? You have indigo, Captain?"

"Oh, yes. On board the *Charlemagne*. The finest American indigo. A hold full of the stuff."

"But, may I see it? I could well be interested in purchasing it myself."

"Oh, Monsieur Boucher," Biddlecomb chuckled, "I don't know if I want to tangle with you again. What think you, Ezra?"

"He's a crafty one, sir. For an innocent American like you. Besides, that Le Rois was mighty interested."

"Please, Captain, I wish only to take a look, and perhaps

we can talk about price over a glass. I have some fine cognac in the boat."

"Well, I suppose if you just wish to look . . ."

Two hours and one bottle of cognac later, Monsieur Boucher was the legal owner of all of the indigo in the *Charlemagne*'s hold. He was considerably poorer as a result, having paid what would seem on sober reflection an extraordinarily high price for the dye. Even as he climbed down into his boat, he seemed a little uncertain as to how he had been talked into buying it all and paying what he had.

Biddlecomb, watching from the quarterdeck, felt not the least qualm about the transaction. Boucher had received some excellent indigo. And perhaps just as importantly, he had learned a valuable lesson about the innocence of the Yankee trader.

CHAPTER
12

Men & Melons are hard to know.

—Poor Richard's Almanack, 1733

To His Excellency the Comte de Vergennes
Minister of Foreign Affairs to His Most Christian Majesty Louis XVI
Versailles

Monsieur,

As you are well aware, a Blessed State of Peace has for some years now existed between my country and yours, well preserved by the Treaty entered into at the terminus of the Last War and to which we have thus far mutually adhered. However, a Threat to that tranquillity now arises, a threat that could prove most injurious to the Peace so beloved by both of our nations.

In the early part of this month the rebel Doctor Benjamin Franklin, a subtle and artful man, arrived in this country to join with his fellow Silas Deane, no doubt with the intention of painting the Situation of the Rebels in the falsest colors. While it in no way pleases us that he has received so Enthusiastic a welcome as he has, it is not our intention to make protest on this point.

We must, however, protest most Strenuously the

presence of a rebel Privateer, the *Charlemagne*, and the harboring of such in the French ports of Quiberon and Nantes, along with two illegally captured British Vessels which the rebels style prizes. As Your Excellency is well aware, the harboring, by one of our countries, of the vessels of war of an enemy of the other, especially if said vessels are allowed to fit out and operate from those places, is quite contrary to all existing Treaties. Allowing prizes to be Condemned and Sold is entirely beyond the pale of acceptable behavior.

I apologize for informing Your Excellency of Treaties of which he is already well aware. I have no doubt that His Most Christian Majesty and those Ministers that Represent Him would never allow such violations to take place, were those violations known to them, and I can therefore only conclude that the rebels have kept you in Ignorance of their plotting.

If it please Your Excellency, it would do much to maintain the Pacific Nature of our current relationship if you were to see that those British vessels illegally captured by the rebels were immediately released and the Rebel Privateer ordered to sail from said Port at the first possible convenience.

I remain Your Obedient and Humble Servant,
David Murray, Seventh Viscount Stormont
Ambassador of Great Britain to the Court of France

To His Excellency Lord Stormont
Ambassador from Great Britain to the Court of France

Sir,

I have received your latest and have given it the most careful consideration, as has His Most Christian Majesty. It is superfluous to say that we are as desirous as you of maintaining the Blessed Peace that currently exists between your country and ours. As to Dr. Franklin and his fellow Commissioners, I have met with them but once, and then briefly. Be assured that France does not entertain any notion of entering into a treaty of any sort with Rebellious British possessions in North America.

I can not pretend to form an opinion offhand concerning British vessels being sold as prizes in French ports, for neither myself nor any in the Ministry to whom I have spoken are aware of nor would we countenance such activity. Please accept my Sincerest assurance that we will investigate this matter to assure ourselves, as well as our most Esteemed Friends in England, that such has not taken place.

As to the harboring of the ships of war belonging to England's Enemies, your Lordship is perfectly aware that such is only permissible when said ships are forced into port under stress of Weather, and allowed to remain only when they are in such Need of Repair that they are unable to put to sea. I am assured that Such is the case with the rebel Privateer *Charlemagne*, and likewise I am assured that said vessel will leave France immediately she is able.

I have no doubt that Your Lordship is sensible to the situation in which France finds herself. It is our sincere desire to avoid offending your country, with whom we share a Love for peace, but likewise I beg you understand that France must be cautious about exposing her trade to the depredations of the Americans, as well as her West Indian possessions and the commerce we enjoy with that nation.

Perhaps it would be of some assistance if Your Lordship could prepare a Memorial protesting the admission of American ships of War and their prizes into French

Ports. Such an official Protest would serve to guide our Ministry in their investigation of this matter.

Your Obedient Servant,
Comte de Vergennes

To Captain Isaac Biddlecomb
Master, United States Brig-of-War *Charlemagne*
Nantes

Sir,

Allow me to acknowledge the receipt of my trunks and thank you for the care and dispatch with which you sent them on after my leaving the ship. It is a great relief to my mind to have them in my possession once more.

The French Ministry has thus far proven very friendly to the American Commissioners, and very well disposed to assist us, though not in so open a fashion as to Offend the British and provoke a war. We have met with the Comte de Vergennes on several occasions, though quite secretly, and he gives his Assurance that our men-of-war will find a welcome in French harbors, so long as it will appear that they are in need of the facilities there. For that reason I beg you will continue with your Improvements of the *Charlemagne* brig, so that it might not look as if you are idly at anchor with no reason for not taking to the Sea. We have given the Minister assurance that no Prizes have been carried into French Ports and it pleases him to believe that, though I am in no doubt that he knows the truth of the Matter.

As to the Disposition of the Prizes, you say that a certain gentleman has made you an offer, however, I can not advise you to accept any such offer now. Affairs between America and France are of such a State that it might be most prejudicial to our affairs if such a sale were to take place and the British Ambassador to raise a protest, as he surely would. Therefore we instruct you not to Sell the Prizes, under any circumstances, until American affairs are on a more Settled and Regular establishment.

Your Obedient and Humble Servant.
B. Franklin

"Uh-oh."

Biddlecomb could think of nothing more to say. He set his coffee mug down and then grabbed at it as it slid away across the desk. It looked as if it were possessed by demons, though in fact it was sliding because the *Charlemagne* carried a five-degree larboard list. There was nothing like a list to make a ship look like a pathetic wreck.

In the silence, Biddlecomb became aware of the noisy grinding of the pumps as they worked nonstop, watch on watch, struggling to keep the hold free of water. The sound had become so constant that he rarely noticed it anymore.

"I take it, sir, there is some problem with the doctor's missive?" Young Temple sat across the desk from Biddlecomb, an identical mug in his hand. A third such mug was clutched in the great paw of Ezra Rumstick, seated against the larboard side of the great cabin and enjoying the more inclined position that the vessel's list provided. Next to him Lieutenant. Faircloth did the same.

"Well, sir, as it happens the prizes are no longer in my possession."

"I see. The doctor thought that might be the case, and so he gave me verbal instructions for you, if indeed it was. The delegation . . . that's Grandfather as well as Mr. Dean and Mr. Lee, feel it would be best if you were to leave France for a time, until things settle a bit. They suggest perhaps a cruise around the British Isles, wherever you think it would be most advantageous to cruise for prizes."

"Prizes? What are we to do with prizes? Its unlikely that any we take around the British Isles will be in condition to be sent to America."

"The doctor reckons any prizes can be sent to France," Temple explained, and then in response to Biddlecomb's confused look added, "Grandfather doesn't want things between England, France, and America to be too much settled."

Biddlecomb leaned back and smiled and looked over at Rumstick, who was smiling as well.

"God bless the good doctor," the first officer said.

"Very well, then," said Biddlecomb, "we shall get under way directly."

"Oh, but, sir," said Temple, "you are not to get under way if it will put your vessel in danger."

"Why should it put us in danger?"

"Sir, the pumps are going constantly just to keep up with the leak. You can see the water discharged all the way from the shore. And the list, sir. The poor ship looks as if she were about to roll over."

"Oh, that. Never you mind about that, young sir. Now, let me write a quick note to the doctor and I will see you over the side. Mr. Rumstick, please see us ready to weigh anchor and set sail. And . . . ah . . . see to the leak and this annoying list."

Half an hour later the *Charlemagne*'s gig returned from ferrying young Temple ashore, and Biddlecomb watched with a sense of anticipation as it was hoisted aboard and stowed down on the booms.

The topsails hung in their gear, the anchor cable was hove to short peak, and the men stood by the capstan, ready to break the anchor out. The casks of water piled on the larboard side of the hold to induce the list were drained and stowed down.

The pump hidden in the forepeak and worked day and night to pump water secretly into the hold so that it could then be ostentatiously pumped out again, was unshipped and secured.

To anyone watching from shore it would have been an amazing sight. In half an hour the *Charlemagne*, a vessel so near to sinking that it could not possibly venture from the port of Nantes, had become a man-of-war ready in all aspects for combat and the open sea.

CHAPTER
13

There is no little enemy.

—POOR RICHARD'S ALMANACK, 1733

IT WAS A SIMPLE PLAN, THE ONE THAT SMITH HAD COME UP WITH, and that was much to Capt. Joe Hynson's liking.

He, Hynson, had merely to aid Nicholson in finding and outfitting a cutter and then help him get the boat to France. Once in France, Hynson would see that he himself was appointed master, or at the very least first officer. He would see that the cutter was loaded to the gunnels with expensive war materials, supplies upon which the rebels were counting, as well as all of the important dispatches that Franklin and the others would be sending. Then he had only to sail out of port and into the arms of the British navy, whom he would have alerted to his departure.

They would treat him gruffly while in the sight of the others, as if he were as much a prisoner as they, and then when they had returned to England, he would be set free, with a handsome reward to boot. To the British he would be a hero and to the Americans a poor, noble prisoner for the cause. He was set no matter who won the war.

As the lieutenant colonel explained it, it seemed simple enough. And it beat the hell out of being disemboweled.

And now that pathetic calf Sam Nicholson was threatening to queer the whole thing.

"Lookee here, Sam," Hynson said, staring out the window

137

of their room and pouring himself a short glass of rum. As a rule he tried to avoid drinking before ten o'clock in the morning, and as a rule he failed. "She was married, you recall, and not likely to leave the old man. You knew that, and what's more, how can you trust some"—he nearly said "whore" but instead said—"woman when you know she's already cuckolded one poor bastard."

As he drank, he looked over at Sam, lying facedown on the bed. They had shared the bed that night, he and Sam, to save money. There was no reason not to. Mrs. Carter had left the day before, absolutely refusing Sam's entreaties to run away with him to America or, indeed, to spend another minute in his company. Hynson was not sure what had happened; there had been no obvious fight. He guessed that the adventurous Mrs. Carter had just grown bored.

At first Hynson had been delighted to be rid of her, but now Nicholson's hangdog act was growing more tiresome even than his moon-calf act had been.

"Come along, Sam. You've your duty, you know," Hynson said, trying another tack. "You mustn't let your personal problems, as painful as they might be, interfere with that." He couldn't believe that Nicholson was getting this worked up over that stupid tart, but he had tact enough not to say so.

Nicholson rolled over with a groan and met Hynson's eyes at last. "You're right, Joe. As usual, you are right and I am a fool. I fear I have not been so attentive in my duties, God help me. You're a good friend, and you've chosen not to notice, but the truth be told, until now I have looked for every excuse to avoid buying a cutter."

Oh, is that a fact? Hynson thought. *We've only looked in every fucking port city on the southern coast. Been through bloody Dover, Folkestone, Portsmouth, Weymouth, Plymouth, and God knows how many festering little ports in between, passed up half a dozen perfectly good boats.*

"Now, Sam, I'll not have you blame yourself," Hynson

said in a soothing tone, sensing that he was making some progress at last. "I've not been too delighted with the boats I've seen, you know. We'll off to Bristol today, get there the day after next. Best bloody cutters in the world, built in Bristol."

"Thank you, Joe." Nicholson smiled and the expression made him look more pathetic still. "No more distractions, I swear to you. From now on it's duty first."

"Good lad." Joe poured himself another drink. Nicholson *was* a good lad, really, if a bit stupid about women. Hynson thought about letting him in on the plan, keeping him out of trouble with the British authorities.

But no, Nicholson wasn't so smart about politics, either. He'd just muck up the whole thing. The concerns of state took precedence over Sam Nicholson, and the concerns of Joe Hynson took precedence over everything.

Isaac Biddlecomb glanced around the quarterdeck and down into the waist to see that all was ready. The sail trimmers were at their stations, with hands in the tops ready to set the studdingsails if that extra speed was called for. The *Charlemagne* was cleared for action, the gun crews at their guns, match smoldering, rags tied around their ears to muffle, even a little, the terrible concussive sound of the cannon. Rumstick prowled the deck, maintaining silence, looking for some fault worth mentioning but finding none.

On the quarterdeck the long tiller was double manned with Second Lieutenant Weatherspoon standing just to weather of the helmsmen and Mr. Midshipman Gerrish standing by the leeward rail where Biddlecomb was so accustomed to seeing Weatherspoon.

At the midshipman's feet lay a canvas bag that contained the Grand Union flag, thirteen alternating red and white stripes with the union jack in the canton, the proper ensign for a United States ship of war. The fly of the flag was hanging out of the bag and bent to the halyard, and Gerrish stood ready to hoist away.

Biddlecomb ran his eyes up to the main royal pole, where just below the gleaming lightning rod flew a flag that was decidedly not the proper flag for the *Charlemagne;* a blue field with the Union Jack in the canton, a British naval ensign.

In truth Isaac was not certain that it was the right flag for a British brig-of-war to fly either. The British navy had so many flags that he was never quite able to figure which was supposed to be flown when. But it looked right to him. And more importantly it looked right to the complacent merchantman with whom they were closing, as evidenced by the fact that she was making no attempt to escape or alter course or speed in any way.

It was just a single ship, which meant that it was not Biddlecomb's most sought-after prize, the Irish linen fleet. Still, it was not a small vessel, and if it carried in its hold the right cargo, it could be valuable indeed.

A mile of water was still between the two. The merchantman was running before the wind on a heading north by northeast, the *Charlemagne* on a taut bowline, starboard tacks aboard, sailing southeast. Biddlecomb had altered course slowly, imperceptibly, from due east, once they had spotted the merchantman and established the heading it was on. Altered course so that the two vessels would pass within a cable length of one another. There was nothing threatening in the *Charlemagne*'s action; they were just two ships crossing paths on a well-traveled bit of ocean.

That bit of ocean was the Irish Sea, which was all the more reason why the merchantman would not guess at his danger. The Irish Sea might contain all of the usual hazards to navigation, including storms, shoals, rocks, fog, and current, but it did not, to anyone's knowledge, harbor American ships of war or privateers.

The simple logistical fact was that without a European

base from which to operate, American ships could not venture into British waters to raid commerce, and no European powers were willing to risk Britain's wrath by harboring them. Or so the thinking went.

Biddlecomb breathed deep. The air was as clean as air could be, blowing cold and twenty knots, pushing the small, gray and white humpbacked clouds across the sky like some great fleet.

He thought of all the ships that had come before him on those waters, those sacred waters, squeezed between Ireland to the west and England to the east. Like many of them, he was an invader here, like the Vikings and the Normans and the Spanish Armada. But he had already penetrated deeper into British water than any of them had ever done.

He was here to show the British that they would never be safe as long as they waged war on Americans.

Not even in the Irish Sea, all but surrounded by the British Isles, would they be safe.

"Fall off a point, Mr. Weatherspoon," Biddlecomb called, then watched with satisfaction as the lieutenant gave the commands to helmsmen and sail trimmers that brought the *Charlemagne* a point more off the wind. He could feel her fabric hum, feel her speed increase as she pounded into the sea, scattering crystalline drops of spray across the quarterdeck.

"Mr. Rumstick, we'll meet her starboard to starboard. See that number one gun is ready to go!"

"Aye, sir!" Rumstick called back.

"God, but this is the finest kind of day, ain't it, Mr. Faircloth?" Isaac said to the marine officer who stood beside him on the quarterdeck, probing to see if Faircloth was still upset. The marines, who were arranged along the quarterdeck partially for the protection of the officers, were now the very men who most wished to see some injury befall their captain. They shot dirty looks back at him and muttered just loud enough to be audible.

At their feet, neatly folded, were their beloved bottle green jackets, ready to be donned the moment permission was granted. Biddlecomb had forbid them to wear the green regimentals while they closed with their quarry. He was flying false colors in hopes of convincing the merchantman that the *Charlemagne* was a British naval vessel, a vessel whose marines would be dressed in red. Even a dull merchant captain would be suspicious if he saw the quarterdeck covered with green uniform coats.

To that end Biddlecomb had sewn white cotton cloth over the red lapels and cuffs of his own uniform coat and exchanged the red waistcoat and blue breeches designated by Congress for the white and white of the Royal Navy.

But that did not mollify the marines. Their commanding officer, Lieutenant Faircloth, had purchased the uniforms himself from his own substantial private fortune, and his men were inordinately proud of them, and equally disgusted at the thought of going into battle without them.

"Aye, sir, lovely day," Faircloth said at last in his usual cheerful tone. Faircloth was bound to see reason eventually, nor could he hold a grudge any longer than he could hold a hundred-pound sack of flour; that is to say, about fifteen or twenty minutes.

The merchantman was less than a quarter mile away, the two vessels closing fast as if racing to be the first to that invisible spot on the ocean where their tracks would cross. She was ship-rigged, over two hundred tons, and as best as Isaac could tell, heavy laden. Despite his attempt at stoicism he felt his lips part in a smile, and the second he tried to suppress the smile, it bloomed into a grin. This ship would be worth quite a bit of money.

He felt the avarice that had driven him during his merchant days stirring once more in his breast.

"He's waving, sir," Weatherspoon said, staring through a glass.

"Beg your pardon?"

"The master of the merchantman, he's waving."

Biddlecomb put his glass to his eye and trained it on the merchantman's quarterdeck. Sure enough, he could make out the ship's master, clad in a long blue coat and cocked hat, waving a pleasant greeting. *Poor bastard*, Biddlecomb thought as he waved back. He felt just a hint of guilt creeping in around the edges of his greed.

"Lord, sir, this is like shooting deer in a park," Faircloth said. "And not a very big park at that."

"Indeed. Well, we ain't here to be sporting, Mr. Faircloth," Biddlecomb said. "Mr. Gerrish, please strike the British colors and hoist our own."

Biddlecomb watched the master of the merchantman as the British colors came down and the Grand Union flag was run up in its place. The waving slowed, then stopped, and though he was still too far away to tell, Biddlecomb imagined that a look of confusion was on the man's face. He had likely never seen the American flag before, but he would have to be slow-witted indeed not to guess what it was.

"Mr. Rumstick, a shot across his bows, if you please." Rumstick waved and called an order forward, and the captain of number one gun, who was already aiming his charge, stepped back and brought the match to the powder. The gun went off with a roar, flinging itself inboard, the captain having in his enthusiasm used a bit more powder than was quite called for.

Biddlecomb saw the shot hit the ocean fifty yards ahead of the merchantman and skip along the surface, sending a series of waterspouts skyward until at last it plowed into the side of a swell and disappeared.

The merchantman wasted not a second in rounding up into the wind and letting her halyards fly. Her sails came down in a great, disorganized mess, hanging in big, useless folds of canvas. Her headway was gone and she sat rocking on that patch of ocean, defenseless and awaiting her fate.

"Well, I guess she's struck," Biddlecomb announced. It

was rather a surprise, after all of that preparation. The marines had laid their muskets aside and were struggling into their coats, but the naval officers at least were paying attention. "Let us heave to and get the longboat over the side."

Ten minutes later Biddlecomb was climbing up onto the merchantman's deck, Weatherspoon at his heels, and a boat filled with marines and the prize crew behind him.

"You are the master of this vessel?" Biddlecomb asked, approaching the man in the blue coat whom he had seen through his glass.

"I am. Capt. Fletcher Page, master of the *White Bird*. And just who, sir, are you?"

"I am Capt. Isaac Biddlecomb, master of the United States brig-of-war *Charlemagne*, and you, sir, are my—"

"Nonsense. There is no United States navy, and there most certainly is no United States navy sailing in these goddamned waters."

"Well, sir, I must disabuse you of that notion. I am a captain in the United States navy, and—"

"No, you are not, sir. There is no such thing."

Biddlecomb stared at Captain Page for a long second before deciding that further argument would be useless. "Very good, sir, then you shall have to content yourself with being the prize of a nonexistent entity. You may tell your underwriter that your ship was whisked away by fairies. Now would you be so kind as to get your papers?"

Page did do that, and quickly too, encouraged no doubt by the speed and efficiency with which Faircloth and his marines rounded up the *White Bird*'s crew and held them at gunpoint along the leeward bulwark, lined up as if before a firing squad. By the time Page returned to the deck, he seemed to be more convinced of the existence of an American navy. The discipline and uniformity of the marines were no doubt helping to stimulate his imagination.

Isaac took the logbook and the handful of papers from Page and leafed through them until he found the bill of lading. The *White Bird* was loaded with brandy, claret, hoops, and a thousand quintals of dried codfish. A very valuable prize, in all.

"Mr. Faircloth, please see the prisoners transferred over to the *Charlemagne.* Mr. Weatherspoon, you have your prize crew and your orders?"

"Aye, sir," Weatherspoon said. "I'm to take the prize to Nantes or Brest, as directly as possible, contact the American commissioners in Paris, and wait word of you, sir."

"You have no concerns about your ability to carry out those orders?"

"No, sir."

"Good. Neither have I," Biddlecomb said, and he meant it. Weatherspoon had not always been the most conscientious student when it came to the intricacies of celestial navigation, but he was a good seaman and had learned a great deal through hard use. Weatherspoon had grown to manhood under Biddlecomb's captaincy, and now he was off in his first command. Isaac felt something akin to paternal stirrings in his heart.

"Captain, sir," Rumstick's voice floated across the water from the *Charlemagne*'s quarterdeck. "Lookout reports two strange sail, bearing south southeast."

"Very good!" Biddlecomb shouted back, then turning to the second lieutenant said, "We'll go across now. Godspeed, Mr. Weatherspoon."

"Thank you, sir." Weatherspoon saluted, then turned to the prize crew and in a voice that sounded to Biddlecomb surprisingly like his own began issuing orders to get the ship under way.

And so it went, with little variation, for the next four days. Faircloth's assessment had been right: taking prizes in the Irish Sea was like shooting deer in a very small park. Biddlecomb was forced to admit as much, though he would admit it only to himself, for saying so out loud would have been terribly unlucky, even for someone who denied having any superstitious parts.

But there was no denying the ease with which they were collecting prizes. Not a day went by that they did not spot a dozen sail at least. Of that dozen they were generally able to intercept four or five, and of that four or five one or two were generally worth taking as prizes.

The others they burned or loaded with the prisoners that they had collected from other ships and sent them on their way. Thus not only were they able to collect prizes, but they had no prisoners to worry about while at sea, nor would they have to concern themselves with the sticky political problem of holding British prisoners in France.

By the fifth day the *Charlemagne*'s decks were looking positively deserted, so many of the men were off in the prizes, bringing the captured merchantmen into ports in France. Of the officers, only Rumstick, Faircloth, Gerrish, and the surgeon remained. Weatherspoon and Sprout, as well as the sailing master, the sailmaker, Woodberry, and two other of the more experienced hands were all off as prize captains. It made Biddlecomb a bit uneasy to be so shorthanded. It was time to end the cruise and sail the *Charlemagne* back to France.

"We're heading all but due south now," Biddlecomb said, nodding toward the *Charlemagne*'s bow, which was at that moment heading straight for France, as well as heading to intercept a large merchantman with which they had been closing for several hours and which was now crossing their path a cable length ahead. "We'll take this one last prize, and then it's off for France."

"Very well, sir," Rumstick said, and anyone who did not know him as well as Biddlecomb did might have thought he genuinely liked the idea. At least until he added, "Must say, I would have thought you'd want to quit when you're ahead. It's always when you say 'just this last one' that things get bunged up."

"Now, Ezra, there is no logical, rational reason to think that's so. Just because it seems to work out that way so often."

"The fact that it seems to work out that way so often ain't enough, Captain?"

"I think perhaps topmast stun's'ls now, Mr. Rumstick," Biddlecomb said, changing the subject.

The first officer went forward to issue orders while Isaac, leaning on the rail, silently cursed him for voicing the very concerns that were silently gnawing at him.

It was just greed, pure greed, that drove him to take one more prize.

But what, after all, was wrong with that? Some of man's greatest enterprises were built on pure greed.

It was stupid to think that he was pushing his luck. The very idea of luck was absurd. Such thinking belonged in the Dark Ages, not in the enlightened days of the eighteenth century. He realized that he was staring at the lightning rod, unconsciously checking to see if it was still intact.

"Oh, for the love of . . . ," he muttered, and then called to Mr. Gerrish at the flag halyard, "Let that son of a bitch see our colors!"

With the studdingsails spread to the fresh breeze, the *Charlemagne* quickly overhauled the slow merchantman, and indeed there was no place for the merchantman to run. The Americans put a shot across her stern, and like the *Charlemagne*'s other victims she rounded up into the wind, letting her yards come down on a run, so fast that the main topsail yard broke clean in two when it stopped short at the end of its lifts.

Ten minutes later Biddlecomb stood at the *Charlemagne*'s gangway, Rumstick beside him. Lined up behind the two men and ready to go down into the boat alongside were the eight men of the prize crew, all that the *Charlemagne* could spare, who would, under Rumstick's command, sail the prize to France. It was all quite routine.

The prize itself looked like a wreck, with its sails hanging like laundry and its main topsail yard broken, but that image was deceiving. She was ship-rigged and new-looking, with six small cannon mounted on her deck, though her crew had apparently not even tried to load them, much less use them for defense. Across her transom Biddlecomb could see the name *Goliath*, picked out in gold leaf.

"We'll stand off and on until you get that main topsail yard straightened out," Biddlecomb said, "then we'll sail in company. If we get separated, you know what to do?"

"Aye, I'm to—"

"On deck!" the lookout aloft interrupted.

"Deck, aye!"

"Sail to leeward! Two, three . . . six sail that I can see, sir, sailing in convoy!"

"Oh, my Lord . . . ," Biddlecomb muttered.

"Isaac, don't think on it," Rumstick said. "This here was the last prize."

"But, Ezra, it's the linen fleet! The Irish linen fleet! It must be. Have you any notion of what it's worth?"

"Isaac . . ."

"Now, see here, Lieutenant. We'll just go and investigate whilst you get that yard replaced. There could be a heavy escort with the fleet, in which case we'll lure them away from you. If not, we'll see what prizes we can scoop up. Once you have the yard straightened out, you get under way and assist as best you can."

"Aye, sir," Rumstick said grudgingly, and good subordinate that he was, he said no more.

"We'll see you in France then, Lieutenant," Biddlecomb said, shaking Rumstick's hand. He watched as his old friend clambered down the boarding steps, Mr. Gerrish and the prize crew climbing down behind him. He wished they would hurry. He was eager to get at the linen fleet, the Irish linen fleet, like some legendary lost treasure there for his taking.

*   *   *

Ezra Rumstick drew his cutlass as he stepped through the merchantman's gangway and, using it like a pointer, gestured at the people standing in clumps around the deck.

"All of you, lay aft, there," he growled. Perhaps twenty people were on deck, mostly sailors but a few well-dressed passengers as well, men and women. They began shuffling toward the quarterdeck, never taking their eyes off their huge, dangerous-looking, cutlass-wielding captor.

The rest of the prize crew, all of them at least as heavily armed as Rumstick, came up behind him and hurried the prisoners along.

"What is the meaning of this? Who are you?" the ship's master demanded, stepping boldly up to Rumstick and thrusting his face as close to the lieutenant's as he could. He was in his sixties with long white hair, bound in a queue. He looked like a man who had started life as a cabin boy and worked his way up to the quarterdeck through a combination of hard work, dependability, and longevity.

Rumstick took a step back. "You the master?"

"Aye. I asked who you are."

"Lt. Ezra Rumstick, of the United States brig *Charlemagne*."

"Pirates! Yankee rebel pirates, here in the damned Irish Sea!"

"Yes, and soon to be in the Atlantic Ocean, if I have aught to say, which I do. Pray send some of your men up to unbend that main topsail. I want that yard on the deck in twenty minutes."

"We'll do nothing of the sort! Help Yankee bastards, indeed."

Staring at that ornery bastard, Rumstick had a vision of himself in thirty years and knew there was no sense in arguing with him.

He pushed the old man aside and addressed the huddled group of seamen. "Listen here, you men! I want that broken yard down and fished in half an hour. If you do it, I'll see you're set ashore in England. If you don't, I'll batten you down right now and I won't let you out until we reach a prison in America, where you'll be held as prisoners of war for the duration. What'll it be?"

It was exactly what Rumstick knew it would be. With curses under their breath and dirty looks at their captors, the seamen, to a man, moved to the mainmast and hauled the topsail up with bunts and clewlines and then clambered into the shrouds and made their way aloft to begin repairs to the damaged rig. They did not move overly fast, or with any great enthusiasm, but they worked at least as fast as Rumstick hoped they would. At that rate it would take an hour or more before they could be under way.

He looked to leeward. The *Charlemagne* was already half a mile away, with studdingsails aloft and alow. Rumstick shook his head at the sight.

He had known Biddlecomb for almost half his lifetime, and he respected him more than any other man he had ever met, with the possible exception of John Adams. But Isaac could get greedy, and his avarice could make him do stupid things. Anyone with any common sense knew when luck was being pushed too far, and when that happened, all the lucky lightning rods in the world wouldn't help.

He hoped that this was not one of those times, but he did not have a good feeling.

"Sir, here are the ship's papers." Midshipman Gerrish handed Rumstick the bundle of official documents that he had apparently collected from the master's cabin.

"Thank you, Mr. Gerrish." Rumstick had entirely forgotten about them, with the distraction of the topsail yard. *Be nice to know what we have here,* he thought as he thumbed through the sheaf, looking for the bill of lading.

He flipped past the crew list and the ship's registry and the list of sea stores and pulled out a sheet marked "Ship *Goliath*, William Sweetman, Master, from Cork to Bristol, January 28, 1777, List of Passengers." He ran his eye down the neatly inscribed names. Men and women were listed there, the same men and women, no doubt, who were now huddled fearfully on the quarterdeck. He counted four women's names on the list and compared that to the four women glaring at him. Five male passengers were on the quarterdeck as well, glaring with equal ferocity.

But on the list of passengers there were not five men, but at least three times that number.

He frowned and ran down the list again. "Lt. John Stevens, Lt. Jas. Larson, Capt. Joshiah Barrett . . ." and on and on the names read. Rumstick looked up at the five men on deck. They were not in uniform, nor did they look like military officers, army or navy.

"Oh, son of a whore," Rumstick said softly. He turned toward his men. "Here, spread out and search belowdecks! These bastards are lying in wait for us," he shouted, but he was too late.

Before the startled Charlemagnes could even catch his meaning, the scuttles fore and aft burst open and more than a dozen men charged the deck, running, shouting, swords and pistols in hand, clad in the scarlet uniforms of the British army.

CHAPTER
14

Experience keeps a dear school,
yet fools will learn in no other.

—Poor Richard's Almanack, 1743

Gerrish was the first to react, and he did not equivocate. He raised his pistol and fired, and the gray-haired captain of light infantry who was leading the charge fell forward, spraying the main hatch with blood as he went down. A woman screamed. The other soldiers behind did not break stride. They rushed past him and raised a cheer like a flank company on a bayonet charge.

"Pistols! Pistols!" Rumstick shouted, jerking his own gun from his shoulder belt. The Charlemagnes were caught unaware—only a few had weapons drawn—and they struggled to pull their pistols before this new enemy was on them, rushing them from fore and aft.

They fired at the same time, British and Americans, with no more then ten feet separating them. For five seconds nothing was to be heard but the twin crack of priming and pistol going off, nothing to be seen beyond the spurts of gray smoke.

And then the smoke was whisked away and Rumstick and Gerrish and a British officer all shouted, "At them!" and those who were not already dead or wounded fell on one another, swords and cutlasses clashing, flailing, and probing through the melee.

Rumstick found himself facing a young officer, a lieutenant, he guessed, some poor bastard whose daddy had just bought him a commission. A stranger to combat. Rumstick could see the fear in his eyes.

The young officer held his sword in the position that some fencing instructor had taught him, a position that had nothing to do with real fighting. Rumstick swept sideways with his cutlass, gripping the handle with two hands, connecting with the lieutenant's sword and knocking it aside with brute force.

Shock on the young officer's face. He tried to bring his sword up again, but in Rumstick's mind their fight was already over. He was looking at his next adversary, an older major who was doubling up on Gerrish, as he thrust at the lieutenant, felt the cutlass bite, heard the lieutenant scream, and twisted and pulled back.

The lieutenant fell. His wound might or might not be fatal, but would certainly put him out of the fight, and Rumstick spared him not a second thought.

Gerrish was being overwhelmed, a lieutenant in front with whom he was fully engaged and the older major coming at him from the side. Rumstick bounded forward just as the major's sword opened up a gash on Gerrish's arm. Rumstick saw Gerrish bare his teeth like a horse, could all but feel the midshipman's pain as Gerrish stepped aside and parried what would have been the coup de grâce.

Rumstick had always thought that Gerrish, pudgy and sardonic, would be useless in a fight, but he saw that he was wrong.

He lunged forward just as the major was drawing back his sword to kill Gerrish and caught the man under the arm with the point of the cutlass. The blade resisted, then plunged into the soldier's body. The man screamed, eyes wide, a horrible sight, and fell as Rumstick pulled the blade free. He would not live for another minute.

Rumstick turned to his next adversary, his heavy cutlass

beating back an attack, his mind as confused as the fight on the deck, unable to concentrate or even form a coherent thought.

He wished that he could leap up on the capstan to see what was happening, to direct the fight from that vantage, but of course he could not.

He thought of Biddlecomb, wondered how Biddlecomb was able to keep thinking in this kind of madness, always able to remain rational. He felt awe, jealousy at his friend's ability, not for the first time.

He did not know what was happening, who was winning. The deck, as far as he could see, was a great struggling crowd of men, red coats and sailors' blue jackets, swords, cutlasses, and pistols.

The Charlemagnes had been caught between two groups of defenders, some coming from forward, some from aft. That was not good.

Rumstick parried a sword thrust, stepped toward the man attacking him, and shoved him hard in the chest, sending him sprawling back into one of his fellow officers, sending them both to the deck.

And in that second's respite he looked around.

The Charlemagnes were being squeezed between the two groups of attackers, and as many of them were down as were still standing.

The *Goliath*'s men were joining in as well, coming down from the main topsail yard, sliding down the backstays, plummeting to deck like birds of prey. They would each have sheath knives, and Rumstick could see those men already on deck grabbing up belaying pins and capstan bars.

He let out a bellow, like a bull, part anger, part frustration, part despair. They could do nothing but fight and die. They could not win, and they certainly could not surrender. He could not. He lifted his cutlass and plunged into it again, flailing back and forth, sweeping away everything in his path, steel and flesh.

He felt the burn of a blade sticking him in the shoulder, but the pain could not get through his rage. He turned and lifted his cutlass and felt the strength drain out of his arm like water through a scupper.

"Aaaaaaah!" he shouted, and tried to lift his arm again, but he could not. He felt another sword thrust, from behind him now.

He half turned, his cutlass dragging on the deck. Saw a sailor winding up with a capstan bar like an ax, saw it start to swing at him. He tried to lift his arm to stop the blow or slow it down. Nothing.

He could only watch, openmouthed and stupid, as the five-foot oak bar arced around and smashed into the side of his head.

It *was* the Irish linen fleet, twenty sail in all, carrying a fortune in cargo from Dublin to various ports in England. Spread out over the horizon were prizes enough to make every man aboard the *Charlemagne* as wealthy as John Hancock. Capturing even one of those ships would earn the brig's company as much as they were likely to make in a lifetime of work.

And from the look of it there was not the slightest chance of their doing so.

Biddlecomb stood on the quarterdeck surveying the scene through his glass. He had thought he was making the fortune of every man aboard, but now he wondered if he had actually managed to bugger them all, finally and completely.

The linen fleet was already beyond reach. They had hauled their wind as soon as they saw him coming, spun on their heels in surprisingly good order and run away, which meant that the sheep now knew that the wolf was about. No doubt the dozens of prisoners he had sent ashore had spread tales of the Yankee raider through all of the harbor towns of Great Britain. There would be no surprising anyone anymore.

But even without the use of surprise the *Charlemagne* would have been able to run down one or two of the linen fleet, were it not for the escort.

She was a genuine British navy brig-of-war, unlike the *Charlemagne*, and fully manned, also unlike the *Charlemagne*, and she was at that moment imposing herself between the *Charlemagne* and the fleeing ships.

"Well, damn," he said, putting the glass down and looking around, at what he did not know. He was sick with his own stupidity; his stomach felt as if he had swallowed a grapeshot. The enemy, no doubt fully manned, was a mile away and closing fast with them, running with the wind astern and studdingsails, which she flashed out with intimidating speed, set aloft and alow.

"Damned stupid fool . . . stupid, stupid," he muttered.

Lieutenant Faircloth, standing on the leeward side of the quarterdeck, felt none of that trepidation. "Are we to engage, sir?" he asked. He looked like a big dog eager for a hunt.

"No, Lieutenant, I fear not. I've made enough of a hash of things for one day. We'll give 'em one broadside to attract their attention, then I shall run like the dog I am with my tail between my legs. The best we can do is draw them away from Rumstick's prize, or sure they will take her back, and our men in prison or hung as pirates."

"Aye, sir." Faircloth was actually disappointed.

"You may as well have your men put on their regimental coats. We're not fooling anyone now."

That seemed to mollify the lieutenant a bit. The marines grinned and shoved one another like schoolboys as they pulled on their beloved coats.

Isaac turned to speak to Lieutenant Rumstick, but of course Rumstick was not there. Nor for that matter were Weatherspoon or Gerrish or half of the Charlemagnes. There would be no fighting the ship with so depleted a crew. God, he hoped there were at least men enough to make a good race of it.

The brig is an escort, it will not leave the fleet too far behind, he assured himself.

The British vessel was no more than a half mile away with the wind right aft. She was running down fast, charging headlong into the fight, as if her captain knew how undermanned his adversary was.

The *Charlemagne* in turn was close hauled, with all plain sail and weather studdingsails set, clawing up to them on a heading that would take them across the enemy's path just before they met. The two men-of-war were converging fast.

"Listen up, you men!" Biddlecomb called down into the waist. "We'll pass starboard to starboard, give 'em a broadside, and then tack, fall off, and set everything we can, draw them away from the prize. Once the guns are fired, I want topmen aloft and all studdingsails set, fast as you can."

In the waist the men were nodding. If they had one advantage, it was the months they had been together as a crew, their experience in handling the brig.

Biddlecomb glanced aloft at the weather leeches, and to his surprise and disgust he saw that the British ensign was still flying from the *Charlemagne*'s mainmast head. So many details that he relied on his officers to attend to went overlooked when they were gone.

Piqued and irritated with himself and with that offensive flag, he drew his sword and with one slashing, irrational, and destructive motion cut the flag halyard in two. He watched with satisfaction as the blue ensign fluttered away downwind, trailing the long halyard as it pulled the thin line through the sheave in the truck. For a good hundred feet the flag remained airborne until at last it collapsed into the ocean and was lost to sight.

Isaac smiled for the first time in an hour. He turned to order someone to run up the Grand Union flag, but no one was there to order, only the helmsman, who was fully engaged, and the marines, who would tangle the thing hopelessly in the rig if they tried to run it aloft.

He bent the flag to the remaining halyard and ran it up himself. He felt like the master of a great house on the day when the servants are off.

By the time he made off the halyard, the enemy was less than a quarter mile off. The Charlemagnes were grim-faced, standing by their guns.

"Stand by, wait for my word."

The two vessels were closing fast now, the British brig rising and falling with the sea, her bow pounding into the deep blue water, sending up a great spray each time. Biddlecomb could see blue uniforms and red uniforms on her quarterdeck, the black muzzles of guns thrust out from the waist, an armament very like that of *Charlemagne*.

One broadside each, and then we are gone, he thought.

The *Charlemagne* came in line with her enemy's bow, a cable length downwind. "Gunners, fire as you bear!"

He did not get to the end of the sentence before the forewardmost gun roared out, flinging roundshot in a straight trajectory right at the oncoming vessel. The second and the third went off, a nearly unbroken wall of noise.

But the enemy was not willing to just take that punishment. They began to turn, presenting their starboard side to the *Charlemagne*, firing one after another as the guns came to bear. Biddlecomb heard the familiar scream of shot, the shudder as it hit the hull.

Below his feet the last of the *Charlemagne*'s guns went off, and then the first was run out again, despite his orders, and fired, and he shouted, "Belay that! Hands to stations for stays!" and the men left the guns and ran to the lines on the pin rails and fife rails. Not enough men were aboard to tack the brig and fire the guns all at once.

He glanced over the leeward side. The *Goliath* was still hove to, her topsail yard still hanging broken with no one that he could see doing anything about it.

Ezra, what in all hell are you about? he wondered. *Please, please, be gone. I do not need your capture on my conscience as well.*

"Ease down the helm!" he called. "Cast off those headsails, come on! Helm's alee! Rise tacks and sheets!"

The men scrambled to carry out the orders as fast as Biddlecomb shouted them, but that was not possible. The headsails flogged as the *Charlemagne* turned up into the wind.

"Mainsail, haul!" Biddlecomb shouted, and the mainyards came around; ragged, uncoordinated, but around they came.

He took a second to look astern. The British brig-of-war had run past them, but no more than one hundred feet before she began to turn as well, to claw back to the *Charlemagne* before the Yankees could get out of point-blank range. She would pass astern of the *Charlemagne* and they would have to endure one more raking broadside as they headed for the horizon.

Then a commotion forward, a shouting from the waist, and Biddlecomb realized that they had missed stays. The brig was hanging in irons, motionless, exposed.

"Headsails! Back the headsails!" Isaac shouted. On the foredeck someone snatched up the headsail sheets, tossed them over the stock of the best bower, hauled them taut.

The enemy was close hauled now, coming up astern of them, and Biddlecomb could see boarders massing in the bows, ready to leap aboard, to sweep the Charlemagnes away with their superior numbers.

The *Charlemagne*'s headsails stopped their flogging as they were sheeted aback, and slowly, slowly, as if she were sailing in tar, the brig began to turn again.

"Turn, turn, damn it," Biddlecomb muttered. "Good enough! Haul of all!"

A shadow moved across the quarterdeck, and above his head the enemy's jibboom rose like a monster from the sea, but Isaac knew it was too late for them to run their bow aboard the *Charlemagne,* and as he watched, the *Charlemagne* began to gather way, to pull ahead of the enemy now just a few yards astern.

"Keep falling off!" he called to the helmsmen, and then, "Sail trimmers, meet her, meet her, square up!" He could not let the British board, that much was certain. Their little crew would be overwhelmed in minutes.

The *Charlemagne* was turning still and the British brig was turning with her, crossing her stern, and as the first of her great guns came up with the *Charlemagne*, it fired.

Round shot tore through the great cabin below Isaac's feet, through the gunroom, and through the bulkhead that sheltered the gunroom from the waist. Blast after blast from the enemy, tearing the full length of the ship, and the men at the braces steeled themselves for each successive shot.

They turned together, the British brig trying to run herself into the *Charlemagne* and the *Charlemagne* trying to avoid her grasp. Not ten feet was between the *Charlemagne*'s transom and the enemy's side.

Biddlecomb ran to the taffrail, leaned over, looked at the distance between the ships. Musket balls from the red-coated marines in the enemy's tops smacked around him, splintering the planks in the deck, but he was too concerned about boarders to even think of sharpshooters.

He looked down and aft. Too close, too close, they would hit for sure.

He turned, ran forward. "Bear up! Bear up!" Biddlecomb shouted, and the confused helmsman began to shift his helm just as the *Charlemagne*'s boom fouled the enemy's main shrouds.

The boom swung across the deck, the *Charlemagne* sloughed around, and the two ships struck, stern to stern, locking together at right angles to one another.

The main chains of the Royal Navy brig crunched into the *Charlemagne*'s transom with a great rending and snapping of wood. Biddlecomb tripped, fell, pulled himself to his knees.

He was looking right across at the enemy's quarterdeck, and the startled British officers were staring back at him.

"Cut us away! Axmen, cut us away!" Biddlecomb shouted, waving toward the boom, gesturing to those men who had snatched up axes. On the enemy's quarterdeck he could hear the British officers calling for grapples to bind the ships together, could hear them as clear as if they were already aboard the *Charlemagne.*

A moment more and the enemy's boarders would be pouring over the side.

The axmen swarmed up to the quarterdeck, hacking at the boom, at anything that held the *Charlemagne* to the enemy. A topmast backstay parted and swung inboard, and one of the axmen was shot down in midstroke by an officer on the British quarterdeck.

A grappling hook sailed through the air and caught on the *Charlemagne*'s boom, and Biddlecomb severed the line with his sword, but another followed, and another and another, too fast for him to cut them all. He heard a cheer, not from his men, and saw the British boarders massing on their own quarterdeck. Faircloth's marines were loading and shooting into them as fast as they could, but that deadly fire did not dampen their ardor in the least.

"Charlemagnes! Prepare to repel boarders! Lay aft! Lay aft!" Biddlecomb shouted, waving his sword over his head and gesturing to the crowd of heavily armed sailors on the enemy's deck.

And then the boarders broke like a wave over their taffrail, leaping across to the *Charlemagne*'s quarterdeck, crashing into the American defenders and sweeping them along. Biddlecomb's sword knocked aside a boarding pike and deflected a cutlass, then another, as he was pushed back by the sheer mass of men.

All around him the Charlemagnes, sailors and marines, struggled to hold back the flood, taking a step back, then another and another as the British threatened to ring them in on all sides.

Biddlecomb saw a pistol come up, aimed at one of his marines, and he slashed with his sword, then turned and hacked at another of the enemy, missing and sinking his blade into the binnacle box. He wrenched it free and leapt back as a pike thrust out, from where he could not tell, and skewered the space that a second before he had occupied.

He took another step back. The boarders were pushing them along, surrounding them, coming at them from three sides.

"Fall back, fall back!" Biddlecomb shouted, taking a step, then another. But they could only fall back so far.

Already the Charlemagnes were leaping down from the quarterdeck to the safety of the waist. Isaac felt himself run up against something hard. He reached back, felt the rail that ran along the break of the quarterdeck.

One by one his men leapt from the quarterdeck down to the waist, pressed by the nearly solid mass of boarders who had all but overwhelmed them.

"Throw down your weapons! Strike! Strike!" one of the British officers called. Biddlecomb saw one of the Charlemagnes fling a cutlass away. Once the spirit of surrender caught, it would sweep over his men fast.

"No!" Biddlecomb screamed. "No quarter!" He hacked at the man in front of him, pushed him aside, and in that fraction of a second before the man recovered, he flung himself over the rail and down into the waist.

He stumbled as he hit the deck, pitched forward, then scrambled to his feet and turned to face the enemy as they poured down off the quarterdeck and pressed their charge forward, outnumbering the Charlemagnes two to one.

The Charlemagnes in turn backed away, stepping faster and faster, some turning their backs and running for the bow. Panic was sweeping over them, and once panic had them Biddlecomb knew they would surrender. He had to get them safe, if even for a minute, long enough to rally them.

"Below! Go below! All of you, down the scuttle!" This at least seemed to the Charlemagnes to be a good idea, and those who were running for the illusionary protection of the bow leapt down the scuttle to the 'tween decks below. Like water through a scupper the Americans disappeared down the ladder, those on deck fighting a rearguard action to cover their retreat.

Only a few of the Charlemagnes were left on deck—Biddlecomb and four others. One turned for the hatch and a boarding pike caught him between the shoulder blades. He arched his back, screamed. Biddlecomb seized the pike, held it, reached out, and thrust the point of his sword into the pikeman's neck.

Then Biddlecomb was alone. No other Americans were left alive on deck. He parried a sword thrust, turned, and dove headfirst down the hatch, felt his shoulder jam on the ladder, felt his feet come over his head as he tumbled and landed in a heap on the deck.

A square patch of light was coming in from the hatch, and then the light was gone and the sharp sounds from the deck above were muffled.

The enemy had clapped the hatch cover over the scuttle, and the Americans were trapped below, trapped aboard their own ship.

CHAPTER
15

When you're an Anvil, hold you still;
When you're a Hammer, strike your Fill.
—POOR RICHARD'S ALMANACK, 1758

"WELL, THIS IS SOMETHING OF AN AWKWARD SITUATION," FAIRcloth said. He was the first to speak.

Biddlecomb pulled himself to his feet, winced as he put his weight on his right knee. He felt as if he had been beaten with a cudgel, ached from half a dozen points of impact, could feel blood running down his leg under his breeches.

One of the marines handed him his sword, which he had dropped in the fall. He took it and nodded his thanks, then looked around at the faces in the gloomy 'tween decks, forty or so men in all. He saw anger and confusion and despondency and fear. Mostly fear.

He looked up at the hatch, shut tight overhead. They were at a standoff, the Charlemagnes and the British. Anyone attacking through the hatch, up or down, would have to attack one man at a time, due to the narrowness of the opening, and they would be killed one man at a time by the defenders, in an almost leisurely manner. Biddlecomb did not imagine that the British overhead cared to do that any more than he did.

"Sir, shall I post guards around the other scuttles?" Faircloth asked. "They might try to rush us."

"No, I have another idea. All of you, follow me. Quietly." With teeth clenched against the pain Biddlecomb pushed his way through the men and led them aft. This idea had come all of eight seconds before, but he moved as if it were what he had been planning to do all along. He knew that it was a great comfort to those men under him to think this was all part of the show.

He limped aft along the berthing deck, crouching low under the beams, listening for some indication of what the British were doing on the weather deck above. They would just guard the hatches, no doubt, ignore the Americans below, and sail the *Charlemagne* into Dublin, less than a day's sail away. They had to act before the victors were able to organize themselves.

The pain in his knee subsided a bit as he walked it out, and he picked up his pace. There was little damage where they were, on that lower deck. The broadsides fired through the transom would have wrecked the great cabin and the officers' quarters on the deck above, but they could not reach the lower deck.

Overhead they heard shouting and a rumble like rolling thunder; heavy guns being moved across the deck. They stopped and listened. The British were repositioning three of the *Charlemagne*'s six-pounders.

"Setting guns to the hatches," Biddlecomb said softly. The British were positioning the guns to fire down the hatches. They would load them with grape or canister shot, and if the Americans were stupid enough to try to charge topside, they would blast them with one horrible discharge, point-blank range. The carnage would be unthinkable.

"Don't worry, men," Biddlecomb reassured them, "we're not going up that way."

They came to a small scuttle aft that led up to the gunroom, that space aft, just outside the great cabin, where the officers lived. Biddlecomb took a few tentative steps up the ladder, poked his head through the hatch, marveled at what the British iron had done.

The gunroom had once consisted of a long table down the center of the deck and small cabins lining either side. Now it consisted of shards of wood, smashed doors, cots flung here and there, and shredded clothing flung about like dead men. A few holes were blasted through the forward bulkhead, and Biddlecomb could see out into the waist, but he knew that the men out there would not be able to see into the dark interior.

"Very well, follow me," he whispered. He climbed up into the gunroom and let the next man come, then led them aft.

The farther back they went, the closer to where the British guns had fired, the worse the destruction became. Biddlecomb was not eager to see what his own cabin looked like, the farthest-aft section of the ship.

He stepped carefully through the jagged rent that had once been the door to the great cabin. The warm, close-packed human smell of the lower deck was entirely gone, washed away by the cold, fresh sea breeze that blew unimpeded through what had once been the stern windows, fashion pieces, and transom, but now was just a hole, rimmed with broken glass and ragged, shattered wood, jutting out at odd angles.

A man behind him gasped and another exclaimed, "Holy mother of God!" and pointed toward a corner of the cabin. It looked to be a scene of some horrible carnage: shattered wood, a great puddle of blood covering the deck and splashed against the bulkhead, some unfortunate soul blasted to pieces, beyond recognition.

"That was my damned wine cabinet," Biddlecomb said. He had just spent two months' wages restocking that cabinet with some of the finest offerings of the Loire Valley, and now it was all no more than a wide, semipermanent stain on the deck.

The badge on the starboard side of the cabin was entirely blown out, as were all of the windows that had once arced across the after end of the cabin. And the only thing visible through that hole was the stern section of the British brig, with which the *Charlemagne* was still entangled and grappled.

Biddlecomb stepped over to the hole that had been the starboard badge and peered out, peered right into the great cabin of the other vessel. She was the *Swallow*, he saw, reading the name carved in her fashion piece. He reached through the hole and ran his fingers over the carved letters, painted white and actually butting against the *Charlemagne*'s side when the ships came together on the swells.

He craned his neck around and looked up through the gap between the ships. A sliver of blue sky was visible between them, no more, and no one on deck looking down. In fact he could see no activity at all on the deck over his head, and he imagined that the British were preoccupied with moving the guns and preparing for the rush that they thought would come through the scuttles from the lower deck.

"Come on, you men. Follow me. Cold steel only, until I say otherwise."

The Charlemagnes at last saw what he had in mind—to board the *Swallow* through the shattered stern section. He could see some men going wide-eyed with disbelief, but most, especially the marines, were grinning with delight. Those few moments below had quelled their panic and any thought of surrender. The fight was back in them now.

Biddlecomb stepped up on a locker gingerly, until he was sure it would bear his weight, then pushing aside a shattered pane of glass, reached through the hole and swung open the unscathed window on the *Swallow*'s larboard badge less than two feet away.

He leaned forward, checking that the *Swallow*'s great cabin was deserted, then stepped easily, unnoticed, from his ship to that of his enemy. He hopped down from the settee in the *Swallow*'s cabin and onto the deck, wincing with the renewed pain in his knee.

Lieutenant Faircloth came behind him, right on his heels, smiling like a boy engaged in some mischief. Isaac ran his eyes over the *Swallow*'s great cabin. The lieutenant in command had taste and money; the cabin was well-appointed, the furniture of the highest order.

The cabin was quite filled by the two score or so Charlemagnes who had poured through the broken windows into the unsuspecting brig.

Biddlecomb held his hands up to attract their attention. When they were all looking at him, pressed shoulder to shoulder in that small space, he held a finger to his lips to indicate silence. He reached down and pulled Faircloth's bayonet from its frog, held it like a dagger, and swung the door of the great cabin open, ready to run the steel through any marine sentry standing there, wondering as he did if he was really capable of so cold-blooded an act, beyond the heat of battle.

He did not have to take that test. The door was unguarded and the gunroom beyond empty.

Biddlecomb made his way forward, stepping carefully. The *Swallow* was flush-decked; the great cabin, gunroom, and berthing deck were all on the same level, unlike the *Charlemagne* with her officers' quarters on the gun deck and the berthing deck below.

A door in the bulkhead at the far end of the gunroom was open, and through it he could see a ladder leading to a scuttle in the deck above. At the base of the ladder was a square patch of light that moved slowly back and forth as the *Swallow* rocked in the swell. Just forward of the ladder was another scuttle that led to the deck beneath them.

At the foot of the ladder Isaac paused and peered cautiously up, trying to see if anyone was on the weather deck above, anyone who might give the alarm.

"Here, who in hell are you?" a voice demanded, not from above but from below, and Biddlecomb nearly leapt off the deck in surprise. He whirled around and thrust out with his sword, stopping the point an inch from the neck of a man who was standing in the hatch at his feet, looking up.

He had gray hair and a round, red face. His corpulent body was covered with an apron that was fairly coated in blood, as were his hands, some dried brown, some still glistening red. As they stood facing each other, Biddlecomb became aware of the agonized groans coming up from the hatch.

"You're the surgeon," he said.

"Yes," said the man below, "and I asked who the hell you were."

"That is not important," Isaac replied, but in that instant the surgeon realized who he was. He turned his face to the hatch above and opened his mouth to shout out a warning, but before he could make a sound Biddlecomb poked his neck with the point of his sword. The surgeon recoiled, and a thin trickle of blood ran down his skin where the steel had pricked him.

"Don't do that, sir, I beg you," Biddlecomb said. "I would not want to kill you."

"Humph," the surgeon said, his lips shut tight. He clearly did not want to be killed.

"You there." Isaac pointed to one of the Charlemagnes who was limping from a nasty gash on the leg. "Stay here and keep an eye on this gentleman. Let him attend to his wounded but don't let him give warning. And you"—Biddlecomb turned to the surgeon—"I'll thank you to dress my man's wound."

With that he turned to the ladder, moving closer and looking up through the hatch. He could see no one. "Those of you with firelocks, load them. Quietly," he said. He put a foot on the lowest rung and stepped up, then on the next and the next. His eyes came level with the deck and he looked around, fore and aft, like some animal peering warily from its burrow.

The *Swallow's* deck was practically deserted. Forward, just out on the bowsprit, he could see a knot of men stowing the headsails. Three more men, one of them a bosun's mate, walked past but paid no attention to him, and he guessed that the top of one head looked pretty much like another. The three men walked back along the *Swallow's* quarterdeck and then over the taffrail to the *Charlemagne*, and the British brig's deck was deserted once again.

"Come on, quick as you can," Biddlecomb said in a loud whisper down the hatch. He scrambled up the last few rungs of the ladder and emerged on deck, standing aside as his men poured up from below. The white pieces of cloth he had sewn over the red lapels on his coat were half torn off, so he tore them away completely and flung them aside. He stood a good chance of being hung as a traitor anyway, so he didn't need the added charge of wearing the enemy's uniform.

As the last of the Charlemagnes came out into the daylight, Biddlecomb led them aft, crouching low so that they would not be seen over the taffrail, moving quick, Faircloth at his side, forty armed, desperate, frightened men behind.

They made it to the very stern of the brig, and Faircloth, kneeling beside Biddlecomb, gestured to his marines to come up. The marines did so, moving quickly in well-drilled order. They were eager to be the first into the fray, and the Charlemagnes seemed quite content to let them have that honor.

Biddlecomb rose slowly and peered over the taffrail. All of the Swallows were there, entirely occupied with their prize, secure in the knowledge that any American still living was locked down below. Four officers were on the quarterdeck, *his* quarterdeck, talking and directing the activities in the waist below. Most of that activity was blocked to his view, but he could see British sailors forward, pushing and hauling one of the great guns toward the forward scuttle.

He heard the gentle rasp of steel on steel. Faircloth's marines were fixing bayonets to their muskets. The bayonet was a rarity in the Continental forces, army or marines, and even more than the uniforms they were a sign of how much money Faircloth had laid out for his men. And in the next five minutes, Biddlecomb imagined, they would all have cause to be glad he did.

"Listen up, you men," Biddlecomb began, then one of the men on the bowsprit yelled out in a voice edged with hysteria, "Hey! Bloody hell! Who the fuck are you, then? Who the fuck are they?"

The officers on the *Charlemagne*'s quarterdeck swung around like startled deer, mouths open.

"Go!" Biddlecomb cried, leaping to his feet and drawing his sword.

"Go! Marines, advance!" Faircloth cried, leaping up as well, jumping the taffrail and landing on the *Charlemagne's* quarterdeck. The British officers looked entirely baffled, but they did recognize a threat when they saw one, and they struggled to draw their swords. The marines, like a green and white wave, came crashing aboard the *Charlemagne*, muskets low, bayonets wavering before them as they advanced, and the officers turned and fled forward, abandoning the quarterdeck to the Americans and shouting to the men in the waist to take up their arms.

"At 'em! Go!" Biddlecomb shouted, and the sailors came over the taffrail as well, right on the heels of the marines.

They raced forward, and Biddlecomb would have led them down into the waist, but Faircloth stopped at the break of the quarterdeck and shouted, "Company, halt!" and the marines stopped at the break as if they had run into a wall.

"Rear rank, take distance!" he shouted, and half the marines stepped back and the other half knelt down on one knee. "Front rank, make ready! Take aim!" In the *Charlemagne's* waist the British sailors were backing away, eyes wide in surprise and fear of what they saw coming. Some held cutlasses or swords as if to ward off the fusillade, some were desperately loading pistols or short-barreled sea-pattern muskets.

"Fire!" Faircloth shouted, and the front rank fired at once, and while still lost in the cloud of gun smoke, they fell to reloading. Panic began to sweep over the British sailors as the hail of lead slammed into their ranks.

"Swallows! To me! At 'em, lads!" An officer held his sword over his head and waved it at the Americans, advancing toward the quarterdeck, his men starting to follow, gathering momentum.

"Rear rank! Make ready! Take aim! Fire!" The rear rank of marines fired and the advance wavered. "Front rank, make ready! Take aim! Fire!"

This was the moment that Faircloth had drilled for, the moment he had waited for, when he could make full use of his disciplined men, and Biddlecomb was happy to let him have it. "Charlemagnes! You men who have pistols, get in here where you can!" He waved to the sailors, and those who had guns crowded in around the marines or leapt up on the bulwark and fired into the British in the waist, giving a chaotic and disorganized sound to Faircloth's well-drilled volleys.

The British were firing back, those who had guns. One of the Charlemagnes was knocked from the shrouds and landed on the channel, twisted between the deadeyes.

"Swallows! At them! Will you stand here and be shot down?" the lieutenant was shouting, waving his sword. The men were rallying, shouting as well and advancing, heedless of the volley from the second rank of marines.

"Marines! Charge!" Faircloth shouted, a cry that carried over all the cacophony on the deck, and with a terrifying cry the marines ran down the steps on either side of the quarterdeck or flung themselves over the rail, racing forward at the startled British sailors.

The two small armies came together like the Red Sea crashing over the Egyptians, with screams and small arms, swords and bayonets. For a second they stopped, locked in struggle, and then Faircloth's marines began pushing the British back.

The Swallows fought hard, valiantly, led with skill by their officers, but it was not enough, not in the face of total surprise, disciplined volleys, and twenty bayonet-wielding marines.

The Swallows screamed and fell as they suffered the horrible wounds doled out by the triangular blades. Three, four of them went down, shrieking that high-pitched scream, and for the rest that was all they could stand.

They fled toward the bows, and for a second Biddlecomb was afraid that they would do what he had done, retreat to the 'tween decks, but the British had secured the hatches and they could not open them in time. Instead they crowded up against the rounded bulwark, some clambering out along the bowsprit to escape the horrible bayonets, and one by one they flung their weapons down and held their hands over their heads.

At last it was quiet. The British lieutenant stepped forward. His coat was ripped, a great swatch of cloth hanging down, blood on the torn white waistcoat beneath. He unbuckled his sword as he approached and with a quick bow handed it to Biddlecomb. "Comdr. John Webber, sir, of His Majesty's brig-of-war *Swallow*. I am your prisoner."

Biddlecomb took the sword. "Capt. Isaac Biddlecomb, of the United States brig-of-war *Charlemagne*." The two officers stood looking at one another. Biddlecomb could see Webber struggling with himself, trying to work up the nerve to ask, trying to decide if it was appropriate, or if Biddlecomb would even answer.

"We came through my great cabin," Biddlecomb explained, relieving the lieutenant's curiosity. "Stepped right from mine into yours and then up your aftermost scuttle."

"Ahhh." Webber nodded, seeing it all in his mind. "Bloody good show." His attitude seemed very positive for a prisoner of war. Biddlecomb wrote it off to his age, which was no more than twenty-one.

"Mr. Faircloth, well done, all of you," Biddlecomb said in a voice loud enough to be heard around the deck. "Please see to these prisoners. Half of them on the prize, half on the *Charlemagne*, if you would. See if there's some secure place below. Keep a good guard on them."

"Aye, sir," said Faircloth, and as the marine began to issue orders, Biddlecomb walked aft to the *Swallow*'s quarterdeck.

It was extraordinary what they had done. They had taken a British man-of-war in the St. George's Channel, nearly within sight of the British coast.

When he brought the *Swallow* as a prize into France, and the French gave him safe haven, the British government would go wild. It might well push the two nations to war, and if that happened, the Spanish would have to join in as well. The Germans were already fighting with the British, though for a price, and eventually the Dutch would have to throw in, and perhaps the Swedes and the Russians as well.

Half of the civilized world at the brink of war, and now just that much closer because he had tried to scoop up the Irish linen fleet.

The thought of the linen fleet made him think of Rumstick, whom he had in the excitement forgotten. He looked to leeward, pleased to see the *Goliath* gone. He found a telescope in the *Swallow*'s binnacle box, climbed up into the main shrouds, and swept the sea to the south.

There was nothing there. From southwest to southeast, the full arc in which a ship bound for France might be found, there was nothing.

Biddlecomb lowered the telescope, frowned at the horizon. Felt the first inkling of concern creep over him. The *Goliath* could not be lost from sight of the deck that soon, not that slab-sided merchantman with a broken main topsail yard.

He searched the western horizon. He could see some of the linen fleet, but not the *Goliath*. It seemed pointless to look to the east; there was nothing in that direction but England, and Rumstick certainly was not heading for England.

He looked anyway. And there she was, nearly hull down on the eastern horizon. He might not even have known it was her, save for the fact that the broken main topsail yard was now gone and she was making way under foresails, main course, and mizzen topsail. She was sailing with the wind abeam almost due east, making for the Bristol Channel.

Biddlecomb felt weak, sick to his stomach.

"Sir?" Faircloth was on the deck behind him. "Sir, the prisoners are secured."

"Thank you, Lieutenant."

"Are you looking for Rumstick, sir? Is he under way?"

"Yes, he is under way. But I doubt very much that he is still in command."

CHAPTER
16

Don't think so much of your own Cunning,
as to forget other Men's: A cunning Man
is overmatch'd by a cunning Man and a Half.

—POOR RICHARD IMPROVED, 1754

THE WATERFRONT OF BRISTOL WAS ABSOLUTELY BUZZING WITH THE
story, both the truthful core of the thing and all the periph-
eral flights of fancy provided by those who told and retold
the tale.

Like Dr. Franklin's lightning rod, there was no greater
conductor of a tale than a seaman, and since the waterfront
of Bristol was composed almost entirely of those and related
elements, with only a little resistance provided by merchants
and underwriters and such, the story crackled and leapt
from quay to quay, from chop shop to alehouse to boardinghouse and brothel.

By the time Sam Nicholson and Joe Hynson concluded
the negotiations for the cutter—a lovely, stout craft, sixty
feet long on deck, about eighty tons burthen, with a nice
sweeping sheer and rigging well set up—they had heard the
story three times. But that did not stop the old former naval
officer who was selling the vessel from telling it again.

"So them goddamned Yankees come aboard, just as bold
as you please, and think they'll take her as easy as you
please! And then as soon as their brig leaves 'em, leaves a

prize crew on board, well, out come all the officers, don't you know, officers from three different regiments posted temporary in Dublin, taking passage home on leave, and they just lays right into 'em and takes 'em all, Yankee sons of bitches!"

The old man spat over the rail into the dark water of the Avon River, on which the town of Bristol was situated. He was hard of hearing, having been a lieutenant in charge of a lower-deck battery of thirty-two-pounders aboard a ship of the line during the last war, or so he had explained.

Hynson guessed that was why he didn't realize that he was talking to Yankee sons of bitches at the moment, or why he could not hear the grunts and sighs that he, Hynson, was letting out every few minutes, indicating a complete lack of interest.

"That's her, there. *Goliath*. Should have seen the mob when them officers come ashore."

Actually, Hynson had seen it, an hour before, two hours after the *Goliath* had dropped her hook in Bristol Harbor. The story had already been widely circulated by the time the merchantman's boat had pulled ashore, filled with red-coated officers, and the people had jammed the quays and the waterfront street to catch a glimpse of the victors, and to cheer them as they stepped ashore. The people yelled as if that dozen men had just subdued all of America.

It made Hynson sick.

"Sir?" Sam Nicholson said to the old man, practically yelling. "Here is the bank draft, sir! I reckon you'll find this is all in order!" He handed the former lieutenant the paperwork and the old man squinted at it, his eyesight apparently as bad as his hearing.

"Very well. This seems to be in order," the old man said at last, then paused and took a long look around the cutter's deck and said, "You made a good deal, boys. She's a fine little ship and I hate to see her go."

"She's a slab-sided, rotten tub and you overcharged us

by a hundred pounds at least, you criminal," Hynson said in a nearly conversational tone. He smiled at the cutter's former owner, who nodded and smiled back. Then louder and more politely Sam Nicholson thanked the man and escorted him to the quay.

"She ain't really a rotten tub, is she, Joe?" Nicholson asked as he rejoined Hynson in the cutter's bow, having seen her former owner ashore.

"No, no. There's nothing wrong with her. I was just getting sick of that old bastard's prattle."

"I reckon you were. I was ready to knock him on the head myself if he said 'Yankee sons of bitches' one more time. But what think you of this story about the *Goliath?*"

"Some stupid bastards, taking prizes off the coast before we get the chance to. Well, looks like they took the wrong ship, the sons of bitches. Serves them right."

"Well, now, they might have been poaching on our property, as it were, but they're Americans. On our side."

"Yes," Hynson said, expelling a long breath, "I reckon you're right. And I reckon their poaching days is about done."

The two men stood silent for a moment, looking at the *Goliath* as she rode at a single anchor a half a mile down the river. She was missing her main topsail yard and her sails were drying to a bowline. As they watched, a small boat pulled up to her side and a single figure climbed up the cleats on her side, but they could see no other activity on her decks. All of the brouhaha that had attended her arrival had come ashore with the army officers who had defended her.

"I was thinking, Joe, we might be able to do something for those men," Nicholson said softly, as if the cutter were filled with eavesdroppers.

"What?" Hynson asked warily.

"Well, we're clearing out for France tonight, once we get a few hands hired on. Why couldn't we try and take those fellows with us? It'd be but a few minutes, board that tub, take the guards by surprise, pistols and cutlasses, set the Americans free, and it's off to France."

Hynson turned and stared at Nicholson. *What the hell have I done?* he thought. He had talked up this duty nonsense as a way of getting young Sam over that Mrs. Carter doxy. Apparently he had overdone it, because now Nicholson was as stupid with patriotism as he had been with love.

"Are you mad?" Hynson asked. "What, you and me storm aboard the merchantman, take on the whole crew by ourselves, set the prisoners free, and then explain to the British seamen that we hired to work the cutter that we're American rebels and would you mind taking us to France with our freed prisoners?"

Nicholson shifted uncomfortably under Hynson's stare. He glanced out at the *Goliath* once more, then back at Hynson. "No, not like that. It'd have to be done with stealth. Trick them somehow into letting the prisoners go. Look." Nicholson brightened as a new idea came to him. "Let's go out to the ship and have a look around. Maybe we can talk to the prisoners."

"How are we supposed to do that? What are—"

"We'll think of something, some story. Come along."

Before Hynson could make further reply, Nicholson was gone, hurrying across his newly acquired cutter's deck and onto the quay.

"Son of a bitch, son of a bitch," Hynson muttered under his breath, but he followed Nicholson nonetheless. He needed Nicholson. All of his plans, Smith and Vardell's plans, depended on Nicholson. There was nothing else he could do.

Ezra Rumstick opened his eyes, looked around the *Goliath*'s forepeak, the small, V-shaped storeroom in the bow section of the hold. The pounding in his head had subsided, was all but gone. For the past twenty-four hours, since he had come to in that place, he had been in such agony that he could hardly speak. But the pain had faded at last, faded enough for him to contemplate their surroundings, and their predicament.

Their surroundings were nothing special: the forepeak of the merchantman was like any of a hundred he had seen. Their captors had not been so foolish as to allow them a lantern; they could do too much mischief with a flame and all of that paint and tar, so the only light was coming from the grating overhead, which as best he could tell communicated with the forecastle.

All of the Americans were crammed down there, eight men in all—Rumstick, Gerrish, and the six men of the prize crew who had survived the fight. Their particular odors mixed with the smell of the tar and linseed oil and marlin to form, in one potent whiff, all of the smells associated with a sailing ship, only more so.

And their predicament, as Rumstick considered it, was even worse than their surroundings.

The *Goliath* was at anchor. He did not need to see beyond the forepeak to know that. That being the case, there was no way to know how many men were now guarding the ship. They could have brought a regiment out from shore, for all he knew.

But it would not take a regiment to guard them. Their only means of escape was through that small hatch, and they could only fit through that one at a time, which meant that it would not take a lot of men and guns to stop them. No, there would be no escape from there. Perhaps later, onshore, but not while aboard the *Goliath*.

Of course there was always the hope that someone would come to their aid, but Rumstick dismissed that as soon as he thought it. That would not happen, and thinking about it would not help.

"Gerrish? Mr. Gerrish, are you there?" he asked.

"Aye, sir. How is your head?"

"Better." They both paused at the sound of feet overhead. The grating was lifted and the light became brighter for a moment, and then it was dark as a figure climbed down the ladder, filling the narrow hatch with his frame.

He stepped down onto the uneven deck and turned. He had the air of someone used to being in command, an experienced military man, though dressed in civilian clothes. He would have been intimidating even without the patch over his left eye, the wicked scar running from under the patch down his left cheek.

"I am Lieutenant Colonel Smith. Which of you is in charge?"

"I am. I'm Lt. Ezra Rumstick, United States Navy."

"United States Navy? Indeed. Pretending to have a navy won't save you from hanging as pirates. What ship are you from?"

There was a pause, and then Rumstick said, "I don't reckon I'll tell you that."

"You don't reckon you'll tell me that? I assure you that it would be better if you told me now. You would save yourselves a great deal of trouble."

"There are laws about how to treat prisoners of war."

"And there are laws about how to treat traitors and pirates."

"Sir?" a voice called down from the deck above. "Boat's putting off, sir, and pulling for us."

Lieutenant Colonel Smith looked annoyed. "Very well. I hate to cut this meeting short, but I'm afraid I must."

"And why is that?" Rumstick asked. "I was just enjoying myself."

Lieutenant Colonel Smith gave him a half smile. "I don't reckon I'll tell you that, but when you and your men are ashore, Lieutenant, then we shall have time for more pleasant discussion." With that, Smith turned and climbed back up the ladder.

When he was gone, Gerrish said, "Why is it, sir, that I think all the pleasure will be his?"

"I can think of folks I'd rather talk to than him," Rumstick agreed. "Lucifer, for one, comes to mind."

Joe Hynson could see a figure climbing down the *Goliath*'s side and back into the boat that had just pulled alongside the ship. He was not thinking about who it was or why he might have visited the ship so briefly. He did not care.

He was sitting in the stern sheets of the wherry that Nicholson had hired to take them out to the *Goliath*. He was thinking of the predicament that Nicholson was leading him into.

If Smith's plan was to work, Hynson needed Nicholson to introduce him in Paris. If Nicholson was apprehended now, then all of Vardell and Smith's plans were shot, and it was prison for him. If he refused to help Nicholson, then he might lose Sam's confidence, get no introduction in Paris, and the same thing would happen.

But if Hynson was caught trying to free the Americans, then Vardell and Smith would think he was a turncoat, and then he would be lucky if prison was the worst that happened to him. If he could not talk Nicholson out of this stupid idea, then he had to see that they pulled it off and got away, and that Vardell and Smith never found out that he had had a hand in it.

"Son of a bitch, son of a bitch," he said again, this time a little louder.

The boatman sat facing them, glancing over his shoulder now and again and correcting his course to the *Goliath*. He and Nicholson exchanged the odd pleasantry, but Hynson had little to say. He was not at all pleased with this thing Nicholson was doing, and as they drew closer, he became more fearful of what would happen once they were aboard, and so he said nothing at all, save for arguing with the boatman over his fare.

They came at last to the *Goliath*'s high side, and the two men scrambled up the boarding cleats. Hynson expected to be challenged from the deck; indeed, he had expected to be challenged just approaching the ship, but no one seemed to pay any attention. Apparently the *Goliath* had seen so much activity that day that two more visitors did not warrant notice.

They stepped through the gangway and onto the deck, amidships. The *Goliath* was a medium-sized merchantman, her decks clean, her running gear hanging in even coils along her fife rails and pin rails, her hatches still battened down. She was entirely unremarkable, save for the main topsail yard, broken in two and lying on the deck, and the large dark patches on her tarpaulins and deck planking where blood had been imperfectly scrubbed away.

"May I help you, gentlemen?" they heard a voice from aft. There was no threat in the tone, not even much curiosity or genuine desire to help.

"Yes, thank you," Sam Nicholson said brightly. "Would you be the master, sir?"

"Master's ashore, sir. I'm the mate. Mr. George Pinkart."

"Mr. Pinkart, pleased to make your acquaintance." Nicholson stepped aft and shook the mate's hand. "I am Mr. Samuel Nicholson, this is Joseph Hynson. We are from the underwriter's office."

"From Lloyd's?"

"Yes, just so. I am head of the American Accounts office. Something of a dull job, nowadays, as you can imagine, not many of our clients venturing to the colonies, what?" Nicholson said with a smile.

Pinkart the mate smiled as well. "I should imagine not. I apologize, sir, for not seeing you aboard, but it has been quite a day, all manner of people coming and going. Fellow just left a few minutes ago, wouldn't even say who he was. But, how may I be of assistance?"

"Well, sir, I was in Bristol to meet with Mr. Hynson here

when we caught wind of what had happened, and being as there are no other Lloyd's people in town, I reckoned I should come and have a look for myself. Particularly as there seems to be some American connection."

Pinkart looked confused. "But, was there not one of your people out here this morning? Just soon after we anchored?"

"Oh, yes, of course," Nicholson said. "I meant no one from the London office. Fellow this morning was from the local office."

Pinkart nodded and seemed to accept this. Not that there was any reason for him to not accept it. Nicholson spoke like a gentleman, and he and Hynson were well dressed in silks and velvets and brilliant gold buckles and gold-headed walking sticks. They had dressed that morning to look like successful American merchantmen, which was, in Nicholson's case, exactly what he was.

"Now tell me," Nicholson continued, "was there any damage to ship or cargo, to speak of?"

"No, sir. As we told the fellow this morning, the main topsail yard broke, but it was rotten in the slings to begin with. Half-hour glass was shot through by a stray bullet, but that was it."

"And the prisoners? Are they still aboard?"

"Aye, sir. There's been no end of argument about who's to take them. Civilian authority don't want them, the army officers say they're prisoners of the Crown, but there's no military authority in town to take charge of them. They're still battened down below, locked in the forepeak, 'til someone figures out where they should go. It makes me damned nervous too, sir, I don't mind telling you."

"I should imagine so. You've a decent guard on them, I suppose?"

"Not much of one. We only have half a dozen hands aboard. Half the crew went ashore first thing, and now there's just what's left of my men to watch over them. I must have said half a dozen times we need more men to guard these ones, but it don't appear anyone was listening. All too busy arguing about whose responsibility it is. But there's only one small hatch into the forepeak, so it only takes one or two men with a few loaded weapons to guard it, do you see?"

"I do indeed. Well, I'll see about having some more men sent out, help you guard those prisoners. I don't think the London office would be too pleased to see them retake the ship!"

Hynson was impressed. He would not have credited Sam Nicholson with that much wit and creativity. Perhaps the lovesick patriot could carry this off after all.

"Now," Nicholson continued, "if you don't mind, I should like to interview the prisoners."

"Interview . . . the prisoners?" This at last caught Pinkart's attention.

"Why, yes. Most important. See what I can find out about this Yankee pirate sailing about in British waters."

Pinkart looked from Nicholson to Hynson and back. Finally he shrugged, as if this was just another in a long string of absurd events, and saying, "This way, gentlemen," he led them down into the gloom of the lower deck and forward.

They made their way past stacks of casks, containing what they could not tell, and into the forecastle, where a bored sailor sat in the light coming through a small hatch overhead. He had two pistols thrust in his belt, which, along with his gold earring, gave him a piratical look, and three muskets leaning against a bunk.

"Mr. Mate," he said with a nod as the three men stepped into the forecastle.

"Johnson," Pinkart replied. "These gentlemen are from Lloyd's. Wants to have a word with the prisoners. They been behaving themselves?"

"Hardly a peep, sir. They was most cordial to that last fellow."

"Good. You escort these gentlemen down into the fore-peak then."

"Oh, no, no," said Hynson, unwilling to let Nicholson do all of the lying. "We can't risk your man being taken as hostage. Us, we're ready for it, you understand. Paid to take that risk."

"Makes sense to me," said Johnson, who did not seem disappointed to be staying behind. He lifted the grating on the small hatch in the deck, and Nicholson and then Hynson found the ladder and climbed down.

The forepeak smelled like every other forepeak Hynson had ever been in—tar and hemp and paint and tallow—but this one had as well a strong smell of men, packed together, which was no wonder as eight prisoners were crammed into that little space. Many of them wore bandages, dark with dried blood, and they glared at the two visitors as they stepped from the ladder and found their footing.

"Now who the bloody hell are you?" asked one of them, apparently their commanding officer, one of those with a bandaged head.

"I am Samuel Nicholson, from the Lloyd's of London office. Who of you is in command here?"

"I am Ezra Rumstick, United States Navy. You sound like an American." There was accusation in his tone, and it made Hynson feel even less comfortable than he was. This Rumstick was a big bastard, bigger even than himself, and he didn't look quite right in the head. He might decide that he was going to take one of the enemy down with him, and who better than a loyalist American?

"My nationality, sir, is of no importance to you—" Nicholson continued, but Hynson interrupted in a whisper.

"Aye, we're Americans. Come to get you out, if we can. I'm Capt. Joe Hynson, from New York, this here's Capt. Sam Nicholson of Maryland. We're just putting on to be from Lloyd's, so we could talk to you."

"Or you're working with that bastard Smith, hoping I'll

tell you what I wouldn't tell him. You might have waited an hour at least before trying this."

"You have the advantage of me, sir," Nicholson said.

"Smith, your boss? Lieutenant Colonel Smith, with the eye patch? The scar? There, sir, I see by your face that you know him." Rumstick looked right at Hynson, who had been trying to hide his shock at hearing Smith's name uttered there in that strange place.

"Smith . . . was here?" Hynson asked, but Rumstick said nothing, just glared at him. At last Hynson continued, "Yes, I know him. He is some sort of spy for the British, involved with their intelligence. I've . . . I've been around a bit, know who these bastards are."

"Well, sir," said Nicholson, "I for one do not know this Smith. But see here, Lieutenant, I am Samuel Nicholson, of the Maryland Nicholsons. My brother James was lately appointed senior captain of the United States Navy. If these credentials are not enough to satisfy you, sir, and I swear to their truth on my word as a gentleman, then we shall bid you good day."

Rumstick looked at one and then the other, as if he were buying a horse from them. Then he turned and met the eyes of another man with a pudgy face and a blue coat like an officer's, but torn down the side. The other man cocked an eyebrow, nodded slightly, but said nothing.

"Very good, then," Rumstick said at last. "This here is Mr. Gerrish, midshipman. Rest of the men are foremast jacks. We're off the United States brig-of-war *Charlemagne*, Capt. Isaac Biddlecomb commanding. You don't need to know more than that."

"Biddlecomb?" Nicholson asked.

"Aye. You know him?"

"By reputation only. And it's quite a reputation, I dare say. And you're . . . Rumstick. Of course."

"Yes, and I'm George Washington," said Gerrish, "and

this is all very flattering, indeed, but to return to the subject, I'm certain I heard something about a rescue?"

"Yes," Nicholson whispered. "It looks as if it shall be easier than I had imagined. There's not much of a guard. The master and the army fellows who retook the prize are ashore. The mate thinks we're really from Lloyd's. I told him we would send out more men to stand guard, protect the ship that we're insuring, you see. We'll come out this evening in our cutter, ostensibly with new guards, and once we're aboard, we'll overwhelm the real guards and off we go, outward bound for France."

Rumstick considered that for a moment. "Sound's simple enough. Simple plan's always the best. What if they take us ashore before then?"

"We'll keep a weather eye out for that, but it don't look like that'll happen. They're all arguing about who should have charge of you and they can't decide. It's only four hours to dark, I think you're safe till then."

"When should we be looking for you?" Rumstick asked.

"We need to get downriver fast, which means we'll need to leave on the first of the ebb tide," Hynson supplied, feeling less and less comfortable about this entire thing. "When the hell is that? We don't know when that is."

"But we do, my dear Hynson," said Nicholson. "You see, I've already found that out. First of the ebb's at nine twenty-five tonight."

Aboard the many vessels that were working their way up and down the Bristol Channel—brigs, sloops, schooners, ships, and the ubiquitous Bristol cutters—no one seemed overly interested in the innocuous brig-of-war *Swallow* as she stood up-channel under topsails and foresail.

Those who passed close might turn a curious eye toward her, but it was a mild curiosity at best, and once they had looked her over, they turned back to hauling their nets or sheets or anchor cables. Too many Royal Navy brigs-of-war were about to raise anyone's interest.

Isaac Biddlecomb, standing on the quarterdeck and wearing the coat of the *Swallow*'s former commanding officer, was delighted and relieved to find that no one cared about him. Sailing in the Irish Sea, he had felt like Daniel in the lion's den. Sailing in the Bristol Channel, he felt like Daniel in the lion's mouth. He did not care to spend one more second there than was required for him to redeem himself in his own eyes for his greed and stupidity.

"You'll want to fall off a point," the pilot said, grunted, really, nodding his head over the leeward side.

"Fall off a point," Biddlecomb said over his shoulder to the helmsman, and the helmsman pushed the tiller over a foot to windward.

"Good. Steady up," the pilot grunted.

They had picked him up at Weston, after following the *Goliath*'s course for twenty hours, right through the night, as she made for some port far up the Bristol Channel. Though the channel was still many miles wide at Weston, and remained so for many miles more, Biddlecomb knew that they would need the guidance of an expert with local knowledge.

It took the pilot about a minute and a half after stepping aboard to realize that something was terribly wrong, but it was too late by then.

He was eventually persuaded to navigate the vessel, persuaded by a promise of fiscal reward if he did so and a prolonged and brutal death if he did not. So exhausted, so utterly unwilling to argue, was Biddlecomb that his threat came across with complete sincerity, so much so that the pilot quickly acquiesced and even Faircloth seemed to believe that his captain was willing to do all of the gruesome things he threatened.

And the pilot had provided them with information about more than just hazards to navigation. In his intercourse with shipping on the channel he had picked up the entire story of the *Goliath*, how she had been captured, recaptured, and most importantly, that she had been taken to Bristol.

"Very good then, pilot," Biddlecomb had said. "Pray take us to Bristol as well."

Biddlecomb leaned now on the quarterdeck rail, staring across the water at the rocky and tree-covered shore as it slipped past. They still had the breeze and the flood tide with them, carrying them northeast to the mouth of the Avon River and Bristol, and that was fortunate, he thought.

He closed his eyes, resting them, and a second later jerked awake as his elbow slid off the rail. He shook his head and blinked hard. He was so tired, so very tired. He had slept little and had done so much in the past thirty hours.

To keep awake he paced back and forth along the quarterdeck. Down in the waist it looked like the aftermath of some horrible battle with the dead strewn around. Biddlecomb had let the hands sleep at quarters, keeping just enough men awake to handle helm and sails.

He looked with envy at them now. He would give anything to lie down and sleep himself, but he could not. If they were to rescue their prize crew from the *Goliath*, they had to strike as quickly as they could. Once the prisoners disappeared into England, there would be no finding them. It might already be too late.

Faircloth stepped up to the quarterdeck and stood for a moment, watching the shoreline and the smattering of small boats between the *Swallow* and the land. He had not slept either, though Biddlecomb had given him permission to do so.

"Tell me, Mr. Faircloth, have you ever been to England before?" Biddlecomb asked.

The marine strode over to where Biddlecomb was standing by the rail. "When I came of an age, I made an appearance for a few seasons in London. Couldn't tolerate it. Bloody decadent, effete goings-on. If you want any further proof of the difference between Americans and Englishmen, you have only to spend a season in London."

"I should imagine."

"And you, Captain? Have you ever been here before?"

"Here? No. I was born and raised in Bristol, Rhode Island, till the age of thirteen in any event, but I've never been to Bristol, England. Been to London on a few occasions, twice as a foremast jack and once as second mate. Rumstick was with me, all three times. I don't reckon we were moving in the same circles you were. We spent most of our time ashore in waterfront establishments, taverns and the like. Decadent to be sure but I wouldn't call them effete."

Faircloth smiled. "I wouldn't think so. I wish I'd been with you. I'll wager you were having a better time than me."

The two men were silent for a moment and then Faircloth said, "Sir, might I ask, what course of action do you intend?"

"Nothing too very elaborate." Biddlecomb did not feel capable of anything too elaborate. "Ship's in Bristol, or so the pilot says and I reckon he's too afraid to lie. We'll anchor at Avonmouth, take two boats upriver. Go right for the prize ship, board her from bow and stern, and overwhelm any guard on board, and pray all the while that they haven't taken Rumstick and the others ashore."

"Very good, sir. And will we try to carry the *Goliath* off with us as well?"

Biddlecomb smiled and shook his head. That would just be greed, and it was his blind greed and stupidity that had got them into this mess in the first place. If he had stuck with the *Goliath* rather than chasing after the linen fleet, then they would all be halfway to France at that very moment. He would not succumb to further avarice and try to take the *Goliath* again.

As it was, he was putting his remaining men into extraordinary danger just to salve his conscience. He knew he wouldn't have tried to effect this kind of rescue for one of the other prize crews, had they been taken.

Or was it his friendship with Rumstick that was leading him to take such extreme measures?

He pushed those considerations aside. "If this breeze holds, we'll be at Avonmouth by nightfall," he told Faircloth. "Start upriver then. We can lie at our oars if need be to kill time until we board."

"And when will that be, sir?"

"We'll need the ebb tide to make certain we can get down-channel. We'll attack the *Goliath* right at the first of the ebb tonight. Nine twenty-five."

CHAPTER
17

Here comes Courage! that seiz'd the lion absent,
And run away from the present mouse.

—POOR RICHARD'S ALMANACK, 1736

JOE HYNSON COULD FEEL EYES ON HIS BACK. HE TURNED SLOWLY, looking up and down the dark waterfront street, looking for whoever it was who was watching him.

A few people were moving about, the usual smattering of whores and drunk sailors and respectable people out for a stroll. But no one that he could see was paying the least attention to him or any of the activity aboard the cutter. None of Smith and Vardell's hired criminals glaring at him, taking note of his apparent treachery. But that did not mean that they were not there, just that they were well hidden.

" 'Ey, Mr. Hynson, you gonna want this 'ere anchor cock-billed or is it alright 'ow it is?'' called one of the hands from forward. They had hired on three men, blue-water sailors between ships, to help them sail the cutter to France.

Of course, they might get no farther than halfway across the river, to where the *Goliath* rode at anchor. Nicholson had suggested that they hire a boat to take them out to the merchantman, free the American prisoners, and then return to the cutter and get under way, but Hynson had rejected the idea outright. That would take too long by half.

If Sam was committed to this stupid idea, which apparently he was, then the best thing was to grab the bastards

193

and get out of Bristol fast. And the best way to do that was to lay the cutter alongside the *Goliath* and tie up to the larger ship. It would be awkward—the cutter had a sparred length of seventy feet—but not overly so.

And more to the point, the cutter would be right there, ready to go, no rowing back and forth after the alarm was sounded.

"Sir?" the sailor said again, patiently reminding Hynson of his question.

"Ah, that's fine as it is." Hynson glared at the sailor, who was coiling down the cat fall and obviously trying to look innocent. *Who do you work for, really?* he thought.

And then he realized he had made a mistake, preoccupied as he was with finding spies. "No, wait a moment, you're right. Cock-bill it."

Think, think, he urged himself. He ran his eyes aloft, up and down the cutter's single mast and along the long boom that jutted out over the taffrail. The mainsail was neatly furled along the length of the boom, and the gaff was resting on top of that. Everything seemed in order.

From somewhere in the town of Bristol a bell rang out nine o'clock. Hynson pulled his watch from his waistcoat and squinted at the face, just visible in the moonlight and the various lanterns burning along the waterfront. Eight fifty-eight. He'd reset the piece of rubbish two hours before and already it had lost two minutes. He considered flinging it into the river and would have, to ease his nerves, if Nicholson had not appeared through the hatch at that moment.

"Nine o'clock, Joe," he said in a soft voice. "Slack water. Twenty-five minutes to the ebb." A smile was playing across his face and it made Hynson want to smack him. Bloody little hero.

Hynson looked fore and aft. None of the British sailors were listening, and none were within earshot.

"Are you certain this is so great an idea, Sam?" he asked instead, forcing his voice to be steady. "I mean, we can probably get them off with no problem, but there's a whole fucking river we have to get down without putting the cutter aground, on a falling tide, I should mention, and then clear down the Bristol Channel. It don't look so good when you examine it more closely."

"I appreciate what you're doing, Joe," Sam said, and said no more.

"Go on." said Hynson. He wanted to find out what Sam thought he was doing.

"Giving me a way out, I mean. Making like you think this is a bad idea, so I can back out if I don't have the nerve for this. But it's all right. I still think we can do it. They haven't taken those poor bastards ashore yet, and we haven't seen any more guards going out to the *Goliath*. I think this won't be too hard at all."

Hynson grunted. He felt sick to his stomach. The night had an unreal quality, as if he were watching someone else risking his neck to help strangers he didn't know just because they were stupid enough to get caught, and he was surprised to find that that someone was him. "Single her up, fore and aft," he growled, giving orders without thinking, "and get them gaskets off. There's breeze enough to get us over to the ship without the run of the tide."

Nicholson was smiling even broader now, enjoying the adventure. "I reckon you're right. I tell you, Joe, this is going to make our reputations. Best thing I ever did, looking you up in London. Hell, I'd never have the courage to try this if you weren't here."

"Good, good, now shut up, would you, so we can get this fucking tub under way?" All the chatter was making Hynson even more nauseous. The hired men had singled up the head and stern fasts, and on Hynson's command they cast them off completely. The cutter drifted away from the quay, a foot, two feet, enough, finally, that Hynson could no longer leap ashore if he so chose. He was committed.

He clenched his teeth and said, "Get that goddamned jib

set. We'll just hold that for now." Then he turned to Sam and said, "That all right, Sam?" They had never officially determined who was in charge.

"That's great, Joe," Nicholson said, and then in a louder voice addressed the sailors. "Now see here, you men. We're bound for France, as you know, but we've a bit of business to do with the mate of that ship over there."

"What, the *Goliath?*" one of the men asked.

"Yes, the *Goliath*. We'll raft alongside for a moment while Joe and I go aboard, and then we're under way. We've worked everything out, you see, so even if things seem a bit . . . ah . . . well, out of the ordinary, don't pay any mind because . . . ah . . . we've worked everything out."

Oh, that was a bloody confidence-inspiring speech, Hynson thought.

The hired men shot dubious glances at one another. "Ain't nothing against the law, is it, Cap'n?" asked the one who had cock-billed the anchor.

"No, no, nothing like that. Course not."

"Humph," was all the reply they got from the sailors as they turned back to their work. Hynson imagined that their chief concern was not the legality of the enterprise but the likelihood of getting caught. This was confirmed a moment later when the same man turned back to them and said, "Didn't say nothing about this when we hired on. We wants double our wages or we take her back to the quay, right now."

"Now see here—" Nicholson began, but Hynson cut him off.

"Very well. And a bonus on top of it when we get to France."

"Right, then," said the sailor, smiling as he turned back to his work. Hynson knew there was no point in arguing with these men. He knew how their minds worked.

With the jib set and drawing in the light offshore breeze, the cutter began to make headway, leaving a small, rippling wake astern. Making no more than a couple of knots through the still water, she pushed down the river, the Avon River, the current stopped by the pressure of the ocean's tide pushing inland.

The lights from the buildings that crowded up to the waterfront cast their shimmering, undulating reflections across the water, and Hynson forgot about those people moving onshore and looked instead for any moving on the water. There was one boat that he could see, far off, pulling slowly toward some unknown destination. A few people moving with a lantern on the deck of a merchantman upriver. And the *Goliath*, silent, seemingly deserted, a single lantern hanging from her mainstay above the waist.

Hynson swallowed hard, wiped his sweating palm on his coat. "Right, here we go," he muttered. He pushed the tiller over and pointed the short bowsprit at the pilot ladder that still hung down the *Goliath*'s side.

Biddlecomb was embarrassed to realize that he had fallen asleep, and further embarrassed to realize that everyone in both boats probably knew it but were not saying anything. The sound of the bells had brought him fully awake, though utterly confused, and he said, "Oh. Oh," in a low, startled voice until it came to him where he was.

He was in the stern sheets of the *Swallow*'s longboat, in a dark part of the Avon River just below the town of Bristol. The boat was held in place against the current by a grapple over the bow, and the sailors and marines crowded on the thwarts were resting as best they could, leaning in various attitudes of relaxation.

Ten feet away, the *Swallow*'s pinnace was also tugging at a line made fast to a grapple. In the moonlight Biddlecomb could see the ghostly forms of white faces over dark jackets—blue for the sailors, and the marines' bottle green.

He had allowed the marines to wear their beloved regimentals, and he himself was wearing the blue coat with red lapels, the red waistcoat, and blue breeches. They weren't trying to fool anyone that night, it was strike fast and go, and either they succeeded or they did not.

As the last of the bells died away, their significance dawned on him. They were chiming out the time. He pulled his watch from his waistcoat and angled it toward the moon. Three minutes past nine. Either the bells were late or his watch was fast. He suspected the latter.

"Mr. Faircloth?" he said in a loud whisper.

"Aye?" came Faircloth's voice from the pinnace.

"We'll get under way now, it's slack water, and approach slowly. I'll go in under *Goliath*'s bow, you under the stern. As quietly as we can. No noise unless they raise the alarm, and then yell like the damned. Understood?"

"Aye, sir." They had been over it many times already, he and Faircloth and the sailors and the marines in the boarding parties, but Biddlecomb wanted to go over it one last time, for the benefit of those members who were not so bright.

Up in the bow the sailors hauled in the dripping anchor line. "Give way, all," Biddlecomb said as he felt the grapple break from the muddy bottom, felt the boat begin to drift. The two banks of oars came down together, pulled, lifted, pulled again, and the longboat gathered headway, moving toward the town of Bristol, silent save for the muffled creak and the drip of the blades in the water. To larboard and a little abaft their beam the pinnace kept pace.

It was a quiet night, the river calm at slack water. Half a dozen merchant ships were at anchor beyond the town, but no one took any notice of their approach.

Biddlecomb was afraid for a moment that he would not be able to identify the *Goliath* from a distance, and he did not care to go searching around through the anchorage, but even from a half a mile away he could see her. He recognized her from the morning before. The absence of her topsail yard made her even more obvious.

He nudged the tiller over, swinging the longboat's bow toward the *Goliath*. He turned his head to see the pinnace following suit.

A boat was rowing slowly about, over half a mile away, only visible now and again as it passed through the illumination of one of the anchor lights. It might have been a guard boat, though Biddlecomb doubted it. There would be no need for a guard boat in a peaceful town such as Bristol, one that did not have a naval base.

There was a cutter as well that he could see, moving slowly under a single headsail, no doubt taking advantage of the ebb tide to drop downriver and into the channel. Just as he would be doing, with any luck, in twenty minutes time.

As they passed the closest of the anchored merchantmen, Biddlecomb ran his eyes over her. It would be such a simple thing to have her, just storm aboard, cut the cable, set topsails, and away you go. But tonight was not the night, and after tonight every seaport town in England would be on guard for Yankee pirates, sneaking in with muffled oars and cold steel.

The *Goliath* was less than a quarter mile away, and Biddlecomb could see no activity on her deck. A single lantern was hanging from her mainstay, casting a light that reached from the foredeck to near the quarterdeck, but he could see no one moving, no one alarmed by their approach.

He glanced over at the cutter. It was moving a bit faster now, her single headsail sheeted in. It seemed odd that they had not set the mainsail as well, but local watermen had their own way of doing things. She passed close to the *Goliath*, disappeared from sight behind the *Goliath*'s high sides. Her hull was lost from sight, but Biddlecomb could still mark her progress by watching her mast as it swept along.

And then suddenly it stopped and he could see the head of her jib flogging as the sheet was let go. The cutter had come alongside the *Goliath* and rafted up. Why would they do such a thing, and at that time of night?

"Oh, son of a bitch," he said, louder than he had intended. He swiveled around until he could see Faircloth in the pinnace. "Faircloth!" His voice seemed surprisingly loud after all the quiet. "Faircloth, I think they're taking the prisoners off her! See that cutter alongside? I think they're moving them! Let's go, double time! Let's go!"

Hynson had felt sick leaving the dock, felt himself calm a bit as the cutter approached the *Goliath*, and then all but puked when Pinkart stuck his head over the bulwark and called out, "Hey there, stand off! Who in hell are you?"

He looked wildly around, wondering if he should fall off and bypass the damned ship all together, head right for the middle of the river, but Nicholson stepped up next to him and unshuttered a lantern, allowing the light to fall on both of their faces. "It's us, sir!" he called out in his grating, cheery tone. "Mr. Nicholson and Mr. Hynson, from Lloyd's? We've finally managed those extra guards we promised!"

"Oh, good evening, sirs," Pinkart called back. "Thought you'd forgotten about us!"

"Oh, no, never. Just had the devil of a time getting things organized. Here, get those fenders over the side." The last he called out to the hired seamen who were standing amidships, looking vaguely amused.

A moment later the cutter came alongside the *Goliath*, the single headsail was cast off, and with a perfectly timed twist of the rudder Hynson brought the fenders lightly against the merchantman's side. The mooring lines were tossed up and with a "Haul!" and "Make fast!" the two vessels were bound together.

Nicholson turned toward Hynson, shielding him from Pinkart's view, and handed him a pistol, which Hynson took and tucked in his belt under his coat. He had another one in his coat pocket, as well as his sword. That would do for any minor skirmish, and he had no intention of becoming involved in anything more than that.

"Shall I go first?" Nicholson asked, as if they were entering some damned ballroom.

"Yes, go," Hynson growled. Nicholson grabbed on to the cleats and scampered up, Hynson following behind.

"We'll be back in a moment. Get ready to cast off them mooring lines and set that motherless mainsail, but fast," he said to the sailors as he headed up toward the *Goliath*'s deck. He stepped through the gangway. Sam and Pinkart were standing a few feet away, talking softly like old shipmates.

"And Mr. Hynson, welcome," Pinkart said. A look of anticipation was on his face, which soon turned to confusion when no more men appeared at the gangway. "Have you not brought more guards with you? I gave three more of my men leave to go ashore since you said you was bringing them, and I'm bloody shorthanded."

"Oh, well," Hynson began, then Nicholson turned toward Pinkart and in one elegant motion pulled his pistol, cocked it, and thrust it into the startled mate's stomach.

"Now see here, Mr. Pinkart," Sam Nicholson said in a low, frightening growl, "we've no desire to hurt you, but you make one sound or one move and I'll blow your guts all over that capstan, is that clear?"

Pinkart looked down at the pistol, eyes wide, and then up at Sam Nicholson. He nodded his head.

"Should we tie him up, Joe?" Nicholson asked, and Hynson, who had not had a coherent thought since stepping aboard, just nodded. After a pause Nicholson added, "Could you find something to tie him with?"

Hynson nodded again and pulled his folding knife from his pocket. He cut off a fathom of the flag halyard, then another, and a moment later they had Pinkart well secured, lashed hand and foot and lying on the deck.

"So far, so good," Nicholson said. "Shall I go below and free them or stay topside as lookout?"

Hynson looked around. Nothing could be seen beyond the circle of light cast off from the lantern, but suddenly he felt vulnerable, exposed, there on the open deck. He could not see anything out in the dark, but he knew that something was there, something menacing. He thought he would scream if he stood there in the open for a second more.

"I'll go below," he said. "I'll go let them bastards out, and then we get the hell off this goddamned ship."

"Are you quite certain . . . ," Nicholson said, but before he could finish Hynson was down the hatch and into the dark 'tween decks.

A bit of light from the lantern on the deck above was finding its way down the hatch and illuminating the first few feet of that walkway between the stacks of casks. Then there was a long dark area, nothing but blackness, and at the end of that a dull light coming from the forecastle where the guard stood.

The guard! He had forgotten about the buggering guard! Here he had volunteered to go below, thinking only about getting off that exposed deck, and now *he* had to deal with the guard. He clenched his teeth and slowly pulled the pistol from his belt and the other from his pocket. He gripped them as best he could with his sweating palms, cocked them slowly, silently, and then took a tentative step toward the light at the end of the dark passage.

There was still the possibility of taking the ship by surprise, even with the appearance of the cutter. They were only thirty yards from the *Goliath*. Biddlecomb could hardly believe that they had come that close without being spotted, even with the oarsmen pulling for all they were worth, trying to get to the merchantman before Rumstick and the others were taken ashore.

He was certain that the boats would be seen, would be challenged, and that he and his men would have to attack up the sides of the ship in the face of determined defenders.

But now the boats were only twenty yards from the *Goliath* and there was no challenge, no surprised face appearing over the bulwark, nothing.

Biddlecomb turned the longboat toward the merchantman's bow as the pinnace swerved away, heading for the stern and the mizzen chains over which Faircloth would lead his men.

One last pull, toss oars, and glide under the figurehead. Silently over the bow and rush aft, cold steel against a surprised guard, and the ship was theirs. He leaned forward, ready to give the command in a whisper, when a shot rang out, a single shot, from somewhere below the *Goliath*'s deck, followed by running feet, a voice shouting, "Joe! Joe! Son of a bitch!"

It was over. The stealth was over and the fighting had begun. All that Biddlecomb could imagine was that Rumstick was leading some kind of resistance, and that meant it was time for them to move.

"Toss oars, hook on there!" he shouted, all thought of silence gone. "Faircloth, go, go! Right at 'em!"

The *Goliath*'s bow loomed over them, the curved headrails terminating in the bust of that giant Philistine warrior. Biddlecomb jumped to his feet, jammed his pistol more securely in his belt, and pushed his sword aside. He put a foot on the tack boomkin shroud, another on the anchor cable, grabbed on to the jibboom guy with one hand and the headrail with the other, and pulled himself up.

With a grunt and a heave he was over the rail and on the *Goliath*'s beakhead, with more men following after him. He clambered up onto the bowsprit, then ran down through the knightheads and onto the merchantman's foredeck. He drew his sword and pistol as he ran, leading the attack, against what he did not know.

"Oh, God damn it!" Hynson said, the smoking pistol still pointed at the overhead. He had not intended to fire the gun, but he had tripped as he burst into the forecastle and it had gone off accidentally, terribly loud in that confined space.

In the dim light he could see the guard, wide-eyed, his hands held up, his own pistol lying on the deck at his feet.

Shit, he's more scared than I am, Hynson thought. From the bunks lining the forecastle he could see faces peering out, three, four men, jerked from their sleep.

"Joe? Joe?" he heard Nicholson's voice calling down.

"It's all right!" he shouted back, and then with a stroke of inspiration added, "Keep the lads on deck and tell them not to shoot. The men below as well!"

He turned to the guard. "Back up, over there." He waved his one still loaded pistol at him and the guard slowly backed away. "All of you, out of them bunks! Out! Now!"

The occupants of the bunks rolled out, standing on the deck in their underclothes, hands in front of them. They looked so ridiculous that Hynson smiled as he gestured with the pistol for them to back off.

This is going well, he thought. *Shooting that pistol was actually a good move, gave me control of the situation. All right. All right.* He stepped over to the small hatch, never taking his eyes from the *Goliath*'s men, and reached down and lifted it. He glanced down into the forepeak and looked Rumstick full in the face.

"Hynson," said Rumstick, and his face broke into a smile. "You came after all."

"Course we came," Hynson said, and was about to add an unpleasant rebuke of Rumstick's lack of faith when the quiet was shattered by shouts, horrible inhuman screams from the deck above, and running feet from forward and aft. A pistol went off and then another, and Hynson was certain he heard Nicholson's voice scream above the others, but what Sam was saying he could not tell.

Not that it mattered. He knew the sound of an attack

when he heard it. "Damn it!" he wailed. "Damn it, damn it!" There was no time, no thought for anything but escape. He was vaguely aware of Rumstick trying to climb out of the forepeak when he slammed the hatch down again. He heard the soft thud of the grating hitting Rumstick on the head, the louder thud of Rumstick hitting the deck below, but by then he was out of the forecastle, running down the dark space between the barrels, screaming, screaming louder even than the men on the deck above.

He flung himself onto the ladder that led topside, a vague notion in his head that the shouting and the running and the gunfire had stopped, but he had no thought for that, only for the cutter and the dark water beyond, where he could lose himself.

He burst onto the deck. Men were everywhere, with weapons—guns, swords, cutlasses—and uniforms as well. The fucking British army. He raced past them, waiting for the sword thrust or the bullet that would cut him down. He saw confused looks as he hurdled past, thought he heard Nicholson call out, "Joe?" as he bolted for the gangway.

The cutter was ten feet from the *Goliath* and moving away. The hired men had cut the mooring lines and set sail, desperate to save their own skins.

"Wait! You cowards! You bloody, goddamned cowards!" Hynson screamed as he raced toward the break in the bulwark. He hit the space running and hurled himself into the air, leaping for the cutter's stern even as it drew away. Cutter, river, it didn't matter as long as he was off that damned ship.

His shoes hit the cutter's taffrail. He teetered, flailing his arms as if trying to fly, and one of the sailors grabbed him by the coat and pulled him into the boat.

He landed in a heap on the deck by the tiller. With a groan he rolled over and looked back at the *Goliath,* disappearing astern. A more beautiful sight he could not recall.

The sailor who had pulled him aboard was at the tiller. He looked down at him, took a long chew of his quid, and spit over the rail. "You can stick your bonus right up your arse, mate," he said. "This is gonna cost you, a lot more than a fucking bonus."

CHAPTER
18

Knaves & Nettles are akin;
Stroke 'em kindly, yet they'll sting.

—POOR RICHARD IMPROVED, 1748

"WHO WAS THAT?" BIDDLECOMB ASKED SAM NICHOLSON AS the two men stood staring at the place where Joe Hynson had leapt from the *Goliath*.

"That was Captain Hynson, my associate."

"Well, what's he about?"

"I have no idea."

As bizarre as that last incident had been, the big man bursting through the hatch and running screaming across the deck and hurling himself overboard, it was just one in a succession of such occurrences on a night that had grown progressively more bizarre.

Once aboard the *Goliath*, Biddlecomb had raced down the bowsprit and onto the foredeck, sword and pistol in hand, rushing into the face of what he expected to be a formidable enemy.

Toward the after end of the ship he could see Faircloth leading his men in an attack from the rear.

And caught between the two waves of boarders—twenty-five men armed and ready for a bloody fight—were just two men, one of whom was bound hand and foot and lying on the deck.

The man who was not tied up had fired one shot, hitting

207

nothing, and had been answered by three shots from the attackers, which also missed, before Biddlecomb ordered them to stop, realizing that the odds of their hitting one of the Charlemagnes were much better than of their hitting the single defender.

"Strike, strike, throw down your arms!" Biddlecomb had shouted, and the one man, confused and afraid, threw his empty pistol to the deck and held his hands over his head.

Biddlecomb put the point of his sword under the man's chin. "Are you it? Are you all the men defending this ship?"

"I am not defending the ship, sir." The man drew himself up and puffed out his chest, like someone trying to put on a good show before a firing squad. "I have captured this vessel. Or had, anyway. I am Samuel Nicholson, of the United States Navy."

"United States Navy?"

"Yes, sir." The man looked Biddlecomb up and down, and his eyebrows came together. The man turned and looked at Faircloth and the other marines, and then, to Biddlecomb's annoyance, he lowered his hands. "You're . . . are you . . . Americans?"

"Yes. Now tell me—"

It was then that the quiet that had returned to the *Goliath* was split by Joe Hynson's scream, and the already confused men on the deck stood and watched, now completely bewildered, as Hynson ran past them and leapt overboard.

"Well, never mind him, we're here for Rumstick and the others," Biddlecomb said. He was about to issue orders for the marines to begin a sweep of the ship when Rumstick appeared through the hatch, his head poking above the deck as he looked tentatively around. His eyes met Biddlecomb's and they stared at one another for a moment before they both broke into foolish grins.

"Ezra, for the love of God!" Biddlecomb stepped over to the hatch, arms wide as Rumstick climbed up on deck. They embraced as if they had not seen one another for a decade, as if they had had no hope of ever seeing one another again, which in their darker moments was true.

"Isaac, what in all hell are you thinking? You put all these men at risk to rescue the likes of us?" Rumstick said, but he was smiling as wide as he could, and Biddlecomb did not believe that Ezra had any genuine objections to the rescue.

Next through the hatch came Gerrish, and behind him came the rest of the prize crew, their faces screwed into expressions that were equal parts joy and confusion.

"Aren't there any guards?" Biddlecomb asked. "There must be more men?"

"They're all cowering in the hold, ran like rabbits once they heard you storming the ship," Rumstick explained. He turned to Nicholson. "Sam, ain't it? Sam Nicholson? Why didn't you tell me this was part of Isaac's plan?"

Nicholson began a stammering explanation but Biddlecomb cut him off. "You're hurt, Ezra!" A nasty cut was on Rumstick's head and his hair and face were streaked with blood.

"Oh, that's from the hatch. In fact, where is that—"

"Sir," Gerrish said, "I don't want to impinge on this joyous occasion, but it might be best if we was to get going. Before someone comes off from the shore or the crew of this ship decides to put up some resistance?"

"Quite right," said Biddlecomb. He turned to issue orders to the boat crews to bring the boats around to the pilot ladder when a voice called out from somewhere in the night, somewhere across the water.

"You there, heave to!" the voice commanded, loud, expecting to be obeyed. Then, a half a minute later: "Heave to, I say, damn you!"

Everyone on the *Goliath*'s deck froze and stared out in the direction from which the voice had come, but they could see little beyond the glow of the lantern. Rumstick reached up and pulled the offending light down and blew out the candle. The dark wrapped around them and made them feel less vulnerable. They could make out some vague image of boats moving through the night, the cutter drawing away.

And then the voice yelled out, "Fire!" and a swivel gun blasted a load of case shot into the night. In the flash of its muzzle they could see the thirty-foot guard boat, filled with men, on which the gun was mounted, as well as the cutter at which it was aimed.

"Son of a bitch!" one of Faircloth's marines shouted in surprise, and another man dropped a cutlass clattering to the deck.

"You boat crews, get those boats around to the side, quick as you can!" Biddlecomb called. The men scrambled fore and aft, going over the sides and down into the boats below.

"Hurry, hurry!" Biddlecomb shouted by way of encouragement. "Let's get out of here. I don't think we're a secret any longer."

"It *was* a guard boat! Damn! Damn!" Joe Hynson screamed, at no one in particular. He felt the blast of the case shot hit the cutter's transom, the hundred or more musket balls that had been packed into the canister smashing into the wood. But he was still lying on the deck where he had fallen, and the low bulwark protected him from the blast.

"Don't you think of heaving to, you whore's son," he growled at the helmsman, but despite the threat he felt the cutter swinging up into the wind. He rolled over, keeping low, and looked up to see what the helmsman was doing.

He was not doing much, as it happened. He had taken the full brunt of the case shot in the back, and the impact had flung him forward onto the cabin top where he was lying, his limbs twisted at odd angles, blood running down the varnished cabin and pooling on the deck. A surprising amount of blood.

"Oh, bloody hell, bloody hell," Hynson groaned as he grabbed the tiller and pulled it amidships, keeping low and turning the cutter downwind again. He could hear the sound of the guard boat approaching, the sound of the oars in the tholes, the rapid creak and drip of oars being worked at double time.

He wanted to peek over the bulwark to see if they were almost on him, but he was certain that they were about to fire that murderous swivel gun again. In his mind he could see himself catching the blast of case shot right square in the face, and the image made him shudder.

"All right, all right, all right, all right," he panted as he held the tiller amidships and peeked forward, trying to see the river past the bowsprit. He couldn't very well get lost—that was the beauty of a river—and as long as he could outrun the guard boat to the channel, he would be all right.

He felt the cutter heel, just a bit, and surge forward as it caught a cat's-paw of wind. He heard the bubbling of water down the length of the hull and the sound of the pursuing oars falling behind. Given even five knots of breeze, the guard boat would never catch him.

The puff of wind that had surged the cutter ahead did not die, as Hynson had feared it would, but continued steady, and the sound of the water alongside became a prolonged and steady note.

"Oh, thank you, thank you," he said with no thought as to whom he was addressing. He glanced up at the dead sailor growing stiff on the cabin top. "Cost me, will it, you dead son of a whore?" he said, and all but laughed.

"He's drawing the guard boat away," Sam Nicholson said softly, awe in his voice. "Do y'see? He's using the cutter as a decoy, drawing the guard boat away to give us the time to escape!"

"Humph," was all Rumstick could say as he held the longboat's painter, keeping the boat steady while the sailors, marines, and freed prisoners climbed down the *Goliath*'s side.

"It's the only thing that makes sense," Nicholson persisted. "Hynson ain't mad, so why else would he act that way?"

"Humph," Rumstick said again, and said nothing else.

"Well, it's working," Biddlecomb said, looking around the deck for any stragglers. "Whether he's intending to do that or not, it's working."

The guard boat had followed the cutter into the dark, until it was lost from sight from the *Goliath's* deck. Apparently the officer in the guard boat, who could not see the *Charlemagne's* boats hidden behind the *Goliath*, had thought the cutter was the enemy to pursue, and pursue it he had.

"Shall we go?" Biddlecomb said, gesturing to the boats below. "Lieutenant Rumstick, would you take command of the pinnace? Mr. Gerrish, come along. Your yachting holiday is over, sir, it's time to return to work."

The guard boat fired again, spraying the after end of the cutter with lead balls, but Hynson was feeling so confident by then, with the steady breeze and the tide that was starting to ebb, that he just laughed and flung profanity into his wake.

Even as the echo of the swivel gun was still bouncing around the brick buildings of Bristol's waterfront, Hynson raised his head and looked aft. The gun having just discharged, he knew that there would be a minute at least before they could do it again, so this was his chance to reconnoiter.

What he saw pleased him, pleased him more than anything he could recall. The guard boat was all but lost in the darkness, so much had the cutter gained on it in the steady breeze. Even as he watched, the boat spun around, giving up the chase, and headed back toward the distant town.

This was working out nicely. If that damned Lieutenant Colonel Smith got hold of him, he could say he had nothing to do with the rescue. It was all Sam Nicholson's doing, which was why he had abandoned Nicholson aboard the

Goliath. If the Americans got hold of him, he could claim he was just trying to draw the guard boat away from the *Goliath* and did just that too. Hynson smiled, a wide smile of relief.

And then he thought of Sam Nicholson. A prisoner of the British.

"Damn it all," he muttered, still on his knees, still looking aft at the retreating guard boat. What could he do? He had had a brief glimpse of the enemy as he raced down the *Goliath*'s deck, desperate to get off before he was taken. From what he had seen of the boarders, they were numerous and well armed.

"I can't fight 'em all," he muttered to himself, "not with this lot," he added, referring to the two hired sailors he had left, who were, as far as he knew, huddled up in the bow as far from the guard boat as they could get. "Bloody cowards, they'd never join in a fight," he assured himself, then a little louder said, "Sorry, Sam, but there isn't a damned thing I can do for you."

As it was, he had his hands full. He had to get the cutter downriver to the channel and then get it to France. Just getting to the channel would be tricky. The alarm was out, and there could be more guard boats. Navigation would be no simple matter.

"Hey, Captain!" one of the hired men called from forward.

"What?"

"I thinks . . . ," he began, and got no further before the cutter eased itself onto a mud bank and with just the slightest of shudders came to a dead stop.

Sometimes things work out, Biddlecomb thought. *There is no reason to think that they don't. Sometimes they do.*

A cable length astern of the longboat and the pinnace, the crowded longboat and pinnace, the *Goliath*'s crew were just starting to emerge from the hold and move tentatively along the deck. A lantern flared up, and then another. They could hear nothing.

"See there, sir," Faircloth said on Biddlecomb's other side. He nodded his head away from the *Goliath* toward the river's far bank.

With some difficulty Biddlecomb twisted around and looked in the direction that the marine lieutenant was indicating. It was the guard boat, just visible in the dark, pulling hard for the *Goliath*. Whether they saw the Americans or not he could not tell, but even if they did, they were paying them no mind.

The two boats pulled on down the river, which grew darker as they left the town astern. The tide had turned and Biddlecomb could feel the current in the play of the tiller, could feel how the water was sweeping the boat along.

That was good.

It was carrying them toward the channel, toward where the *Swallow* lay at anchor at Avonmouth, toward where the *Charlemagne*—under the command of able-bodied seaman Ferguson, the most qualified man left aboard—was beating back and forth at the mouth of the Bristol Channel, awaiting the return of her men. All they had to do now was get downriver without running aground. He could not envision any threat beyond that.

And then a gun fired, no more than fifty feet ahead. Biddlecomb heard the frightening buzz of a musket ball passing close by his ear.

"Good Lord!" he shouted in surprise. "Back water! Back water, all!"

From out of the dark came a voice, the voice of the shooter, Biddlecomb imagined, high-pitched and tight. "Stand off, you! Stand off or by God I'll fire into you, by God but I will!"

Then it was quiet again, unnaturally so, as both sides listened and wondered what to do next. And then Sam

Nicholson called out hesitatingly, "Joe? Joe Hynson, is that you?"

Quiet again, and then: "Sam Nicholson? That you in that boat?"

"Yes, it is. I got the prisoners with me."

In the dark they heard Joe Hynson clear his throat and spit. When he spoke again, his voice was half an octave deeper.

"Well, it's about damned time you got here! How long did you think I could fight off that guard boat, all by myself?"

CHAPTER
19

The first Mistake in publick Business,
is the going into it.

— POOR RICHARD IMPROVED, 1758

To His Excellency the Comte de Vergennes
Minister of Foreign Affairs to His Most Christian Majesty
Louis XVI
Versailles

Monsieur,

I pray Your Excellency will indulge me and give me leave
to remind you of several of the points made in your last
missive to me. At that time I was assured of the Ministry's
complete ignorance regarding the Harboring of English vessels, illegally taken by the Rebels, in French Ports. I was
given as well the Ministry's assurance that they would investigate any rumors of said vessels being condemned and
sold as prizes.

I was further assured that the Rebel privateer *Charlemagne,*
under the command of one Isaac Biddlecomb, was allowed
to stay in Nantes due only to her need of repair, which
rendered her unable to keep the sea.

Sir, I do not know what your investigation has revealed,
but I have of late received word from an unimpeachable
Source that the two prizes taken by the Rebels, far from
being returned to their rightful owners, were sold as Prizes

and have effectively disappeared from consideration. What is more, the privateer *Charlemagne*, after receiving substantial repairs in Nantes, has been despatched on a cruise of Great Britain's Sovereign waters, and has already taken a significant number of prizes which have been sent, with all local contrivance, into various ports in France!

However desirous His Majesty King George may be to maintain the present Peace, He cannot from His Respect to His own Honor, and His Regard to the Interest of his Trading subjects submit to such strong and public instances of support and protection shewn to the Rebels by a Nation that at the same time professes in the strongest terms its Desire to maintain the present Harmony subsisting between the two Crowns. The shelter given to the armed vessels of the Rebels, the facility that they have of disposing of their prizes by the connivance of government, and the conveniences allowed them to refit are such irrefragable proofs of support, that scarcely more could be done if there was an avowed Alliance betwixt France and them, and that we were in a state of War with your kingdom.

The Views of the Rebels are evident: they know that the Honor of this Country and the proper Feelings of the People in general will not submit to such open violation of solemn Treaties and established Laws acknowledged by all Nations. The necessary Consequence must be war, which is the object they have in view and they are not delicate in the choice of means that might bring about an end so much desired by them.

I beg your Excellency will not allow the artful and illegal manipulations of Dr. Franklin and his fellow Rebels to bring our Great Nations into a Conflict which we must regret.

Your Obedient, Humble Servant,
David Murray, Seventh Viscount Stormont
Ambassador of Great Britain to the Court of France

James L. Nelson

To Messrs. Franklin, Deane, and Lee
American Commissioners to France

Sirs:

Yesterday I had the honor of receiving a note from His Excellency, Viscount Stormont, protesting in no uncertain language the alleged Condemnation and Sale in French Ports, most specifically Nantes, of prizes taken by the privateer *Charlemagne*. What is more, Lord Stormont alleges that the said *Charlemagne* is currently cruising in England and sending further Prizes into Convenient Harbors on the French Coast.

You are too well informed, gentlemen, and too penetrating not to see how this conduct affects the dignity of the King, my Master, at the same time it offends the neutrality which His Majesty professes. I expect, therefore, from your equity, that you will be the first to condemn a conduct so opposite to the duties of hospitality and decency. The King cannot dissemble it, and it is by his express order, gentlemen, that I acquaint you, that orders have been sent to the ports where it is likely the said privateer will seek refuge that all persons involved in any affront to His Majesty's professed neutrality should be sequestered and detained until sufficient security can be obtained that they will return directly to their country, and not expose themselves, by new acts of hostility, to the necessity of seeking an asylum in our ports.

What I have the honor to inform you, gentlemen, of the King's disposition, by no means changes the assurances which I have been authorized to make you, at the time of your arrival, and which I again renew, for the security of your residence, or for the continued felicity and respect that our King and nation have for all the people of America and your noble struggle.

I remain your Obedient and Humble Servant,
Comte de Vergennes

218

Memorandum for the Comte de Vergennes
Minister of Foreign Affairs to His Most Christian Majesty
Louis XVI
From the American Commissioners

Your Excellency,

We have ordered no prizes into the ports of France, nor
do we know of any that have entered, for any other purpose than to provide themselves with necessaries until
they could sail for America, or some Port in Europe, for
a Market. We were informed this was not inconsistent
with the Treaty between France and Great Britain, and
that it would not be disagreeable to this Court; and further
than this we have not thought of proceeding. The *Charlemagne* has orders to cruise in the open Sea, and by no
means near the Coast of France, and tho' we are well
assured that a number of British Men of War are at this
instant cruising near the Coast of France for intercepting
the Commerce of America, yet it *Charlemagne* has taken a
station offensive to the Commerce of France, it is without
our Orders or Knowledge, and we shall advise the Captain of his Error. Though we learn his Cruise has been on
the Coast of Spain and Portugal, and the vessels he has
taken, one charged with Cod fish, one with Flour, demonstrate that the Cruise has not been on the Coast of France,
nor detrimental to its Commerce.

Your Excellency, it is by no account our Desire or Intention to provoke your great nation into a conflict which
you have by treaty sought to avoid. We wish only for
the Customary Considerations extended by international
protocol to all nations in conflict by other nations which
choose to take a stance of neutrality in that conflict. We
will do nothing ourselves to jeopardize that neutrality,
nor suffer anything to be done by those over whom we
have Authority, to the extent that we are able, to likewise

jeopardize that neutrality, allowing of course for the difficulty in communicating with our Naval Officers while they are absent from Port.

We Remain your Humble and Obedient Servants,
S. Deane
B. Franklin

CHAPTER
20

Avarice and happiness never saw each other,
How then should they become acquainted?

—Poor Richard's Almanack, 1734

"Good morning, Commodore Biddlecomb."

Mr. Midshipman Gerrish, returned to duty aboard the *Charlemagne*, saluted and stepped aside as Biddlecomb made his way, stiffly, up the quarterdeck ladder and aft.

Biddlecomb chose for the moment to ignore Gerrish's joke, to ignore Gerrish, for that matter, as well as every other person aboard the brig. Such was his prerogative as captain.

Instead he breathed deep in the morning wind, ten knots of it out of the southwest with just a hint of spring's warmth and a promise to build over the next day or so. The skies overhead were a fine, clear blue, dotted with clouds, the sea rolling along in a great blue disk from horizon to horizon.

Nothing but sea, no land at all, which was much to his liking. Land's End, the southwestern tip of England, was somewhere far over the larboard quarter, a hundred leagues or more. That was good. He had seen enough of England for a while.

The *Charlemagne* was on a course to weather Ushant. Once safely around that island they would haul their wind and stand into the Bay of Biscay and make for L'Orient or Nantes, the port from which they had sailed.

He turned his eyes inboard and aloft. They were close

hauled with all plain sail set up to the topgallants, as well as all of her fore-and-aft canvas: jibs, staysails, and mainsail. The brilliant morning sun seemed to illuminate all the imperfections in her top-hamper, the tar stains on the sails, the patches and new panels made of clean white canvas against the older gray cloth, the great smudges down the center of each sail where the canvas had rubbed against the slush on the masts.

But for all that she was beautiful, all tautness and symmetry and perfection. The windward rigging was a series of quivering, tight, straight lines running up and up the masts in fine geometric relation, while the leeward rigging bowed away in gentle, organic curves, as if taking its ease, not having to bear the strain of wind in canvas, for that moment at least.

It was mathematics and art all at once.

Only a landsman could be distracted by or even notice the tar and the slush, those surface imperfections that had nothing to do with the real ship. Biddlecomb's eyes saw only the curve of the sails, the tension of the rigging, the trueness of the masts, and the bow of the yards. That part of the ship, the real part, was perfection.

And the captain looked upon the rig, Biddlecomb thought, *and he saw it was good*. He smiled to himself at the allusion. *Getting a bit full of ourselves, aren't we?* But the perfect morning and the loveliness of his own vessel had put him in a good mood, which was fortunate for the iconoclastic Mr. Gerrish.

"I thank you, Mr. Gerrish, for your kindness in promoting me," he said at last, taking his eyes from the top-hamper. "I was not aware that you had such authority."

"I thought it only proper, sir, given the squadron now under your command."

Gerrish's face was, as usual, all but devoid of expression, which made it difficult for one who did not understand him to know when he was joking. It drove Rumstick to distraction. But Biddlecomb had Gerrish figured out, and he liked him, though one had to be in the right mood for Gerrish's humor.

"It's a dubious squadron at best," Biddlecomb said. "I've three vessels under my command, and about enough men to man a bumboat, if the bumboat isn't too particular about evolutions."

The two men turned and looked at the other vessels in the ad hoc squadron. Two cable lengths astern was the *Swallow*, carrying sail nearly identical to the *Charlemagne*'s, though in better shape, thanks to the enormous resources of the British navy. Rumstick was in command of her, but from where they stood, they could see nothing of her deck beyond the great clouds of canvas that drove her in the *Charlemagne*'s wake.

"I think perhaps before we sell *Swallow* we shall swap sails with her," Biddlecomb said.

"I should think just a little recutting here and there and they will do admirably," Gerrish agreed.

Astern of *Swallow*, and having a harder time of it in the chop, was the cutter, under the seeming joint command of Hynson and Nicholson. They were sticking with the brigs more for their protection than anything else—they were not officially under Biddlecomb's authority—and sailing in convoy as they were was forcing the bigger vessels to slow down. Had it not been for the need to keep the cutter in their wake, *Charlemagne* and *Swallow* would have set studdingsails to that blessed breeze and quickly put another hundred leagues between themselves and Great Britain.

There had been little difficulty in getting the cutter off the mud bank. Biddlecomb had set the prize crew aboard her and ordered them to stand by the taffrail, and the weight had all but lifted the bow free. After that it was a simple matter for the boats to tow her off and lead her downriver, forging ahead to seek out the open channel. Hynson's two hired British seamen were set ashore in Avonmouth, along with the body of the third, and Biddlecomb had loaned the two Americans three of the Charlemagnes as crew to help get them to France.

He had little choice in the matter, as he saw his duty, but still it was a generosity he could ill afford. Both the *Charlemagne* and the *Swallow* were dangerously short of men. True, they both carried twice the number of men that Biddlecomb would have thought proper during his days as a merchant seaman, but he had learned since then how many were required to sail and fight a man-of-war, even a small one.

Not that he had any intention of fighting, even with three armed vessels at his disposal. They had had a hard month's cruise, ships and men, and now both were tired. Half his men were off in prizes, three were aboard the cutter, and the rest split between the two brigs.

No, it was France for them, a safe harbor, a well-supplied dockyard and a distribution of prize money.

"Sail ho! On deck there, sail ho!" the lookout sang out from high aloft.

Biddlecomb's and Gerrish's eyes met. "Indeed?" said Biddlecomb, and then turning his face to the crosstrees called out, "Where away? What d'ya make of her?"

There was a pause and then, "Fine on the weather bow! Ship-rigged, sir, standing northeast with the wind betwixt two sheets . . . just topsails and topgallants showing, but she looks like a big one!"

Biddlecomb stared silently at the horizon, fine on the weather bow. Of course he could not see the strange sail from deck, but it helped his concentration to stare off at the empty distance.

They were near the mouth of the English Channel, that doorway through which passed all of the shipping bound for the ports in southern England, including London, as well as all the ports on the east coast of Great Britain.

But that was not all. Every vessel bound away for northern France or the Netherlands or the Scandinavian countries or the Baltic Sea would have to pass that way. It was arguably the busiest spot of ocean in the world, which meant the strange sail could be anything. Absolutely anything.

Including, of course, a big British man-of-war. And that was what Biddlecomb had to assume it was. That was what he would assume, he knew, if he had any brains at all, if he had any ability to learn from his past mistakes. He would haul his wind immediately and make for Brest or St.-Malo or Cherbourg.

On the other hand, there was just as much chance that she was a British East Indiaman, homeward bound from India or the Orient with the Lord knows what kind of riches stuffed in her hold. A big fat, wallowing Indiaman that could probably be induced to strike just by the sight of three armed American vessels. There would be no way for a big Indiaman to know how many men were aboard those three vessels. He would have to assume they were fully manned. And then it was only a day and a half or so to France.

"God, I'm an idiot. God help me, I am such a fool," Biddlecomb muttered. He turned to Gerrish and the helmsman. "We'll maintain this heading. Draw a little closer, see what this fellow is."

An hour later the stranger's topgallant sails were visible from the quarterdeck, at first just flashing and then disappearing below the horizon as the *Charlemagne* rose and fell on the sea, and then remaining steady, as if they were a fixed mark, a buoy or a headland.

Then slowly the topsails made their appearance, grayish white against the blue sky. An hour after that the men on the *Charlemagne*'s deck had their first glimpse of her courses, and Biddlecomb knew that it was time for him to go aloft.

He slung the big signal telescope over his shoulder and clambered up into the main shrouds and made his way up that familiar route: main shrouds, futtock shrouds, maintop, and then up the narrowing topmast shrouds to the crosstrees at the doubling of topmast and topgallant.

He nodded a greeting to the lookout and then looked down to the deck below. From that perspective, looking down on the narrow hull from so high aloft, the vessel always seemed entirely too top-heavy, as if she should roll over at any moment. He looked aft, at the lovely sight of the *Swallow* bowling along in their wake. She was even more beautiful from that perspective. Even the little cutter looked good against the deep blue of the open ocean.

But he was procrastinating, and he knew it. He had gone aloft because he knew that he would now be able to see this stranger's hull from that height, and here he was looking at everything but that. Because he was afraid of what he would see.

He breathed deep and expelled the air in a sigh and then stuck the telescope between two shrouds, resting it on a ratline, and aimed at the not so distant ship. It appeared in the lens, a gray and blue smudge, and he twisted the glass until it came into focus.

He stared for half a minute. *Of course, of course,* he thought.

It was a man-of-war. Not only a man-of-war, but a big one, a two-decker, a seventy-four at least. When she and *Charlemagne* rose in unison, he could just make out the two rows of gunports down her side. In that respect he was fortunate—had there been just one row, he might still have believed her to be an Indiaman, heavily armed as they were. But no Indiaman had two gun decks.

He glanced up at the lightning rod, still as brilliantly polished as ever. "We could use some help now," he said to the thing as he grabbed on to the backstay and slid back to the quarterdeck.

As loath as he was to lose a second in what he knew would be a long and probably futile attempt to outrun the big ship, Biddlecomb ordered the foresail clewed up and allowed the *Swallow* to draw alongside. Rumstick was standing on the prize's quarterdeck.

"You've seen that strange sail?" Biddlecomb shouted across the twenty-foot gap between the vessels.

"Aye!"

"She's a British man-of-war. Two-decker!"

"Aye!" Rumstick shouted back. He did not sound surprised.

"We'll have to split up! You run away southeast, make for L'Orient or Nantes! Should be near enough in a day to pick up a pilot! I'll make easting and hope he comes after me! Tell Hynson and Nicholson they can do whatever the hell they want, but I would suggest running off north by east!"

"Aye, sir! Godspeed!" Rumstick called, and then as the *Charlemagne* set her foresail once again, the *Swallow* clewed hers up to speak to the cutter.

"Fall off," Biddlecomb ordered the helmsman. The bow of the *Charlemagne* turned away, turned toward France, and kept turning until the man-of-war was right astern of them and they were sailing as directly away from her as possible.

"Mr. Gerrish, French colors, if you please. Then get the carpenter's mate and as many hands as you need and see about rigging up a stern chaser. You can run it out the great cabin, I reckon that would be most convenient. I want it ready to fire in fifteen minutes."

It was a tall order and Biddlecomb could see some pithy remark coming to life in Gerrish's head. The midshipman opened his mouth, noticed Biddlecomb's expression, closed it again, and then said, "Aye, aye, sir!" and raced forward.

"Smart man," Biddlecomb said.

It took only thirteen minutes to get the gun aft, rig it, and ready it for firing, a neat piece of work. Biddlecomb ordered studdingsails set, then ducked below, into his great cabin, which was now quite crowded with gun and crew, busily loading the weapon. He looked past the black barrel at the man-of-war astern.

She had set studdingsails aloft and alow, making her seem

half again as big as she was, and she was already big enough. The French colors apparently were not fooling her, not when the little squadron split up and began to run. Too suspicious looking by half. But Biddlecomb could not let the seventy-four get within cannon shot, not if he could help it.

But he could only help it for so long. The man-of-war, with her long waterline and towering masts, would be considerably faster than the *Charlemagne* and the *Swallow*. The only advantage the smaller brigs had was their shallow draft, which did them no good on the open ocean.

He would not let Rumstick be captured again, not if he could do anything to prevent it. If they split up, the seventy-four could only capture one of them, and this time it would be the *Charlemagne*. It was the least he could do to atone for his consistent stupidity.

"Ready, sir." The gunner stepped back.

"Very good," Biddlecomb said, then bent over and peered through the shattered stern windows again. The seventy-four was almost hull up from that level. She was closing fast. He could see the *Swallow* to the southward, through the gaping hole that had once been the *Charlemagne*'s badge. She was already half a mile away and running like a rabbit for the coast of France.

"Godspeed," Biddlecomb muttered, and looked back at the seventy-four. If they fired, then the charade of being a French brig-of-war was over.

"Oh, to hell with it, they don't believe a bit of it anyway," he muttered, and then to the gunner said, "You may fire when you bear."

"Aye, sir . . ." The gunner regarded him as if he were a simpleton, worthy of pity. "Sir, you know the seventy-four's twice again as far as this gun will shoot?"

"I am aware of that. I want only to attract their attention."

The gunner nodded, sighted down the barrel, then stepped aside and put the match to the touchhole. The great gun went off with a terrific roar, much louder than on the open deck, and leapt back against its breechings, which thankfully held, as did the hastily sunk eyebolts in the transom.

"That should convince them to ignore the *Swallow* and the cutter, I imagine," Biddlecomb observed.

He indulged himself in another half minute of staring at the seventy-four, then straightened and said to the gunner, "Pray, continue firing. Another five rounds should do it, then secure the gun."

He turned to Gerrish. "Get some hands together and start the fresh water and pump it overboard, then let's jettison all the food, save for three days' rations. Carpenter's stores can go by the board, as well as those two spare six-pounders in the hold."

"Aye, sir," said Gerrish. He hurried forward to organize the Charlemagnes while Biddlecomb returned to the quarterdeck.

No sooner had he stepped aft than the stern chaser went off beneath his feet. He could not resist turning and watching for the fall of the shot, but he could see nothing and he doubted they had hit. As close as the man-of-war seemed, it was still extreme range for the long six-pounder.

A few minutes, and Biddlecomb heard the first tentative clanking of the bilge pump. The noise grew steadier, less chaotic, as the man working the brakes got into the rhythm of the thing, and seconds later the first gush of fresh water burst from the spout of the pump and ran in a small river down the deck and out the scuppers. It had been quite pure, by shipboard standards, having only been in the casks for a month or so, but now it was filthy and brown after cycling through the bilges.

Up from the main hatch, which a second work party had broken open, and dangling from slings on the stay tackle, came a cask of fresh water, followed by another. They were set down and lashed to the foremast fife rail and their heads broken open.

229

"Unlimited fresh water, until it's gone," Biddlecomb announced to the men in the waist, and more than a few stuck their cups in the barrels and gulped greedily. That was a rare treat. There was nothing, save for rum, that was as tightly rationed as fresh water.

Once the seventy-four was within close pistol range, Isaac figured he would serve out the rum the same way.

When the men had quenched their omnipresent thirst, they turned back to the stay tackle, and soon barrels of beef and pork and dried peas were coming up and over the side.

The stern chaser went off again, and again Biddlecomb turned to see the fall of the shot, but could not. He wondered if the British would start their fresh water as well, or jettison supplies. If they were out for a long patrol, then they could not afford to do so. And the unhappy truth of the matter was they did not have to, not to catch the *Charlemagne*.

The morning turned at last to afternoon, with the ringing of eight bells and the taking of noon sights and the men sent below for their dinner. Indeed, there was no break in the routine, save for the specter of the great ship off in their wake.

The hard work that had gone into making the *Charlemagne* faster had lifted the men's spirits. Biddlecomb was pleased to hear the buzz of conversation, even the occasional laugh, as the men went about their business. As long as the men had hope, they would work hard and take orders, and as long as they did that, Biddlecomb knew, then there was reason for hope.

Swallow and the cutter were safe, at least. They had both disappeared over the horizon an hour before, the *Swallow* to the south, bound for Nantes, most likely, and the cutter sailing north, going God knows where. And the seventy-four had stayed steadfastly on the *Charlemagne*'s tail.

And now all the *Charlemagne* had to do was to close with the coast of France and they would be safe. This man-of-war would not dare chase them far into French waters; that would be an act of war, a violation of French sovereignty, a political faux pas that no senior captain would risk. Or so Biddlecomb hoped.

The noon sight put them no more than one hundred miles from Cape Finistère, which lay just a little south of due east. One hundred miles, less than twenty-four hours of sailing if the wind held, which it looked as if it would.

Biddlecomb turned again to look at the man-of-war. It was gaining on them, to be sure, but gaining slowly, ever so slowly, as they lightened the *Charlemagne* and carried all of the sail that they safely could, and then some. This chase would not be over soon.

He frowned and shook his head. *Here we go again*, he thought. *Here we bloody go again.*

CHAPTER
21

Christianity commands us to pass by injuries;
Policy, to let them pass by us.

—POOR RICHARD'S ALMANAC, 1741

BY THE END OF THE SECOND DOGWATCH THEY HAD THROWN OVER-
board just about everything that they could do without, including nearly all of the food and water, the spare spars
and lumber, the great-cabin furniture, and half of the powder and shot.

Anyone at all attuned to the brig's motion could tell that
lightening her thus had made her livelier underfoot, and she
was tearing through the water just about as fast as she
could. They were now lacking only sufficient wind for her
to reach the maximum speed she could physically attain,
around eleven knots.

The sun fell lower and lower in the west, illuminating the
seventy-four in their wake with an orange glow, making her
look for a time as if she were on fire, a happy thought but
too much to reasonably wish for. Biddlecomb could vaguely
recall a saying about lightning striking twice, and in this
case it would literally be true. But the saying had to do with
the unlikelihood of that event, and to that extent it was
applicable to their situation.

He took a deep breath, let it out, and looked around.
There was a surprising degree of normality aboard the *Charlemagne*. They had not cleared for action, not gone to quar-

ters—there was no need, since there was no possibility of fighting the big man-of-war—and so the men went about their routine, changing watches, having supper, sitting around the forecastle head yarning or doing their fancy ropework while the light held.

Only the constant noise of the pumps, working to keep every drop of water out of the bilges, signaled anything beyond the ordinary. The chase had gone on with little change for long enough that the men were bored with it. They acted as if they were unaware of the threat in their wake.

Biddlecomb, to his chagrin, did not have the luxury of ignoring the big ship astern. That was the price he paid for the many, many benefits of command. So he pulled his eyes from the men lounging about forward and looked again at the enemy behind.

She was about two and a half miles astern, perhaps a little more. Biddlecomb had to hold his hand up to shield the low-hanging sun from his eyes so that he could look at her. Her sails and high sides glowed orange with those last rays lighting her from behind, and he had to admit that she was a beautiful sight. He wondered if, somewhere on the acres of quarterdeck she sported, a British captain was looking at the little *Charlemagne* and thinking the same thing. Probably not.

She was gaining on them, of course, but even being as pessimistic as he could—a wise policy, he had long ago discovered—he had to admit that she was not overhauling them as quickly as he thought she would. The *Charlemagne* was absolutely flying through the water, and it was entirely possible that the seventy-four was not quite as fast as he had imagined she would be. Her bottom could be quite foul. He nodded his head slowly. Perhaps, perhaps.

Perhaps they would raise the coast of France at first light. Perhaps the seventy-four would still be far enough astern that they could run into shallow water where the big ship would dare not follow, like a rabbit into a brier patch. Perhaps the captain of the British man-of-war would not wish to risk an international incident, the kind over which wars were begun, just to run down an impudent Yankee brig.

Perhaps.

Or perhaps not.

In any event, their best hope was to get into French waters, and since they were already on the most direct course for France, there was nothing to do but to keep running and wait and see. It would do no good to alter course, not even after dark when the move would not be seen, since that would only delay their arrival in that neutral country.

"Mr. Gerrish," Biddlecomb said at last, "pray send someone down to the wreckage I call a great cabin and fetch up my hammock chair. I hope it was not thrown overboard."

"I believe it was spared, sir," Gerrish said, and a minute later a seaman appeared with the folding hammock chair, a clever contraption run up for Biddlecomb by the carpenter, and unfolded it on the quarterdeck. Just the sight of it made Biddlecomb realize how very, very tired he was. With a stifled moan he eased himself into the seat and stretched his weary legs, the first time he had been off his feet in ten hours.

"Sir, if you'd care to sleep, I could have some of the men rig your cot, or a hammock, if you wish," Gerrish volunteered. There was genuine concern in his voice, the most sincere note Biddlecomb had ever heard the midshipman utter.

"Thank you, Mr. Gerrish. Thank you, but no, I believe I'll keep the deck tonight."

That was just another item on the bill that every captain paid, the times when the men under him slept and woke, watch by watch, while he remained on deck throughout, ready to take command in an instant. Ready for the moment when things might happen too fast for a subordinate to come below and wake him.

Biddlecomb spent the night pacing the quarterdeck or reclined in his hammock chair, snatching sleep in ten- and fifteen-minute increments when things were quiet and a reliable man was on the quarterdeck.

But the moment did not come when he would have to snap awake or step into the breach of panic and chaos and take firm command. Indeed, the *Charlemagne's* routine seemed even more normal once the sun set, once the seventy-four disappeared from view and the stars appeared overhead, comforting in their familiarity.

The wind held steady and strong through the night, calling for no adjustments of the many sails flying aloft. The ship soon took on that odd quiet that a ship at sea has during the hours of dark, when the sound of the pump or someone speaking in a normal tone seems unnaturally loud. It was, in fact, a peaceful night, as peaceful as any that Biddlecomb had experienced at sea.

Six A.M., four bells in the morning watch, and the first gray light of dawn made a weak showing in the east.

"Sir," Gerrish said, "shall we clear for action?" That was their morning routine, as much as holystoning or eating breakfast.

"Of course." A useless gesture, but not doing so would give the men the impression that their cause was hopeless. It would break their routine, which was the backbone of discipline, and give them time to speculate about their pending capture. "But tell the cook to keep the galley fires burning." Hot food did much for discipline as well.

"Aye, sir." Gerrish stepped forward and gave the order, and half a minute, a quarter of a minute later, the peaceful ship was alive with the well-trained crew hustling to clear away and get to dawn quarters.

It took twenty-five minutes with the reduced company, and when at last they were done, standing at their stations, there was light enough for Biddlecomb to see clear to the bow.

And what he saw did not impress him: a fraction of the men he had started out with, who, no matter how well disciplined or ready to fight they were, were still too few in number even to take on a vessel equal in size to the *Charlemagne*.

He looked astern. It was still too dark to see more than a half cable or so, but at least he knew that the seventy-four was not as close as that. Another ten minutes and he would know just how close she was.

The sun grew nearer and nearer to the eastern edge of the world, and the black night resolved into blue-gray dawn, and the seventy-four slowly emerged from the gloom. She had studdingsails set aloft and alow, a bone in her teeth, exactly as she had been at sunset, only closer. Much closer. A half a mile astern, just a half a mile.

Biddlecomb pressed his lips together and stared at her, letting his disappointment run off. He had hoped that the captain of that big ship would not have had the nerve to stand on toward the coast in the dark with everything set. He had hoped the man would reduce sail so that if he did hit something, he would hit it more slowly.

But that was not the case. Apparently he would stop at nothing to capture this rebel who had fired at him. Biddlecomb wondered if that included causing an international crisis.

"Land, ho!"

The cry from aloft startled Biddlecomb from his reveries.

Land. Of course. That was what he had been hoping for. He turned and looked forward, and there, illuminated by the rising sun, long and low and black, was the coast of France, the nearest point not ten miles distant.

"That fellow was very foolish," Gerrish said, nodding toward the seventy-four, "standing on under full sail all night like that. Look how close he has come to piling up on the coast of France."

"Very foolish, indeed," Biddlecomb agreed. "Where does the navy get these people?"

The two men stood silent for a moment and stared at the big ship. It was a beautiful morning, with the sun revealing a light blue sky and a promise of warmth in the air. It should have been a joyous time. They were almost to France, where they had sent a number of rich prizes. He had made a successful cruise, losing precious few men for all he had accomplished. He had fought and taken a British naval vessel of superior strength.

He resented the son of a bitch astern who was ruining it all.

But that was absurd, of course, and he pushed those thoughts aside. "Mr. Gerrish, let us send the men to their breakfast. If they can all be fed and back at quarters in one glass, I should be delighted. And once breakfast is finished, have the gunner start in with the stern chaser again."

The men stood down to the watch on deck, while the watch below went below to eat. With *Charlemagne*'s full complement it would have been impossible to feed everyone in half an hour, but now it was easily done. By the time the last of the men had come up from below, and Biddlecomb had finished wolfing down his own breakfast, standing on the quarterdeck and setting the pewter plate on the binnacle box, they had nearly halved the distance between themselves and the shore.

Isaac had just put his spoon down and wiped his mouth with his napkin when the seventy-four fired her bow chaser, as if they had shown him the courtesy of waiting for him to finish eating before blowing him to hell. The ball plunged into the ocean wide of the mark and far astern.

The chaser was probably a twelve-pounder, or a long nine, and if so, they were firing at fairly long range. What was more, a bow chaser could not be brought to bear on a ship directly in line with the one firing. It was one of the first lessons Biddlecomb had learned in the art of naval warfare.

Gerrish, pudgy and red-faced, looking less like a naval officer than any other officer Biddlecomb had ever seen, stepped up onto the quarterdeck just as the *Charlemagne*'s stern chaser went off. It was extreme range and then some for the *Charlemagne*'s guns as well, but it did no harm to fire thus and even bolstered the men's spirits a bit, shooting back, particularly now that they were under fire themselves.

"You must know this coast well, sir," Gerrish commented, looking past the *Charlemagne*'s bow toward Cape Finistère, five miles away and fine on the starboard bow.

"Why do you say that?"

"Well, closing with it as you are, going for the shallow water with everything set. You must have confidence that there is enough water there to . . ." Gerrish began to falter. "You do, sir, do you not?"

"In point of fact I've never been here before. Don't even have a chart of this area."

"Well, sir, if I may be so bold . . . how do you intend to navigate close in?"

"I am not certain, Mr. Gerrish," Biddlecomb replied honestly. "I think we should send a hand aloft to polish that lightning rod, and perhaps something will come along."

And as it happened something did come along, half an hour later, just as the seventy-four was starting to find its range, dropping round shot close enough on occasion to splash the quarterdeck with the spout of water thrown up by the spent ball.

"On deck! Sail—" The lookout's "ho" was lost in the blast of their own stern chaser, but once the concussion had subsided, he continued, "Schooner, just coming around the headland, sir! Might see it from deck!"

"There, sir," Gerrish said as the two men crouched down and peered forward, under the foresail, "just below the starboard spritsail yardarm."

Biddlecomb saw it as well, a schooner, well clear of the land and standing toward them, close hauled, the gap between the two vessels closing fast. He put a glass to his eye and surveyed the little vessel for a moment.

"If I am not mistaken, this is a pilot boat," he said. "I think perhaps our polishing has paid off."

Gerrish looked at him with a puzzled expression, as if this time it was he who did not know if someone was joking. "Have we time to stop and pick up a pilot, sir?"

"No, but neither do we have any choice."

Ten minutes later, with the *Charlemagne* charging down on them, the schooner hove to and put a boat over the side. Biddlecomb sent all hands aloft to take in studdingsails, then to braces and bowlines and clew garnets. They had to have a pilot, which meant they had to heave to for him, but they did not have a spare second to waste. This would have to be the fastest heave to and go in the history of seafaring.

They swooped down abeam of the schooner, and Biddlecomb ordered the helm over and the main braces hauled, turning the brig up into the wind until the mainsails came aback. No sooner was the brig hove to then the schooner's boat was alongside. Biddlecomb leaned over the rail, expecting to see the pilot coming up the cleats, but to his annoyance he saw the man still in the stern sheets of the boat.

"*Bonjour, Capitaine,*" the pilot called with an insouciant wave of his hand, after the French fashion. "Do you have need of a pilot, *monsieur?*"

"*Bonjour,* yes, pray come aboard immediately."

The seventy-four fired again and scored their first hit, the ball smashing weakly into the taffrail and breaking off a piece of the cap before falling into the sea.

The pilot shrugged and held up his hands. "It is very dangerous, *Capitaine,* as you see. I do not think I can pilot you for my usual fee, *comprendez-vous?*"

"*Oui,* I *comprendez,*" *you coy, mercenary bastard,* Biddlecomb added silently. "Whatever you require, *monsieur*, just please come aboard."

"I think, perhaps, three thousand livres, *monsieur?*"

"Yes, yes, fine, now come aboard, please," Biddlecomb said, not really listening to the price to which he had agreed, but looking instead for the fall of the seventy-four's next shot. It missed, but not by much, the shot falling in line with the quarterdeck and fifteen feet off.

As soon as the pilot had two hands and one foot on the *Charlemagne*'s cleats, Biddlecomb ordered the helm over and the mainsails braced around.

The brig gathered way once again, but the sails, which had been trimmed to perfection, were now all askew, and all of the wonderful momentum that the ship had built was gone. It would take half an hour at least before the *Charlemagne* was back up to the speed she was making before.

Biddlecomb glared at the French pilot as he stepped gingerly aft. Quite a profusion of silver was on his clothing, buckles, and buttons, and he wore on his hip a delicate sword, and on his head a long, white, powdered wig. He looked for all the world as if he should be at court, and not on the quarterdeck of a brig-of-war, and the distaste with which he regarded his surroundings suggested that he felt the same way.

You better be worth it, you bastard, you better be worth the distance I lost and whatever the hell I agreed to pay you, Biddlecomb thought as he extended his hand and, smiling, said, "Welcome aboard, Monsieur Pilot. Welcome aboard the United States brig-of-war *Charlemagne*. I am Capt. Isaac Biddlecomb."

"*Enchanté, Monsieur Capitaine,*" said the pilot, sounding something less then *enchanted,* and giving Biddlecomb's hand a lifeless shake.

"As you can see, Monsieur Pilot, we are being pursued quite vigorously by yonder seventy-four."

The pilot glanced astern and then dismissed the big ship

with a wave of his hand. "Bah. Zat is the *Burford*, she is of no consequence. She will tack away soon, not enough water for her."

"Yes, I intended to go close inshore—"

"No, *Monsieur Capitaine*, we will bear up now, two points to larboard. Zere is not enough water for you, either."

Biddlecomb considered that for a moment. The last thing he wished to do was bear up to larboard, to turn away from the land, however slightly, and present the seventy-four, the *Burford*, apparently, with a bigger target.

But this was the kind of local knowledge for which he had risked so much in picking up the pilot to begin with.

"Helmsman, bear up, two points to larboard."

They were still making off the braces when the *Burford* fired again, reminding Biddlecomb of why he did not want to turn. It was not just the bow chaser this time, but the forwardmost guns as well, which would now bear on the *Charlemagne* since the two ships were no longer directly in line with one another. A heavy ball struck the brig's side, smashing in a plank and lodging there, while two more splashed nearby.

Gerrish leaned over the rail and looked down at the shot, then looked askance at the pilot. The pilot in turn gave the seventy-four another dismissive wave of the hand. "He will tack away, *monsieur*, do not fear. He is afraid of the shallow water. Besides, he is now violating French neutrality. There will be much trouble for him."

But if the *Burford*'s captain was in fact as afraid as the pilot suggested, then he was doing a fine job of covering it up. He altered course two points to larboard as well, paralleling the *Charlemagne*, which took him away from the treacherous shallows and made it easier for his forward guns to bear on the rebel.

They banged out again, three almost at once, and a hole appeared in the *Charlemagne*'s mainsail, directly over the helmsman's head. Gerrish ducked involuntarily at the sound of the round shot screaming by, then smiled sheepishly. The pilot, for his part, looked bored.

He's a cool one, Biddlecomb thought, trying not to think about how much of a mistake it might have been to alter course.

"Pilot, tell me, how much water is there, right up to the shore?"

"Not enough for you, *Capitaine.*"

Biddlecomb paused, breathed deep, let the annoyance pass. "And how much would that be?" he said at last when he felt he could safely speak.

The pilot shrugged, apparently a favorite gesture. "A fathom? Perhaps a bit more? But there are shoals as well."

Biddlecomb nodded, looking back at the *Burford.* They could not keep on the way they were. They were moving away from the safety of the land and closer to a place where the guns of the big ship would bear. He stepped up to the break of the quarterdeck.

"Hands to the braces, stations for wearing ship! Helmsman, bring her head around, starboard tack."

"*Capitaine,* what are you doing?" the pilot demanded, and was nearly trampled by a gang of men coming aft to haul the main boom from starboard to larboard.

The *Charlemagne* turned slowly, the yards bracing around, the jibboom finally pointing toward the green coast of France. The long boom and mainsail swung over the quarterdeck, the men struggling at the sheet to keep the huge sail under control as they eased it out over the larboard side.

"Mr. Gerrish, get a hand lead going, if you would." Biddlecomb turned to the livid Frenchman at his side. "Pilot, I can't keep running out to sea, it'll put us right under the *Burford's* guns. I have to try to scrape him off against the coast, *comprendez?* Here's your chance to do some real piloting."

"*Merde!* The bottom, it shoals like son of bitch! You have deep water, and then, nothing. A fathom, no more."

"Well, sir, we draw a fathom and a half, fully loaded, but we've lightened considerably. We just might make it."

The *Charlemagne* flew toward the shoreline, now less than a mile away, as if intent on killing herself.

"No bottom! No bottom, this line!" called the seaman heaving the lead from the mainchains as he hauled the lead line in for another cast.

"When the bottom comes, *Capitaine*, it will come fast," the pilot said.

"Then you tell us when to fall off, pilot," Biddlecomb instructed, "and we'll follow your sage advice." He turned his back to the Frenchman and looked at the seventy-four, now little more than two cable lengths astern. There had been little reason for hope before, now there was even less, with the big ship coming right up their wake.

Turning toward the shore had helped. It had forced the *Burford* to turn as well, to keep closing with the *Charlemagne*. But the captain of the big ship did not dare close as fast with the shore as Biddlecomb did. And now only his bow chaser would bear.

But that one gun was hitting more often than not. It banged out as Biddlecomb was watching, and the screaming round shot clipped the *Charlemagne*'s starboard main yard-arm, smashing the studdingsail boom and turning that beautiful sail into so much flogging canvas.

"Three fathoms! Three fathoms!" the leadsman sang out.

"You must fall off now, *Capitaine*. Now it begins to shoal," the pilot said.

"Are you quite certain?" Biddlecomb asked, stalling, suspecting that the pilot was being a bit too cautious.

"*Oui*, you must fall off. Turn to leeward, *maintenant!*"

"But I would like to close more with the shoreline, if at all possible."

The pilot stamped his finely shod foot on the deck. "*Merde alors!* Turn ze goddamned *bateau!*"

"Two fathoms! Two fathoms and shoaling!"

"Very well. Helmsman, fall off, two points. Hands to braces! Mind the men aloft!" A party of men were already swarming over the main yardarm, straightening away the damage as best they could. The loss of that studdingsail would not help in this race.

As much as he tried, Biddlecomb could not resist turning and looking once more at the *Burford*. "Son of a bitch," he muttered.

That captain, whoever he was, was absolutely composed of nerve. He was standing on as if he were in the middle of the ocean, even though his ship had to draw three and a half fathoms at least, even though he was in utter violation of every treaty and convention regarding the national sovereignty of France. It seemed he would stop at nothing to have the rebel as his prisoner, and if something didn't happen soon, he would have his way.

Well, we best make something happen, Biddlecomb thought. "Mr. Gerrish, we'll throw the guns over the side. I know, I know, I'm loath to do it, but we're desperate now, and the guns won't do us any good against that big bastard."

"Aye, sir," said Gerrish, resigned. "Um, how should I . . ."

"Fetch Ferguson, tell him what I want to do. He'll know how."

Five minutes later Ferguson had the number one gun ready to go, the trunnions sitting on the upper edge of the carriage, levered out of the semicircular notches in which they rested, a tackle rigged from the cascabel to an eyebolt in the bulwark, handspikes under the breech. Gathered around him, like apprentices watching the master, were the other gun captains, learning how to toss their beloved guns away.

"On the down roll," Ferguson said, ". . . wait for it . . . heave!" and as the *Charlemagne* rolled her starboard side down, the men on the tackle and the handspikes heaved. Two thousand four hundred pounds of long six-pounder cannon shot from the gunport and plunged into the sea, leaving nothing but a foaming, rippling patch that soon disappeared in their wake.

"We commend thy body to the deep," someone muttered.

The gun captains ran to their guns, ran to perform the last service to the weapons they had come to love, and soon, one by one, starboard side and then larboard, the great guns flew from the ports, leaving a trail of iron along the bottom of the ocean in just under two fathoms of water.

And still the *Burford* gained on them.

"You cannot win, *Monsieur Capitaine,*" the pilot said with yet another in his long series of shrugs. "I do not see how you can win. You throw the guns over, but still she is faster than you."

"I thought you said he would tack away, said he wouldn't dare come in this close," Biddlecomb replied, to which the pilot just shrugged, as Biddlecomb knew he would.

"Perhaps it is time to haul down the flag, no?" the pilot asked.

Easy for you to say, ain't it? Biddlecomb thought. *Poor innocent neutral that you are.* "No," was all he said.

They stood on for another hour, and in that time the *Burford* closed the gap to a cable and a half, the round shot whistling over their heads and now and again carrying something away, though failing, thankfully, to hit anything vital. The *Charlemagne*'s stern chaser, spared the fate of its fellow guns, continued to bang out all the while, slamming balls into the seventy-four's bow, but likewise failing to strike anything that would slow them down.

"Mr. Gerrish, pray fetch the carpenter aft," Biddlecomb said, and when the carpenter had shuffled up to the quarterdeck, Isaac said, "Chips, let us knock the wedges out of the masts. That should buy us a bit of speed."

"Aye, sir," the carpenter agreed.

"And I've heard that one can get a bit more speed by sawing through the chief deck beams. Get some flexibility into the hull."

"I've heard the same, sir," the carpenter said with a skeptical tone, "but I ain't seen it done and got no idea if it'd work."

"Let's find out, shall we? Go ahead and saw through the main beam and, say, two forward of that and two aft."

The carpenter paused for a moment. He had a proprietorial regard for the *Charlemagne*'s hull, as a carpenter should, and he was not happy about the damage he was being asked to cause, but neither did he wish to argue with his captain.

The pilot, however, felt no such restraint. "Saw the beams? Are you mad? The whole ship, she will fall apart, she will twist herself to pieces!"

"Oh, I doubt that, pilot. But let us see who is right."

The carpenter hurried off forward, and not five minutes later the *Charlemagne* was filled with the sound of sledges pounding the wedges out from around the masts and saws attacking the beams. The pilot folded his arms and leaned against the bulwark in a sulk, apparently unused to having his expertise so thoroughly ignored.

Biddlecomb for his part tried not to think about the bad bargain he had made, losing all that time heaving to, to pick the man up. He looked forward with pleasure to the moment when the pilot asked for his fee and he could laugh in his face. He even thought about going below and putting the pilot's name on the ship's books. That way, if they were taken, the British would consider him a rebel volunteer and thus a prisoner of war as well and lock him up with the rest.

But that was too cruel, even for the mood he was in. Nor could he risk being locked in the same cell as that man.

At last the sawing stopped, and Biddlecomb could feel the difference underfoot, the motion in the quarterdeck planks as the *Charlemagne* flexed with the rolling sea. Half a mile off the starboard side was the coast of France, rocky and wooded with the odd house here or there. It seemed to fly past. And a cable length astern the *Burford* was inching up, all but on top of them. Once her broadsides would bear, it would be over.

"You must wear ship now, *Capitaine*," the pilot said, still sulky, like a child being forced to apologize.

"And why is that?"

"There is a reef, a half mile ahead. It extends out from the shore, a quarter of a mile. You must make your head now northeast by east, one quarter east, if you do not wish to tear ze bottom out."

And then, as if to emphasize the point, the lookout shouted, "Breaker! Breakers ahead!"—that most terrifying of cries.

Biddlecomb glared at the pilot for a moment, but the pilot, seemingly intent on his fingernails, ignored him. "We have to stay directly ahead of the *Burford*. If we turn, then so will they, and we will put ourselves right under their broadsides. Why did you not mention this before?"

"If you had not turned back toward shore, against my advice, you would have weathered the reef on the old tack. Now . . . ?" The pilot shrugged.

"How much water is over this reef?"

"Not enough for you, *Capitaine*."

"How much?" Biddlecomb growled.

The pilot looked up, met his eyes, and the two men glared at one another until the pilot said, "Less than a fathom."

"Less than a fathom at low water," Biddlecomb corrected. "We are not at low water now."

"We are not at high water either, *monsieur*. Ze flood is perhaps half through."

"Very well."

The first glimmer of panic flashed in the pilot's eyes. He stood up from leaning against the bulwark and took a step toward Biddlecomb. "What do you intend, *monsieur*? If you do not wear ship now, you will come more under the *Burford*'s guns when you do."

"I don't believe we will wear ship at all," Biddlecomb said.

"You cannot pass over that reef. There is not enough water," the pilot insisted, and this time it was Biddlecomb's turn to shrug.

For four minutes they stood on, hurdling down on the reef hidden beneath the Atlantic. But not hidden entirely; Biddlecomb could see the line of ripples on the water, the slight irregularity on the surface, the occasional flash of white that marked some anomaly below. He thought of the *Burford* charging up astern. Did her captain know about this reef? If not, the next ten minutes would be most dramatic indeed.

"You have sawn your beams in two, *Capitaine*," the pilot said at last, as if Biddlecomb did not know this. "Ze ship is much weakened. She cannot now withstand hitting the reef."

"We will not wear ship, pilot."

Silence again, the line of ripples only two cable lengths ahead, the *Burford* one cable length astern. The round shot from her bow chaser continued to fly overhead, a shot every forty-five seconds, and a new hole in a sail, another line cut in two and flailing in the wind.

Biddlecomb glanced at the pilot's face. His eyes were starting to bulge and his hands were clasping and unclasping. He looked as if some great internal pressure was pushing outward, threatening to blow him apart. Finally he could stand it no longer.

"*Merde alors, Capitaine!* You cannot cross this reef!"

"We have no choice."

"You *have* a choice! Bring to, haul down the flag! No one is hurt!" The pilot was practically screaming now.

"You mean *you* are not hurt," Biddlecomb corrected.

"*Capitaine*, bring to, haul down the flag!"

"No." Biddlecomb turned his back to the pilot and looked forward, looking for the line of ripples over the reef. He could not see it, and for a second he was confused, until he realized that they were almost directly on top of it, the great band of water, lighter than the rest, stretching away from under the bow north and south.

The *Charlemagne* charged ahead. He could see the variegated shades beneath the water as the reef reached up to the surface and the brig swept over it.

"Hold on!" he managed to yell, then he felt the keel strike, abaft the mainmast, just below his feet. He pitched forward, saw the deck coming up at him, saw his hands go out as he broke his fall. Around him the others were thrown down as well, Gerrish and the helmsman side by side hitting the deck, the French pilot in a flurry of finery, like a game bird shot in flight, the men in the waist.

Biddlecomb rolled over, scrambling to his feet, waiting to hear the rending sound of the ship breaking her back on the reef, of masts and yards tumbling down, of the brig slewing around and dying on the rocks. But he heard none of it. He heard nothing but the shouting and talking of men and the familiar sound of water rushing down their side.

He stood and looked astern. The *Burford* was still behind them, but now so was the reef line, the ominous marks on the sea. They had passed over it, hit, and continued on.

The helmsman scrambled across the deck on hands and knees. He grabbed the tiller just as it started to swing.

"The rudder, is it all right?" Biddlecomb called.

The helmsman gave the tiller a tentative push to larboard and starboard. "I felt it jump clean out of its gudgeons, sir, but it must have popped right back in. Feels all right."

"Thank the Lord," Biddlecomb said, and suddenly the air was filled with the sound of a broadside going off, a full blast from the side of a big ship, the scream of round shot, a sound from the grave, the sound of death passing by. The *Burford* had rounded up half a cable length short of the reef and let loose with one last parting effort.

Apparently her captain knew about the reef.

A few more holes in the sails, and a piece taken out of the larboard main channel, and that was all the damage that that last broadside achieved. The seventy-four did not stop in her turn but continued to round up, turning close-hauled to claw away from the ledge over which she could never pass.

It would take them half a day to sail around the far end of the submerged obstruction and continue the pursuit, but Biddlecomb doubted that they would bother.

The *Charlemagne* was silent, silent as a congregation that has just witnessed a miracle, as they stared at the *Burford* sailing away from them.

Well, I reckon we won, Biddlecomb thought, and the thought surprised him. They had won. Not because they had actually defeated the seventy-four. No, they won because they had not lost.

CHAPTER
22

Came you from Court? for in your mien
A self-important air is seen.

—Poor Richard's Almanack, 1743

The Hôtel de Valentinois in the town of Passy, where the famed Dr. Franklin was staying, was very like the home that Joe Hynson had imagined himself owning in his wilder flights of fancy—and they were wild indeed—but it was unlike anything that he had ever actually seen before.

The ceiling of the dining room, in which he was standing at that moment and trying to look unimpressed, was twenty-five feet from the floor. It was elaborately carved and molded, though the molding could have been *trompe l'oeil*—he could no longer tell, having been fooled several times already. In the middle of the ceiling was a lovely fresco featuring a scene of heaven, from the middle of which hung a crystal chandelier sporting hundreds of candles, all exactly the same length, all burning bright and illuminating the room wonderfully.

And there was much to illuminate, for, as beautiful as the ceiling was, it was still just the ceiling, never intended to be the focus of the room, and it seemed almost plebeian compared with the rest of the space. The walls, at eye level and above, were covered in rich red cloth, silks and velvet, as best Hynson could judge, and set off with doorways and mirrors and paintings, the frames of which were all done up with gold leaf.

The polished marble floor was nearly lost under expensive carpets and the feet of the many guests of M. de Chaumont, the owner of the Hôtel de Valentinois, who packed the room. They were all of the aristocracy in one manner or another, which, Hynson was coming to realize, was not that noteworthy in France, where it seemed there were nearly as many aristocrats as commoners.

Their sheer numbers, however, did not prevent them from acting the part of the nobility. Each of the guests was dressed in the latest fashion, the men wearing long silk coats and delicate swords on their hips, and wigs thick with powder and piled so high as to prevent their wearing their hats, which they carried under their arms instead.

The women's dresses occupied a significant portion of the floor space, held out by hoops and false hips, cork rumps and buns. Their faces were white, an unnatural shade of white, unlike the working women of England and America, with their ruddier complexions, whom Hynson was used to. Their hair and wigs were piled into extraordinary constructions, rising high over their heads and supporting all manner of feathers and birds and flowers and whatever else caught their fancy.

Hynson noticed two women across the floor whose hair was not piled quite so high, but rather was molded into a shape much like a hatbox and rising no more than a foot above their heads. "Look here, Dr. Franklin," Hynson said, interrupting some conversation the doctor was carrying on in French, "those women there, their hair looks a damn sight like that fur cap of yours!"

Hynson had meant this as a joke, a humorous observation of the bizarre taste of the French, but Franklin flushed a light shade of red and said, "Actually, I believe it is not a coincidence. I am embarrassed to say it, but that is something of a fashion nowadays for the ladies to wear their hair to resemble my cap. It is called doing one's hair *à la Franklin.*"

"Oh," Hynson said, now embarrassed himself.

It was not the first faux pas he had committed since arriving in France, not even close, and he knew that others had noticed his mistakes. Franklin had already witnessed several.

The worst had been just an hour before, when they first arrived at the party, leaving the wing of the Hôtel that Franklin and Silas Deane occupied and walking around to the front of the expansive building, there to make their entrance. Hynson, wanting not to look like a Yankee bumpkin, had bowed deep, leg extended, to the gentleman who had greeted them, thinking, from the elegance of the man's dress, that he was M. de Chaumont.

As it happened, the man was a servant, not even the house butler, and even Franklin, generally stoic when it served, had not been able to suppress a smile.

It was just another in a series of ordeals for Hynson, starting with their getting to France. The sight of the big man-of-war, a seventy-four at least, had absolutely filled him with terror. After his part in freeing the American prisoners off the *Goliath,* he was not sure how Smith and Vardell and that lot would treat him.

But to his great relief the big ship went after the *Charlemagne* and completely ignored the cutter, leaving them free to scamper into Le Havre unmolested and take a carriage to Paris. There, with Nicholson's fat purse, for the Nicholsons were a wealthy family, they had purchased clothing fit for an appearance at Versailles, just in case the American commissioners wished to present the bold American seafarers at court.

All the while Sam Nicholson had been talking about Franklin, the great Franklin, with whom he had concocted all of these plans for armed cutters and the like. Every shop on every street corner from Le Havre to Paris sold pictures, prints, busts, engravings, medallions, and plaques featuring Franklin's face. It seemed all of France was mad for the Yankee philosopher. So when at last they met with the man, in his wing of the Hôtel de Valentinois, Hynson had some mighty large expectations.

But the flesh-and-blood Franklin—gray hair, and not much of it, unpowdered and unwigged; simple, even rustic clothes; soft-spoken with none of the commanding nature of great men—was something of a disappointment. Hynson had expected Richard the Lion Heart and he had got Poor Richard instead.

What was more, Franklin had been unwilling to discuss plans for the cutter, saying simply that there were other considerations before the vessel was sent to America. If he failed to send the boat to America, loaded with stores and dispatches, then Smith's plan would fall apart and he, Hynson, would be blamed.

He was near panic by the time Franklin invited them to the party at the Hôtel, and only the prospect of that affair finally took Hynson's mind from his troubles.

"Gar-son," Hynson said in his best French, waving a servant over to him. He drained the last gulp from his crystal champagne glass and placed it on the man's tray, then snatched up another. He could not recall how many glasses of the stuff he had had—it went down so easily, unlike the rotgut that was more his usual drink. He took a mouthful and went back to regarding Franklin.

Hynson had the idea that Franklin, dressed more for a Quaker meeting than a Paris *soirée*, would be shunned, laughed at, and ignored by the other, more elegant guests.

But once they had entered the ballroom, once Hynson had paid his most humble respects to the doorman, he had found just the opposite was true. The gentlemen swarmed to Franklin, each vying for his ear, seeming to hang on every word he said. He was, in fact, the center of attention, despite his entirely inelegant appearance, his plain brown suit and simple white collar, his head unadorned by hat or wig, his thin, gray hair hanging straight, unpowdered and unstyled.

And more annoying still, the women flocked to the old man as well, women of all descriptions, many of whom—most of whom—were young and beautiful, in an aristocratic manner that was unlike any of the women Hynson had ever had. They held Franklin's hands and his arms, kissed his cheeks, and called him "Papa." It was almost more than Joe Hynson could take.

I should try that Quaker tack next time, Hynson thought. He swallowed the last of the champagne in his glass and cast his eye around the room. The party was turning into something of a bore. Everyone spoke French, everyone but Hynson, and it seemed there was no one with whom he could converse.

Even Nicholson, who spoke a passable French, had deserted him in favor of some young coquette, and Joe cursed him for a rude and thoughtless cad, though he would have done the same had the linguistic skills been reversed.

He took an unsteady step toward the table spread with food. The champagne, he surmised, and the heat of the room were having an effect on his head.

A little of that beef'll set things right, he thought, then heard Franklin's deep, soft voice saying, "Captain Hynson, pray come and meet these gentlemen."

Hynson turned and made his way to the doctor's side. "I have been telling these gentlemen all about your exploits in Bristol, freeing those American prisoners," Franklin said, and judging from the looks on the men's faces Hynson guessed he had been telling them good things. He felt a renewed affection for the old man.

"We have a long struggle ahead of us, and every patriot must do his part," Hynson said, and waited while Franklin translated in halting French.

When Franklin had finished, the Frenchmen raised their glasses to him, with various "*Oui*'"s and "*Bien*'"s. Another waiter sailed by, and Hynson snatched up a fresh glass of champagne. In the balcony overhead a quartet played away at an airy piece.

This ain't so bad, Hynson thought, swallowing half the glass in one gulp. It occurred to him that if he did indeed fulfill Vardell and Smith's plan, then it was back to Mrs. Jump's with him. He would spend the rest of his life living in squalor on some pathetic pension and rutting with the scrawny Isabella.

However, if he was genuinely an American patriot, then a lifestyle such as the one he was presently enjoying might be his lot. He could learn to speak French, if Sam Nicholson and the old fart Franklin could. And then which of these lovelies would he be bedding?

"Monsieur Hynson?"

He turned at the sound of his name, pronounced in a feminine voice, and found himself looking down at a gorgeous, petite young woman, eighteen or nineteen years old, no more, though with the wig and the makeup it was often hard to tell. She beamed up at him with big white teeth, set off by red lips, and a look in her eye that was something between hero worship and lust.

"Yes, I'm Hynson."

"Capitain Hynson, who free the prisoners?"

"Wee," Hynson said, thinking, *Damn me if I ain't picking up this language already.*

"Oh, *Capitain,* I 'ave heard many stories, but I would much love to hear from you, *oui?*"

"Why, certainly. You see, I was in—"

"Oh, *monsieur,* it is so hot in here. Could we step out into ze garden?" The young woman tilted her head and looked up at him through long lashes.

"But, of course," Hynson said, making a quick bow. He held out his arm, indicating the way, but the young woman had already swept past him, headed in the opposite direction, so Hynson followed her.

They pushed through the elegant crowd, past the table heaped with meats and fowl of all kinds, cheese, pastries, sweets, and ices. They stepped into a short, darkened hallway that communicated with the dining room and out a big double set of glass doors, propped open to allow some circulation of air into the crowded room inside.

They walked in silence, and all the while Hynson wondered about his extraordinary turn of luck. He had heard about French women, particularly the rich, bored ones, and he imagined he was going to learn something of the truth that evening. He had to imagine this young doxy had more on her mind than hearing the story of how he had rescued the prisoners aboard the *Goliath*, as fascinating as that was.

They were halfway across the huge formal garden attached to the house, cool and sweet-smelling in the night air, when Hynson decided that he would not return to England at all, would not carry out that bastard Lieutenant Colonel Smith's plans.

He would remain in France, be an American patriot, and reap the substantial rewards that went along with that distinction.

The night was quiet, that far from the house, the loudest sound the enticing rustle of silk skirts, the most obvious smell the perfume from the young woman's neck. They walked down a half dozen steps at the far end of the garden and onto the green lawn that rolled away like the sea in the night.

The girl was walking two steps in front of him. She glanced back now and again, smiling, as if to give him further encouragement, as if he needed it. The sounds of the party could only just be heard at that distance, and Hynson knew that to anyone watching from the house he and the girl were invisible in the dark.

Does she mean for us to do it right here, right on the grass, rutting like wild animals? Hynson wondered. The thought aroused him.

257

"Evening, Hynson," a voice called out, clipped and British, nearby.

"What the—" Hynson nearly leapt off the ground. He whirled around just as Lieutenant Colonel Smith stepped from the shadows of the shrubbery and into the pale moonlight.

"What the hell?" Hynson said again, turning back to make certain that the girl was still there, but she was already up the stairs and running back toward the house.

"What the . . . goddamn you, that little bunter was going to—"

"No, she wasn't, Hynson. Believe me."

Hynson turned to look for the girl again, but she was already gone, having disappeared back into the big Hôtel. He turned back to Smith. "What are you doing here? How did you know where I was?"

"I always know where you are. What you're about. I know about your part in rescuing the rebel prisoners. I know when you arrived in Le Havre. I even know in which shop Sam Nicholson bought those fine clothes for you."

"There was nothing I could do to stop them from rescuing them prisoners," Hynson began, starting to feel the knife edge of panic on his throat. The black patch over Smith's eye looked like a gaping hole in his head. His scar seemed to shine in the pale light. "They would have suspected me—"

Smith held up his hand. "I know what happened in Bristol. I know that you were none too . . . heroic . . . in your efforts. That doesn't concern me."

"Oh." Hynson felt himself relax, just a bit. "That little tart," he asked, nodding in the direction the French girl had run, "she works for you?"

For a moment Smith was silent, considering Hynson, wearing the look of a man who realizes he got the bad end of a bargain. "There are many people who work for me," he answered cryptically, "on both sides of the Channel. Pray remember that."

"Very well. What are you doing here?"

"I am here, Hynson, to make certain that you do not get too enamored of these luxurious surroundings. That you do not forget the bargain we made."

"I ain't forgot, but I can't get that old bastard Franklin to commit to when he'll send the cutter out. Some damned thing happened, I don't know what."

"The commissioners got word of the rebel Washington's success at Trenton, and they're waiting for French reaction to the news. These things happen, I understand."

"In the meantime," Smith continued, "I expect you to find out what you can about the commissioners' affairs. Any stray conversation, any documents left lying around, anything that might be of use. I expect diligence, and I expect you will not betray me, because, Hynson, and mark this well, if a death sentence for treason is passed on you, it *will* be carried out. Whether it's a gallows at Tyburn or a knife in a back alley in Paris, it *will* be carried out."

Hynson stared at Lieutenant Colonel Smith, transfixed, like a rat looking at a cobra. He tried to swallow but could not. All vestiges of his former arousal were gone, and he wondered briefly if he would ever feel aroused again, if he would ever feel anything but his present panic.

"Yes, sir," he croaked at last.

"Damn me, look at all them Frogs, sir," Midshipman Gerrish exclaimed, looking through his telescope at the waterfront of Le Havre, less than a mile away and getting closer with each minute.

"Frogs?" asked Biddlecomb.

"Frenchmen, sir. There's Frenchmen lining the street there and it looks as if they're here to welcome us."

Biddlecomb put his own glass to his eye. Sure enough, the waterfront was thronged with people, and they did seem to be watching the *Charlemagne.* Some in fact were waving their hands, some waving French flags and some the Grand

Union flag, identical to the one that flew at the *Charlemagne*'s mainmast head, only smaller.

"Why do you call them 'Frogs'?" asked Lieutenant Faircloth. The three officers were standing together on the quarterdeck, each as resplendent as he could be in his best uniform, which, in Faircloth's case at least, was quite resplendent indeed. "I thought 'Frogs' were Dutchmen."

"I've heard the term applied to Dutchmen as well. But I think it is most commonly used for Frenchmen, nowadays."

"I see."

It was nearly twenty-four hours since they had seen the last of the *Burford*, and in that time the *Charlemagne* had made her way across the mouth of the Golfe de Saint-Malo, weathered the Pointe de Barfleur, and was now standing into the port of Le Havre under top sails and topgallants.

And from the look of it, word of their exploits had preceded them. It appeared that the whole town had turned out to cheer their arrival.

"They eat them, you know, sir," Gerrish said matter-of-factly.

"Who?"

"The French. They eat them."

"The French eat Dutchmen?"

"No, sir, the French eat frogs. Frogs' legs, specifically the back legs on those big ones, what we call bullfrogs back home."

"The French have always had some strange notions as to what constitutes food," Biddlecomb said as he ran his glass over the crowd.

"I think I should rather eat Dutchmen," Faircloth offered.

"Remind me of the frogs next time I complain about salt horse," Biddlecomb said.

Small boats were swarming around the *Charlemagne* like mosquitoes on a summer night, crammed with sightseers, but there were none of an official nature, as far as Biddlecomb could tell, so he stood on. He was entirely ignorant of the political situation in France. He was reminded of the story of Francis Drake, returning from his circumnavigation and asking if Elizabeth was still alive, not knowing if he was to be knighted or beheaded.

But like Drake, Biddlecomb had no choice but to make landfall. The *Charlemagne* was now quite defenseless with her food, water, and great guns at the bottom of the ocean and her main beams sawn in two. She was in no position to remain at sea.

He ran his glass up to the low fort situated above the town, with its commanding view of the harbor and entrances. At the top of the flagpole the white ensign of Bourbon France waved languidly, with the same unhurried ease as the people it represented.

"Mr. Gerrish, let us stick our toes in the political waters," Biddlecomb said, snapping his telescope closed. "Pray dip the ensign to the fort."

Gerrish unwound the flag halyard from its belaying pin and hauled the Grand Union flag down past the crosstrees. His eyes were fixed on the fort's ensign, as were all of the others on the quarterdeck, as well as those of the men forward who understood the significance of the moment. If the fort did not return their salute, then it could well mean that they were not welcome in France, in which case Biddlecomb did not know what he would do.

For half a minute nothing happened, and Biddlecomb was just beginning to feel the pangs of trepidation when the French ensign jerked and dipped as well.

There was a palpable easing of tension on the quarterdeck as the three officers exchanged smiles. "I guess we are all still friends, sir," Faircloth said.

"I guess so," Biddlecomb replied, and then calling forward said, "Ferguson, let us proceed with the salute!"

"Aye, sir," Ferguson called back, and touched the match to the trail of powder on the one remaining gun, the former stern chaser, now once again on the weather deck.

The gun went off with a roar, lower and flatter than a shotted weapon, and rolled back from the gunport a foot or so, with none of the drama of a shotted cannon flinging itself inboard with the recoil.

The gun crew swarmed over the gun, hauling it inboard and swabbing it out, preparing to reload. Ideally, each gun of the salute would come about three seconds from the last, but with only one gun it would take a little longer.

Twelve times the gun crew reloaded and fired, for a total of thirteen guns saluting the fort. A great cloud of gray smoke trailed astern of the *Charlemagne*, making her look as if she were on fire.

When the last of the American's guns went off, all eyes turned once more toward the fort, and this time the response was immediate, one gun after another returning the salute. The sight of the gray smoke erupting from the distant guns made Biddlecomb want to look for the fall of the shot; the habit was so ingrained that it was difficult for him not to turn his head.

"I wish everyone who fired guns at us was this well intentioned," Gerrish observed.

The salute from the fort took considerably less time than that from the *Charlemagne*.

"You may anchor over there, *Capitain*," the French pilot said when it was finished, pointing toward what was obviously the anchorage. He had become most helpful after the *Charlemagne* had made it over the reef, hoping no doubt to salvage both his reputation and his fee.

"Thank you, pilot," Biddlecomb said, and then to the helmsman added, "Bear up a point. Let us pass just astern of the brigantine, there. The yellow one."

They stood on deeper into the harbor, with Ferguson up in the bow supervising the cock-billing of the anchor and all sundry hands aloft, putting harbor stows in the foresail and topgallants.

At last they rounded up into the breeze, dropped the fore

topsail, and as the brig gathered sternway, let go the anchor. The anchor hawse paid out slowly through the hawse hole, coming at last to a stop, and the *Charlemagne* ceased her motion, no longer under way, no longer in danger, safe at last in neutral France.

From the town of Le Havre the people cheered and pistols fired into the air. The Charlemagnes on deck lined the rail and waved back, and those aloft waved with what free hands they had, each man aboard no doubt trying to gauge how much this newfound celebrity would be worth in terms of free alcohol and women.

"Damn me, sir, ain't this just like when we came into New London?" Faircloth asked. "After the New Providence expedition?"

"Very like," Biddlecomb agreed, "though I'd venture we've earned it more this time."

"On deck! Boat putting off!" the lookout called. "Official-looking boat, that is," he amended, to differentiate this boat from the dozens of others swarming around.

Biddlecomb ran his glass over the waterfront. There was no mistaking Le Havre for anything but a major European port city.

The quays were jammed with ships, yardarm to yardarm, the mainyards cock-billed to keep them from fouling their neighbors.

Through the tangle of masts, crowding down to the water, ancient brick buildings, four and five stories tall, shoulder to shoulder, signs with pictures of charts, pictures of sails, pictures of sextants, pictures of tankards. And between them, worn gray cobblestone streets, streets that had felt the wheels of Norman carts and perhaps Roman chariots. Streets that were crowded all day long with the busy people of Le Havre, nearly all of whom made their living from the sea, in one way or another.

That was the scene that Isaac saw through his glass, searching, searching, until he came at last to the boat that the lookout had spotted. It was a barge, long and white, with identically clad seamen at the oars and an official in uniform in the stern sheets. This would have caused Biddlecomb a fair amount of concern had they not received the fort's salute, indicating that America and France were still on friendly terms.

"*Capitain*, I must leave now, so it is time you paid me my fee," the pilot said with all the cheek he could muster.

"Your fee?" Biddlecomb was incredulous, but before he could continue, Faircloth interrupted.

"Sir, should we have a side party for this Frog coming out?"

"Indeed. Full captain's honors should do."

Biddlecomb turned back to the pilot, but now Gerrish was there. "Sir, would you like the boats over?"

"Yes, get them both over, please. And let us break open the hatches and get some air below. And we'll need to organize a watering party, we're all but dry. I'll see about fresh food as well."

"*Monsieur*," the pilot said, vying for Biddlecomb's attention, and Biddlecomb wished dearly to give it to him, having a number of things he wished to say, but he was interrupted by Sgt. Able Dawes barking, " 'Ten-shun!" and the marines coming to attention in a beautifully coordinated clash of shoes and muskets.

Biddlecomb raced forward, down the quarterdeck ladder, the pilot on his heels.

"*Monsieur Capitain*, I must . . . ," the pilot was saying as the visiting dignitary stepped up the cleats and onto the *Charlemagne*'s deck. He was dressed in an immaculate uniform: a blue coat trimmed out with gold, gold epaulets on the shoulders, scarlet waistcoat and breeches. A small medallion was pinned to his lapel, featuring a portrait of a man who looked surprisingly like Dr. Franklin. He stepped past the two lines of marines as half of his well-armed boat crew came up behind him. Biddlecomb removed his hat and bowed in salute.

"Are you Captain . . . Biddlecomb?" the dignitary asked, pronouncing the name with great difficulty.

"I am, *monsieur.*"

"Good day, sir. I am Captain Gourlade, intendant of the Port of Le Havre."

At this news the pilot stepped forward and began to address the intendant in rapid French, but the intendant cut him off in midsentence with something that Biddlecomb did not understand but guessed, judging from the pilot's expression, was quite insulting.

"Captain"—the intendant turned back to Biddlecomb—"I understand that on your latest cruise you have taken some English prizes, which you have sent into French ports?"

"That is correct."

"Then I beg you will forgive me this inconvenience, Captain," the intendant said, bowing a shallow bow, "but I fear I must place you under arrest."

CHAPTER
23

*We must all hang together, or assuredly
we shall all hang separately.*

—BENJAMIN FRANKLIN
AT THE SIGNING OF THE
DECLARATION OF INDEPENDENCE

JOE HYNSON MOVED AS QUIETLY AS HE COULD, CONCENTRATING
more on the noises coming from below stairs than on the
papers in front of him. He was in Franklin's office, had been
meeting with the doctor, when Franklin was called away by
the arrival of some associate or other.

Left alone, Hynson recognized his chance to see if anything of import was lying open on the old man's desk, anything that he could feed to Smith to keep him sated for the
time being. Smith had told him to look for something, had
made it clear what the consequences might be for not fulfill-
ing his role for British intelligence, so Hynson tore eagerly
through the stacks of paper, searching for something to
pass on.

He had been spending a fair amount of time with Franklin
and the other commissioners, Silas Deane and Arthur Lee,
and the numerous satellite patriots who whirled around
them, some with official commissions, most just hangers-on.
It was a fascinating place, Paris and the Hôtel de Valentinois, full of rumor and court intrigue and high politics, just

the kind of air Hynson loved to breathe, the type of place he felt he belonged.

At that morning's meeting, which had just been interrupted, Hynson had approached Franklin once again about using the cutter to carry arms and dispatches to America. He pushed as hard as he dared, not wanting to sound over-eager, and not really wanting to leave Passy and Paris, but also not wanting to disappoint Smith.

Franklin had told him the truth of the matter at last. Apparently General Washington, who for the past year had been retreating all over New York and New Jersey, had decided on a bold move. On Christmas night he had taken his entire army, then stationed in Philadelphia, over the Delaware River and hit the Hessians in Trenton, New Jersey. Hit them hard. For the first time since the evacuation of Boston the Americans were on the offensive, and a great deal of excitement surrounded that event.

More, Hynson thought, than was quite warranted.

But the upshot of all that, as far as the commissioners were concerned, was a renewed interest on the part of the French court in siding with the Americans, since now the hope sparked that the Americans could actually win, or at least not lose. And so the commissioners were holding off with their precious dispatches to the Continental Congress in hopes of receiving some official word from Versailles, or some further news from America that would goad the French into a decision.

The cutter would have to wait.

Hynson heard some sounds from below stairs, a muffled greeting of someone at the door, and he stepped up his search.

Franklin's explanation of the delay had not been news to Hynson. Smith had actually told him the reason before he heard it from Franklin, which meant that Smith had eyes and ears everywhere. There was no telling who was working for the bastard. Just thinking about it made Hynson's stomach sour.

He did not genuinely expect to find anything important lying on top of the desk. No one would be that careless, but at least he could tell Smith that he had looked.

For that reason he was quite surprised to find a number of important and very secret documents there, shoved into piles as if they were old shopping lists. Letters to the Compte de Vergennes and from that worthy to the commissioners, letters to and from various American ship captains in France, letters from Thomas Morris, who, Hynson understood, was responsible for selling American prizes in France.

There were even notes concerning a letter from Lord Stormont to William Eden, which meant that Smith was not the only one running spies. Franklin apparently had his own people, people within the British embassy who were keeping their eyes open. That information alone should be worth a month of freedom from Smith's harassment.

From beyond the door, which Franklin had thankfully left ajar, Hynson heard the click of the old man's walking stick on the marble stairs and, faintly, the tread of Franklin's visitor, accompanying the old man upstairs. Franklin wore soft leather slippers at home, much like the footwear of the Red Indians, since his gout had flared up again.

Hynson quickly replaced the papers—there was no need to put them in any order since they had not been in any order before—and sat down once more in his former casual, slouching position.

"Ah, Captain Hynson," Franklin said as he stepped into the room, "here's an old comrade of yours." And much to Hynson's shock and dismay, which he struggled to mask, Capt. Isaac Biddlecomb followed the old man into the room.

Biddlecomb looked like hell. His uniform, which might once have been his best, was wrinkled and covered with dust, apparently from hard riding. His face had the pale, lined quality of one who has not slept in some time. But still there were those sharp, dark eyes that seemed to take in far more than they revealed, the strong jaw and set mouth of someone who would not easily be manipulated. He made Hynson uncomfortable, even more so now that Hynson did not know what Biddlecomb thought of him.

Biddlecomb nodded a greeting. "Hynson, good to see you again, sir. I thought that I saw your cutter in Le Havre. I am delighted to see you made it safe to France."

"And you, sir," Hynson replied. Biddlecomb sounded civil enough, if a bit cool, but of course he did not look as if he was in any shape to be effusive in his greeting. "We're safe thanks to you, drawing that two-decker off with your stern chaser. But I had heard . . . ah," Hynson continued, thinking, *Damn me, I should have kept my mouth shut,* "I heard you was arrested, sir."

"I was. I have escaped. It is one of the points I wished to discuss with Dr. Franklin."

Please, Lord, do not let them send me away, Hynson thought, realizing what a wealth of information might be forthcoming.

"Oh course you do," Franklin said, sitting heavily in his high-backed wing chair and swinging his gouty foot up onto a stool. "Have a seat, Captain Biddlecomb." He gestured toward another chair, close by his, and Biddlecomb sat. "Captain Hynson, might I impose on you to fetch us all a glass of wine. There is some excellent Bordeaux in the cabinet there. Pray forgive my lack of hospitality, but I really cannot stand on my poor foot for a second longer."

"Think nothing of it, sir," said Hynson, trying not to show his relief, to remain as stony faced as Biddlecomb. He stepped over to the cabinet and pulled out three glasses and the uncorked bottle as Biddlecomb and Franklin fell into discussion.

"I needn't tell you how distressing this is, sir," Biddlecomb began, angry, "being arrested and taken away like a common criminal on the deck of my own ship. How detrimental that is to a captain's authority."

"I understand entirely, Captain. But, sir, you must understand the delicacy of the situation here. The French are very much on our side, particularly after what General Washington has done in Trenton, but they are not ready to go to war with Britain. When we tread too hard on British toes, as you have done, the French must make some gesture to show the British that they are truly neutral. Understand, sir, that we all applaud your efforts, but they are precisely why the French arrested you."

"Gesture, indeed. I should say that placing an American naval officer under arrest is more than a gesture, it is an act of war against the United States."

Hynson distributed the glasses and then sat as well, joining the circle, afraid that he would be asked to leave, but no one paid him any attention. Franklin regarded Biddlecomb with a slight smile, a paternal expression.

"Now, Captain," Franklin said, "pray, won't you tell us of your escape? How did you manage it?"

"Well, sir, it was purely through the carelessness of the guards. I was imprisoned for two days, with no means of escape that I could find. Then on the morning of the third day, yesterday, that is, after breakfast, the guard failed to fully close the door to my cell. The lock didn't engage. Once he was gone, I simply opened the door and made my way out. I was lucky not to encounter any other of the guards."

"I see," said Franklin, putting the tips of his fingers together and forming an arch like the back of a Portuguese man-of-war. "And do you think, Captain, that it was entirely an accident that the door was left ajar? That no guards were about? That there was a saddled horse for you to . . . borrow . . . just without the prison door?"

At that Biddlecomb looked stunned. "Do you mean to say . . ."

Franklin waved his hand in a gesture of dismissal. "We must play these silly games, I fear, and I am sorry that you were made to be a player against your will, after all you have done. But I am glad you have come, for we must discuss what is to be done with you and your bold Charlemagnes."

"Bold we may be," said Biddlecomb, sounding more appeased, "but we're helpless as well. The *Charlemagne* suffered considerable damage in the past weeks. And we had to throw all of our great guns overboard."

"Oh, dear," said Franklin. "That is a bit of a problem. If we try to rearm your vessel in France, Lord Stormont will become absolutely rabid. I think perhaps it is time we sent you back to America."

Halloa, thought Hynson, seeing the first glimmer of a possibility.

"I should be delighted to return to America, and I think I speak for my men as well. We can repair the damage to the brig, but with no cannon we dare not venture even beyond the port of Le Havre."

"Sirs, if I may," Hynson interrupted, "this might be an answer to a number of problems. As the doctor knows, I am particularly interested in seeing the American troops supplied from France. Been trying to run a load of guns across myself, but there have been delays. No one's fault, it just happens.

"But think on this. We repair the *Charlemagne* and, instead of rearming her we seal over the gunports, repaint her and rename her, something French, and there you have it: a French merchantman that no British man-of-war would dare stop for fear of violating French neutrality. Run up a French ensign and that should be disguise enough to get you past the cruisers in the Channel, and once you're in open water, it's downhill to home, with the *Charlemagne*'s hold filled with small arms, powder, whatever. Hell, she could take dispatches as well, and then when there was further news, Doctor, you could send me in the cutter."

Hynson made himself shut up, lest his enthusiasm give him away, but it was not easy. The more he talked the more he realized how perfect this was. Here was the American ship, loaded with arms and dispatches, that he had promised to Smith. The British would like nothing more than to capture the notorious rebel pirate Isaac Biddlecomb, particularly after his raiding in the Irish Sea, and here was Joe Hynson, throwing the man himself into the deal, at no additional charge.

And best of all, he, Joe Hynson, would not be aboard. For, despite all of Smith's promises of decent treatment once he had been separated from the other prisoners, Hynson did not trust him. He thought it just as likely that after capture he would be treated as just another rebel, or worse.

He glanced at Biddlecomb and Franklin. The two men were pondering the idea, which was good. He was desperate to further his argument, desperate to push them over the edge of a decision, but he knew that now was the time to keep quiet. He found himself squirming in his seat with the effort.

"You might even turn the *Charlemagne* into a snow," Hynson said at last, unable to contain himself any longer. "Bend a sail on the mainyard, add a snow mast, no great effort, and then it would be even less likely that she could be recognized."

"The plan has merit," said Franklin at last. "Were there any hope of getting guns for your ship, Captain, I should never send you out unarmed, but I fear that it is impossible, politically. What think you of Captain Hynson's plan?"

Biddlecomb took a sip of his wine. "I believe it could

work. Clearly if we cannot use force to get out of France, we must use guile. Of course there are spies everywhere. We would have to take the cargo on board and do all the work as quickly as we can, before word spreads too far. But it could be done."

Hynson put his wineglass up to his lips to mask the smile that was threatening to break out. When at last he felt he had his delight under control, he said, "I would like very much to help in the organization of this thing. I believe I could be of some assistance, and I think the experience would be invaluable for me, for the time when I'm running supplies to America."

"Of course, Hynson, of course, we can use all the help we can get," Biddlecomb said, but his mind was elsewhere, no doubt turning the plan over in his head, probing it for flaws, weaknesses.

"Yes," he said at last. "I reckon it's the way. Even with guns we couldn't fight through a serious cordon of British men-of-war. And even though the British haven't been over-worried about French neutrality—chased the *Charlemagne* almost onto the beach at Cape Finistère—still we can hope they won't have the audacity to stop and search a French merchantman. Might even ship a few French sailors, some-one who can converse in French if one of them hauls up within hailing distance."

"That's a very good idea, Captain," Hynson said brightly, so brightly that it caused Biddlecomb to regard him curi-ously, which in turn made Hynson silently curse himself. In a more somber tone he added, "When might we return to Le Havre, do you think?"

"As soon as possible, I should imagine. I trust, Doctor, that I won't be thrown in jail again?"

"No, sir, we can see to that. We can see to all the supplies you will need as well: food, water, lumber for repairs, paint for disguise. The French will be more than eager to assist in anything that gets you out of their country. Anything but guns. They have been quite clear on that point."

"Well, sir," said Biddlecomb, "I share their enthusiasm for my leaving France, and I should think, if supplies are forthcoming, that we will be able to sail in a fortnight. Captain Hynson, I believe you offered your assistance?"

"Oh, yes," said Joe Hynson, and to himself added, *Oh yes, oh yes, oh yes!*

CHAPTER
24

He that would rise at Court, must begin by Creeping.

—POOR RICHARD IMPROVED, 1757

THE HONORABLE DAVID MURRAY, SEVENTH VISCOUNT STORMONT, British ambassador to France, was lost in the halls of Versailles.

He followed his escort, a palace servant in a long, powdered wig, down a short set of wide marble stairs bounded by marble handrails a foot wide. The walls and ceiling rose two stories above their heads, every inch tricked out in gilded molding and marble inlay and paintings and *trompe-l'oeil.*

A right turn at the bottom of the stairs and down a hall way of mirrors and gold frames, huge chandeliers hung at regular intervals. The black and white tiles of the marble floor were polished so bright they looked as if they were under half an inch of pure, clear water.

It was unreal, too much by half, by much more than half. Stormont was no stranger to Versailles—he had been there many times, officially and otherwise—but never did he fail to marvel at the excess. He felt rustic and awkward in those surroundings, like a county squire in a Fielding novel. And though he was dressed in his finest, which did no disgrace to his office, still his clothing was not half as elaborate as that of the servant whom he followed. To Lord Stormont's thinking, nothing confirmed the superiority of the British character over that of the decadent French more than did Versailles.

The servant led them around a corner, which, by the ambassador's calculation, would put them outside the suite of the Comte de Vergennes, but instead it led to yet another hall with yet another staircase at the far end.

Stormont was completely lost, as he was every time he visited the palace.

He found Versailles a gold-encrusted labyrinth in which he could never get his bearings. He did not think it was a failing on his part. He was convinced that the servants led him to the Vergennes suite by a different route every time he came to call, for the sole purpose of preventing him from ever being able to navigate those halls on his own.

The thought crossed his mind that the next time he came to visit, he would bring an ax and chop notches in the various columns and moldings to mark his trail, the way he understood was done by the woodsmen. That thought would have made him smile had he not been so very angry.

Up the staircase at the far end of the hall, right turn at the top, down another short hallway, and finally they arrived at a place that Stormont recognized, the suite of the French foreign minister, Charles Gravier, le Comte de Vergennes.

The servant opened the door, bowed, and gestured for Stormont to enter, all in one motion that also included undertones of obsequiousness and arrogance, all melded into one seamless package. Damned Frenchmen.

The Comte de Vergennes's suite was done up in the new style known as *Louis Seize*, with white and gold paneling, elaborate gold crown molding around the edge of the ceiling, twenty feet overhead, a fireplace with mantel trimmed out in gold and supporting an elaborate clock, which in turn was supported by a host of little gold cherubs and eagles and such, the entire thing reflected in the ten-foot-high mirror behind it. It was what passed for simple elegance in the court of Louis XVI.

Vergennes was seated across the main room at a big, round table, conversing with two other gentlemen of the court. He looked up, caught Stormont's eye, and nodded in acknowledgment of his entrance, then turned back to the two men beside him.

Stormont wondered how long he would be kept waiting. Vergennes was tricky. He was not stupid, despite his being as great a dandy as any at court, and he played this game of foreign affairs with skill.

But Lord Stormont was equally skilled. He understood, for instance, that the amount of time he was kept waiting was in inverse proportion to the confidence Vergennes had in his position on whatever issue was in dispute. If Vergennes felt he had the upper hand, he would see Stormont immediately. If he felt his position was weak, he would make Stormont wait, in hopes of throwing him off. And it had worked, until Stormont had smoked the tactic.

The Englishman ran his eyes around the room. Perhaps half a dozen people were there, mostly secretaries scribbling away at desks scattered around, each desk worth more than a British scrivener would earn in a year. He glanced quickly at the foreign minister and the two gentlemen with whom he was conversing. They showed no sign of breaking up the meeting.

He was being made to wait.

Good.

The Americans had been allowed to go too far, and Vergennes knew it.

Stormont took the opportunity of the delay to run over the words he had prepared that morning. He would greet Vergennes with righteous indignation at the French government's flouting of their neutrality. He knew from experience that his righteous indignation worked better when rehearsed.

At length Vergennes stood and the two gentlemen did likewise, and Vergennes bid them good day. They collected up their various papers and folders and left the suite, and Vergennes approached the British ambassador, his expression friendly, if serious.

He was dressed, as usual, in a suit that was almost entirely white and picked out here and there with bright embroidery, as if his clothing was designed to match the decor of his suite, and as far as Stormont knew, it was. He bowed slightly and Stormont did the same.

"My Lord Stormont, how very good of you to come."

"The pleasure is mine, sir. We have much to discuss." Stormont did not try to hide the irritation that he felt, and he could see his tone register with Vergennes.

"But of course. Will you accompany me into my closet?" Vergennes crossed the room and opened a nearly invisible door, and Stormont followed him into the room beyond.

The closet, which was Vergennes's private office, was a smaller version of the main room in the suite, though it was by no means small. After closing the door, Vergennes sat behind his big desk and gestured to Stormont to take a seat in front. Stormont sat and crossed his legs and before Vergennes could begin said, "I am outraged, sir, absolutely outraged, at the assistance that the American rebels have received from your government. They have been given safe harbor, allowed to buy weapons, supplies, sell their prizes, which no reasonable person could consider legitimate—"

"*Monsieur*"—Vergennes held up his hands in protest— "please do not mistake the actions of private citizens with the actions of the government. The people are quite partial to the Americans, it is true, but there is nothing we can do about that. As to the government, I gave you my assurance that the American captain Biddlecomb would be placed under arrest and that was done, despite the risk we run of antagonizing the Americans and the danger to our West Indian possessions."

"I understand that Biddlecomb was arrested, and I am grateful for that," Stormont said. He also understood that Biddlecomb had been allowed to escape, but he would not tip his hand so far as to say so. "However, the rebel ship *Charlemagne* remains in Le Havre and her officers are treated as heroes by the people there, given every imaginable succor."

At that Vergennes shrugged. "As I say, I cannot regulate how the people feel toward Americans. And please recall, sir, that the *Charlemagne* was driven into Le Havre by your own ship."

"And five of her 'prizes' have arrived in France, at Nantes and Brest and L'Orient, and for all I know they have been sold already."

Vergennes looked surprised at that news, a look that Stormont found entirely unconvincing. "I know nothing of that. I will look into it." Vergennes scribbled a note to himself. "If you would care to make a formal protest, I shall see it receives the proper attention."

"Perhaps I will do that, sir, though I have observed, with great regret, that when I have made representations to you, they have been attended to at the moment, and fair promises made, but some secret, invisible influence has always countered my representations and rendered your promises without effect." Not that the influence was really that invisible. Its likeness was everywhere, and its name was Franklin.

"Orders are given, *monsieur*, but often are eluded."

"You will not seriously tell a man who has spent so much of his life in France that any officer in this country dares to disobey the king's commands." Stormont leaned forward, considered standing, but did not. He was ready for this moment. He had rehearsed all morning for it.

"The facts are clear. We know the *Charlemagne* is gone

into Le Havre, an English man-of-war chased her, but when he came near your coast, he stopped the pursuit, so different, sir, is our conduct from yours.

"The harboring of these armed vessels, suffering them to make what use of your ports they will, where they are sure to find not only asylum, but the most cordial reception and every assistance, your turning a blind eye to the harboring and sale of what the rebels are pleased to call prizes, are so direct a violation of the laws of nations, of every treaty, that, to speak plainly, sir, it is a little short of direct hostility.

"You know, sir, as well as I do, that all human things have bounds beyond which they cannot go. We are now come to the utmost verge of these bounds, and we must either return to peace and harmony, or pass the line, and proceed to an immediate rupture."

The two men were silent for a moment, each holding the other's eyes, unflinching. Stormont had cried "havoc," had allowed the French foreign minister to see just how far he had pushed his old enemy. Now there was nothing but to make amends or let slip the dogs of war.

Vergennes was the first to break the silence. "What is it you wish us to do, *monsieur?*"

"The *Charlemagne* must be ordered to leave France and never to use her ports again as a haven for attacking English shipping."

"I understand that the *Charlemagne* suffered much damage, sir, running from your man-of-war. A chase which took your countrymen much further into French waters than perhaps you realize. In all humanity we cannot force the Americans to leave in a vessel that is not fit to keep the sea."

Stormont was ready for that tack. It had been used before. "The Americans have received every conceivable kind of aid and material. There is no reason to believe that their vessel has not been sufficiently repaired."

Vergennes leaned back in his chair and laced his fingers together. He was angry. But Stormont had it on good authority that Vergennes was also angry with the American commissioners, as well he might be, for it was their playing free and easy with French neutrality and friendship that had put him in his present, awkward position. That was good. Perhaps he would be less willing to protect the precious rebel privateer.

"The king, my master, has no wish to harm the blessed peace that exists between the two crowns," Vergennes began slowly, "but neither will he be forced to abandon a friendship that he has professed toward the Americans. However, if I represent to him the numerous violations of French neutrality that you claim the American ship *Charlemagne* has perpetrated, I think it likely he will acquiesce in the measure to your request."

The Frenchman was dancing, something the French seemed to do as often verbally as they did physically, but Stormont needed more than that. The morning before he had received a letter from William Eden detailing the rebels' plan to sneak the *Charlemagne*, disguised as a French merchantman, past the cordon of British men-of-war.

It was frightening, the amount of detail that Eden knew. He clearly had more than one highly placed operative in the American commissioners' offices. That in turn made Stormont wonder who in his own embassy was working for Vergennes, or Franklin.

Stormont envisioned a vast underworld of spies, operating before his eyes, there, but invisible, like the world of spirits. It made him uncomfortable, though he understood how essential that ghostly world was to the world of diplomacy and warfare.

Here was yet another example: plans laid out by Franklin and the rebel pirate Biddlecomb, laid out in total secrecy, and somehow Eden knew every note and verse. The undersecretary had dispatched five ships, the *Speedwell*, the *Coura-*

geous, the *Royal Oak*, the *Ranger*, and the *Hector* to patrol off Le Havre. Biddlecomb could not slip past them all.

But neither could they remain on station indefinitely. The rebel had to be made to leave Le Havre soon. That was Stormont's part of the operation.

"I need your assurance, sir, that the *Charlemagne* will be made to leave France and ordered not to return. Such an assurance is required by *my* king, *my* master."

It was the kind of ultimatum that Vergennes hated, the kind that made him furious, and Stormont could see it was having that effect again. But he also knew that France, and young Louis XVI, only three years on the throne, were not ready to go to war for a bunch of republican farmers and backwoodsmen who were in any event most likely to lose.

"You cannot ask us to send the American out into the jaws of your men-of-war, *monsieur*."

"Our men-of-war will not violate French neutrality by operating in French water. I believe the *Burford*'s giving up her chase proved that. What happens on the open sea is no concern of France."

There was a long pause, a charged quiet, like wrestlers holding one another in such a way that neither can move. And then Vergennes said, "I believe that I can safely give my assurance that the American will be ordered to leave within twenty-four hours."

"I thank you, sir, in the name of all peace-loving Englishmen."

That was enough for Stormont's satisfaction. If Vergennes had said he would *ask* the Americans to leave within twenty-four hours, then that could have meant as much as two months. By saying he would *order* the Americans to leave within twenty-four hours, it was reasonable to assume that the *Charlemagne* would be gone within a week.

That would be fine. The five British ships could remain

on station for a week, throwing a screen across the Baie de la Seine. A screen through which nothing could pass undetected, including an unarmed rebel brig-of-war disguised as a French merchantman. She would be a worthy prize, loaded with secret dispatches and military stores.

And with her they would snag the rebel pirate Biddlecomb, and that would be the end of yet another irritant. A major irritant at that.

CHAPTER
25

Alas! that Heroes ever were made!
The Plague, and the Hero, are both of a Trade!
Yet the Plague spares our Goods, which the Hero does not;
So a Plague take such Heroes and let their Fames rot.

—POOR RICHARD IMPROVED, 1748

THE *CHARLEMAGNE* WAS FINALLY READY TO PUT TO SEA, SIX DAYS after she had been given twenty-four hours to clear out of Le Havre.

Captain Gourlade, intendant of the port, was courtesy itself, never even mentioning, during the several times that he and Biddlecomb met, that Biddlecomb was an escaped prisoner and liable to arrest. But even the Frenchman's seemingly boundless courtesy grew strained as one day turned into the next and the *Charlemagne* remained in the harbor.

Biddlecomb did what he could to mollify the officials. He unmoored the brig, hauling one of the two anchors aboard and leaving the vessel swinging at a single hook, as if they were on the verge of leaving. He shifted his berth one day and left the sails hanging in their gear, rather than stowed in neat harbor furls. Each of these little signs of progress helped pacify Gourlade, whom, Biddlecomb suspected, was being pressured from Paris to see the Americans gone.

And those little gestures were nothing in comparison to

the real work that the Charlemagnes were doing to ready themselves for sea. Lumber was sent aboard, given to the Americans on credit by one of the many merchants ashore who were enthusiastic supporters of their cause, and it was quickly absorbed into the fabric of the ship. Bulwark planking was torn out and reworked. All of the gunports, which were gaping empty like missing teeth in a smile, were eliminated, so the bulwarks formed a smooth, unbroken line from the break of quarterdeck to bow, merchantman fashion.

The formerly oiled sides were painted black and trimmed out with white and yellow and red, from the main wale to the rails. A square sail for the mainyard was hurriedly fashioned and bent on the yard. A snow mast, stepped on deck abaft the mainmast and terminating under the maintop, was put in place, turning the brig *Charlemagne* into a snow, per Hynson's clever suggestion.

Great balks of timber were wrestled below and fashioned into replacements for the sawn beams, then forced into place alongside the crippled ones. In the great cabin, a half a dozen French artisans labored to rebuild, again, the shattered stern section.

From Nantes and L'Orient and Brest and St.-Malo those Charlemagnes who had been sent off as prize crews began to drift in, directed to Le Havre by the American commissioners, to whom they had been told to report. Rumstick and Weatherspoon and their bands came back on the second day, a joyful reunion, and were put to work immediately.

On the fifth day, after a fretful visit by Capitaine Gourlade, the stores began to arrive. Fresh water, beef, pork, dried peas, flour, live chickens, pigs, and goats—all lightered out to the *Charlemagne* and hoisted aboard, stowed down in the hold or forward in the manger or thrust squawking into coops on the quarterdeck. The stores, like the lumber, were provided by those many people ashore who, for reasons that none of the Americans could fathom, were dedicated to the cause of American independence.

And those same people vied every night to have the American officers as their guests at dinner and dances and the various other functions so loved by the French. The Americans, Biddlecomb included, were delighted at first to accept, finding the center of attention an agreeable place to be. And by the time they had grown tired of it, and exhausted all the time from the work and the late-night entertainment, they were not able to refuse, for fear of offending the very people on whom they relied. So they worked and celebrated and prayed for the day when they could get to sea.

The cargo began to arrive six days after they had been ordered to leave. It too was lightered out and loaded aboard and stowed down, not in the hold of the brig-of-war *Charlemagne*, for such a vessel no longer existed, but aboard the French merchant snow *Les Deux Frères*. The disguise was complete, even down to the fashion piece with the French name carved into it, fitted into the gap in the transom where the name *Charlemagne* had been before the *Swallow* had shot it away.

The *Charlemagne*'s carpenter had garnered quite a bit of experience in carving name boards since their arrival in France.

The cargo was a mixed lot, consisting of cordage, barrel hoops, wine, cloth, and shoes, all of which would be welcome in the United States. But happy as the Congress would be to see those things, they would be happier by far with the last of the consignment: eighty crates containing two thousand .69-caliber, long land-pattern French muskets, direct from the armory of Louis XVI.

And not just the muskets, but a dozen barrels of powder as well, along with barrels of flints, barrels of shot, and crates full of bullet molds, bayonets, spare locks and barrels, all the things that would maintain the efficacy of those two thousand weapons. Short of declaring war on England, there was no more effective aid that the French court could give to the Continental Congress.

"Lovely, just lovely," Rumstick said, aiming an unloaded musket at some distant target and snapping the flint against the frizzen. A shower of sparks fell from the lock and trailed down to the deck, vanishing before they hit the wood.

"I'll still take a Brown Bess over any Frog musket," said Faircloth, taking a weapon from the open crate on the quarterdeck and hefting it on his hand, "but these are decent guns, I'll warrant. All these different calibers are going to give some poor quartermaster fits."

"It's the bayonets that'll make a difference," said Sam Nicholson, who had spent every day of the past week aboard the *Charlemagne*, helping with the fitting out.

"In any event," said Biddlecomb, "the relative merits of the guns are not our concern. We are only a poor French merchantman, hired to bring them to the beleaguered Americans. Slack water's in two hours. The last of these will be stowed down by then, and then I believe we shall sail. This wind should hold fair for the rest of the day."

"But Joe Hynson's not yet returned from Paris with dispatches," Nicholson said "though he should be here shortly."

"Right. Hynson."

Hynson had been as invaluable as Nicholson over the past week, helping out in every aspect of the preparations. He had acted as courier as well, between the American commissioners and the *Charlemagne*, kindly volunteering to carry any messages too secret to be trusted to the mails. He had gone down to Paris for last-minute dispatches and correspondence from Franklin and the others. They could not sail until he returned.

"Ezra, might I impose on you to go around to Hynson's rooms and see if he has returned. We have to weigh in two hours, we can't delay a moment beyond that without causing an international crisis."

"Certainly. And if he ain't there, I'll wait on him at that little tavern they got there," Rumstick said. *Or that little whorehouse just up the road,* he thought. They could put whatever uniform they wanted on him, give him any fancy title they pleased, but he was still at heart a sailor, and he was comfortable with that.

"Temperance, Lieutenant, temperance. I would not wish to have to drag you out of some bawdy house, half drunk like a common sailor."

"Never in life, sir."

Rumstick took the captain's gig across the harbor and brought it along the slimy, ancient stone steps of the quay. "You lot stay with the boat," he said to the four-man boat crew. "I may be a few hours, and you damned well better be here when I get back. And you better be sober too."

With that he tugged his uniform into place, adjusted his sword, and headed off down the narrow street. The boat crew would get into some mischief, of that he was certain. Probably take turns as lookout while the rest ran off to some grog shop or brothel.

He held out no hope that they would be entirely sober when he returned, but as long as they were passable, he would let it go. A sailor could get into a great deal of mischief in two hours. Hell, if Hynson was not at his rooms, Rumstick doubted that he himself would be entirely sober on his return.

The streets were narrow and walled in by three-story buildings on either side, worse even than the most confined streets in Boston, and far more crowded. Rumstick shouldered his way along the high sidewalk, smiling and returning the greetings of all those who greeted him, those who recognized him as one of the heroic American naval officers.

He came at last to the Charlevoix, the inn at which Hynson had been staying while in Le Havre. It was a nice place; big, airy rooms looked out over a central court ringed with flowers and bushes of a type Rumstick had never seen. The accommodations were not cheap, and Rumstick wondered if perhaps Hynson was being a bit free with the commissioners' money. Franklin and the others, he knew, were constantly plagued with fiscal problems.

He climbed up the wooden stairs to the balcony that circled the courtyard and walked halfway around until he came to Hynson's door. He knocked, then knocked again. There was no answer so he went back down to the courtyard and found the innkeeper in the tavern that opened onto the street.

"Bon joor, missier," he said in the best French he possessed. The innkeeper was stoking up a fire in the fireplace that occupied all of one wall of the tavern. The mantel was lined with various bits of crockery, and above that hung a larger-than-life-size portrait of Benjamin Franklin. "Ah . . . speak English?"

"*Anglais? Non, monsieur, je ne parle pas anglais,*" the innkeeper said, straightening and turning toward him. He turned his head and yelled into the back room, "*Jean-Claude, viens ici!*"

Jean-Claude came in from the back room, wiping his hands on his apron. He was the innkeeper's son, or so Rumstick guessed. He looked like a younger version of the innkeeper.

"*Bonjour, monsieur,*" Jean-Claude said. "I . . . am . . . speak English."

That statement thoroughly confused Rumstick, until he realized that the boy meant that he spoke English. *Damn me,* he thought, *why is it every time Biddlecomb talks to these foreigners he finds one speaks perfect English and I never do?*

"I'm looking for Captain Hynson, Joe Hynson, has a room upstairs?" Rumstick said, speaking loud and slow, as he was wont to do when addressing foreigners and blind people.

Jean-Claude turned and spoke to the innkeeper in French so rapid that Rumstick wondered how anyone, including a Frenchman, could understand. There seemed to be no discernible gap between one word and the next.

The innkeeper replied and Jean-Claude said, "Capitaine Hynson was here . . . one hour past. 'As left again *avec l'autre* American, ze other American. But not far. 'Is horse is still in stable."

" 'Other American'? What other American?"

More lightning-fast French and then Jean-Claude said, "My father does not know name. A . . . tall man, *avec* . . . patch over his eye and . . . *cicatrice* . . . scar, come down from the patch." He held a hand over his eye to demonstrate the patch and with his other hand traced the route of the scar emerging from under the patch.

Rumstick felt as if he had been punched in the stomach. There was no mistaking the description. Lieutenant Colonel Smith, the officious bastard who had tried to question him aboard the *Goliath*.

But that was not possible.

And yet . . . Hynson had blanched when Rumstick mentioned Smith, back in the *Goliath*'s forepeak. Said he knew who Smith was, knew him by reputation. Perhaps it ran a little deeper than that.

Rumstick considered how the "hero" Joe Hynson had dropped that hatch on his head and run screaming from the forecastle. With all the praise Hynson had received for drawing the guard boat off, Rumstick had not felt comfortable pointing out that Hynson couldn't have known about the boat's existence when he first abandoned them in the forepeak. Since the escape had gone off well in the end, Rumstick had let the issue drop. But he had never been comfortable around Joe Hynson. And now this.

"Your father said 'the other American.' Is he certain this fellow with the eye patch was American?"

Jean-Claude translated that, and when he was done, his

father shrugged and replied. "My father says they both talk English. He cannot tell American from a British. Is all the same."

Rumstick nodded. "I know the fellow, the one with the patch. Old friend of mine. Do you think you could let me into Captain Hynson's room, so I could wait for him there?"

The innkeeper did not seem to have a problem with that request, and five minutes later he opened Hynson's door and let Rumstick in.

Rumstick closed the door behind him and looked around the room in the dim light leaking in through the closed shutters. Empty bottles were strewn around, wine bottles, and though Rumstick knew little about wine he did not think those bottles had contained rotgut. They looked like the kind of expensive drink he had grown accustomed to being served by the wealthier citizens of Le Havre.

Along with the bottles were various articles of clothing heaped here and there, looking like sleeping animals in the semidarkness. Rumstick stepped cautiously around the room, pushing clothing aside with his toe, rifling through the drawers of the small desk in the corner, but he could find nothing that might prove Hynson's treason.

Not that he needed any proof. Hynson, he suspected, would give himself away once he was confronted. The big man had never struck him as a stony-faced liar. In fact, Rumstick had secretly suspected that Joe Hynson was something of a coward. He had never voiced those suspicions, for they were, in his mind, the worst accusation that a man could make, and he would not make them without irrefutable proof.

He searched the entire room, but nothing incriminating was there, save for the evidence of Hynson's high living. He pulled out his pocket watch and held it up to a tiny shaft of light coming in from the window. He had less than an hour before Biddlecomb wanted to sail. He had to be back by then or the *Charlemagne* would sail without him. Isaac would have no choice.

He leaned against the wall beside the door and waited. Perhaps Hynson would return in the next hour, and then they could both return to the *Charlemagne* where Hynson could do a bit of explaining.

The room was entirely silent. Rumstick could hear the sounds from the street outside the window, the carts rolling by and the people talking and yelling in their odd, musical language.

But his mind was on Hynson, and the amount of damage that he might have done. He knew everything, absolutely everything. Hell, it was Hynson's idea to turn the *Charlemagne* into a snow, something they had all thought was so damned clever. If he had betrayed it all to the British, then the Charlemagnes would be sailing right into a trap, with no guns to defend themselves and a disguise that was already compromised.

He heard the sound of shoes on the wooden steps, shoes on the balcony outside the door. He tensed up, his hand on the hilt of his sword. It could be anyone, going to any of the rooms on that floor.

But it wasn't. The shoes stopped outside the door and Rumstick heard a key inserted into the keyhole, heard it twist in the lock. The door swung open—Rumstick had to step back to avoid being hit—and Joe Hynson came shuffling in, slamming the door behind him. He was alone.

"Meeting come off all right, Joe?"

Hynson gasped and swung around at the sound of Rumstick's voice. His eyes were wide and he stammered for a second, then he seemed to relax as he recognized the man in the shadows. "Rumstick, sweet Jesus, you startled me! What are you doing here?"

"I came to see if the commissioners had any last dispatches. I didn't know you was going to be out, meeting

with Lieutenant Colonel Smith. The one you yourself said
was a British spy."

"Lieutenant Colonel . . . ? Oh, come now, sir! Why should
I meet with him?"

If Hynson had been a good liar, then Rumstick would
have been all at sea as to how to proceed. Biddlecomb
could always tell when a man was lying, but Rumstick
could not. By his own admission he could be quite gullible
at times.

But fortunately for Rumstick, Hynson was not a good liar,
not a good liar at all, at least not when faced with the possibility of bodily injury. The sweat was already standing out
on his forehead, and as he talked, he glanced furtively
around, as if seeking a means of escape. His eyes shifted
over to the door several times.

"Funny you should look at the door, Joe, 'cause that's
where we're going." Hynson was a big son of a bitch, almost
as big as Rumstick, but it never even occurred to Rumstick
to be intimidated by him. "I think we best go back to the
ship and you can tell Captain Biddlecomb everything you've
been about."

"Ah . . . all right, very good, but . . . ," Hynson stammered, looking around again.

Rumstick, not the most patient of men, had had enough.
He took a step forward, reaching out for Hynson's arm, but
Hynson leapt back and grabbed the chair that was in front
of the small desk. He drew it back like an ax, spilling clothes
and bottles from the seat and smashed it down, shattering
it over Rumstick's head and upraised arm.

The force of the blow drove Rumstick to the floor. He felt
the room shudder as Hynson bounded past, leaping for the
door. He heard the click of the doorknob turning.

He pushed himself to a crouching position and launched
himself at Hynson, slamming into the big man at waist level
and knocking him sideways. Together they fell across a little
table just inside the door, which collapsed under them as if

it were made of stiff paper. They landed on the wreckage with a crash that made the room shudder again, Hynson on the bottom, Rumstick on top of him.

Hynson was cursing and slamming his huge fist into Rumstick's head. He may have been a coward, but he was a strong one, and his unadulterated terror made him stronger still. Rumstick felt his head swimming with the blows. He pushed himself up and raised his right hand as Hynson swung a meaty fist at his face. He caught the fist in his crushing grip and twisted. He could feel bones pop and rend as he wrenched Hynson's arm around, and Hynson's curses turned into screams that grew higher and higher in pitch.

Rumstick let go of Hynson's arm and grabbed him by the collar of his coat, rolling back and using the momentum to jerk Hynson to his feet. They stood there for a second, face-to-face, and then Rumstick flung Hynson across the room. Hynson tripped on his sea chest and fell sprawling across the top of the small desk, blocking the fall with his damaged hand and screaming anew.

The door to the room flew open and sunlight streamed in, and standing silhouetted in the light were two men, one behind the other. The first held a cudgel in his hand. They paused, looking in at Rumstick and Hynson while Rumstick and Hynson stared back. The room was silent for a second, two seconds, as if the intruders did not know whom to attack, and the two Americans did not know if they were facing friend or foe.

And then with a shout the man with the cudgel charged at Rumstick, weapon upraised. He was no more than two feet away, swinging the heavy club, when Rumstick stepped toward him and smashed his fist into the man's face. He felt the man's nose collapse under the blow, felt his entire body lift off the floor and careen into his accomplice behind.

But Rumstick was not thinking about the attackers. Indeed, they were but a distraction to his main purpose, which was Hynson.

And Hynson was getting away. From the corner of his eye Rumstick saw the traitor push himself off the desk and race for the door. He skirted around the two men, who were all but entwined in one another, and charged for the daylight beyond.

"Son of a bitch!" Rumstick bellowed. The two strangers were free of one another and stood shoulder to shoulder between him and the fleeing Hynson.

Rumstick whirled around, picked up the desk, and swung it at the two men. It broke apart on their heads, knocking them sideways, leaving Rumstick holding nothing but the two legs with which he had grasped it.

He could hear Hynson's heavy tread on the wooden balcony outside as the man raced for the steps. Rumstick charged for the door, but one of the men had recovered enough to step in his way, grabbing him by the collar, trying to wrestle him aside. Rumstick broke one of the desk legs over his head, then the other. He grabbed the man's wrist and twisted it, forcing him to spin around or have his arm wrenched out of the socket.

Holding the assailant in front of him like a shield, Rumstick ran through the door. He stopped half a foot from the edge of the balcony and pushed, hurling the man through the flimsy wood railing and launching him out over the courtyard.

He was aware of a scream as the man fell, aware of the dull thud that his body made hitting the gravel in the courtyard below, but he did not linger to watch the fun. He charged along the balcony and down the stairs, desperate to catch up with Hynson before the traitor lost himself in the streets of Le Havre.

He was already lost to Rumstick's sight, but he could have gone only one way, and that was through the front gate.

Rumstick raced toward the street, pulling his sword as he ran.

"*Monsieur . . .* ," the innkeeper called as Rumstick ran past, but Rumstick ignored him. He pushed out into the street, looking left and then right. He paused, his breath coming fast, his sword in his hand.

Hynson was gone. There was no sign of him. He had disappeared into the crowds and the crowds had closed over him, like a body dropped into the sea.

From the direction of the harbor he heard the flat, low boom of a gun fired across the water. It could only be one thing: the *Charlemagne*'s recall gun. The one remaining cannon that Biddlecomb had set up in the great cabin as a stern chaser, hidden from view, and now calling Rumstick back to the ship.

It was time to go. He could not go hunting for the traitor Hynson. He could dally no more.

"Hynson, you son of a whore! So help me, one of these days I'll find you and I'll kill you, you bastard!" he shouted at the top of his lungs, but his threats got him no more than a few odd stares from the Frenchmen passing in the streets.

He slid his sword back into its scabbard and headed off toward the waterfront.

CHAPTER
26

Hope and a red rag are baits for men and mackerel.

—POOR RICHARD'S ALMANACK, 1742

COMDR. RICHARD MIDDLETON OF HIS MAJESTY'S SLOOP OF WAR *Hector* was not a happy man. Not a happy man at all. He leaned against the weather rail of his ship's small quarter-deck, staring out at the black night and the few points of light from the coast of France, and considered the many affronts that he had suffered.

The *Hector* was one of them. True, she was a command, his largest to date and a new-built vessel at that. She was his first ship-rigged command as well, after a series of schooners and brigs. True, she was well armed, with eighteen six-pounders lining the larboard and starboard sides of the waist.

But she was not a post ship, and he was there because he was not a post captain. He was still a mere lieutenant, which was not necessarily unusual for someone twenty-four years of age, like himself, but which was nonetheless, in his opinion, grossly unfair.

The *Hector* rolled in a long, ungraceful, drunken wallow, causing all of the top-hamper to bang and rattle and flog, the peculiar motion of a vessel in a long swell with little wind. It had been that way for a few hours now, ever since the eight knots of breeze had fallen to five, then four, and then at last to mere puffs that rarely reached two.

With the rising sun they would get the land breeze, but for the moment there was nothing to do but wallow, barely maintaining steerageway. Two weeks before, the motion would have had Commander Middleton puking through the stern windows in the privacy of his great cabin, but he was reacclimated now, and the sicking roll was no more than an annoyance.

The ship rolled back and overhead the sails snapped full in a cat's-paw of wind. The sun would appear in an hour and then he would be able to see where he was, exactly. Somewhere north of Le Havre, near the Cap d'Antifer. On station. And that, his station, was the greatest annoyance of all.

The Hector constituted the easternmost man-of-war in the line of pickets that stretched like a net across the Baie de la Seine. They were there to stop a single ship, an American rebel that had raided the Irish Sea and given the inhabitants of the coast and the merchants and underwriters in London an apoplexy.

The four others, all more powerful than the Hector, were stationed to the west, each supposedly maintaining visual contact with the vessels on their flanks. At night they sailed north along the track that any vessel leaving Le Havre would take. At first light they tacked about and retraced their course. Nothing could slip past them.

The Hector of course had only one ship on her flank, the Royal Oak to the west, while the coast of France was to the east of her. Middleton's orders were to keep both in sight, which he would have done if the captain of the Royal Oak, in his zeal, had not insisted on running off to the westward, where he—and Middleton—knew that the action would be. Thus the Hector was left to patrol all alone in her empty spot of ocean. A spot that Middleton believed with all his heart would remain empty for as long as he was there.

The first glimmer of dawn lit the hills of the French coast from behind, making them stand out at last from the dark

298

night, and Middleton ordered the drummer to beat to quarters. The boy stepped up to the break of the quarterdeck, drumsticks held high, and with a flourish he brought them down on the skin of the drum and beat his tattoo.

It was a thrilling sound, and it never failed to stir Middleton and ease whatever funk he was in. Unconsciously his foot tapped out the flourishes of the drum: one, two, three. And then came the blast of the bosun's calls, screaming down the hatches, the shouts of the bosun and his mates. One second, two seconds, three seconds, and then the pounding of feet on the ladders, feet on the decks as 160 men turned out and scrambled to quarters. There was a beautiful rhythm to the thing, and it made Middleton less miserable than he was.

At least until he considered the futility of the exercise. He was perhaps three miles from the coast of France, which meant that he was actually north and east of Le Havre. The rebel privateer would not be sailing north and east out of Le Havre. That was almost the opposite of the direction he would want to go. He would go west, toward America, toward the other ships in the squadron. That was why the captain of the *Royal Oak* was forever disappearing in that direction. There was no chance the rebel would sail into the *Hector*'s end of the net.

That was the greatest injustice of all.

It was to be a rich prize too, loaded with military stores and gold coin, or so the rumor went, and commanded by the pirate Biddlecomb. The man who captured him would be set for life. Knighted, most likely. Certainly made post, if he was not already.

But Middleton had no hope of participating in the capture of the rebel. No hope of sharing the glory, and only a slim hope of sharing the prize money. If he was not in sight for the capture, then he would get nothing. He would be cheated out of all of it, all of it that should, by rights, be his, after all of the loyalty he had shown the Royal Navy. It simply was not fair.

The drummer stopped his roll and the bosun and his mates left off their calls and the *Hector* was filled with the sounds of the guns running in and the tools being laid out and the chain slings being rigged aloft.

It had occurred to Middleton to order the ship be cleared in silence, but he decided it was not worth the breath it would take to pass the order. They were at the far end of the line, shuffled off to the place where they would have no share of the glory, or the prize money, treated with unwarranted contempt by the squadron's commodore.

They were exiles. There was no one there to hear them.

"Do you hear that?" Biddlecomb asked.

He and Rumstick and Faircloth and Weatherspoon stood together on the quarterdeck, straining to hear beyond the rattle and bang of the *Charlemagne's* top-hamper as the former brig, now a snow, rolled in the swell, a confused sea coming in from the English Channel and rebounding off the nearby coast of France.

"Aye," said Rumstick. "Sounded like a bosun's call, but it's gone now. Might have been drums as well."

"Mr. Faircloth?"

"Yes, sir, I believe I heard it too, but I'll not swear to it."

Biddlecomb turned to Rumstick and opened his mouth and nearly said, "Let us maintain silence when we clear for action," then realized that they would be doing no such thing. They were a French merchantman, *Les Deux Frères*. There was nothing to clear. They had no great guns, save for the one hidden in the great cabin. They did not even have gunports. He would have to think of something else.

"It could be a Frog, sir," Gerrish supplied from the leeward rail. "We're still in French waters."

"That's true. It could be a Frog," Biddlecomb said, though he did not for a moment believe that it was. For one thing, there would be no reason for a French man-of-war to go to dawn quarters; France was not at war with anyone. For another, a British man-of-war was exactly the thing he would expect to find, after learning of their betrayal, though he had hoped with an almost religious fervor that he would not.

Rumstick's news about Hynson had come as a profound shock, so profound that it had taken a few moments for Biddlecomb to fathom the full implications of the man's treachery. Hynson knew everything, and if he had gone turncoat, then the British would know everything as well. They would know about the cargo, the lack of guns, the *Charlemagne*'s disguise. They would know that the Americans had to sail soon, that their welcome in France was entirely exhausted. All the Royal Navy had to do was to stretch a line of pickets across the Baie de la Seine and wait.

The *Charlemagne/Les Deux Frères* had sailed from Le Havre the day before. They had no choice. Captain Gourlade had made that entirely clear. He was unaware of any British patrols, he assured them, and thus he could not allow the Americans to stay an hour longer. He could not let them remain until nightfall to sail under the cover of darkness. Gourlade was receiving emphatic orders from Paris, Biddlecomb was certain. A company of French infantry was seen assembling on the quay. The situation was turning ugly, ugly on an international scale.

They had weighed anchor and stood out of Le Havre with all plain sail set, visible evidence of their desire to comply with French wishes.

What was not visible were the three cables and the sea anchor dragging astern, slowing them down enough that they would not clear the harbor until it was nearly dark.

The British ships on patrol would not know that Hynson's treachery had been discovered. They would expect their quarry to sail on a heading just north of west, the most direct course for America. Thus the Charlemagnes' one hope of eluding the British pickets would be to sail in the direction that they would least expect. So once the sun was down they hauled the drogue and the cables aboard and turned north and east, skirting the coast of France, heading in fact more toward Sweden than the United States. It was not much of a chance, but it was all they had.

Biddlecomb sent a hand aloft to polish the lightning rod. Keep the men's spirits up, he said.

They had had a good run through the night, feeling their way along the coast with the lead line going in the chains. Then two hours before dawn the wind turned fluky and then all but died away, leaving them to roll and slat in the swell.

Biddlecomb assured himself that the land breeze would fill in with the rising sun. He resisted the urge to thrust a penknife into the mainmast but secretly hoped that somebody else would.

"There, sir," Rumstick said, cocking an ear outboard. "That wasn't from us. That sounded like a hatch dropping."

Biddlecomb nodded. He had heard it as well and it was not the banging of the *Charlemagne*'s spars. It had come from somewhere out in the dark.

"Damn it all," he said. The sun was starting to rise. He could just make out the loom of the hills on the coast. In ten minutes they would be able to see whoever it was out there, and whoever it was would see them.

"Very well, listen here," he said to his officers. "We've nothing to clear for action, save the stern chaser, so we may as well get that ready. As for the rest, the best we can do is put on our disguise and hope the land breeze will carry us away before any British patrol can figure out who we are.

"I want only the officers and ten handpicked men on deck. No uniforms, obviously. Civilian clothes only. Make sure that Frenchman, Bellême, we brought along is aft with me. I think he's still asleep. And make certain he's dressed like a merchant captain. Everyone else is to remain belowdecks."

The officers nodded and replied, "Aye, aye," and hurried off to see the orders complied with. His instructions concerning uniforms had been in the nature of a reminder, particularly for Faircloth and his marines, since all of the officers were already in civilian clothes.

Biddlecomb himself was wearing battered old shoes, wool stockings, and slop trousers. Against the chill of the morning he wore a much faded blue coat over his wool shirt and waistcoat. On his head was a battered cocked hat. They were much the same clothes he had worn to sea during his many years as a mate aboard merchantmen, and such he was again, or so he hoped the British would think.

François Ouellette, le Comte de Bellême, staggered up to the quarterdeck, rubbing sleep from both eyes with his knuckles. He tripped over the last step and almost fell, saving himself by grabbing a handful of the main topsail halyard for support. He smiled an embarrassed smile and crossed over to where Biddlecomb stood.

"*Bon martin, Capitaine Biddlecomb,*" he said brightly, giving a quick bow. Bellême was a young man, perhaps twenty-five years old, and a minor aristocrat, one of hundreds who had volunteered to serve in the American army. There was a certain romance about the struggling colonials, fighting for liberty against France's old enemy, that attracted the young gentlemen. And along with the romance there was the chance for glory, as well as the possibility of free land in America if the rebels won, which led the sons of the aristocracy to deluge Franklin and the others with requests for commissions.

It was the same problem faced by the United States navy. There was never a dearth of people who were willing to be officers.

But Bellême could at least speak English, which was what had prompted Franklin to issue him a commission at a time when he was denying them to those who could not. The American commissioners in France had been assured that Washington already had all of the non-English-speaking French officers he might want.

"Good morning, *monsieur*," Biddlecomb greeted him. "I have reason to suspect that there is a British man-of-war somewhere to seaward of us. If that is the case, then we shall have to play at being a merchantman once there is light enough for him to see us. In about a quarter of an hour."

"Very good, *Capitaine*."

Biddlecomb made a quick inspection of the Frenchman's outfit. The expensive, ornate clothing that he had worn since coming aboard two days before was gone. Now he wore a plain, homespun coat and unadorned cocked hat, canvas breeches, and old shoes with dull brass buckles.

"I compliment you on your dress, *monsieur*. You look every inch the poor merchant captain."

"*Merci, Capitaine.* These clothes, they are the genuine article. When I heard of our little game we play, I purchased these from a ship captain in Le Havre for many times what they are worth, the thief."

Isaac smiled. "Well done." Bellême was clever, he thought ahead. Biddlecomb was starting to like him. "Now, *monsieur*, if you would stand over there, at the weather rail, and look as if you are in command."

"As you wish, *Capitaine*. And by your leave I shall refrain from bowing or saluting anymore."

"I would expect no less from the captain of *Les Deux Frères*."

Bellême smiled and retreated to the weather rail of the quarterdeck, clasping his hands behind his back and running his eyes aloft in what Biddlecomb realized was an imitation of himself.

From his unaccustomed position at the leeward rail Biddlecomb looked forward along the *Charlemagne*'s deck. He could see almost to the bowsprit. The black sky of night was giving way to the dark blue of dawn, and to the east it was lighter still. It would be but a matter of moments before he could see the other ship out there, and the other ship could see them.

The *Charlemagne* rolled and slatted, and in the relative quiet Biddlecomb felt anxiety seeping in, like water through old caulking. As much as they had done to repair the brig, she was not in good shape. They had no guns with which to fight.

He felt exposed and vulnerable. It was like one of his bad dreams, the one in which he realized he had come to an elegant ball with no clothes on.

Commander Middleton stared out to the eastward, now utterly oblivious to everything but the dark shape resolving out of the night. When he first became aware of it, he could not tell what it was, how big or how far away. He had felt a touch of panic when he considered that it might be some island or exposed rock, that he might not be anywhere near where he thought he was. But as the dawn approached, he had become more and more convinced that it was in fact a ship of some sort.

And now the sun was just behind the distant hills and the night had turned into the misty half-darkness of the moments before dawn, and he was certain that it was a ship.

Actually, not a ship. The profile was too short for it to be a ship. It was something smaller, a schooner or a brig or a snow.

"It can't be, it can't be. It simply can't be," he muttered to himself. The chance that it was the rebel was extremely remote. Hundreds of ships were coming in and out of Le Havre. Why would the rebel be there, so far to the east? But all the logic in the world could not quash his building excitement.

He pulled his eyes from the strange vessel at last and turned forward. "Starboard battery, run out!" he shouted.

The gun crews leaned into their train tackles and the great guns began to rumble toward their ports.

"No, belay that!" he shouted. "Run them in again!" It would have a greater effect on this stranger to actually see the guns come running out. It was an intimidating sight, would scare them half to death. He ignored the few contemptuous looks thrown his way as the men hauled the guns back in again.

At last the upper rim of the sun broke free of the hills, sending its blinding rays across the water and turning the sky a robin's egg blue. Middleton put his telescope to his eye and studied the stranger, half a mile away.

She was a snow, to be sure. She had her square mainsail set as well as her big gaff-headed trysail. Her yards were braced on larboard tack, and he could clearly see the snow mast abaft the main.

It was a snow that he was looking for. The intelligence that they had received had indicated as much. And the hull of this strange snow was black with white, yellow, and red trim, just as the rebel vessel was reported to be. He could see no gunports, which was again what he had been told to expect.

The rebel had no guns. He was defenseless. The *Hector* might as well have been a first-rate ship of the line for all the resistance the Yankee could put up.

Middleton felt his excitement building with each passing second. He had them. And no other ship of the squadron was in sight.

They would strike to him in the next hour, or he would blow them to hell, where all such traitors were bound to go.

CHAPTER
27

Wars bring scars.

—Poor Richard's Almanack, 1745

Biddlecomb ordered the yards braced around as the first puff of the land breeze blew over the starboard side and set the canvas flogging. The *Charlemagne* heeled a trifle and surged ahead, then came more upright as the puff passed them by, the breeze diminishing but not disappearing.

The wind was the only good thing that the dawn had brought with it. The spreading light had revealed the ghostly outline of a ship, half a mile or so to seaward. The rising sun painted it gold and made it stand out in sharp relief from the blue green water. It was a sloop of war. A British sloop of war.

"Mr. Weatherspoon, go below and tell Gerrish what's acting. Have him give the word to the men," Biddlecomb instructed. All but fifteen of the Charlemagnes were stowed down on the 'tween decks with Mr. Midshipman Gerrish there to maintain some order. It would not be fair to keep them uninformed of what was happening. Not fair and not wise, for their imaginations would conjure up scenarios much worse than the one they actually faced.

Though how it could be much worse, Biddlecomb could not imagine. An enemy vessel was half a mile away, and they were defenseless. What was more, their backs were up against the coast of France. There was no route of escape.

"Rumstick, could I trouble you to run up that French ensign?" Biddlecomb and Rumstick were both loitering on the quarterdeck, dressed in the working clothes of mates aboard a merchantman.

"Aye, sir." Rumstick pulled the tightly bundled flag from the locker, bent it to the flag halyard, and ran it aloft. The dark ball of cloth hit the main truck and he jerked the halyard, breaking it free. It flapped limply in the breeze, a blue field with a white cross and a shield with three fleurs-de-lis in the center. The French merchantman's ensign.

"They will not dare to fire on us now, eh, *Capitaine?*" Bellême said from his position at the weather rail. "Us, a neutral French merchantman!"

"I wish I were as certain, *Capitaine,*" Biddlecomb replied. The land breeze had reached the sloop and she had braced around as well, and like the *Charlemagne* she was starting to make some headway, leaving a weak and irregular wake astern. But she was heading up as well, turning her bow toward the coast of France, turning to intercept the Americans.

Biddlecomb clasped his hands behind his back and stared out at the sloop of war, forcing himself to look dispassionately at their situation, to examine their circumstance like a sculptor examining his subject from every angle. What would the British captain be thinking? No doubt he had a solid description of *Les Deux Frères*. Hynson could have provided every detail, down to the paint scheme and the slapped-together square mainsail.

"On deck!" the lookout called from where he stood on the main topgallant yard. "No sail in sight, sir, save for the sloop!"

No sail in sight. Very well. That was at least something in their favor. It was just the *Charlemagne* and this sloop. This sloop that could blow them to pieces while they could do nothing to stop him. They could not run and they could not fight. Biddlecomb could not imagine what they would do, other than surrender.

"Look at this son of a bitch," Bellême observed. " 'E makes for us like this was 'is fucking ocean. 'E is in French waters, does 'e not know that, the arrogant son of a bitch?"

"I'm certain he knows, *monsieur,* and equally certain that he does not care," Biddlecomb replied, never taking his eyes from the sloop. And yet . . .

How certain was he really of that? How certain was this British captain that he was looking at the *Charlemagne* in disguise?

Sure, he had Hynson's description, a snow painted black with certain colored trim, but that was in no way unique. Hell, Biddlecomb himself had seen half a dozen vessels in the past two months that would fit that description, had chosen that color scheme exactly because it was so ubiquitous.

Would this British officer be so certain that he would be willing to cannonade them and possibly sink an innocent French merchantman? In French territorial waters?

A sloop of war would be commanded by a lieutenant, which meant that he was likely to be fairly young and fairly inexperienced. But he would have to be stupid as well not to realize that firing on a neutral merchantman could possibly start a war with France. It would certainly be the end of his career.

Biddlecomb reached for the hilt of his sword, which he tended to worry at moments like that, but it was not there. Mates aboard merchantmen did not wear swords. He glanced down at the deck where he had laid it, ready to strap on if need be.

He felt the soles of his feet tingle, a welcome sensation. It meant that a plan was forming, somewhere deep inside, and in a moment it would come to the surface. So far it always had.

It did not seem possible that this British captain would

stand off and blow them apart. He would have to be certain that he had the right snow. What was more, he would want them as a prize, not as a sunken wreck. No, the only thing for him to do was to make *Les Deux Frères* heave to and search her.

And if she would not heave to? Board her.

And they could defend the *Charlemagne* against boarders. They had no great guns with which to fight a ship-to-ship duel, but in a hand-to-hand fight they had just the thing: a fair-sized crew of seasoned men, and two thousand brand-new .69-caliber muskets.

Commander Middleton was practically dancing with delight. The French merchantman's ensign did not fool him, not for a second. He ordered the helmsman to bear up, turning the sloop onto a course to intercept the snow.

This was the rebel pirate out of Le Havre. It had to be. Unarmed, loaded with booty, and not another British vessel in sight. He thought of the captain of the *Royal Oak,* somewhere off to the west, looking for this very ship, and the thought made him more delighted still.

The rebel had caught a puff and surged ahead, but soon the breeze reached the *Hector* as well, causing the sails to flog and then fill as the sloop made uneven headway. She heeled to leeward and for a few seconds Middleton heard the sound of water gurgling down her side, and then she came upright as the breeze faded away.

But the wind was no matter. They were both getting the same uneven puffs, the *Hector* and the rebel snow, and the *Hector,* ship-rigged and longer on the waterline, would always be the faster vessel.

The breeze gave another breath and then filled in, blowing more steady, if not strong, and the *Hector*'s motion through the water grew more even. It was full daylight now and the two vessels were plainly visible to one another.

Now I'll make them piss their britches, Middleton thought.

He stepped up to the break of the quarterdeck. "Starboard battery, run out!" he shouted.

The men on the starboard battery did not move as quickly as they had the last time, and Middleton thought, with not a little pique, that they expected him to change his mind again. Well, he would not. He had settled on a course of action, and that was the course he would take, unwavering in his resolve.

The nine big guns along the starboard side rolled up the slightly inclined deck, making the entire vessel tremble. Middleton could feel the tremor through the leather of his shoes. Nine long six-pounders, staring cold and mercilessly at the rebel. *It would scare me*, he thought, *if I were the American pirate.*

But the snow had not altered course, had not reacted at all to the battery running out. The commander felt a vague sense of disappointment.

Silly. The Yankees weren't likely to just give up because he had run his guns out. It would take more than that. Not much, but more than that.

For half an hour they stood on, the rebel brig maintaining her course, heading north by east along the coast, heading vaguely in the direction of the Baltic. The *Hector* continued to close until the distance between the two vessels was no more than a quarter mile. Nearly point-blank range for the long six-pounders.

Middleton swept the snow's deck with his glass. No uniforms in sight, but he would not expect to see any. Not many men on deck either, for a man-of-war, and those who were visible were wearing fairly tatty clothes, as best as he could tell.

Well, that was also what he would expect. They were pretending to be a merchantman. The rest of the crew was no doubt below.

But despite the logic of that explanation, Middleton felt a vaguely uneasy stirring in his gut. His former delight ebbed away, and in its place came a nebulous uncertainty. How sure was he, really, that this was the Yankee in disguise?

For a vessel in inescapable peril they seemed awfully non-chalant. They had made no move to escape, had not altered course or sail trim. In fact, they seemed to be going about their normal business, with all the lethargy of real Frenchmen. Through his glass Middleton could see the sail-maker and his mates stretching a sail out in the waist for repairs. It looked like a hundred French merchantmen he had seen.

Was he certain enough to fire on them?

Coming on the heels of his former delight, these thoughts made him increasingly desperate. He felt the despair build-ing, felt that if he let go, he might begin to weep with frustration.

Calm yourself, calm yourself, he thought, sucking in a chest-ful of cool morning air. You need only make them heave to, board them, and search them to find out if it's the Yankee or not, and a shot across the bow will make them heave to. No call for violence until you know exactly who they are.

That line of thought calmed him enough that he was able to look inboard again. "Lieutenant," he snapped at the first officer, "please see to that loo'rd main topsail brace."

Another fifteen minutes and the *Hector* and the suspected rebel were within hailing distance, no more than one hun-dred yards separating them. The slight lead that the snow had gained in the early puffs was now lost to the *Hector*'s superior speed, and Middleton had to rise tacks and sheets and slow the sloop down to keep from overshooting the quarry.

He stepped up to the weather rail and put his speaking trumpet to his lips. "Hoay, the snow! What vessel is that?"

He waited, but no reply came. He saw some activity on the deck, foremast hands staring over at them, some confer-ence among the officers on the quarterdeck. The man he had assumed was the captain, the one who had been standing alone at the weather side, came down to the leeward, the side closest to the *Hector*, but still he made no reply.

Can't ignore your troubles and hope they'll flee, Middleton thought, his former delight returning. "I say, what vessel is that?" he called again.

This time he could see the captain put his speaking trumpet to his lips. *"Je ne parle pas anglais!"* the man shouted back, but Middleton, who spoke not a word of French, could not make out what he was saying.

"Oh, damn it," he muttered in frustration. "Lieutenant, have we anyone on board who speaks French?" He should have thought of this before.

"Lessard, sir, captain of the foretop. He's a Guernseyman. I believe he speaks the lingo."

Four minutes later Lessard appeared on the quarterdeck and saluted.

"Do you speak French, Lessard?" Middleton asked.

"Yes, sir."

"Good. Take this speaking trumpet and ask the snow what vessel it is."

Lessard put the speaking trumpet to his mouth and shouted some gibberish across the water. More gibberish came back.

"He says she's *Le Comte de Vergennes* out of Brest bound for the Baltic," Lessard reported.

"Le Comte de Vergennes? Are you certain?"

"That's what he said, sir."

Le Comte de Vergennes? The report from the spy said the Yankees were calling themselves *Les Deux Frères.* This genuinely confused the issue. What was more, the snow seemed to be named for the French foreign minister, which might mean that he owned the vessel or had some interest in it, which further meant that there would be a world of pain for him if he fired on it and they were indeed who they said they were.

And if they were not? If they were in fact the American

rebels and he let them slip away? What would happen when word of that got out? Middleton stamped his foot on the deck and shouted, "Damn it! Damn it all! Damn it to hell!" in pure frustration, and once more his inability to decide on a course of action moved him almost to tears.

"That was a good idea, sir, that *Comte de Vergennes* thing," Rumstick said in a low voice. "They ain't had anything to say to that."

"So far, at any rate," Biddlecomb agreed. It had occurred to him that if Hynson had betrayed all of the other information, he had no doubt betrayed the false name as well. Giving a name that the British would not expect would only make them that much more uncertain.

"Is Mr. Sprout finished?"

"Aye, sir," said Weatherspoon, sitting on the deck and pretending to long-splice a buntline.

"Good. Just in time." The sloop of war's superior speed had caused her to surge ahead of the *Charlemagne*, blocking her view of the *Charlemagne*'s transom and giving the bosun a chance to lean out of the great cabin windows unobserved and paint out the name *Les Deux Frères*. But now the sloop had clewed up her courses and slowed down to match the Americans' speed.

The number two main topsail was spread out in the waist as the sailmaker and three men pretended to overhaul it. It shifted and moved as if something living were trapped underneath as the men in the hold pulled the hatch covers off, their activity hidden by the canvas.

From the hold itself came the rending sound of the lid being pried off yet another case of muskets. The screech cut through the undercurrent of sound coming up from below, the sound made by sixty men loading and priming muskets, testing locks, charging them with bayonets, and laying them aside as quietly as they could. It seemed impossible to Biddlecomb that the British could not hear the noise, but nothing in their actions indicated that they could.

The sloop of war was half a cable away. Biddlecomb could see perfectly all of the activity on her decks, the men at the great guns, the officers on the quarterdeck.

"It's your move," he muttered, and as if in response to that came a voice through a speaking trumpet, demanding, insistent, and French.

"What did he say?" Biddlecomb whispered to Bellême.

" 'E orders us to heave to, 'e says he will board us, the arrogant dog."

"That's the attitude. Tell him you will not heave to for such a search. This is a French ship in French waters and you will not submit to such a humiliation."

Bellême smiled and put the speaking trumpet to his mouth and shouted out some quick-fire French. There was a pause and then the French speaker on the British ship called back, and to whatever he said, Bellême replied, *"Non!"*

Biddlecomb saw a swirl of activity on the sloop's deck. He could imagine the orders flying along the length of the vessel. "How sure are you, you son of a bitch?" Biddlecomb asked out loud.

A gun fired from the sloop's side, the ball whooshing fifty feet forward of the *Charlemagne's* bow.

Bellême reacted superbly, screeching in French like a madman. Biddlecomb spun the flag halyard off the pin and jerked the French ensign up and down as if trying to emphasize the vessel's nationality.

Another order in French from the sloop, followed by a protracted, nearly hysterical reply from le Comte de Bellême.

"Rumstick, get that swivel gun up here and load it with grape," Biddlecomb hissed. Rumstick ran off forward and a moment later returned cradling a swivel gun in his arms like a baby. Weatherspoon followed behind with the attendant tools and shot. Rumstick slipped the rod of the swivel into a hole bored in the quarterdeck rail for that purpose, and Weatherspoon shoved cartridge, wadding, and grape-shot down the barrel.

"This ain't going to do much at this range," Rumstick said. "I don't reckon it'll even reach."

"That's all right. I don't want to hurt anyone. I want to confuse them a little more."

The rebels, if such they were, were not doing as instructed. Every demand was met with a refusal. In French. Middleton gnawed on his thumbnail as he stared across the water at them, growing angrier and angrier. All he asked was that they heave to and allow him to board. If they had nothing to hide, then that should not be a problem. But even a shot across their bows had failed to move them.

"Bastards. Sons of bitches," Middleton muttered. He was loosing his patience and did not know what to do next.

And then a swivel gun banged out from the snow's quarterdeck, a pathetic little pop of defiance. Middleton saw the water cut up by grapeshot, which landed twenty feet shy of the *Hector*'s side, but that was enough for him.

"Starboard battery, fire as you bear!" he shouted.

"Sir . . . ," the first officer said, his brows furrowed, but he got no further, his words cut off by the blast of the starboard battery, going off as one. Pieces of the snow's bulwark were blasted away, her boom shot clean in two. They were less than a hundred yards away, they could not miss. Middleton saw the sailmaker tossed across the deck, a dead and bloody corpse.

"Shoot at me, you son of a whore?" Middleton nearly shouted. The gun crews were swabbing out and reloading their great guns. "Give it to them again!" he shouted into the waist.

"Sir, forgive me, sir," the first officer said, "but you are quite certain that this is the rebel pirate?"

"Well . . . ," Middleton stammered. "Well, they shot at us, damn it, who else might they be?"

"I don't know, sir. I mean, if you are quite convinced . . ."

Bloody hell, the commander thought. *Perhaps I was a bit too hasty . . .*

He turned and looked at the snow and unconsciously stuck his thumbnail between his teeth and gnawed on it again. The few men on deck were running around like lunatics, the French captain screaming at them in Frog. No more men had come up from below.

He turned back to the *Hector*'s waist to order the gunners to cease fire just as they fired again, the full broadside once again going off as one. The snow's foremast leaned away from the *Hector*, the shrouds parting one after another until the entire mast collapsed over the snow's far side, tearing the main topgallant gear down with it.

The *Hector*'s gun crews cheered. Middleton felt sick to his stomach.

"Cut that mess away!" Biddlecomb hissed to the men in the waist, wondering why he was clinging to the charade of being a Frenchman. This British captain was not fooled, that much was clear. He was willing to stand off and blow them to pieces, something Biddlecomb, in his stupidity, had been certain he would not do.

He considered ordering the men up from below to help clear away the wreckage. And the dead and the wounded. But he decided against it. No advantage was to be gained in clearing things away more quickly. There never was anyplace that they could run; now with the foremast gone they did not even have the means. He might as well let the remaining men stay safely below, out of the hail of iron.

Bellême was doing a beautiful job, like a good actor who would not step out of character. He was standing on the quarterdeck rail, steadying himself with the backstay and screaming in French at the British ship. Rumstick had found another French ensign and was waving it back and forth. They could not put on a more convincing show, but the British captain did not seem to be buying it.

They could hold out a little longer, but not much. If the sloop of war continued to pound them like that, then they would have to strike or be slaughtered. Biddlecomb had not yet decided which it would be.

"Well, I reckon that's taught them not to fire on a British vessel, eh?" Middleton asked the quarterdeck in general, but received no reply. He was grinning, a wide, toothy grin, and he hoped that it masked the fact that he was more frightened then he had ever been before.

Not frightened for his life; French or American, the snow was unarmed and posed no threat. He was frightened for his reputation, and his career.

If that was indeed the rebel, then he was about to become England's greatest naval hero.

He did not want to think about what he would become if it was not.

"We'll board them now, the rascals, and make certain that they are the rebels. Helmsman, run us alongside. Lieutenant, pray see the boarding parties are armed and ready to go. Just half of the first party will do. They don't seem to have much fight left in them."

"Aye, sir," said the first officer. He seemed angry and upset, and Middleton guessed that he was afraid that if he, Middleton, went down, the first oficer would go down with him.

"Coward, bloody coward," Middleton muttered. He made a mental note that if this was indeed the rebel pirate, and he became the hero he knew he would, he would give his first officer none of the credit, none whatsoever. Bloody indecisive man.

Biddlecomb waited for the next broadside, but it did not come. Rather the British sloop bore up even more, heading more directly for the *Charlemagne*, and Biddlecomb felt a spark of his former optimism flair and glow. Perhaps they were going to board after all. Lord knew, the *Charlemagne* had not shown enough fight to make him want to stand off and fire from a safe distance.

Come on, then, come on, he thought. *We have no teeth that you can see.*

He considered what would happen in the next few mo ments. All that the Americans had on their side was surprise, and surprise did not last long. The Charlemagnes had to win in the first thirty seconds or they would not win at all. And that meant he had to have an enemy that was enraged, that was moved to attack en masse.

"Mr. Rumstick," he said in a loud whisper. "Mr. Weatherspoon, come here. We have to get ready to goad this bastard, and goad him hard."

Fifty yards, forty yards, thirty yards. The land breeze had filled in to a steady ten knots, and the *Hector* seemed to be absolutely flying down on the snow. Of course it helped that the snow was dead in the water, her foremast gone by the board and her main sails flogging uselessly, all the braces torn out when the foremast fell.

"Sir, sir, look!" the first officer cried. "Are they striking?"

Middleton looked over at the snow. Sure enough the French ensign was fluttering down from the mainmast head, hauled down by one of the mates on the quarterdeck.

"Hah!" Middleton shouted in triumph. "Stuck already, the . . ." He paused as he saw another bundle of canvas hit the main truck, hauled up on the second flag halyard. A jerk of the line and another ensign broke out, flapping nobly in the wind, twice the size of the French merchant's flag. Red stripes and white stripes, the union jack in the canton. The rebel's ensign. They called it the Grand Union flag.

"Son of a bitch!" Middleton shouted. He could feel his face going red, and before he could say another word, the

Yankee's swivel gun banged out again, this time spraying the *Hector* with grape. A man in the waist fell screaming and clutching a bloody shoulder.

Muskets appeared over the snow's bulwark, six or seven of them, and the Yankee sailors fired, to no effect, and then fell to reloading.

"Yankees!" Middleton shouted. "You see, I knew they were bloody Yankees! Knew it from the start! Fire on me, will you?" He was working himself into a rage, but more than anger he felt relief, rich, pure relief, the sweetest sensation he had ever felt. It was to be heroism for him, and not ruination at all.

He considered another broadside but dismissed it. They were almost on top of the rebels, they outnumbered them five to one, with the boarding parties ready to swarm over the side. And more importantly, he did not want to damage his prize any more than he already had.

"All boarders, listen to me! I want you to all go over at once, first and second parties at once! No mercy for these Yankee bastards, no quarter, just roll right over them!"

From the waist the Hectors cheered and cheered, as excited as was Middleton by the sight of the damned rebel flag. Twenty yards, fifteen yards, ten yards. He could see the pathetic handful of musketmen backing away from the bulwark, retreating to the far side, terrified of the storm of men who were about to charge.

"Lay us right alongside, Quartermaster," Middleton shouted.

"Aye, sir," said the quartermaster. Five yards. The tip of the *Hector*'s jibboom would have speared the rebel's fore shrouds if the fore shrouds had not been shot away.

"Fall off! Fall off!" shouted the quartermaster, and the *Hector* swung to leeward, coming parallel with the crippled snow just as the two vessels slammed together with a shudder and the crunch of smashing wood and the shriek of twisting iron.

"Boarders, away!" Middleton shouted. He was Caesar, he was Alexander the Great, on the verge of his greatest victory.

He leapt into the *Hector*'s main shrouds, from where he could best leap onto the rebel's quarterdeck. The captain, the infamous Captain Biddlecomb, he wanted for himself. He was actually thinking of the wording for his report, which he knew would be published in the *Gazette*, as the first of his boarders swarmed over the side.

The Hectors were a terrifying sight, cutlasses and axes waving over their heads, massed at the sloop's rail. The few Yankees in the waist shrank back, moving around the sail still spread out across the main hatch.

This was going to be too easy.

"Boarders, away!" Middleton screamed again, tensed for the leap to the rebel's quarterdeck.

Four of the Yankees grabbed at the sail and pulled it away, revealing the missing gratings, the gaping black hole of the main hatch.

What in hell? Middleton paused even as his men poured over the rebel's battered bulwark and down onto their deck.

And then from the dark hole stood forty men, rising like ghosts, muskets in their hands.

The Hectors seemed to freeze, shouts died on their lips.

Someone yelled, "Fire!" and all forty muskets went off, blasting a shower of lead into the British boarders, only feet away. The Yankees hurled the spent muskets at their enemy and then from the darkness of the hold more were handed up.

The British backed away. Panic began to swirl through the packed men as through a herd of sheep when the wolves are on them. The Americans fired again, blowing great holes in the tightly grouped boarders. Men screamed. Men fell and died.

"No! God damn it, no!" Middleton shouted. He flung himself into the rebel's shrouds, swung inboard, and landed on the enemy's deck. "At 'em! At 'em! Shoot them down!" he screamed, and waved his sword at the hatch.

The Hectors lurched forward, and here and there a pistol banged out and one of the Americans was knocked aside, but now the rebels had yet another round of fresh muskets. They fired and more of the boarders fell. They flung the guns at the Hectors and more were handed up from below. More muskets, more muskets. Where were the goddamned muskets coming from?

"At them! At them! Kill the sons of bitches!" Middleton screamed, and this time the commands penetrated his men's dreamlike shock. Someone raised a cutlass and shouted, then another and another, and the boarders surged forward again at the moment that the Americans were reaching for their fresh muskets, at the moment that the Americans had no weapons at the ready, and the fight began anew.

Biddlecomb stood on the weather side at the break of the quarterdeck and watched the slaughter. It was horrible, but it was working. The British had stormed the *Charlemagne*, nearly every man had leapt onto the enemy deck, and now they were being shot down in ranks. Blood soaked the waist and ran in rivulets along the waterways. The air stank of burnt powder and the coppery smell of blood. He thought he might be sick.

No momentum was left in the British attack. They had run into Biddlecomb's wall of lead and stopped. The officer leading the attack had gone down in the first volley, and now the boarders were staggering around, shocked, dazed, leaderless, making the odd swipe at resistance as volley after volley was fired into them.

Rumstick was leading the fight in the waist. He had been one of those to draw the sail back, and now he was engaging the flanks of the attack with the five men that he had, and though they were greatly outnumbered, they were adding to the enemy's nightmarish confusion.

Then there was a voice of command, shouting down at them. Biddlecomb looked across the quarterdeck. The commander of the sloop had clambered aboard and now he was rallying his men, driving them to attack.

And the men were listening, flinging themselves at the Charlemagnes in the hatch, by sheer good luck at exactly the moment that his men had no guns at the ready. He saw cutlasses rise and fall, saw one of his men struck down under a heavy blade.

He had to stop that bastard, the commander, who had managed to rally his men at the very second they were about to fold. But first it was time for Faircloth.

He turned aft. "Mr. Weatherspoon!" he shouted, but before he could say more, Bellême pulled his sword and charged forward. Biddlecomb had told him to stay out of the fight—if they lost, it would not do to have a Frenchman aboard as a participant—but apparently Monsieur Ouellette could stand it no longer. "I am at them, *Capitaine* Biddlecomb!" he shouted, and ran past, down the steps to the waist and into the fray.

Biddlecomb watched him rush by and stopped, his gaze drawn to the British commander, who stood opposite him on the quarterdeck. The commander was staring at him, eyes wide. He saw the man's lips form the word "Biddlecomb." He pulled a pistol from his belt and fired. The ball whizzed past Biddlecomb's ear—it could not have been more than inches—but Biddlecomb was too numbed to care.

The commander's sword was dangling from his wrist. With a twist of his hand he grabbed it up, and with a scream of defiance he charged across the deck.

Biddlecomb saw his own sword come up, saw the point of the British officer's weapon coming at him. It did not seem real, it did not seem like a threat, and indeed Biddlecomb could see from that stumbling attack that the man was no swordsman.

He brought his own sword up to meet the attack, catching

the point of the commander's blade and turning it aside. The British officer came to a clumsy halt, and Biddlecomb grabbed him by the coat and pushed him aside, stepping back to gain fighting distance.

He thrust out at the lieutenant and the man stumbled again, falling sideways and slashing out wildly, knocking Biddlecomb's blade aside. He was clawing at a second pistol in his belt.

Biddlecomb recovered from the blow to his sword, prepared to lunge. Behind him he could hear the furious sound of one hundred and more men locked in battle, but how it was going he did not know, nor could he turn and look.

He lunged at the commander, but the man was able to twist away from the sword point, roll, find his feet again.

And then at Biddlecomb's back, shouts closed in, feet were on the quarterdeck. He turned. Boarders pushed their way aft, pushing toward him.

A cutlass came down and he turned the blade aside, sidestepping a slash from a boarding ax. He darted forward, stabbing the first attacker in the gut. The man shrieked, doubled over, and Biddlecomb shoved him hard into the next man behind, sending them all sprawling down the ladder.

The door to the after scuttle burst open and from below came a horrible scream, a high-pitched whooping, like Red Indians on the warpath, and Faircloth's green-coated marines came charging onto the waist.

More screaming from forward and more of the marines poured up from the forwardmost hatch, pausing to find targets, firing, and then plunging into the fight with bayonets.

Biddlecomb whirled around as the British officer jerked the pistol from his belt. Biddlecomb hit the gun with the flat of his sword and sent it tumbling across the deck. He slashed the man's arm. The officer screamed and grabbed at the wound, and Biddlecomb drove the point of his sword into the man's side. He screamed again, doubled over.

Isaac turned, ran down the ladder to the waist. The men

that he had shoved down the steps were getting to their feet, save for the one he had wounded. Another was on his knees, getting up, when Biddlecomb kicked him hard in the face and sent him sprawling back again.

The fighting was general and hand-to-hand. The Charlemagnes from the hold, those still alive, had gained the deck with their last round of muskets, muskets with bayonets fixed.

The waist was filled with struggling men, ax and cutlass against sword, musket, and bayonet.

And in that fight the bayonet was king. No one could stand up long against eighteen inches of stiletto-sharp steel at the end of a five-foot musket, wielded with the momentum gained from the nine-pound weight of the gun. One of the boarders dropped his weapon and raised his arms, and then another, and Biddlecomb knew that surrender would sweep the enemy like wildfire.

"Strike!" he shouted. "Throw down your weapons!" Some men fought on, a pistol fired, then another from behind him, but one by one the British complied, throwing their weapons aside and raising their hands. More and more weapons were flung away, swords, pistols clattering on the deck, hands in the air, and then the fight was over.

Far less than half of those who had stormed over the side were still standing, hands in the air. The majority of them lay wounded, dead, or dying in the great pools of blood, more even than could soak into the porous wood of the deck.

Biddlecomb thought for a moment that the Charlemagnes might cheer. He hoped they would not. The sight of the slaughter on the brig's decks did not make him feel like cheering, and apparently the others felt the same.

The rebels were silent as they herded the remaining boarders forward while others, under Rumstick's command, climbed over to the British sloop to haul down their ensign. They found the sloop's surgeon at his station in the cockpit and told him he would be most needed aboard the *Charlemagne*.

Biddlecomb wiped his bloody sword on the shirt of some dead British sailor and slid it back into his sheath. Another sword was waiting for him, the sword of the commander with whom he had fought. But he would not take it. The man had fought bravely and hard. Losing to an unarmed snow would be humiliation enough for him. At least he should not lose his sword.

Biddlecomb stepped wearily up to the quarterdeck. He would have to confront the officer, find out what he could from the man.

He found him where he had left him, lying by the weather rail of the quarterdeck. His hair was matted with blood, which spread out around him across the deck like a great red halo. A neat hole was in the right side of his head. The left side of his head was all but gone. His right hand still clutched the spent pistol.

Biddlecomb turned his face outboard. In a morning chockful of horrors, why was this so bad?

Because it was so utterly unnecessary.

He didn't even know the commander's name, what did it matter? He was not the only one to die that day, not the last who would die in that war.

A mile away was the coast of France, peaceful and green. Biddlecomb let the tears roll down his cheek. They felt cool in the offshore breeze.

CHAPTER
28

A ship under sail and a big-bellied Woman,
Are the handsomest two things that can be seen common.

—POOR RICHARD'S ALMANACK, 1735

SHE SCREAMED AGAIN, SO LOUD THAT THE CLOSED DOOR DID NOT seem to muffle the sound in the least. Biddlecomb leaned forward in the winged chair in the hall just outside the bedroom. He put his face in his hands and rocked back and forth and muttered, "Please, God, please, God, please, Jesus, help her."

William Stanton stood beside him and put his hand on Isaac's shoulder. "It's all right, son, it's all right. Not a thing to worry about."

"Oh, please, God . . . ," Isaac said again. William did not sound so certain. Just as Isaac's father had not sounded so certain, all those years ago. "This is how . . . my mother . . ."

"I know, Isaac. I know."

He could hear the heavy breathing again from the bedroom. Earlier, hours before, when it had first started, Virginia's breathing had sounded the way it sounded when they were making love, and Isaac had felt himself becoming aroused, which in turn made him feel guilty. Why, he did not know.

But then the screaming started and had continued intermittently for several hours, and any sense of arousal was long gone, and in its place was a kind of profound terror that Biddlecomb had never known before, not in all the times he had fought his way aloft in a raging storm or paced a deck with the air torn apart around him by flying metal.

It was suddenly quiet again in the bedroom. Isaac turned his head toward the door to better hear. He knew what he was listening for: the panicked sound of the midwife's voice, the sharp orders to her assistant, the door's flying open with demands for this and that.

But he did not hear any of that. Rather he heard voices in low and soothing tones, too low to make out the words. That was something, at least. Something to give him hope.

It was a very different United States to which the *Charlemagne* had returned in the summer of 1777. Early in the campaigning season Howe had failed in his attempts to entrap Washington in New Jersey, and finally he abandoned the state to the rebels. He embarked his army on the huge fleet of transports at his disposal and put to sea. Where he was bound was something of a mystery. Reported sightings of the fleet came in from points north and south. It was rumored that he intended to take Philadelphia.

Gen. John Burgoyne had arrived in Canada and was pushing south to Albany in hopes of taking that city and cutting New England off from the rest of the rebellious states. Why he thought taking Albany would accomplish that goal was another mystery, but that, apparently, was his strategy. In his way stood the Americans: Schuyler, Gates, Morgan, and Arnold.

Commodore Hopkins's battered squadron had remained mostly idle, moored in Providence, Rhode Island, for all the time that the *Charlemagne* was absent. But naval affairs had continued apace. The young Scots former first lieutenant of the *Alfred*, John Paul Jones, having distinguished himself with command of the little *Providence*, was given command of a new-built sloop of war, the *Ranger*.

All along the seaboard from New Hampshire to Maryland

thirteen new frigates were under construction. Some, indeed, were already at sea.

And the Charlemagnes had missed it all.

Once the *Hector* was theirs, they had worked like men possessed, cutting away the wreckage of the *Charlemagne*'s foremast, setting up a jury rig, attending as best they could to the wounded and commending the dead to the deep.

They had loaded all of the British prisoners in the boats from the *Hector* and the *Charlemagne* and sent them off to the coast of France. They set sail on the *Hector* and with the *Charlemagne* in tow had made the best of their way north and east, away from the patrols that were still searching for *Les Deux Frères*.

They had improved the *Charlemagne*'s jury rig, enough to allow her to sail on her own, enough to get her to Amsterdam. There she stood in, in her French guise, though the Dutch, to be sure, were no more concerned with neutrality than were the French. Perhaps even less.

In Amsterdam they had a new foremast stepped. From there the two vessels sailed north, around Scotland by way of the inhospitable North Sea.

Twice they saw British patrols, but the Hectors had neglected to throw their signal books overboard, and as a result the Americans were able to interpret their enemy's signals and respond accordingly. In the first case they simply flew their identification number and signaled that they were carrying dispatches, and the distant ship left them alone. In the second they were ordered to close with the flag, but they pretended not to see the signal and nothing more came of it.

In late July they arrived in Boston, sailing unmolested into the harbor and warping up to the Long Wharf. It was the first time in ten years that Biddlecomb had seen that city free of the British army.

And those patriots who still occupied the town hailed the *Charlemagne*'s victory and toasted the victors from France.

The Navy Board of the Eastern Department was based in Boston; this three-man committee, of which William Stanton was now a member, had not even existed when the *Charlemagne* had sailed.

They authorized the purchase of the *Hector* and distributed prize money to the Charlemagnes. It was the first prize money they had ever seen, and according to Stanton, all that they were likely to see, despite the numerous prizes they had taken. The American prize agent in France, Thomas Morris, was a drunkard and a thief, and there simply was no more money to hand out.

But Isaac cared little about that. His only thought, from the moment that Cape Cod came up over the horizon, was Virginia, and those thoughts were a powerful mix of love and carnal desire.

His thoughts had been with her many times over the intervening months, of course, during those long stretches at sea when there is little to do, for a captain, at least. He had received two letters from her. They were chatty and gossipy, describing the social and political scene in Philadelphia, the move to Boston, William Stanton's new position. Only at the end did they turn to wild professions of love.

He had written back three long letters, which in retrospect did not seem like much. He had no idea whether she had received them or not.

With each mile made good toward America, he became more and more desperate to see her.

The dock lines were not even doubled up when he left the two vessels in Rumstick's charge and hired a horse to ride to the Stantons' rented house in Cambridge.

Virginia was radiant, beautiful, overcome with joy at his return. Virginia was nine months pregnant.

"Oh, my love, my love," she said, pressed against him, the tears running down her cheeks and soaking into his shirt. "I was so afraid something would go wrong, I couldn't bear to tell you."

Isaac did not know what to feel. The whole thing was beyond feeling. He had known joy before, and anticipation and love, but it was not like this. This was something else, something much greater.

A week later she went into labor. The contractions started and Isaac stood by her bed. Virginia grimaced with each one, and then gasped and clenched his hand as they grew worse by the hour, and then let out little cries and then stifled screams.

At last the midwife threw him out of the room. He paced and punched his fist into his open palm and tried to smile at his father-in-law.

He had only experienced this proximity to childbirth once before. That was when he was twelve and his mother had given birth to his sister. Neither had lived through it.

At least he had had the joy of his marriage to Virginia, he told himself, and the joy of the past week. It was a happiness that he had not experienced since the death of his parents sixteen years before. It was a joy that he could always carry with him and remember as he spent the rest of his life alone.

Because he was going to lose Virginia and his baby. He knew it. Each scream, each gasp, just reinforced that. How could he expect anything else? How, after all the death on his hands, could he expect anything but loneliness for himself?

He stood up from the chair and resumed his pacing. He was sick of the fear. It was like waiting for his own execution; as horrible and final as it would be, he wished that it would just come.

"Isaac, it'll be all right," William said again. His voice sounded like a dream.

The screaming grew louder, grew to a crescendo. He heard the midwife's voice, loud, commanding. He knew that sound. It was the sound of death.

Not death like death in a battle, killers killing killers, but innocent death, undeserving death. He was the one who deserved to die, and here he was, safer than he had been in nine months, helpless to stop the death on the other side of the door.

Then it was silent. Biddlecomb glanced at Stanton. Their eyes met. Stanton was white. Sweat was standing out on his forehead.

And then from the other side of the door came a cry, a tiny cry, weak yet demanding, and the soft sound of voices again. It was not a sound that Isaac could identify. He looked questioningly at William, and William was smiling like a fool.

"It's a baby, Isaac! Don't you recognize that sound? It's your baby, son!"

"My . . . baby?"

The midwife opened the bedroom door. Isaac had no notion of how long he had been standing there. "Captain, you can come in now," she said.

Biddlecomb shuffled through the door. There was a vaguely unreal quality to the room, the house, the people moving around. He did not seem able to get anything in focus. When he tried to concentrate on something, it seemed to slip away from him.

Virginia was in the big bed, propped up by a great mountain of pillows. Her hair was soaked with sweat. She looked awful, tired, but she was smiling, and she seemed to have a life in her eyes that Isaac had never seen before.

In her arms was a bundle of cloth. Isaac stepped closer. Framed by the cloth was a face, a tiny, pink face, squinting and crying, a little shock of dark hair peeking out from under the swaddling clothes.

"It's your son, Isaac," Virginia said. "I'd like to name him John William Biddlecomb. Your son."

"My son . . . ," Isaac muttered numbly. He did not quite understand what that meant. "My son."

He reached out a tentative finger and stroked the tiny

332

cheek. John William Biddlecomb opened his eyes, and Isaac expected him to bawl anew, but he did not. Rather, he looked up at his father with big eyes, a face astounded by what it saw, at the profound experience he had just had. Isaac pulled his hand back and Virginia took it and squeezed it and he squeezed back.

He knew what it meant.

My son.

He knew intellectually and now he was beginning to understand it as well. It meant that he had a family. It meant that he was not alone in the world any longer. He had a family.

He stepped closer and cupped John Biddlecomb's tiny head in his hand. His foot came down on something under the bed, something round and hard, like a staff.

He frowned, trying to remember. Then he smiled. At himself. At his foolishness.

It was the lightning rod. Franklin's lightning rod. He had taken it down from the *Charlemagne*'s main truck, put it under the bed a week before. Just in case.

Historical Note

*Historians relate, not so much what is done,
but what they would have believed.*

—POOR RICHARD'S ALMANACK, 1738

IT WAS SAID OF BENJAMIN FRANKLIN THAT HE DEARLY LOVED THE truth, which was why he used it so sparingly. And indeed the political entanglements of a lifetime's work garnered him any number of enemies who would characterize him as disingenuous, or, as Britain's ambassador to France Lord Stormont was to describe him, a "subtle, artful man, devoid of all truth . . . a dangerous engine."

Likewise he had many friends who considered him a worldly, kind, and deeply intellectual man. Neither description was entirely wrong.

Franklin was in his seventies when he was sent as American commissioner to France. During his long life he had achieved significant fame both in America and in Europe for his electrical experiments, his scientific writing, his *Poor Richard's Almanack*, and chiefly for his development of the lightning rod. He knew and corresponded with many of the great thinkers of the eighteenth century including Edmund Burke, David Hume, and Voltaire. At

the outbreak of the American Revolution he was already
a hero to the French, which made him the ideal choice for
his post.

Franklin had a backwoods, folksy quality about him that
the effete, decadent French court found absolutely charming.
His dress was simple, he wore his thin, gray hair long and
unpowdered. He did not wear a wig. He was the homespun
philosopher, Poor Richard in the flesh. The overly civilized
court of Louis XVI found this simple, rustic American a
refreshing novelty.

In reality, of course, Franklin was anything but simple
and rustic. He had spent a good part of his life living in
London and France and traveling widely. While in London
he had served as agent for several American colonies and
became adept at the subtle art of politics. Nor was Philadelphia, the largest city in America at the time, quite the backwoods, frontier town that the French envisioned.

Part of the commissioner's long-term goals was to involve
France in the war with England. Nor were the French unwilling to join, eager as they were to do any harm they
could to their old enemy. In 1777, Franklin wrote to the
Continental Congress:

This [French] Court continues the same conduct that it
has held ever since our arrival. It professes to England
a resolution to observe all treaties, and proves it by
restoring prizes too openly brought into their ports, im-
prisoning such persons as are found to be concerned in
fitting out armed vessels against England from France,
warning frequently those from America to depart. . . .
To us it privately professes a real friendship, wishes
success to our cause, winks at the supplies we obtain
here, as much as it can without giving open grounds
for complaint to England, privately affords us every essential aids and goes on preparing for war.

Before they would go to war, however, the French needed some assurances that the rebels could actually win. This was something that Franklin could not provide, nor was anything happening military-wise that might lead the French to believe that such was the case. In truth, until Washington's brilliant offensive in Trenton, it did not seem at all likely that the Americans would win.

Understanding that the French would not be led into war, Franklin and the other commissioners tried to push them. Helping them in this effort was Capt. Lambert Wickes, a thirty-four-year-old Maryland man, captain in the Continental navy and master of the ship *Reprisal.*

Wickes had already distinguished himself before the Continental Congress ordered him to carry Franklin to France aboard the *Reprisal.* Once there, Franklin set Wickes cruising against the British in the English Channel and the Irish Sea. Wickes was an energetic and effective commerce raider, scooping up British merchant ships under the noses of the British navy, and literally within sight of the British Isles, and carrying them back to France as prizes.

The British were understandably furious at this practice, and their fury was directed primarily at the French, who were blatantly violating their neutrality by allowing that to happen.

The French, in turn, did not always appreciate the Americans' efforts to involve them in the fight. On a number of occasions the commissioners' actions brought about diplomatic crises between England and France that nearly led to declarations of war. On those occasions the French foreign minister, le Comte de Vergennes, was forced to bow to British wishes regarding restoration of prizes and the arrest or expulsion of offending American sailors from France, an embarrassment to him and his country. He made no attempt to hide his displeasure with the Americans' activities.

When political pressure grew too great, Wickes was sent back to America. On the way, the much battered *Reprisal* foundered and all hands were lost, save the cook. Had he lived longer, Wickes might well have ranked with John Paul Jones in our national memory. As it stands, he is one of an unhappy number of sailors who fought for their country's freedom and whose names are all but forgotten.

Until late 1777, France and England performed a delicate balancing act between peace and war. Then, in that year, General Burgoyne was forced to surrender at the Battle of Saratoga, and the French were finally willing to believe that the Americans could indeed win the war and were thus willing to join in the fight. When they did, the little insurrection in the American colonies became a world war.

Joe Hynson, Sam Nicholson, John Vardell, Lieutenant Colonel Smith, Mrs. Jump, and Isabella Cleghorn are not products of the author's imagination but actual people, and the recruitment of Joe Hynson as a British spy happened much as described in this book. Hynson never did receive an American command, nor did he want one, so fruitful did he find his position with the American commissioners. His final act of treason was to steal the letters and dispatches from the American commissioners to the Continental Congress, with which he absconded to England where he received a pension from the king for his efforts.

Hynson was far from being the only spy in the American camp. In fact, quite a bit of spying was going on, on both sides. This was facilitated by the fact that England and France were ostensibly at peace, so travel was easy and legal between the two countries. Likewise, England was at war only with the rebellious Americans; those still loyal to the Crown were considered English citizens and as such were free to come and go in England. And it was hard to tell at a glance if a colonist was loyal or not.

Biographer Ronald W. Clark has observed that "much of the espionage activity was conducted, on both sides, at a simple, somewhat Boy Scout level." Franklin was much to blame for the copious leaks, being very casual in his approach to security. A friend of his, William Alexander, wrote to him saying, "Forgive me, dear Doctor, for noticing that your papers seem to lye a little loosely around your house. You ought to consider yourself as surrounded by spies and amidst people who can make a cable from a thread. Would not a spare half-hour per day enable your grandson to arrange all of your papers, useless or not, so that you could come at them sooner, and not one be visible to a prying eye?" Of course even such precautions as those would have been futile since Franklin's personal secretary and confidant, Dr. Edward Bancroft, was also in the British employ.

As to the other historically significant events that Isaac Biddlecomb had the good fortune to witness in this volume . . .

The Battle of Long Island was one of several situations during the American Revolution in which Washington's leadership, skill, and pure luck saved him from falling into a hole that he himself had dug. By deploying his troops with their backs to the East River, Washington allowed himself to be trapped when Howe and his seasoned British regulars easily overran the American defenses.

The storm that came up the night after the first day of fighting left the Americans vulnerable to a bayonet charge. It was extremely difficult to load and fire a musket in the rain, but a bayonet works just as well wet or dry, and only the British had those weapons in great numbers. Fortunately for Washington, the memory of Bunker Hill was still fresh in Howe's mind, and he did not care to ever again charge entrenched Americans.

John Adams recognized immediately the historic significance of the adoption of the Declaration of Independence. Writing to his wife, Abigail, he said that the date

will be the most memorable epocha in the history of America. I am apt to believe that it will be celebrated by succeeding generations as the great anniversary festival. It ought to be commemorated as the day of deliverance, by solemn acts of devotion to God Almighty. It ought to be solemnized with pomp and parade, with shows, games, sports, guns, bells, bonfires and illuminations, from one end of this continent to the other, from this time forward, forevermore.

His words were amazingly prescient, and had he mentioned barbecues (a term in use during the eighteenth century), he would have been 100 percent accurate in predicting future Independence Day celebrations.

It is interesting to note, however, that Adams thought that the day of celebration would be the second of July, the day that the Continental Congress voted in favor of independence, and not the fourth, when the Declaration of Independence was actually approved, following several revisions. The Declaration was read in public for the first time on July 8, 1776.

As to the birth of John William Biddlecomb, I will leave it to those readers who, like the author, have young children to appreciate what kind of trouble Isaac is in for now.

Glossary

Note: See diagram of brig (Page X) for names and illustrations of all sails and spars.

aback: said of a sail when the wind is striking it on the wrong side and, in the case of a square sail, pressing it back against the mast.

abaft: nearer the back of the ship, farther aft, behind.

abeam: at right angles to the ship's centerline.

aft: toward the stern of the ship, as opposed to *fore.*

afterguard: men stationed aft to work the aftermost sails.

apron: a curved timber situated above the joint between the keel, which forms the bottom of a ship, and the stem, which forms the bow.

backstay: long ropes leading from the topmast and topgallant mastheads down to the channels. Backstays work with shrouds to support the masts from behind.

badge: small, ornamental windows on either side of the great cabin, much like small QUARTER GALLERIES.

beakhead: a small deck forward of the forecastle, which overhangs the bow. The crew's latrine was located there, hence in current usage the term *head* for a marine toilet.

beam reach: sailing with the wind abeam.

belay: to make a rope fast to a belaying pin, cleat, or other such device. Also used as a general command to stop or cancel, e.g., "Belay that last order!"

belaying pin: a wooden pin, later made of metal, generally about twenty inches in length to which lines were made fast, or "belayed." They were arranged in pin rails along the inside of the bulwark and in fife rails around the masts.

bells: method by which time was marked on ship board. Each day was generally divided into five four-hour "watches" and two two-hour "dogwatches." After the first half hour of a watch, one bell was rung, then another for each additional half hour until eight bells and the change of watch, when the process was begun again.

binnacle: a large wooden box, just forward of the helm, housing the compass, half-hour glass for timing the watches, and candles to light the compass at night.

bitts: heavy timber frame near the bow to which the end of the anchor cable is made fast, hence the term *bitter end.*

block: nautical term for a pulley.

boatswain (bosun): warrant officer in charge of boats, sails, and rigging. Also responsible for relaying orders and seeing them carried out, not unlike a sergeant in the military.

boatswain's call: a small, unusually shaped whistle with a high, piercing sound with which the boatswain relayed orders by playing any of a number of recognizable tunes. Also played as a salute.

boatswain's chair: a wooden seat with a rope sling attached. Used for hoisting men aloft or over the side for work.

boom: the spar to which the lower edge of a fore-and-aft sail is attached. Special studdingsail booms are used for those sails.

boomkin: a short spar projecting out at an angle from the bow at the end of which is attached a block through which the fore tack is led.

booms: spare spars, generally stowed amidships on raised gallows upon which the boats were often stored.

bow: the rounded, forwardmost part of a ship or boat.

bow chaser: a cannon situated near the bow to fire as directly forward as possible.

bower: one of two primary anchors stored near the bow, designated best bower and small bower.

bowline: line attached to a bridle that is in turn attached to the vertical edge of a square sail. The bowline is hauled taut when sailing close-hauled to keep the edge of the sail tight and prevent shivering. Also, a common knot used to put a loop in the end of a rope.

brace: line attached to the end of the yard that, when hauled upon, turns the yard horizontally to present the sail at the most favorable angle to the wind. Also, to perform the action of bracing the yards.

brake: the handle of a ship's pump.

break: the edge of a raised deck closest to the center of the ship.

breast hook: Thick timbers mounted perpendicular to the **stem** to reinforce the bow.

breast line: a dock line running from the bow or stern to the dock at right angles to the centerline of the vessel.

breeching: rope used to secure a cannon to the side of a ship and prevent it from recoiling too far.

brig: a two-masted vessel, square-rigged on fore and main with a large fore-and-aft mainsail supported by boom and gaff and made fast to the after side of the mainmast.

brow: a substantial gangway used to board a ship when tied to a dock.

bulwark: wall-like structure, generally of waist height or higher, built around the outer edge of the weather decks.

bumboat: privately owned boat used to carry out to anchored vessels vegetables, liquor, and other items for sale.

buntlines: lines running from the lower edge of a square sail to the yard above and used to haul the bunt, or body of the sail, up to the yard, generally in preparation for furling.

cable: A large, strong rope. As a unit of measure, 120 fathoms or 240 yards, generally the length of a cable.

cable tier: a section of the lowest deck in a ship in which the cables are stored.

cant frame: frames at the bow and stern of a vessel that are not set at right angles to the keel.

cap: a heavy wooden block through which an upper mast passes, designed to hold the upper mast in place against the mast below it. Forms the upper part of the DOUBLING.

caprail: wooden rail that is fastened to the top edge of the bulwark.

capstan: a heavy wooden cylinder, pierced with holes to accept wooden bars. The capstan is turned by means of pushing on the bars and is thus used to raise the anchor or move other heavy objects.

cascabel: the knob at the end of a cannon opposite the muzzle to which the breeching is fastened.

case shot: a type of shot used in cannons consisting of a quantity of musket balls in a tin cylinder called a canister. When fired, the canister blows apart creating a shotgun effect.

cathead: short, strong wooden beam that projects out over the bow, one on either side of the ship, used to suspend the anchor clear of the ship when hauling it up or letting it go.

cat-o'-nine-tails (cat): a whip composed of a rope handle around an inch in diameter and two feet in length to which was attached nine tails, also around two feet in length. "Flogging" with the cat was the most common punishment meted out in the navy.

ceiling: the inside planking or "inner wall" of a ship.

chains: strong links or iron plates used to fasten the deadeyes to the hull. The lower parts of the chains are bolted to the hull, the upper ends are fastened to the chainwale, or CHANNEL. They are generally referred to as forechains, mainchains, and mizzenchains for those respective masts.

channel: corruption of *chainwale*. Broad, thick planks extending from both sides of the ship at the base of each mast to which the shrouds are attached.

chevaux-de-frise: underwater obstructions, generally consisting of iron-tipped poles, firmly secured and designed to tear the bottom out of a passing ship.

clear for action: the process by which a ship is prepared for an engagement. Also the order that is given to prepare the ship.

cleats: steps nailed onto a ship's side from the waterline to the GANGWAY for the purpose of climbing aboard.

clew: either of the two lower corners of a square sail or the lower aft corner of a fore-and-aft sail. To clew up is to haul the corners of the sail up to the yard by means of the clewlines.

clewline: (pronounced *clew-lin*) lines running from the clews of a square sail to the yard above and used to haul the clews up, generally in preparation for furling. On lower, or course, sails the clewlines are called clew garnets.

close hauled: said of a vessel that is sailing as nearly into the wind as she is able, her sails hauled as close to her centerline as they can go.

cock-bill: said of a yard that is adjusted so as not to be horizontal. Said of an anchor when it is hanging from the cathead by the ring stopper only.

conn: to direct the helmsman in the steering of the ship.

course: the largest sails; in the case of square sails, those hung from the lowest, or course, yards and loose-footed. The foresail and mainsail are courses.

crosstrees: horizontal wooden bars, situated at right angles to the ship's centerline and located at the junction of the lower and the upper masts. Between the lower mast and the topmast they support the TOP, between the topmast and the topgallant mast they stand alone to spread the shrouds and provide a perch for the lookout.

cutter: a small vessel rigged as a SLOOP and much favored by smugglers. Also a small boat used aboard men-of-war.

deadeye: a round, flattish wooden block pierced with three holes through which a LANYARD is rove. Deadeyes and lanyards are used to secure and adjust standing rigging, most commonly the SHROUDS.

dead reckoning: from *deduced reckoning*. Calculating a vessel's position through an estimate of speed and drift.

dirk: a small sword, more like a large dagger, worn by junior officers.

dogwatch: two-hour watches from 4 to 6 P.M. (first dog watch) and 6 to 8 P.M. (second dogwatch).

doubling: the section where two masts overlap, such as the lower mast and the topmast just above the top.

driver: a temporary sail, much like a studdingsail, hoisted to the gaff on the aftermost fore-and-aft sail.

elm tree pump: an older-style pump, generally used as a bilge pump, consisting of a piston in a wooden cylinder that reached from the deck to the bilge.

fall: the loose end of a system of blocks and tackle, the part upon which one pulls.

fathom: six feet.

fife rail: wooden rails, found generally at the base of the masts and pierced with holes to accept belaying pins.

first rate: the largest class of naval ship, carrying one hundred or more guns. Ships were rated from first to sixth rates depending on the number of guns. Sloops, brigs, schooners, and other small vessels were not rated.

fish: long sections of wood bound around a weak or broken SPAR to reinforce it, much like a splint on a broken limb. Also, the process of affixing fishes to the spar.

flemish: to coil a rope neatly down in concentric circles with the end being in the middle of the coil.

fore and aft: parallel to the centerline of the ship. In reference to sails, those that are set parallel to the centerline and are not attached to yards. Also used to mean the entire deck encompassed, e.g., "Silence, fore and aft!"

forecastle: pronounced *fo'c'sle*. The forward part of the upper deck, forward of the foremast, in some vessels raised above the upper deck. Also, the space enclosed by this deck.

In the merchant service the forecastle was the living quarters for the seamen.

forestay: standing rigging primarily responsible for preventing the foremast from falling back when the foresails are ABACK. Runs from under the foretop to the bowsprit.

forward: pronounced *for'ed*. Toward the bow, or front of the ship. To send an officer forward implied disrating: sending him from the officers' quarters aft to the sailors' quarters forward.

fother: to attempt to stop a leak in a vessel by means of placing a sail or other material on the outside of the ship over the leaking area. The sail is held in place by the pressure of the incoming water.

frigate: vessels of the fifth or sixth rate, generally fast and well armed for their size, carrying between twenty and thirty-six guns.

furl: the process of bundling a sail tightly against the YARD, stay, or mast to which it is attached and lashing it in place with GASKETS.

futtock shrouds: short, heavy pieces of standing rigging connected on one end to the topmast shrouds at the outer edge of the TOP and on the other to the lower shrouds, designed to bear the pressure on the topmast shrouds. When fitted with RATLINES, they allow men going aloft to climb around the outside of the top, though doing so requires them to hang backward at as much as a forty-five-degree angle.

gammoning: heavy lines used to lash the bow sprit down and counteract the pull of the STAYS.

gangway: light deck planking laid over the WAIST between the QUARTERDECK and the FORECASTLE on either side of a ship, over the guns, to allow movement from one to the other without having to descend into the waist. Also, the part of the ship's side from which people come aboard or leave, provided with an opening in the bulwark and steps on the vessel's side.

gantline: pronounced *gant-lin*. A line run from the deck to a block aloft and back to the deck used for hauling aloft articles such as rigging. Thus, when the rig is "sent down to a gantline," it has been entirely disassembled save for the gantline, which will be used to haul it up again.

garboard: the first set of planks, next to the keel, on a ship or boat's bottom.

gasket: a short, braided piece of rope attached to the yard and used to secure the furled sail.

gig: small boat generally rowed with six or fewer oars.

glim: a small candle.

grapeshot: a cluster of round, iron shot, generally nine in all, and wrapped in canvas. Upon firing the grapeshot would spread out for a shotgun effect. Used against men and light hulls.

grating: hatch cover composed of perpendicular, interlocking wood pieces, much like a heavy wood screen. It allowed light and air below while still providing cover for the hatch. Gratings were covered with tarpaulins in rough or wet weather.

gripe: to securely lash a boat in the place in which it is stowed by the use of heavy ropes called gripes.

gudgeon: one-half of the hinge mechanism for a rudder. The gudgeon is fixed to the sternpost and has a rounded opening that accepts the PINTLE on the rudder.

gunwale: pronounced *gun-el*. The upper edge of a ship's side.

halyard: any line used to raise a sail or a yard or gaff to which a sail is attached.

headsails: those sails set forward of the fore mast.

heaver: a device like a wooden mallet used as a lever for tightening small lines.

heave to: to adjust the sails in such a way that some are full and some aback with the result being that the vessel is stopped in the water.

hoay, holloa: the hail to gain someone's attention and the answer acknowledging that hail.

hogshead: a large cask, twice the size of a standard barrel. Capacity varied but was generally around one hundred gallons.

holystone: a flat stone used for cleaning a ship's decks.

hood-end: The end of a plank on a ship's hull that fits into a rabbet, or notch, in the STEM or sternpost.

hoy: a small vessel, chiefly used near the coast to transport passengers or supplies to another vessel.

hull down: said of a ship when her hull is still hidden below the horizon and only her masts or superstructure are visible.

jolly boat: a small workboat.

lanyard: line run through the holes in the DEADEYES to secure and adjust the SHROUDS. Also, any short line used to secure or adjust an item on shipboard.

larboard: Until the nineteenth century the term designating the left side of a vessel when facing forward. The term *port* is now used.

leech: the side edges of a square sail or the after edge of a fore-and-aft sail.

leeward: pronounced *loo-ard*. Downwind.

letters of marque: a commission given to private citizens in times of war to take and make prizes of enemy vessels. Also, any vessel that holds such a commission.

lifelines: ropes run the length of the deck, or along booms or yards, for the seamen to hold on to in rough weather.

lifts: ropes running from the ends of the yards to the mast, used to support the yard when lowered or when men are employed thereon.

limber holes: holes cut through the lower timbers in a ship's hull allowing otherwise trapped water to run through to the pumps.

line: term used for a rope that has been put to a specific use.

log: device used to measure a vessel's speed.

longboat: the largest boat carried on shipboard.

lugsail: a small square sail used on a boat.

mainstay: standing rigging primarily responsible for preventing the mainmast from falling back when the main sails are aback. Runs from under the maintop to the bow.

make and mend: time allotted to the seamen to make new clothing or mend their existing ones.

marlinespike: an iron spike used in knotting and splicing rope.

mizzen: large fore and aft sail, hung from a gaff abaft the mizzenmast.

mizzenmast: the aftermost mast on a three-masted ship.

painter: a rope in the bow of a boat used to tie the boat in place. Also, one who paints, a never-ending task on shipboard.

parceling: strips of canvas wrapped around standing rigging prior to SERVING.

partners: heavy wooden frames surrounding the holes in the deck through which the masts and CAPSTAN pass.

pawls: wooden or iron bars that prevent a windlass or capstan from rotating backward.

pintles: pins attached to the rudder that fit in the GUDGEONS and form the hinge on which the rudder pivots.

plain sail: all regular working sails, excluding upper staysails, studdingsails, ringtails, etc.

port: the left side of the ship when facing forward. In the eighteenth century the word was used in helm directions only until it later supplanted LARBOARD in general use.

post: in the Royal Navy, to be given official rank of captain, often called a post captain, and thereby qualified to command a ship of twenty guns or larger.

privateer: vessel built or fitted out expressly to operate under a LETTERS OF MARQUE.

quadrant: instrument used to take the altitude of the sun or other celestial bodies in order to determine the latitude of a place. Forerunner to the modern sextant.

quarter: the area of the ship, larboard or starboard, that runs from the main shrouds aft. Also, the middle section of a YARD, between the SLINGS and the YARDARM.

quarterdeck: a raised deck running from the stern of the vessel as far forward, approximately, as the main mast. The primary duty station of the ship's officers, comparable to the bridge on a modern ship.

quarter gallery: a small, enclosed balcony with windows located on either side of the great cabin aft and projecting out slightly from the side of the ship. Traditionally contained the head, or toilet, for use by those occupying the great cabin.

quoin: a wedge under the breech of a cannon used when aiming to elevate or depress the muzzle.

ratline: pronounced *ratlin.* Small lines tied between the shrouds, horizontal to the deck, forming a sort of rope ladder on which the men can climb aloft.

reef: to reduce the area of sail by pulling a section of the sail up to the yard and tying it in place.

reef point: small lines threaded through eyes in the sail for the purpose of tying the reef in the sail.

rigging: any of the many lines used aboard the ship. *Standing rigging* is employed to hold the masts in place and is only occasionally adjusted. *Running rigging* is used to manipulate the sails and is frequently adjusted, as needed.

ringbolt: an iron bolt through which is fitted an iron ring.

ring stopper: short line on the CATHEAD used to hold the anchor prior to letting it go.

ringtail: a type of studdingsail rigged from the mainsail gaff and down along the after edge of the mainsail.

round seizing: a type of lashing used to bind two larger lines together.

run: to sail with the wind coming over the stern, or nearly over the stern, of the vessel.

running rigging: see RIGGING.

sailing master: warrant officer responsible for charts and navigation, among other duties.

scantlings: the dimensions of any piece of timber used in shipbuilding with regard to its breadth and thickness.

schooner: (eighteenth-century usage) a small, two-masted vessel with fore-and-aft sails on foremast and mainmast and occasionally one or more square sails on the foremast.

scuppers: small holes pierced through the bulwark at the level of the deck to allow water to run overboard.

scuttle: any small, generally covered hatchway through a ship's deck.

service: a tight wrapping of spun yarn put around standing rigging to protect it from the elements.

serving mallet: a tool shaped like a long-handled mallet used to apply SERVICE to rigging.

sheet: line attached to the CLEW of a square sail to pull the sail down and hold it in place when the sail is set. On a fore-and-aft sail the sheet is attached to the BOOM or the sail itself and is used to trim the sail closer or farther away from the ship's centerline to achieve the best angle to the wind.

ship: a vessel of three masts, square-rigged on all masts. *To ship* is to put something in place, thus shipping capstan bars means to put them in their slots in the capstan.

short peak: indicates that the vessel is above the anchor and the anchor is ready to be pulled from the bottom.

shrouds: heavy ropes leading from a masthead aft and down to support the mast when the wind is from abeam or farther aft.

slack water: period at the turn of the tide when there is no tidal current.

slings: the middle section of a yard.

sloop: a small vessel with one mast.

sloop of war: small man-of-war, generally ship rigged and commanded by a lieutenant.

slop chest: purser's stores, including clothing, tobacco, and other items, that the purser sold to the crew and deducted the price from their wages.

snatch block: a block with a hinged side that can be opened to admit a rope.

snow: a two-masted vessel, square-rigged on the foremast and the mainmast, like a brig, but generally larger than a brig and setting a square sail on the mainyard. Snows have a short mast just behind the mainmast, stepped on the deck and terminating under the maintop, on which is set a big gaff-headed fore-and-aft sail called a trysail.

soundings: water shallow enough to measure with a depth-gauge device, traditionally a lead line. Being "in soundings" generally means a vessel is close to shore.

spar: general term for all masts, yards, booms, gaffs, etc.

spring: a line passed from the stern of a vessel and made fast to the anchor cable. When the spring is hauled upon the vessel turns.

spring stay: a smaller stay used as a backup to a larger one.

spritsail topsail: a light sail set outboard of the spritsail.

spun yarn: small line used primarily for SERVICE or seizings.

standing rigging: see RIGGING

starboard: the right side of the vessel when facing forward.

start: to open, in reference to a cask.

stay: standing rigging used to support the mast on the forward part and prevent it from falling back, especially when the sails are ABACK. Also, to *stay a vessel* means to tack; thus *missing stays* means failing to get the bow through the wind.

stay tackle: system of blocks generally rigged from the MAIN-STAY and used for hoisting boats or items stored in the hold.

stem: the heavy timber in the bow of the ship into which the planking at the bow terminates.

step: the process of putting a mast in place. Also, a block of wood fixed to the bottom of a ship to accept the base or heel of the mast.

stern chasers: cannons directed aft to fire on a pursuing vessel.

stern sheets: the area of a boat between the stern and the aftermost of the rowers' seats, generally fitted with benches to accommodate passengers.

sternway: the motion of a ship going backward through the water, the opposite of *headway.*

stow: as relates to sails, the same as FURL.

swifter: a rope tied to the ends of the capstan bars to hold them in place when shipped.

tack: to turn a vessel onto a new course in such a way that her bow passes through the wind. Also used to indicate the relation of a ship to wind; e.g., a ship on a "starboard tack" has the wind coming over the starboard side.

taffrail: the upper part of a ship's stern.

tampion: a plug put in the end of a cannon to prevent water from getting into the barrel.

tarpaulin hat: wide, flat-brimmed canvas hat, coated in tar for waterproofing, favored by sailors.

tender: small vessel that operates in conjunction with a larger man-of-war.

tholes: pins driven into the upper edge of a boat's side to hold the oars in place when rowing.

thwart: seat or bench in a boat on which the rowers sit.

tiller: the bar attached to the rudder and used to turn the rudder in steering.

top: a platform at the junction of the lower mast and the topmast.

top-hamper: general term for all of the spars, rigging, and sails; all the equipment above the level of the deck.

train tackle: arrangement of BLOCKS and tackle attached to the back end of a gun carriage and used to haul the gun inboard.

truck: a round button of wood that serves as a cap on the highest point of a mast.

trunnions: short, round arms that project from either side of a cannon and upon which the cannon rests and tilts.

truss: heavy rope used to hold a yard against a mast or bowsprit.

'tween decks: (corruption of *between decks*) the deck between the uppermost and the lowermost decks.

waist: the area of the ship between the quarterdeck and the forecastle.

waister: men stationed in the waist of the vessel for sail evolutions. Generally, inexperienced, old, or just plain dumb seamen were designated waisters.

warp: a small rope used to move a vessel by hauling it through the water. Also, to move a vessel by means of warps.

water sail: a light-air sail set under a boom.

waterways: long pieces of timber running fore and aft along where the deck meets the upper edge of the hull. The SCUPPERS are cut through the waterways.

wear: to turn the vessel from one TACK to another by turning the stern through the wind. Slower but safer than tacking.

weather: the same as *windward*, thus "a ship to weather" is the same as "a ship to windward." Also describes the side of the ship over which the wind is blowing.

weather deck: upper deck, one that is exposed to the weather.

weft: used to mean a flag, generally the ensign, tied in a long roll and hoisted for the purpose of signaling.

whip: a tackle formed by a rope run through a single fixed block.

wooding: laying in stores of wood for cooking fuel.

woolding: a tight winding of rope around a mast or yard.

worming: small pieces of rope laid between the strands of a larger rope to strengthen it and allow it to better withstand chaffing. Also, putting worming in place.

yard: long, horizontal spars suspended from the masts and from which the sails are spread.

yardarm: the extreme ends of a yard.